Praise for the first novel in
Conn Iggulden's spellbinding Emperor series

EMPEROR
THE GATES OF ROME

"*Emperor* is stunning. . . . Words like 'brilliant,' 'sumptuous' and 'enchanting' jostle to be used, but scarcely convey the way Iggulden brings the schoolbook tale to life. . . . Iggulden knows that history derives from 'story.' And this story has barely begun. *The Gates of Rome* is its first, exhilarating, installment. Don't miss it."
—*Los Angeles Times*

"A swashbuckling adventure story . . . dramatic historical fiction to keep adults turning pages like enthralled kids . . . a spirited, entertaining read. Iggulden is a grand storyteller."
—*USA Today*

"Fast-moving, action-oriented . . . intricate and compelling."
—*Publishers Weekly*

"[Iggulden] excels at describing battle scenes both small-scale and epic. . . . Tantalizing." —*Seattle Times*

"An absorbing portrait of ancient Roman life and history, well written and full of suspense—even for those who know the ending." —*Kirkus Reviews*

"A brilliant, tough-as-nails story. I wish I'd written it. It left me wanting more. A novel of vivid characters, stunning action and unrelenting pace."
—Bernard Cornwell

"*Emperor* rules. . . . What a find. A first-time author who writes—wonderfully! *Emperor* combines the fantasy of Harry Potter with the historical details of John Jakes. Books don't get better than this." —*Contra Costa Times*

BY CONN IGGULDEN

Emperor: The Gates of Rome
Emperor: The Death of Kings

EROR

TH OF KINGS

Volume 2 in the Emperor Series

Conn Iggulden

A DELL BOOK

EMPEROR: THE DEATH OF KINGS
A Dell Book

PUBLISHING HISTORY
Delacorte hardcover edition published March 2004
Dell mass market edition / February 2005

Published by
Bantam Dell
A Division of Random House, Inc.
New York, New York

Library of Congress Catalog Card Number: 2003055547

ISBN 0-440-24095-6

Printed in the United States of America
Published simultaneously in Canada

www.bantamdell.com

OPM 10 9 8 7 6 5

To my father, who recited "Vitai Lampada"
with a gleam in his eye.
Also to my mother, who showed me that
history was a collection of wonderful
stories, with dates.

ACKNOWLEDGMENTS

A growing number of people have been kind enough to read rough versions of chapters, sections, and drafts, often many times over. Nick Sayers and Tim Waller at HarperCollins have guided these books through various versions with a skill I am beginning to take for granted. In addition, I have to thank Joel, Tony, my brother David, my parents, Victoria, Ella, and Clive, in no particular order. Thank you all for your interest and contributions.

PART ONE

CHAPTER 1

The fort of Mytilene loomed above them on the hill. Points of light moved on the walls as sentries walked their paths in the darkness. The oak-and-iron gate was shut and the single road that led up the sheer slopes was heavily guarded.

Gaditicus had left only twenty of his men on the galley. As soon as the rest of the century had disembarked, he had ordered the corvus bridge pulled in and *Accipiter* slid back from the dark island, the oars barely splashing in the still seawaters.

The galley would be safe from attack while they were gone. With all lights forbidden, she was a blot of darkness that enemy ships would miss unless they came right into the small island harbor.

Julius stood with his unit, waiting for orders. Grimly, he controlled his excitement at seeing action at last after six months of coastal patrol. Even with the advantage of surprise, the fort looked solid and dangerous and he knew scaling the walls was likely to be bloody. Once more, he examined the equipment, testing each rung of the ladders he had been issued, moving amongst the men to make sure they had cloths tied around their sandals for silence and better grip on the climb. There was nothing out of place, but his men submitted to the checks without complaint, as they had twice before since landing. He knew they would not disgrace him. Four were long-term soldiers, including Pelitas, who had ten years of galley experience behind him. Julius had made him the Second in the unit as soon as he realized the man had the respect of most of the crew. He had previously been overlooked for promotion, but Julius had seen the quality behind the casual approach to uniform and the quite astonishingly ugly face on the man. Pelitas had quickly become a staunch supporter of the new young tesserarius.

The other six had been picked up in Roman ports around Greece, as *Accipiter* made up her full complement. No doubt some of them had dark histories, but the requirements for a clean record were often ignored for galley soldiers. Men with debts or disagreements with officers knew their last chance for a salary was at sea, but Julius had no complaints. His ten men had all seen battle, and to listen to them tell their stories was like a summary of the progress of Rome in the last twenty years. They were brutal and hard, and Julius enjoyed the luxury of knowing they wouldn't shirk or turn away from the dirty jobs—like clearing the Mytilene fort of rebels on a summer night.

Gaditicus walked through the units, speaking to each officer. Suetonius nodded at whatever he was told and saluted. Julius watched his old neighbor, feeling fresh dislike but unable to pin it to any one thing in the young watch officer. For a year, they had worked together with a frosty politeness that now seemed unbreakable. Suetonius still saw him as the young boy he and his friends had tied and beaten a lifetime before. He knew nothing of his experiences since then and had sneered as Julius told the men what it was like to come into Rome at the head of a Triumph with Marius. The events in the capital were only distant rumor to the men on board, and Julius felt he wasn't believed by some of Tonius's friends. It was galling, but the first hint of tension or fighting between units would have meant demotion to the ranks. Julius had kept his silence, even when he heard Suetonius telling the story of how he had once left the other tesserarius swinging from a tree after cracking his head a few times. His tone had made the incident seem nothing more than a little rough fun between boys. He had felt Julius's gaze on him at the end and pretended surprise, winking at his Second as they went back to their duties.

As Gaditicus walked over to the last of his units, Julius could see Suetonius grinning behind his shoulder. He kept his own eyes on the centurion and saluted stiffly as he stood to attention. Gaditicus nodded to him, returning the salute with a quick motion of his right forearm.

"If they don't know we're here, we should be able to burn out that little nest before dawn. If they've been warned, we'll be fighting for every step. Make sure the armor and swords are muffled. I don't want them giving the alarm while we're on the exposed flanks of that place."

"Yes, sir," Julius replied smartly.

"Your men will attack the south side. The slope's a little easier there. Bring the ladders in quickly and have a man at the bottom of each one to hold them steady so you don't have to waste time looking for a firm footing. I'm sending Suetonius's men to kill the gate sentries. There are four of them, so it could be noisy. If you hear shouts before you're close to the wall, sprint. We must not give them time to organize. Understand? Good. Any questions?"

"Do we know how many are in there, sir?" Julius asked.

Gaditicus looked surprised. "We're taking that fort whether they have fifty or five hundred! They haven't paid taxes for two years and the local governor has been murdered. Do you think we should wait for reinforcements?"

Julius colored with embarrassment. "No, sir."

Gaditicus chuckled bitterly. "The navy is stretched thin enough as it is. You'll get used to never having enough men and ships if you live through tonight. Now, move to your position and take a wide berth around the fort, using cover. Understand?"

"Yes, sir," Julius replied, saluting again. Being an officer, even the lowest rank, was difficult at the best of times. He was expected to know his business, as if the ability came with the rank. He had never assaulted a fortress before by day or night, but was supposed to make decisions on the instant that could mean life or death for his men. He turned to them and felt a fresh surge of determination. He would not let them down.

"You heard the centurion. Silent progress, split formation. Let's go."

As one, they thumped their right fists into their leather breastplates in acknowledgment. Julius winced at the small sound they made.

"And none of that noisy business either. Until we are in the fort, any orders I give are not to be acknowledged. I don't want you singing out 'Yes, sir' when we're trying to move silently, all right?"

One or two grinned, but the tension was palpable as they made their slow and careful way through the cover. Two other units detached with them, leaving Gaditicus to command the frontal attack once the sentries had their throats cut.

Julius was thankful for the endless training drills as he saw the smooth way the men separated in pairs, with four of the long ladders to each unit. The soldiers could run up the wide rungs at almost full speed, and it would take only seconds to reach the top of the black walls and get into the fort. Then it would be vicious. With no way of knowing how many rebels faced them, the legionaries would be looking to kill as many as possible in the first few moments.

He signaled with a flat palm for the men to crouch as one of the sentry torches stopped close to their position. Sounds would carry easily, despite the rhythmic screech of the crickets in the grass. After a few moments, the sentry light moved on again and Julius caught the eyes of the closest officers, nodding to each other to begin the attack.

He stood and his heart beat faster. His men rose with him, one of them grunting slightly with the weight of the sturdy ladder. They began to trot up the broken rock of the south approach. Despite the muffling cloths on their sandals and armor, the thud of feet seemed loud to Julius as he broke into a light run beside his men. Pelitas was in the lead, at the head of the first ladder, but the order changed second by second as they scrambled up the uneven surface, denied even the light of the moon to see the ground. Gaditicus had chosen the night well.

Each of the ladders was passed quickly through the hands of the man in front, the trailing end planted close to the wall for maximum height. The first man held it steady while the second swarmed up into the darkness. In only a few seconds, the first group was over and the second ready to go, their climb made harder as the ladders slipped and scraped on the stone. Julius caught one as it moved, and bunched his shoulders to hold it until the weight at the top had gone, appreciating the sharp reality of levers in the process. All along the line, the soldiers were disappearing into the fort and still the alarm had not been given.

He shifted the ladder until the padded head caught on something, and gripped it tightly as he climbed, having to lean close with the sharp angle. He didn't pause at the top in case archers were sighting on him. There was no time to judge the situation as he slid over the crown and dropped into the darkness below.

He hit and rolled to find his men around him, waiting. Before them was a short stretch of scrub grass, grown long over ancient stones. It was a killing ground for archers and they needed to be out of it quickly. Julius saw the other units had not paused and had crossed to the inner wall. He frowned. It stood as tall as the first, only twenty feet away, but this time the ladders were outside and they were trapped between them, as the ancient designers had planned. He swore softly to himself as the men looked to him for a quick decision.

Then a bell began to ring in the fort, the heavy tones booming out into the darkness.

"What now, sir?" Pelitas said, his voice sounding bored.

Julius took a deep breath, feeling his own nerves settle slightly. "We're dead if we stay here, and they'll be throwing torches down soon to light us up for archers. You're best in the rigging, Peli, so get your armor off and see if you can carry a rope up the inner wall. The stones are old, there should be a few gaps for you." He turned to the others as Pelitas began to undo the lacing that held his armor together.

"We need to get that ladder back. If Peli falls, we'll be easy targets for the archers. It's a fifteen-foot wall, but we should be able to lift the lightest pair of you to the top, where they can reach over and drag it up."

He ignored the growing sounds of panic and battle inside the fort. At least the rebels were concentrating on Gaditicus's attack, but time had to be running out for the soldiers on his side.

The men understood the plan quickly and the heaviest three linked arms and braced their backs against the dark stones of the outer wall. Two more climbed up them and turned carefully so they too were able to lean against the wall behind them. The three at the bottom grunted as the weight came to bear on their armor. The metal plates bit into the men's shoulders with the weight from above, but without them there was a good chance of snapping a collarbone. They bore the discomfort in silence, but Julius saw they could not hold for long.

He turned to the last pair, who had taken off their armor and stripped down to underclothing and bare feet. Both grinned with excitement as Julius nodded to them, and they set about climbing the tower of men with the same speed and efficiency that they brought to the rigging of *Accipiter*. He drew his sword as he waited for them, straining to see into the darkness above.

      *   *   *

Twenty feet away, on the inner wall, Pelitas pressed his face against the cold, dry stone and began a short and desperate prayer. His fingers shook as they held a tiny space between slabs, and he fought not to make any noise as he heaved himself higher, his feet scrabbling for purchase. His breath hissed between his teeth, so loudly he felt sure someone would come to investigate. For a moment, he regretted bringing the heavy gladius as well as the rope wrapped around his chest, though he couldn't think of anything worse than reaching the top without a weapon. Falling off onto his head in a great crash was a similarly unpleasant prospect, however.

Above him, he could see a dark lip of stone dimly outlined against the glow of torches as the fort sprang to defend itself from the fifty led by Gaditicus. He sneered silently to himself. Professional soldiers would already have sent scouts around the perimeter to check for a second force or an ambush. It was good to take pride in your work, he thought.

His hand searched blindly above, finally finding a good grip where a corner had crumbled away over the centuries. His arms quivered with exhaustion as Pelitas placed a palm at last on the top slab and hung for a moment, listening for anyone standing close enough to gut him as he pulled himself into the inner fort.

There was nothing, even when he held his breath to listen. He nodded to himself and clenched his jaw as if he could bite through the fear he always felt at these times, then heaved up, swinging his legs around and in. He dropped quickly into a crouch and drew the gladius inch by inch, to avoid sound.

He was in a well of shadow that left him invisible on the

edge of a narrow platform with steps leading down to the other buildings on two sides. The remains of a meal on the ground showed him there had been a sentry in place, but the man had obviously gone to repel the front attack instead of staying where he had been told. In his head, Pelitas tutted at the lack of discipline.

Moving slowly, he unwound the heavy rope from his chest and shoulders and tied one end to a rusted iron ring set in the stone. He tugged on it and smiled, letting the loops drop into the dark.

*   *   *

Julius saw that one of the other units was pressed close to the inner wall, with the last following his idea to retrieve the ladders. Next time, they would have a rope attached to the top rung to throw over the wall, the last man pulling the whole thing after them, but it was easy to be wise in hindsight. Gaditicus should have spent more time learning the layout of the fort, though that was difficult enough, as nothing overlooked the steep Mytilene hill. Julius dismissed the doubt as disloyal, but a part of him knew that if *he* were ordering the attack, he would not have sent his men to take the fort until he knew everything there was to know about it.

The faces of the three men at the bottom of the tower were streaked in sweat and contorted with shuddering pain. Above, he could hear scratching sounds and then the length of ladder came sliding down to them. Quickly, Julius braced it against the wall and the tower dismantled down it, leaving the three at the bottom gasping in relief and rolling their shoulders against cramp. Julius went to each of them, clapping arms in thanks and whispering the next stage. Together, they crossed to the inner wall.

A voice yelled close in the darkness of the inner fort above them, and Julius's heart hammered. He did not understand the words, but the panic was obvious. Surprise had finally gone but they had the ladder, and as he flattened himself against the wall, he saw Pelitas hadn't failed or fallen.

"Move the ladder a few feet and make it steady. Three to climb the rope here. The rest with me."

They ran to the new point and suddenly the air was cut with arrows whistling overhead, punching into the bodies of the other group bringing their ladder over. Screams sounded as the Romans were picked off. Julius counted at least five archers above, their job made easier as torches were lit and thrown down into the killing ground. There was still darkness under the inner wall, and he guessed the rebels thought they were defending the first assault and didn't know the Romans were already below them.

Julius stepped onto the ladder, gripping his gladius tightly as he climbed the wide rungs. A memory flashed into his mind of the riot that had killed his father years before. So this is what it was like to be first up a wall! He pushed the thoughts aside as he came to the top and quickly threw himself down to miss an axe aimed to decapitate him. Losing balance, he scrabbled on the wall for a terrifying moment and then he was in.

There was no time to take stock of the position. He blocked another axe blow and kicked out hard as the weight of the weapon swung the wielder to one side. It crashed down on stone and his sword slid easily into the heaving chest of the enemy. Something hit him on the helmet, snapping his cheek-guard. His vision blurred and his sword came up to block automatically. He felt wet blood run down his neck and chest to his stomach but ignored it. More of his unit reached the narrow walkway, and the cutting began properly.

Three of his unit formed a tight wedge around the top of the ladder, their light armor denting under heavy blows. Julius saw a gladius jerked up into a jaw from below, impaling one of the rebels.

The men they faced wore no common uniform. Some

sported ancient armor and wielded strange blades, while others carried hatchets or spears. They were Greek in appearance and shouted to each other in that liquid language. It was messy and Julius could only swear as one of his men fell with a cry, blood spattering darkly in the torchlight. Footsteps crashed and echoed all round the fort. It sounded as if there was an army in there, all running to this point. Two more of his men made the walkway and launched into the fight, pushing the enemy back.

Julius jabbed his gladius tip into a man's throat in a lunge Renius had taught him years before. He hit hard and furiously and his opponents flailed and died. Whatever they were, the men they faced were winning only with numbers. The Roman skill and training was making the core of soldiers round the ladder almost impossible to break.

Yet they were tiring. Julius saw one of his men yell in frustration and fear as his sword jammed between the plates of an ornate set of armor, probably handed down from generation to generation since the time of Alexander. The Roman wrenched at it viciously, almost knocking the armored rebel from his feet with the movement. His angry shout changed abruptly to a scream, and Julius could see the rebel punching a short dagger into his man's groin under the armor. Finally the Roman went limp, leaving his gladius still wedged.

"To me!" Julius shouted to his men. Together they could force a path along the narrow walkway and move deeper into the fort. He saw steps nearby and motioned to them. More men fell to him and he began to enjoy the fight. The sword was a good weight. The armor gave him a sense of being invulnerable, and with the hot blood of action in his system, it sat lightly on him.

A sudden blow to his head removed the damaged helmet, and he could feel the cool night air on his sweating skin. It was a pleasure, and he chuckled for a moment as he stepped in and barged into a man's shield, knocking him into the path of his fellows.

"*Accipiter!*" he shouted suddenly. Hawk. It would do. He heard voices echo it and roared it again, ducking under a recurved sword that looked more like a farm implement than a weapon of war. His return stroke cut the man's thighs open, dropping him bawling on the stones.

The other legionaries gathered around him. He saw eight of his unit had made the wall, and there were six others who had survived the archers. They stood together and the rebels began to waver in their rushing as the bodies piled around them.

"Soldiers of Rome, *we* are," grunted one of them. "Best in the world. Come on, don't hang back."

Julius grinned at him and took up the shout of the galley name when it was begun again. He hoped Pelitas would hear them. Somehow, he didn't doubt the ugly bastard had survived.

*   *   *

Pelitas had found a cloak on a hook and used it to cover his tunic and drawn sword. He felt vulnerable without his armor, but the men who clattered past didn't even glance at him. He heard the legionaries growl and shout their challenges nearby and realized it was time to join the fight.

He lifted a torch from a wall bracket and joined the enemy rush to the clash of blades. Gods, there were a lot of them! The inner fort was a maze of broken walls and empty rooms, the sort of place that took hours to clear, with every step open to ambush and arrow fire. He rounded a corner in the darkness, ignored and anonymous for precious moments. He moved quickly, trying not to lose his sense of direction in twists and turns, and then found himself on the north wall, near a group of archers who were firing carefully, their expressions serious and calm. Presumably, the remnants of Gaditicus's force were still out there, though he could hear Roman orders snapped out in the yard by the main gate. Some had got in, but the battle was far from over.

Half the town must have holed up in the fort, he thought angrily as he approached the archers. One looked up sharply at his approach, but only nodded, firing unhurriedly into the mass of men below them.

As he aimed, Pelitas charged, knocking two of the men headfirst to the stones below. They hit with a crash and the other three archers turned in horror to see him as he threw back the cloak and raised the short gladius.

"Evening, lads," he said, his voice calm and cheerful. One step brought his sword into the chest of the closest. He kneed the body off the wall and then an arrow thumped into him, tearing straight through his side. Only the flights jutted from his stomach and he groaned as his left hand plucked at them, almost without his control. Viciously, he swiped the gladius through the throat of the closest archer, who was raising his own arrow.

It was the last and farthest from him who had fired the shaft. Feverishly, he tried to notch another, but fear made him clumsy and Pelitas reached him, sword held out for the thrust. The man backed away in panic and screamed as he fell from the wall. Pelitas went down slowly onto one knee, his breathing rasping painfully. There was no one near and he laid down his sword, reaching around himself to try and snap the arrow. He would not remove it completely. All the soldiers had seen the rush of blood that could kill you when you did. The thought of catching it every time he turned made his eyes water.

His grip was slippery and he could only bend the wooden shaft, a low moan of agony escaping him. His side was soaked in blood and he felt dizzy as he tried to stand up.

Growling softly, he eased the arrow back through himself, so it wasn't sticking so far out behind.

"Have to find the others," he muttered, taking a deep breath. His hands quivered with the beginnings of shock, so he gripped the gladius as tightly as possible and wrapped his other fist in a fold of the cloak.

*   *   *

Gaditicus backhanded a man in the teeth as he ran at him, following through with a short thrust into the ribs. The fort was filled with rebels, more than the small island would support, he was sure. The rebellion must have picked up firebrands from the mainland, but it was too late to worry now. He remembered the young officer's question about numbers and how he'd scorned it. Perhaps he should have organized reinforcements. The outcome of the night wasn't easy to predict.

It had started well, with the sentries taken quickly, almost in the same heartbeat. He had ten men over the ladders and the gate open before anyone inside knew what was happening. Then the dark buildings had vomited soldiers at them, pulling on their armor as they ran. The narrow walkways and steps made the maze an archer's dream, with only the poor light holding their casualties down to flesh wounds, though he'd lost one man to a shaft into his mouth, straight through his skull.

He could hear his men panting as they pressed close to a wall in darkness behind him. Some torches had been lit, but apart from the occasional arrow fired blindly, the enemy had retreated for the moment into the side buildings. Anyone rushing down the path between them was going to be cut to pieces before they made a few paces, but equally they could not leave the shelter to engage the legionaries. It was a temporary lull and Gaditicus was pleased to have the chance to get his breath back. He missed the fitness of the land legions. No matter how you drilled and exercised on a ship, a few minutes of fighting and running left you exhausted. Or maybe it was just age, he acknowledged wryly to himself.

"They've gone to ground," he muttered. It would be bitter from now on, killing from building to building, losing one of theirs for every one or two of the enemy. It was too easy for the rebels to wait inside a door or a window and stab the first thing to come through.

Gaditicus was turning to the soldier behind to give orders when the man looked down, his mouth dropping in horror. The stones were covered in shining liquid that streamed quickly through the group and sluiced down between the fort buildings. There was no time to make a plan.

"Run!" Gaditicus yelled to the group. "Get high! Gods, run!"

Some of the younger men gaped, not understanding, but the experienced ones didn't wait to find out. Gaditicus was at the back, trying not to think about the archers waiting for just this moment. He heard the crackle and whoosh of fire as they lit the sticky fluid and arrows whined past him, taking a legionary in the lower back. The soldier staggered on for a moment before collapsing. Gaditicus stopped to help him, but as he turned his head he saw flames racing toward them. He drew his sword quickly through the soldier's throat, knowing it was better than burning. He could feel the heat on his back and panic filled him as he rose from the body. His sandals were wet with the stuff and he knew the fire could not be quenched. He ran blindly after his men.

At full pounding sprint, the group of soldiers rounded a corner and charged on, straight at a group of three crouched archers. All three panicked and only one took the shot, sending an arrow above their heads. The archers were cut down and trampled almost without slowing.

On sheets of flame, the fort became visible. Gaditicus

and the others roared in anger and in relief at being alive, the sound fueling their strength and frightening the enemy.

The path ended in a courtyard and this time the waiting archers fired smoothly, destroying the front four men and sending the second row sprawling over their dead companions. The yard was full of the rebels, and with a baying cry to answer the Romans in ferocity, they came on, howling.

*   *   *

Julius froze as he saw the flames explode along a row of squat buildings to his left. The sheltering darkness became flickering gold and shadow, and three men in an alcove were suddenly visible a few paces ahead. They were cut down and behind them an open doorway was revealed, leading into the bowels of the fort. It was the decision of a second and Julius ran straight through it, ripping his sword through the guts of a man waiting inside before he could strike. His followers never hesitated. Without knowing the fort, they could spend fruitless minutes searching for ways to reach their comrades with Gaditicus. The most important thing was to keep moving and kill anyone they came across.

After the light of the fire, it was frighteningly dark inside the fortress. Steps led down to a row of empty rooms, and at the end was another set, with a single oil lamp on the wall. Julius grabbed it, swearing as the hot liquid spattered onto his skin. His men clattered behind him and at the bottom Julius threw himself down as arrows hit stone around him and shattered, sending stinging fragments into their midst.

The long, low room they entered had three men in it. Two looked terrified at the dirty, blood-covered soldiers, and the third was tied to a chair, a prisoner. Julius saw by his robe that he was a Roman. His face and body were battered and swollen, but his eyes were alive with sudden hope.

Julius raced across the room, swaying to avoid another shaft fired poorly and in haste. Almost with contempt, he reached the two men and cut the archer across the throat. The other tried to stab him, but the breastplate took the blow easily and his backhand cut sent the man crashing to the floor.

Julius rested the point of his gladius on the stones and leaned on it, suddenly tired. His breathing came in great gasps and he noticed how silent the place was, how far below the main fort they were.

"That was well done," said the man in the chair.

Julius glanced at him. Up close, he saw the man had been brutally tortured. His face was swollen and twisted and his fingers had been broken, jutting at obscene angles. Trembling shook the man's body and Julius guessed he was trying not to lose what little control he had left.

"Cut his bonds," he ordered, and helped the prisoner to his feet as he came free, noting how unsteady he was. One of the man's hands touched the arm of the chair, and he gave out a moan of agony, his eyes rolling up in his head for a second before he steadied under Julius's grip.

"Who are you?" Julius said, wondering what they were going to do with the man.

"Governor Paulus. You might say . . . this is my fort." The man closed his eyes as he spoke, overwhelmed by exhaustion and relief. Julius saw his courage and felt a touch of respect.

"Not yet it isn't, sir," Julius replied. "There's a lot of fighting above and we have to get back to it. I suggest we find you somewhere safe to wait it out. You don't look quite up to joining in."

In fact the man looked bloodless, his skin slack and gray. He was about fifty years old, with heavy shoulders and a sagging stomach. He might once have been a warrior, Julius judged, but time and soft living had taken his strength, at least of the body.

The governor stood straighter, the effort of will obvious. "I'll go with you as far as I can. My hands are smashed, so I can't fight, but I want to get out of this stinking pest-hole, at least."

Julius nodded quickly, signaling to two of the men. "Take his arms, gently, carry him if you have to. We have to get back to help Gaditicus."

With that, Julius was clattering up the steps, his mind already on the battle above.

"Come on, sir. Lean on my shoulder," said one of the last pair as he took the weight. The governor cried out as his broken hands moved, then gritted his teeth against the pain.

"Get me out quickly," he ordered curtly. "Who was the officer who freed me?"

"That was Caesar, sir," the soldier replied as they began the slow trip. By the end of the first flight of stairs, the pain had forced the governor into unconsciousness and they were able to go much faster.

CHAPTER 2

Sulla smiled and drank deeply from a silver goblet. His cheeks were flushed with the effects of the wine, and his eyes frightened Cornelia as she sat on the couch he had provided.

His men had collected her in the heat of the afternoon, when she felt the heaviness of her pregnancy most painfully. She tried to hide her discomfort and fear of the Dictator of Rome, but her hands shook slightly on the lip of the glass of cool white wine he had offered her. She sipped sparingly to please him, wanting nothing more than to be out of his gilded chambers and back in the safety of her own home.

His eyes watched her every move and she could not hold the gaze as the silence stretched between them.

"Are you comfortable?" he asked, and there was a slurred edge to his words that sent a thrill of panic coursing through her.

Be calm, she told herself. The child will feel your fear. Think of Julius. He would want you to be strong.

When she spoke, her voice was almost steady.

"Your men have thought of everything. They were very courteous to me, though they did not say why you desired my presence."

"Desired? What a strange choice of word," he replied

softly. "Most men would never use the word for a woman, what, weeks from giving birth?"

Cornelia looked at him blankly and he emptied his cup, smacking his lips together with pleasure. He rose from his seat without warning, turning his back to her as he refilled his cup from an amphora, letting the stopper fall and roll on the marble floor unheeded.

She watched it spiral and come to rest, as if hypnotized. As it became still, he spoke again, his voice languid and intimate.

"I have heard that a woman is never more beautiful than when she is pregnant, but that is not always true, is it?"

He stepped closer to her, gesturing with the goblet as he spoke, slopping drops over the rim.

"I . . . do not know, sir, it . . ."

"Oh, I have seen them. Rat-haired heifers that amble and bellow, their skin blotched and sweating. Common women, of common stock, whereas the true Roman lady, well . . ."

He pressed even closer to her and it was all she could do not to pull away from him. There was a glitter to his eyes and suddenly she thought of screaming, but who would come? Who would *dare* come?

"The Roman lady is a ripe fruit, her skin glowing, her hair shining and lustrous."

His voice was a husky murmur, and as he spoke he reached out and pressed his hand against the swelling of the child.

"Please . . ." she whispered, but he seemed not to hear. His hand trailed over her, feeling the heavy roundness.

"Ah yes, you have that beauty, Cornelia."

"Please, I am tired. I would like to go home now. My husband . . ."

"Julius? A very undisciplined young man. He refused to give you up, did you know? I can see why, now."

His fingers reached up to her breasts. Swollen and painful as they were at this late stage, they were held only loosely in the *mamillare,* and she closed her eyes in helpless misery as she felt his hands easing over her flesh. Tears came swiftly into her eyes.

"What a de*licious* weight," he whispered, his voice ugly with passion. Without warning, he bent and pressed his mouth on hers, shoving his fat tongue between her lips. The taste of stale wine made her gag in reflex, and then he pulled away, wiping loose lips with the back of his hand.

"Please don't hurt the baby," she said, her voice breaking. Tears streamed out and the sight of them seemed to disgust Sulla. His mouth twisted in irritation and he turned away.

"Take yourself home. Your nose is running and the moment is spoiled. There will be another time."

He filled his cup from the amphora yet again as she left the room, her sobs almost choking her and her eyes blind with shining tears.

*   *   *

Julius roared as his men charged into the small yard where Gaditicus fought the last of the rebels. As his legionaries hit the rebel flank, there was instant panic in the darkness and the Romans took advantage, bodies falling quickly, ripped apart by their swords. Within seconds, there were fewer than twenty facing the legionaries, and Gaditicus shouted, his voice a bellow of authority.

"Drop your weapons!"

A second of hesitation followed, then a clatter as swords and daggers fell to the tiles and the enemy were still at last, chests heaving, drenched in sweat, but beginning to feel that moment of joyous disbelief that comes when a man realizes he has survived where others have fallen.

The legionaries moved to surround them, their faces hard.

Gaditicus waited until the rebels' swords had been taken and they stood in a huddled and sullen group.

"Now kill them all," he snapped, and the legionaries

threw themselves in one last time. There were screams, but it was over quickly and the small yard was quiet.

Julius breathed deeply, trying to clear his lungs of the smells of smoke and blood and opening bowels. He coughed and spat on the stone floor, before wiping his gladius on a body. The blade was nicked and scarred, almost useless. It would take hours to rub out the flaws, and he would be better exchanging it quietly for another from the stores. His stomach heaved slightly and he concentrated even harder on the blade and the work to be done before they could return to *Accipiter*. He had seen bodies piled high before and it was that memory of the morning after his father's death that made him suddenly believe he could smell burning flesh in his nostrils.

"I think that's the last of them," Gaditicus said, panting. He was pale with exhaustion and stood bent over with his hands on his knees for support.

"We'll wait for dawn before checking every doorway, in case a few more are hiding in the shadows." He rose straight, wincing as his back stretched and clicked. "Your men were late in support, Caesar. We were naked for a while."

Julius nodded. He thought of saying what it had taken to get to the centurion at all, but kept his mouth tightly shut. Suetonius grinned at him. He was dabbing a cloth to a gash on his cheek. Julius hoped the stitches would hurt.

"He was delayed rescuing me, Centurion," a voice said. The governor had recovered consciousness, leaning heavily on the shoulders of the two men carrying him. His hands were purple and impossibly swollen, hardly like hands at all.

Gaditicus took in the Roman style of the filthy toga, stiff with blood and dirt. The eyes were tired but the voice was clear enough, despite the broken lips.

"Governor Paulus?" Gaditicus asked. He saluted when the governor nodded.

"We heard you were dead, sir," Gaditicus said.

"Yes . . . it seemed that way to me for a while."

The governor's head lifted and his mouth twisted in a slight smile.

"Welcome to Mytilene fort, gentlemen."

*   *   *

Clodia sobbed as Tubruk put his arm around her in the empty kitchens.

"I don't know what to do," she said, her voice muffled by his tunic. "He's been *at* her and *at* her all through the pregnancy."

"Shhh ... come on." Tubruk patted her back, trying to control the fear that had leapt in him when he first saw Clodia's dusty, tearstained face. He didn't know Cornelia's nurse well, but what he had seen had given him an impression of a solid, sensible woman who would not be crying over nothing.

"What is it, love? Come and sit down and tell me what's going on."

He kept his voice as calm as he could, but it was a struggle. Gods, was the baby dead? It was due any time and childbirth was always risky. He felt coldness touch him. He had told Julius he would keep an eye on them while he was away from the city, but everything had seemed fine. Cornelia had been a little withdrawn in the last months, but many a young girl felt fear with the ordeal of her first birth ahead of her.

Clodia allowed herself to be guided to a bench next to the ovens. She sat without checking the seat for grease or soot, which worried Tubruk even further. He poured a cup of pressed apple juice for her, and she gulped at it, her sobs subsiding to shudders.

"Tell me the problem," Tubruk said. "Most things can be solved, no matter how bad they might seem."

He waited patiently for her to finish drinking and gently took the cup from her limp hand.

"It's Sulla," she whispered. "He's been tormenting Cornelia. She won't tell me all the details, but he has his men bring her to him at any time of the day or night, pregnant as she is, and she comes back in tears."

Tubruk paled in anger. "Has he hurt her? Hurt the child?" he pressed, stepping closer.

Clodia leaned away from his intensity, her mouth quivering with returning force. "Not yet, but every time is worse. She told me he is always drunk and he...places his hands on her."

Tubruk closed his eyes for a moment, knowing he had to remain calm. The only outward sign was a clenched fist, but when he spoke again, his eyes glittered dangerously.

"Does her father know?"

Clodia took his arm in a sudden grip. "Cinna must not know! It would break him. He would not be able to meet Sulla in the Senate without accusations, and he would be killed if he said anything in public. He cannot be told!"

Her voice rose higher as she spoke and Tubruk patted her hand reassuringly.

"He won't learn it from me."

"I have no one else to turn to but you, to help me protect her," Clodia said brokenly, her eyes pleading.

"You've done right, love. She carries a child of this house. I need to know everything that has happened, do you understand? There must be no mistake in this. Do you see how important that is?"

She nodded, wiping her eyes roughly.

"I hope so," he continued. "As the Dictator of Rome, Sulla is almost untouchable under the law. Oh, we could bring a case to the Senate, but not one of them would dare to argue the prosecution. It would mean death for anyone who tried. That is the reality of their precious 'equal law.' And what is his crime? In law, nothing, but if he has touched her and frightened her, then the gods call for punishment even if the Senate would not."

Clodia nodded again. "I understand that—"

"You *must* understand," he interrupted sharply, his voice

hard and low, "because it means that anything we do will be outside the law, and if it is any sort of attack on the body of Sulla himself, then to fail would mean the deaths of Cinna, you, me, Julius's mother, servants, slaves, Cornelia and the child—everybody. Julius would be tracked down no matter where he hid."

"You will kill Sulla?" Clodia whispered, moving closer.

"If everything is as you say, I will certainly kill him," he promised, and for a moment, she could see the gladiator he had once been, frightening and grim.

"Good, it is what he deserves. Cornelia will be able to put these dark months behind her and bear the child in peace." She dabbed at her eyes and some of the grief and worry eased from her visibly.

"Does she know you have come to me?" he asked quietly.

Clodia shook her head.

"Good. Don't tell her what I have said. She is too close to birth for these fears."

"And . . . afterward?"

Tubruk scratched the short crop of hair on the back of his head. "Never. Let her believe it was one of his enemies. He has enough of them. Keep it a secret, Clodia. He has supporters who will be calling for blood for years later if the truth comes out. One wrong word from you to another, who then tells a friend, and the guards will be at the gate to take Cornelia and the child away for torture before the next dawn."

"I will not tell," she whispered, holding his gaze for long seconds. At last she looked away and he sighed as he sat on the bench next to her.

"Now, start from the beginning and don't leave anything out. Pregnant girls often imagine things, and before I risk everything I love, I need to be sure."

They sat and talked for an hour in quiet voices. By the end, the hand she placed on his arm marked the beginning of a shy attraction, despite the ugliness of the subject they discussed.

*   *   *

"I had intended to be on the next tide out to sea," Gaditicus had said sourly. "Not to take part in a parade."

"You believed me to be a corpse then," Governor Paulus had replied. "As I am battered but alive, I feel it necessary to show the support of Rome that stands with me. It will discourage . . . further attempts on my dignity."

"Sir, every young fighter on the whole island must have been holed up in that fort—and a fair few from the mainland as well. Half the families in the town will be grieving for the loss of a son or father. We have shown them well enough what disobedience to Rome means. They will not rebel again."

"You think not?" Paulus had replied, smiling wryly. "How little you know these people. They have been fighting against their conquerors since Athens was the center of the world. Now Rome is here and they fight on. Those who died will have left sons to take up arms as soon as they are able. It is a difficult province."

Discipline had prevented Gaditicus from arguing further. He longed to be back at sea in *Accipiter,* but Paulus had insisted, even demanding four of the legionaries to stay with him permanently as guards. Gaditicus had nearly walked back to the ship at that order, but a few of the older men had volunteered, preferring the easier duty to pirate hunting.

"Don't forget what happened to his last set of guards," Gaditicus had warned them, but it was a hollow threat, as well they knew after the rebels' pyre lifted a stream of black smoke high enough to be seen for miles. The job would take them safely to retirement.

Gaditicus cursed under his breath. He was going to be very short of good men for the next year. The old man Caesar had brought on board with him had turned out to be good with wounds, so a few of the injured might be saved from an early release and poverty. He wasn't a miracle worker, though, and some of the crippled ones would have to be put off at the next port, there to wait for a slow merchant ship to take them back to Rome. The galley century had lost a third of its men in Mytilene. Promotions would have to be made, but they couldn't replace twenty-seven dead in the fighting, fourteen of them competent *hastati* who had served on *Accipiter* for more than ten years.

Gaditicus sighed to himself. Good men lost just to smoke out a few young hotheads trying to live the stories their grandfathers told. He could imagine the speeches they had made, whereas the truth was that Rome brought them civilization and a glimpse of what man could achieve. All the rebels fought for was the right to live in mud huts and scratch their arses, did they but know it. He didn't expect them to be grateful, he had lived too long and seen too much for that, but he demanded their respect, and the ill-planned mess at the fort had shown precious little of that. Eighty-nine enemy bodies had been burned at dawn. The Roman dead were carried back to the ship for burial at sea.

It was with such angry thoughts buzzing around in his head that he marched into the town of Mytilene in his best armor, with the rest of his depleted century shining behind him. Rain threatened in the form of dark, heavy clouds, and the stiflingly hot air matched his mood perfectly.

Julius marched stiffly after the battering he had taken the night before. It amazed him how many small cuts and scrapes he had picked up without noticing. His chest was purple all down the left side, and a shiny yellow lump stood out on one of his ribs. He would have Cabera look at it back on *Accipiter*, but he didn't think it was broken.

He disagreed with Gaditicus over the need for the march. The centurion was happy to break a rebellion and vanish, leaving someone else to handle the politics, but it was important to remind the town that the governor, above all else, was not to be touched.

He glanced over at Paulus, taking in the heavily ban-
daged hands and the still-swollen face. Julius admired that he
had refused to be carried in a litter, determined to show himself unbeaten after his torture. Fair enough that the man
wanted to come back to town at the head of a small army.
There were men like him all over Roman lands. They had little support from the Senate and were like small kings who
nonetheless depended on the goodwill of the locals to make
things happen as they wanted. When that goodwill failed,
Julius knew, a thousand small things could make life very difficult. No wood or food delivered except at sword-point,
roads damaged, small fires set. Nothing to turn out the guards
for, but constant irritations, like burrs caught in the skin.

From what the governor said of the life, Paulus seemed to
enjoy the challenges. Julius had been surprised to note that
his main feeling was not anger at his ordeal, but sadness that
people he had trusted had turned against him. Julius wondered if he would be so trusting in the future.

The legionaries marched through the town, ignoring the
stares and sudden movement as mothers cleared playing children from their path. Most of the Romans were feeling the
aches of the night before and were pleased to reach the governor's home in the center. They formed a square in front of the
building, and Julius saw one of the benefits of the post Paulus
held, in the beauty of the white walls and ornamental pools. It
was a piece of Rome, transplanted into the Greek countryside.

Paulus laughed aloud as his children came running to
greet him. He went down on one knee, letting them embrace
him while he kept his broken hands clear. His wife too came
out to see him, and Julius could see tears in her eyes, even
from the second rank. A lucky man.

"Tesserarius Caesar, stand forward," Gaditicus ordered,
startling Julius out of his thoughts. Julius moved quickly
and saluted. Gaditicus looked him over, his expression unreadable.

Paulus disappeared into his home with his family, and all the ranks waited patiently for him, happy enough to stand in the warmth of the afternoon sunshine with no jobs to be done.

Julius's mind churned, wondering why he had been ordered to stand out alone and how Suetonius would feel if it was a promotion. The governor was not able to order Gaditicus to give him a new post, but his recommendation was unlikely to be ignored.

At last Paulus returned, his wife walking out with him. He filled his lungs to address all the men together, and his voice was warm and strong.

"You have restored me to my position and my family. Rome thanks you for your service. Centurion Gaditicus has agreed that you may take a meal here. My servants are preparing my best food and drink for you all." He paused and his gaze fell on Julius.

"I witnessed great bravery last night, from one man in particular who risked his own life to save mine. To him, I award the honor wreath, to mark his courage. Rome has brave sons and I stand here today to prove it."

His wife stepped forward and lifted a circlet of green oak leaves. Julius unfroze and, when Gaditicus nodded at him, removed his helmet to accept it. He blushed and suddenly the men cheered, though whether it was at the honor to one of their own or the food to come, he wasn't sure.

"Thank you, I-I . . ." he stammered.

Paulus's wife put her hand on his own and Julius could see where face paint covered dark circles of worry under her eyes.

"You brought him back to me."

Gaditicus barked out the orders to remove helmets and follow the governor to where his staff were setting up the meal. He held Julius back for a moment, and when it was quiet, he asked to see the circlet. Julius handed it to him quickly, trying not to shout out loud with the excitement he felt.

Gaditicus turned the band of dark leaves over in his hands. "Do you deserve it?" he asked quietly.

Julius hesitated. He knew he had risked his life and rushed two men on his own down in the lowest room of the fort, but it was a prize he had not expected.

"Not more than a lot of the men, sir," he replied.

Gaditicus looked closely at him, then nodded, satisfied. "That's a good line, though I will say I was pleased to see you when you flanked the bastards last night." He grinned at Julius's rapidly changing expressions, from delight to embarrassment.

"Will you wear it under your helmet, or perched on top?"

Julius felt flustered. "I . . . I hadn't thought. I suppose I will leave it on the ship if there's action."

"Are you sure, now? Pirates will run scared of a man with leaves on his head, perhaps?"

Julius flushed again and Gaditicus laughed, clapping him on the shoulder.

"I'm only teasing you, lad. It is a rare honor. I'll have to promote you, of course. I can't have a lowly watch officer with an honor wreath. I will give you a twenty to command."

"Thank you, sir," Julius replied, his spirits lifting even further.

Gaditicus rubbed the leaves between his fingers thoughtfully. "You will have to wear this in the city sometime. It will be expected of you, at least once."

"Why, sir? I don't know the ritual."

"It's what I would do, anyway. The laws of Rome, lad. If you walk into a public event with an honor wreath, everyone must stand. *Every*one, even the Senate."

The centurion chuckled to himself. "What a sight that would be. Come in when you're settled. I'll make sure they keep some wine for you. It looks like you could do with a drink."

CHAPTER 3

In the gray evening light, Brutus scrambled down the side of the building, tearing most of the climbing roses with him. His foot caught in a loop of thorns at the bottom, and he fell flat, his sword skidding over the cobbles with a clatter. Wincing, he freed himself before struggling to his feet. He could hear another roar of anger above his head as Livia's father approached the window and glared down at the intruder. Brutus looked up at him as he tugged at his *bracae*, yelping as the cloth snagged on a thorn deep in his thigh.

Livia's father was a bull-like man who carried a heavy axe like a hatchet and was obviously considering whether he could hit Brutus with a good throw.

"I'll find you, whelp!" the man bellowed down at him, practically frothing through his beard in rage.

Brutus backed away out of range and tried to pick up his fallen gladius without taking his eyes off the red-faced Greek. He hitched up his bracae with one hand and found the hilt with the other, wishing he had kept his sandals on for the athletic tumbling about with Livia. If her father was trying to protect her innocence, he was about three years too late, Brutus thought. He considered sharing the information with the man out of spite, but she'd played fair by the young Roman, though she really should have checked the house before dragging him into her room as he passed. As she'd been naked, it had seemed only politeness for him to remove his sandals before they collapsed on the bed, though that courtesy would make escape through the sleepy town something of a problem.

No doubt Renius was still snoring in the room for which Brutus had paid. After five days sleeping in the open, both men had been happy enough to break the journey with a chance for a hot bath and a shave, but it looked as if only Renius would be enjoying those comforts while Brutus went for the hills.

Brutus shifted from one foot to the other uncomfortably as he considered his choices. He cursed Renius under his breath, partly for sleeping during a crisis, but mainly for convincing him that a horse would eat through their savings by the time they reached the coast and found a berth for Rome. Renius had said that a legionary could march the distance without any trouble, but even a thin pony would have been handy for a quick escape.

The angry beard vanished above, and while Brutus hesitated, Livia appeared at the window, her skin still flushed from their activities. It was a good healthy glow, Brutus noted idly, appreciating the way she rested her breasts on the sill.

"Get away!" she called in a harsh whisper. "He's coming down after you!"

"Throw my sandals down, then. I can't run like this," he hissed back. After a moment, the articles came flying at him and he laced them in a frenzy, already able to hear the clump of her father's tread as he came to the door.

Brutus heard the man's pleased exclamation to find him still in the yard. Without looking back, he sprinted away, skidding as the iron studs of his soles met the cobbles. Behind, Livia's father shouted for the town to stop him, which seemed to cause a stir of excitement in the locals about their business. Brutus groaned as he ran. Already there were answering yells and he could hear a number of others had joined the pursuit.

Feverishly, he tried to remember the streets he'd wandered through only hours before, thankful to find anything with cheap rooms and hot food. Livia's father had seemed pleasant enough then, though he hadn't been carrying the axe when he showed the tired men to his cheapest room.

Brutus thumped into a wall as he turned a corner at full speed, dodging round a cart and knocking away the grasping hands of its owner. Which way to get out? The town seemed like a labyrinth. He took roads to the left and right without daring to look back, his breath rasping in his throat. So far, Livia had been worth his trouble, but if he was killed, she wasn't his choice for the last woman in his life. He hoped the father would take his anger out on Renius and wished them both luck.

The alleyway he ran down came to a dead end around a corner. A cat scrambled from him as he halted against the nearest stone wall and prepared to risk a glance back. There was nowhere to run, but perhaps he'd lost them for the moment. He strained his ears before inching toward the edge, hearing nothing more threatening than the cat's complaints disappearing into the distance.

He eased one eye around the wall and pulled back at once. The alley seemed filled with men, all heading his way. Brutus dropped down into a crouch and risked a second glance at them, hoping he wouldn't be seen so low down.

A voice called out in recognition and Brutus groaned again as he pulled back. He'd picked up a little Greek in his time with the Bronze Fist, but hardly enough to talk his way out of the situation.

He made his decision and stood, firming his grip on the sword hilt, his other hand falling to the scabbard where he could fling it away. It was a fine blade that he'd won in a legion tournament, and he would have to show the farmers that he'd earned it. He hitched up his bracae one more time and took a deep breath before stepping out into the alley to face them.

There were five of them, their faces filled with the enthusiasm of children as they rushed down the alley. Brutus pulled away the scabbard with a flourish, in case they were in any doubt about his intentions. With great solemnity, he lowered the point at the men, and they pulled up as one. The moment held and Brutus thought furiously. Livia's father had yet to appear and there could be a chance to win free of the younger men before he arrived to encourage them. They might be open to persuasion and even bribery.

The largest of them stepped forward, careful to remain outside the range of the unwavering sword in Brutus's hands.

"Livia is my wife," the man said in clear Latin.

Brutus blinked at him. "Does she know?" he asked.

The man's face colored in anger and he produced a dagger from his belt. The others followed his example, revealing clubs and blades that they waved at Brutus while beckoning him forward to meet them.

Before they could rush him, Brutus spoke quickly, trying to sound calm and unruffled by the threat.

"I could kill every one of you, but all I want is to be allowed to go on my way in peace. I'm a legion champion with this pretty blade, and not one of you will leave this alley alive if you make the wrong decision."

Four of them listened with blank faces until Livia's husband translated the speech. Brutus waited patiently, hoping for a favorable response. Instead, they chuckled and began to edge closer to him. Brutus took a step back.

"Livia is a healthy girl with normal appetites," he said. "She seduced me, not the other way around. There is nothing worth killing for in this."

He waited with the others for the translation to begin, but the husband remained silent. Then the man said something in Greek, which Brutus barely followed. Part of it was certainly to try to keep him alive, which he approved, but the last part involved him being "given to the women," which sounded distinctly unpleasant.

Livia's husband leered at Brutus. "Catching a criminal means a festival for us. You will be the middle . . . the heart of it?"

As Brutus began to frame a reply, they rushed him with a flurry of blows, and though he pricked one of them with his gladius, a whistling club connected behind his ear and knocked him unconscious.

          *   *   *

He woke to a slow creaking and a feeling of dizziness. For a moment, he kept his eyes closed, trying to sense his whereabouts without letting unseen watchers know he was alert. There was a breeze playing about a fair portion of his body, and he had a sudden suspicion that his clothes had been removed. There could be no reasonable explanation for this, and his eyes snapped open despite his intentions.

He was hanging upside down, suspended by the feet from a wooden scaffold in the center of the town. A surreptitious glance upward confirmed the fact that he was naked. Everything hurt, and for a moment a memory of being hung from a tree when he was a boy came back to make him shudder.

It was dark and somewhere nearby he could hear sounds of revelry. He swallowed painfully at the thought of being part of some pagan ritual and strained at the ropes that held him. Blood pounded in his head with the effort, but there was no give in the knots.

His movement made him spin in a slow circle, and he was able to see the whole of the square at intervals. Every house was lit in a show of life far greater than the dull little place he had imagined on arrival. No doubt they were all boiling pig heads and blowing the dust off homemade wines, he thought dismally.

For a moment, he despaired. His armor was back in the room with Renius, and his sword had vanished. He had no sandals and his savings would no doubt fund the very celebration that would be the end of him. Even if he could escape, he was naked and penniless in a strange land. He cursed Renius with some enthusiasm.

"After a refreshing sleep, I have a good stretch and look out the window," Renius said by his ear. Brutus had to wait for a moment until he swung round to face him.

The old gladiator was shaved and clean and clearly enjoying himself.

" 'Surely,' I say to myself. 'Surely that figure hanging by his feet can't be the same popular young soldier I came in with?' "

"Look, I'm sure you'll tell a very amusing story to your cronies, but I'd appreciate it if you'd stop rehearsing it and just cut me down before someone stops you."

The creaking ropes carried Brutus away again. Without a word of warning, Renius sliced the ropes and spilled Brutus onto the ground. Shouts sounded around them and Brutus struggled to rise, pulling himself upright against the scaffold.

"My legs won't take my weight!" he said, trying to rub at each one in turn with desperate energy. Renius sniffed, looking around.

"They'd better. With one arm, I can hardly carry you and keep them off at the same time. Keep rubbing. We may have to bluff it through."

"If we had a horse, you could tie me to the saddle," Brutus retorted, rubbing furiously. Renius shrugged.

"No time for that. Your armor's in this bag. They brought your kit back to the rooming house, and I swiped it on my way out. Take your sword and brace yourself against the scaffold. Here they come." He passed over the blade, and for all his nude helplessness, Brutus felt a little comfort from the familiar hilt.

The crowd gathered quickly, Livia's father at the head, carrying his axe in both hands. He tensed enormously powerful shoulders and jerked the blades in Renius's direction.

"You came in with the one who attacked my daughter. I'll give you one chance to gather your things and move on. He stays here."

Renius stood still for a moment, then took a sharp pace forward, sinking his gladius into the man's chest so that it stood out behind him. He pulled it out and the man fell facedown on the cobbles, the axe head clattering noisily.

"Who else says he stays here?" Renius said, looking around the crowd. They had frozen at the sudden killing and there was no response. Renius nodded sternly at them, speaking slowly and clearly.

"No one was attacked. From the noises I heard, the girl was as enthusiastic as my idiot friend." Renius ignored Brutus's sharp intake of breath at his back, keeping his sweeping gaze locked on the crowd. They barely heard him. The gladiator had killed without a thought and that held the people still.

"Are you ready to go?" Renius murmured.

Brutus tested his legs gingerly, wincing at the fire of returning circulation. He began to pull his garments on as quickly as possible, the armor clanking loudly as he searched the bag with one hand.

"As soon as I'm dressed."

He knew the crowd's stupor couldn't last, but still jumped as Livia came shoving through the people, her voice shrill.

"What are you doing standing there?" she screamed at the crowd. "Look at my father! Who will kill his murderers?"

Behind her back, Brutus rose, his sword ready. The sweet smile he remembered from the afternoon had twisted into hatred as she screamed abuse at her own people. None of them met her eyes, their desire for vengeance cooled by the sprawled figure at her feet.

At the edge of the crowd, her husband turned his back on her and stalked away into the darkness. As she saw who it was, Livia turned on Renius, raining blows on his face and body. His only arm held the sword and as Brutus saw the muscles tense, he reached forward and pulled her away.

"Go home," he snapped at her. Instead, her hands reached for his eyes and Brutus shoved her roughly. She fell to the ground near her father's body and clung to it, weeping.

Renius and Brutus looked at each other and the thinning crowd.

"Leave her," Renius said.

Together, the two men crossed the square and made their way in silence through the town. It seemed hours before they reached the edge of the houses and looked out on a valley leading down to a river in the distance.

"We should push on. By dawn they'll be swearing blood feud and coming after us," Renius said, finally sheathing his sword.

"Did you really hear . . . ?" Brutus asked, looking away.

"You woke me up with your grunting, yes," Renius replied. "Your quick tumble could still kill us if they send out decent trackers. In her father's house!"

Brutus scowled at his companion. "You killed him, don't forget," he muttered.

"And you'd still be there if I hadn't. Now march. We need to cover as much ground as possible before daylight. And the next time a pretty girl looks twice at you, start running. They're more trouble than they're worth."

Silently disagreeing, the two men set off down the hill.

CHAPTER 4

"N ot wearing your wreath? I heard you slept with it," Suetonius sneered as Julius came on watch.

Julius ignored him, knowing that a response would lead to yet another exchange that would bring the two young officers closer to open hostility. For the moment, Suetonius at least made the pretense of courtesy when the other men were near enough to hear, but when they stood watch on their own, each second dawn, the bitterness in the man came to the surface. On the first day at sea after leaving the island, one of the men had tied a circlet of leaves to the tip of *Accipiter*'s mast, as if the whole ship had earned the honor. More than a few of the legionaries had waited around to see Julius catch sight of it, and his delighted grin brought a cheer out of them. Suetonius had smiled with the others, but the dislike in his eyes had deepened even further from that moment.

Julius kept his eyes on the sea and the distant African coast, changing balance slightly with the movements of *Accipiter* as the galley moved in the swell. Despite Suetonius's snide remark, he had not worn the circlet since leaving the town of Mytilene, except for trying it on once or twice in the privacy of his tiny bunk below the decks. The oak leaves had already begun to brown and curl, but that didn't matter. He had been given the right to wear it and would have a fresh one bound when he next saw Rome.

It was easy to ignore Suetonius with the daydream of striding into the Circus Maximus on a race day and seeing thousands of Romans stand, first only as they saw him, then in waves stretching farther away until the whole crowd was on its feet. He smiled slightly to himself, and Suetonius snorted in irritation.

Even in the dawn quiet, the oars rose and fell rhythmically below them as *Accipiter* wallowed through the waves. Julius knew by now that she was not a nimble ship, having seen two pirates disappear over the horizon with apparent ease in the months since Mytilene. The shallow draught had little bite in the water, and even with the twin steering oars, *Accipiter* lumbered through changes in direction. Her one strength was sudden acceleration under the oars, but even with two hundred slaves their best speed was no more than a brisk stroll on land. Gaditicus seemed untroubled by their inability to close with the enemy. It was enough to chase them away from the coastal towns and major trade lanes, but it was not what Julius had hoped for when he joined the ship. He'd had visions of swift and merciless hunting, and it was galling to realize that the Roman skill for land war did not extend to the seas.

Julius looked over the side to where the double oars lifted high and dipped in unison, carving their way through the still waters. He wondered how they could work the massive blades so steadily for hour after hour without exhaustion, even with three slaves to each one. He had been down to the oar deck a few times in the course of his duties, but it was crowded and foul. The bilges stank of wastes that were washed through twice a day with buckets of seawater, and the smell had made his stomach heave. The slaves were fed more than the legionaries, it was said, but watching the rise and fall of the beams in the water, he could see why it was needed.

On the great deck, the blistering heat of the African coast was cut by a stiff breeze as *Accipiter* fought through a westerly wind. At least from that vantage point, Julius could feel *Accipiter* was a ship designed for battle, if not speed. The open deck was clear of any obstruction, a wide expanse of wood that had been whitened by the beating sun over decades. Only the far end housed a raised structure, with cabins for Gaditicus and Prax. The rest of the century slept in cramped quarters below, their equipment stored in the armory where it quickly could be snatched up. Regular drills meant they could go from sleep to battle-readiness in less than one turn of the sandglass. It was a well-disciplined crew, Julius mused to himself. If they could ever catch another ship, they would be deadly.

"Officer on deck!" Suetonius barked suddenly by his ear and Julius came to attention with a start. Gaditicus had chosen a much older man as his *optio,* and Julius guessed Prax couldn't have more than a year or two before retirement. He had the beginnings of a soft belly that had to be belted tightly each morning, but he was a decent enough officer and had noted the tension between Suetonius and Julius in the first few weeks on board. It was Prax who had arranged that they stand dawn watch together, for some reason he chose not to share with them.

He nodded to the two of them amiably as he walked the long deck, making his morning inspection. He checked every rope that ran to the flapping square sail above them and went down on one knee to make sure the deck catapults were solidly bound and unmoving. Only after the careful inspection was finished did he approach the young officers, returning their salutes without ceremony. He scanned the horizon and smiled to himself, rubbing his freshly shaved chin in satisfaction.

"Four ... no, five sails," he said cheerfully. "The trade of nations. Not much of a wind to stir those who rely on it alone, though."

Over the months, Julius had come to realize that the genial outlook hid a mind that knew everything that went on in *Accipiter*, above and below decks, and his advice was usually valuable after you had waited through the casual openings. Suetonius thought he was a fool but appeared to be listening with avid interest, a manner he adopted for all the senior officers.

Prax continued, nodding to himself, "We'll need the oars to get to Thapsus, but it's a clear run up the coast then. After dropping off the pay-chests, we should make Sicily in a few weeks if we don't have to chase the raiders off our waters in the meantime. A beautiful place, Sicily."

Julius nodded, comfortable with Prax in a way that would have been impossible with the captain, despite the moment of familiarity after Mytilene. Prax had not been present at the storming of the fort, but he seemed not to have minded. Julius supposed he was happy enough with the light duties on *Accipiter* as he waited to retire and be dropped off at a legion near Rome to collect his outstanding pay. That was one benefit of hunting pirates with Gaditicus. The seventy-five denarii the legionaries were paid each month mounted up without much opportunity to spend it. Even after expenses for equipment and the tithe to the widows and burials fund, there would be a tidy sum available for most men when their time was up. If they hadn't gambled it all away by then, of course.

"Sir, why do we use ships that can't catch the enemy? We could clear out the Mare Internum in less than a year if we forced them to close with us."

Prax smiled, seemingly delighted by the question. "Close with us? Oh, it happens, but they're better seamen than we are, you know. There's every chance they'll ram and sink us before we can send our men over. Of course, if we can get the legionaries on their decks, the fight is won."

He blew air out slowly through puffed cheeks as he tried to explain. "It's more than just lighter, faster ships we need—

though Rome won't be sending funds to lay keels for them in my lifetime—it's a professional crew to man the oars. Those three vertical banks they use so precisely, can you imagine what our muscular slaves would do with them? They'd be a splintered mess the first time we tried to hit our best speed. With our way, we don't need to train experts, and from the point of view of the Senate we don't need to pay salaries to them either. One sum to buy the slaves, and the ship practically runs herself thereafter. And we do sink a few of them, though there always seem to be more."

"It just seems...frustrating at times," Julius said. He wanted to say it was madness for the most powerful nation in the world to be outsailed by half the ships on the oceans, but Prax kept a reserve that prevented the comment, despite his friendliness. There was a line not to be crossed by a junior, though it was less obvious than with some.

"We are of the land, gentlemen, though some like myself come to love the sea in the end. The Senate sees our ships as transport to take our soldiers to fight on other lands, as we did recently at the fort. They may come to realize that it is as important to rule the waves, but as I said, not in my lifetime. In the meantime, *Accipiter* is a little heavy and slow, but so am I and she's twice my age."

Suetonius laughed dutifully, making Julius wince, but Prax seemed not to notice. Julius felt a breath of memory at Prax's words. He remembered Tubruk had said something similar once, making him hold the dark earth of the estate in his hands and think of the generations that had fed it with their blood. It seemed a lifetime of experience away. His father had been alive then and Marius had still been a consul with a bright future. He wondered if someone was tending their graves. For a moment, the dark currents of worry that were always washing against his thoughts came to the surface. He reassured himself, as he always did, that Tubruk would look after Cornelia and his mother. He trusted no one else half as much as that man.

Prax stiffened slightly as his gaze swept the coast. His amiable expression disappeared, replaced by hardness.

"Get below and sound the call-out, Suetonius. I want every man on deck ready for action in five minutes."

Wide-eyed, Suetonius saluted smartly and strode to the steep steps, climbing nimbly down. Julius looked where Prax pointed and he narrowed his eyes. On the coast, a pall of black smoke was rising into the morning air, almost unmoved by wind.

"Pirates, sir?" he asked quickly, guessing the answer.

Prax nodded. "Looks like they've raided a village. We may be able to catch them as they come away from shore. You could get your chance to 'close' with them, Caesar."

*   *   *

Accipiter was stripped for action. Every loose piece of equipment was stowed away securely; the catapults were winched down and stones and oil prepared for firing. The legionaries gathered quickly and a picked team assembled the corvus, hammering iron spikes between the sections until the great boarding ramp was ready, standing high above the deck. When the holding ropes were released, it would fall outward onto the timbers of an enemy ship, embedding its holding spike immovably. Over it would come the best fighters on *Accipiter,* smashing into the pirates as fast as possible to make a space where the rest could jump on board. It was a perilous business, but after every action the places for those first over were hotly contested and changed hands in gambling games as a high stake in dreary months.

Below, the slave master called for double time and the oars moved in a more urgent rhythm. With the wind coming off the coast, the sail was dropped and reefed neatly. Swords were checked for cracks and nicks. Armor was tied tightly and a growing excitement could be felt on board, held down by the long-accustomed discipline.

The burning village was on the edge of a natural inlet, and they sighted the pirate ship as it cleared the rocky promontories and reached the open sea. Gaditicus ordered full attack speed to cut down the enemy's room to maneuver as much as possible. Caught as they were against the coast, there was little the pirate ship could do to avoid *Accipiter* as she surged forward, and a cheer went up from the Romans, the boredom of slow travel from port to port disappearing in the freshening breeze.

Julius watched the enemy ship closely, thinking of the differences Prax had explained. He could see the triple columns of oars cut the choppy sea in perfect unison despite their differing lengths. She was taller and narrower than *Accipiter* and carried a long bronze spike off the prow that Julius knew could punch through even the heavy cedar planking of the Roman ships. Prax was right, the outcome was never certain, but there was no escape for this one. They would close and drop the corvus solidly, putting the finest fighting men in the world onto the enemy deck. He regretted that he hadn't managed to secure a place for himself, but they had all been allocated since before the landing at Mytilene.

Lost in thought and anticipation as he was, he did not at first hear the sudden changes in the lookout calls. When he looked up, he took a step back from the rail without realizing it. There was another ship coming out of the inlet as they passed it in pursuit of the first. It was coming straight at them and Julius could see the ram emerge from the waves as it crashed through them at full speed, with sail taut and straining to aid the oarsmen. The bronze spike was at the waterline and the deck was filled with armed men, more than the swift pirates usually carried. He saw in a second that the smoke had been a ruse. It was a trap and they had sprung it neatly.

Gaditicus didn't hesitate, taking in the threat and issuing orders to his officers without missing a beat.

"Increase the stroke to the third mark! They'll go right by us," he barked and the drummer below beat out his second fastest rhythm. The ramming speed above it could only be used in a brief burst before the slaves began to collapse, but even the slightly slower attack pace was a brutal strain. Hearts had torn before in battles, and when that happened, the body could foul the other rowers and put an entire oar out of sequence.

The first ship was quickly growing closer and Julius realized they had reversed oars and were moving into the attack. It had been a well-planned ruse to draw the Roman ship close to the shore. No doubt the chests of silver in the hold were the prize, but they would not be won easily.

"Fire catapults at the first ship on my order. . . . Now!" Gaditicus shouted, then followed the path of the rocks as they soared overhead.

The lookout at the prow called, "Two points down!" to the two teams, and the heavy weapons were moved quickly. Sturdy pegs under them were hammered through their holes and others placed to hold the new angle. All this as the winches were wound back once more, with legionaries sweating as they heaved against the tension of a rope of horsehair twice as thick as a man's thigh.

The pirate vessel loomed as the catapults released again. This time, the porous stones were drenched in oil and burned as they curved toward the enemy trireme, leaving smoke trails in the air behind. They struck the enemy deck with cracks that could be heard on *Accipiter,* and the legionaries working the catapults cheered as they wound them back again.

The second trireme rushed toward them and Julius was sure the ram would spear *Accipiter* in the last few feet of her stern, leaving them unable to move or even counterattack by boarding. They would be picked off by arrow fire, pinned and helpless. As that thought struck him, he called to his men to bring up the shields to pass out. In boarding, they were more of a hindrance than a help, but with *Accipiter* caught between two ships that were moving into arrow range, they would be needed desperately.

A few seconds later, arrows began to spit into the air from both of the enemy triremes. There was no order or aiming to them, just the steady firing high into the air with the hope of pinning a legionary under one of the long black shafts.

The ramming ship alone would have slid astern in clear seas, but obstructed from the front by the first trireme, *Accipiter* had to dodge, with all the oars on one side ordered to reverse. The strokes were clumsy, but it was faster than simply having them raised clear while the other side brought *Accipiter* round. It slowed them down, but Gaditicus had seen the need to head for the outside line, or he would be caught between the two ships as the second pulled alongside.

Accipiter crunched past the prow of the first trireme, shuddering as the speed fell off. Gaditicus had the slave master ready for the move, and belowdecks the oars were pulled in quickly. The professionals of the trireme were not fast enough. *Accipiter* snapped the beams in groups of three as she passed, each one smashing men into bloody pulps, deep in the heart of the enemy vessel.

Before the Roman ship had traveled more than half the length of the trireme's oars, the bronze ram of the second smashed into *Accipiter* with the cracking roar of broken timbers. The whole ship groaned at the impact, like a living animal. The slaves below began to scream in a horrific chorus of terror. They were all chained to their benches, and if *Accipiter* went down, so did they.

Arrow fire cut into *Accipiter*'s deck, but there, if nowhere else, was the evidence of lack of army discipline. Julius thanked his luck that they hadn't the training to fire volleys as he ducked under a shaft that whined nastily over his head. The shields protected the men from most of the shots, and then the heavy corvus was leaning out and over, seeming to hang in the air for a moment when the ropes were cut, then smashing down into the enemy deck, its spike holding it as solid as the retribution to come.

The first of the legionaries ran over the causeway, smashing into those who waited, yelling defiance at them. The usual advantage of numbers was gone against either of the two attacking ships. Both seemed packed with fighters, their armor and weapons a mixture of old and new from the whole of the coastal ports.

Julius found Cabera at his side, his usual smile missing. The old man had taken up a dagger and shield, but otherwise wore his habitual robe, which Gaditicus had allowed as long as it was checked for lice twice a month.

"Better to stay with you than down in the dark, I think," Cabera muttered as he took in the unfolding chaos. Both ducked suddenly under their stiff wooden shields as arrows hummed past them. One shaft struck near Julius's hand, rocking him back. He whistled softly as he saw the barbed head had come through.

Heavy bronze hooks clattered onto the planking, trailing writhing coils. Men began to leap onto *Accipiter*'s decks and the noise of battle sounded all around, clashing swords and shouts of triumph and despair.

Julius saw Suetonius spread his men out in a line to meet the attackers. Quickly, he ordered his twenty in to support, though he suspected they would have run in without him if he had been slow. There could be no surrender with *Accipiter* holed, and every man there knew it. Their attacks were ferocious in their intensity and the first over the corvus cleared the decks before them, ignoring wounds.

Cabera stayed with him as he moved in to engage, and Julius felt comfort from his presence, reminding him of other battles they had survived together. Perhaps the old healer was a good-luck charm, he thought, and then he was moving into the arc of enemy blades and cutting them down without conscious will, his body moving in rhythms that Renius had taught him year after hard year.

Julius ducked under a hatchet and shoved the wielder when he was off balance, sending him sprawling by the feet of Pelitas, who stamped hard without thinking, in the legionary's classic battlefield reaction. If it's upright, cut it down. If it's down, stamp it flat.

The corvus was packed with soldiers as they jostled and shoved to get over. They were an easy target for archers, and Julius could see a group of bowmen against the far rail of the trireme taking shots when they could see through their own men. It was devastatingly effective fire at that short range, and more than a dozen legionaries went down before those on board cut the archers apart like so much wheat, in a bloody frenzy. Julius nodded with pleasure as he saw it. He felt the same hatred for archers that all legionaries felt who had known the terror and frustration of their long-range attacks.

The second trireme had backed oars and pulled almost free of *Accipiter*, the damage done. Gaditicus watched them maneuver as he held back units to repel their assault when it came. The situation was changing too rapidly to predict, though he did know the pirates couldn't stand off. *Accipiter* could be sinking, but she would not begin to settle for minutes more and the legionaries could yet fight their way clear onto the other trireme, taking command there. It wasn't impossible that they could salvage some sort of victory if they had an hour and were left alone, which is why he knew there would be another attack as soon as the second ship could clear its ram and bring its fighters close enough to board. He swore to himself as the last cracking timber sounded and the sharp prow pulled away from *Accipiter*, with the new orders to their oarsmen shouted quickly in what sounded like a mixture of Greek and dog Latin.

Gaditicus sent his remaining reserve of soldiers to the

other side of *Accipiter*, guessing they would board on the opposite side to split the defenders. It was a sensible move and served its purpose, though if the first trireme could be taken quickly enough, then all his men could be brought to repel the new attack and the day might not be lost. Gaditicus clenched his fist over the hilt of his gladius in what he knew was useless indignation. Should he have expected them to meet him fairly and be cut to pieces by his soldiers? They were thieves and beggars, after the silver in his holds, and it felt as if small dogs were bringing down the Roman wolf. His hand shook with emotion as he saw the bank of oars pulled in on one side and the second trireme scull toward his beloved ship. He could still hear the screaming of the slaves below in a constant chorus of terror that wore at his nerves.

Julius took a blow on his armor and grunted as he reversed his sword through a man's face. Before he could take in his position, a bearded giant stepped toward him. Julius felt a touch of fear as he saw the enormous height and shoulders of the warrior carrying a weighty metalworker's hammer that was stained red with blood and hair. The man's teeth were bared and he bellowed as he brought the weapon over his shoulder in a downward blow. Julius backed away, bringing his arm up to parry in reflex. He felt the bones of his wrist snap from the impact and cried out in pain.

Cabera darted quickly between them and sank his dagger into the man's neck, but the warrior only roared and brought the hammer back round to sweep the frail healer away. Julius reached for his own dagger with his left hand, trying to ignore the agony of grating bones. He felt dizzy and suddenly detached, but the enormous man was still dangerous, though blood fountained from the neck wound.

The bull-like figure staggered erect and swung again in blind pain. The hammer connected solidly with Julius's head with a dull crack, and he collapsed. Blood pooled slowly from his nose and ears as the fight went on around him.

CHAPTER 5

Brutus took a deep breath of clean mountain air as he looked back at their pursuers. With Greece spread out below them and the slopes covered with tiny purple blooms lifting a rich scent into the wind, it seemed wrong to be dwelling on death and revenge. Yet, as Renius had predicted, the group of riders contained at least one good tracker, and over the last five days they had remained doggedly on their trail despite a number of attempts to lose them.

Renius sat on a mossy rock nearby with his shoulder stump exposed, rubbing grease into the scarred flesh, as he did every morning. Brutus felt guilty each time he saw it, remembering the fight in the training yard of Julius's estate. He thought he could even remember the blow that had severed the nerves of the arm, but there was no calling it back after all this time. Though the flesh had formed a pink pad of callus, raw patches would appear that needed to be salved. The only real relief came when Renius was forced to leave the leather cap off and let the air get to the skin, but he hated the curious looks it brought and shoved the cap back on whenever he could.

"They're getting closer," Brutus said. He didn't need to explain; the five men following had been in both their thoughts ever since first sighting them.

The sun-hammered beauty of the mountains concealed a poor soil that attracted few farmers. The only signs of life were the small figures of the hunters making their slow way up. Brutus knew they could not stay ahead of horses for much longer, and as soon as they reached the plains below, the Romans would be run down and killed. Both of them were approaching exhaustion and the last of the dry food had gone that morning.

Brutus eyed the vegetation that clung to life on the craggy slopes, wondering if any of it was edible. He'd heard of soldiers eating the singing crickets that haunted each tuft and clump of grass, but it wouldn't be worth it to catch one at a time. They couldn't go another day without food, and their waterskins were less than half full. Gold coins still filled his belt pouch, but the nearest Roman city was more than a hundred miles away across the Thessaly plain and they'd never make it. The future looked bleak unless Renius could come up with an idea, but the old gladiator was silent, apparently content to while away an hour rubbing his stump. As Brutus watched, Renius pulled one of the dark flowers and squeezed its juice onto the hairy pad that hung from his shoulder. The old gladiator was always testing herbs for their soothing effect, but as usual, he sniffed with disappointment and let the broken petals fall out of his good hand.

Renius's calm expression suddenly infuriated Brutus. With a pair of horses under them, the pursuers from the village would never have come close. It was not in Renius's nature to regret past decisions, but every pace gained on the footsore Romans made Brutus grunt in irritation.

"How can you just sit there while they climb up to us? The immortal Renius, victor of hundreds of bouts to the death, cut to pieces by a few ragged Greeks on a hilltop."

Renius looked at him, unmoved, then shrugged. "The slope will cut down their advantage. Horses aren't much good up here."

"So we're making a stand then?" Brutus demanded, feeling vast relief that Renius had some sort of plan.

"They won't be here for hours yet. If I were you, I'd sit down in the shade and rest. You'll find sharpening my sword will calm your nerves."

Brutus scowled at him, but still took up the older man's gladius and began to work a stone along the edges in long strokes.

"There are five of them, remember," he said after a while.

Renius ignored him, fitting the leather cup over his stump with a grunt. He held one end of the tying thong in his teeth and knotted it with the ease of long practice while Brutus looked on.

"Eighty-nine," Renius said suddenly.

"What?"

"I killed eighty-nine men in the bouts in Rome. Not hundreds."

He rose smoothly to his feet and there was nothing of an old man in his movement. It had taken a long time to retrain his body to balance without the weight of his left arm, but he had beaten that loss as he had beaten everything else that stood against him in his life. Brutus remembered the moment Cabera had pressed his hands into the gray flesh of Renius's chest and seen the color change as the body stiffened in a sudden rush of returning life. Cabera had sat back on his heels in silent awe as they watched the old man's hair darken, as if even death couldn't keep its grip on him. The gods had saved the old gladiator, perhaps so he in turn could save another young Roman on a hilltop in Greece. Brutus felt his own confidence build, forgetting the hunger and exhaustion that racked him.

"There are only five today," Brutus said. "And I am the best of my generation, you know. There is not a man alive who can beat me with a sword."

Renius grunted at this. "I was the best of my generation, lad, and from what I can see, the standard has slipped a bit since then. Still, we may yet surprise them."

*   *   *

Cornelia groaned in pain as the midwife rubbed golden olive oil into her thighs, helping the muscles to uncramp. Clodia handed her a warm drink of milk and honey wine, and she emptied the cup almost without tasting it, holding it out for more even as the next contraction built in her. She shuddered and cried out.

The midwife continued to lather oil over her in wide, slow strokes, holding a cloth of the softest wool in her hands, which she dipped into a bowl of the liquid.

"Not long now," she said. "You are doing very well. The honey and wine should help with the pain, but it will soon be time to move you over to the chair for the birth. Clodia, fetch more cloths and the sponge in case there's bleeding. There shouldn't be much. You are very strong and your hips are a good size for this work."

Cornelia could only moan in response, breathing in short gasps as the contraction came on fully. She clenched her teeth and gripped the sides of the hard bed, pushing down with her hips. The midwife shook her head slightly.

"Don't start pushing yet, dear. The baby is just thinking about coming out. It's dropped down into position and needs to rest. I'll tell you when to start pressing her out."

"Her?" Cornelia gasped between heavy breaths.

The midwife nodded. "Boys are always easier births. It's girls who take as long as this." She thanked Clodia as the sponge and cloths were placed next to the wooden birthing chair, ready for the last stages of the labor.

Clodia reached out and took Cornelia's hand, rubbing it tenderly. A door to the room opened quietly and Aurelia entered, moving quickly to the bed and taking the other hand in her own tight grip. Clodia watched her covertly. Tubruk had told her all about the woman's problems so that she would be able to deal with any difficulty, but Cornelia's labor seemed to focus Aurelia's attention and it was right that she should be present at the birth of her grandchild. With Tubruk gone from the house to complete the business they had discussed, Clodia knew it would fall on her to remove Aurelia if she began her sickness before the birth was over. None of her own servants would dare, but it was not a task Clodia relished and she sent a quick prayer to the household gods that it would not be necessary.

"We think it will be a daughter," Clodia told her as Julius's mother took up station on the other side.

Aurelia did not reply. For a moment, Clodia wondered if her stiffness was because she was the lady of the house and Clodia only a slave, but dismissed the idea. The rules were relaxed during a labor and Tubruk had said she had trouble with the small things that people took for granted.

Cornelia cried out and the midwife nodded sharply.

"It's time," she said, then spoke sharply to Aurelia: "Are you up to helping us, dear?"

When there was no answer, the midwife asked again, much louder. Aurelia seemed to come out of a daze.

"I'd like to help," she said quietly, and the midwife paused for a moment, weighing her up. Then she shrugged.

"All right, but it could be hours. If you're not up to it, send in a strong girl to help in your stead. Understand?"

Aurelia nodded, her attention again on Cornelia as she got into position to help take her weight over to the chair. As Clodia too began to lift, she marveled at the confidence the midwife showed. Of course, she was a freedwoman, so the days of her slavery were long behind, but there was not an ounce of deference in her manner. Clodia rather liked her and resolved to be as strong herself as was needed.

The chair was built solidly and had arrived on a cart with the midwife a few days before. Together, they walked Cornelia to where it stood, close to the bed. She gripped the arms tightly, letting her whole weight fall on the narrow curve of the seat. The midwife knelt in front of Cornelia, pushing her legs gently apart over the deep crescent cut into the old wood.

"Press yourself against the back of the chair," she advised, then turned to Clodia. "Don't let it tip backward. I'll have another job for you when the baby is showing her head, but for the moment, that's your task, understood?"

Clodia took up position with the weight of her hip braced against the chair back.

"Aurelia? I want you to push down on the abdomen when I say, not before. Is that clear?"

Aurelia placed her hands on the swollen belly and waited patiently, her eyes clear.

"It's starting again," Cornelia said, wincing.

"That's as it should be, my girl. The baby wants to come out. Let it build and I'll tell you when to push." Her hands rubbed more oil into Cornelia and she smiled.

"Shouldn't be long now. Ready? Now, girl, push! Aurelia, press down gently."

Together, they pressed and Cornelia wailed in pain. Again and again they tensed and released until the contraction had gone and Cornelia was drenched in perspiration, her hair wet and dark.

"Getting the head out is the worst of it," the midwife said. "You're doing well, dear. A lot of women scream all the way through. Clodia, I want you to press a piece of cloth against her bottom during the spasms. She won't thank us if there are grapes hanging there at the end."

Clodia did as she was told, reaching down between the chair back and Cornelia and holding the pad steady.

"Not long now, Cornelia," she said comfortingly.

Cornelia managed a weak smile. Then the contractions built again, a tightening of every muscle that was frightening in its power. She had never known anything like it and almost felt a spectator in her own body as it moved to rhythms of its own, with a strength she didn't know she had. She felt the pressure build and build, then suddenly disappear, leaving her exhausted.

"No more," she whispered.

"I have the head, dear. The rest is easier," the midwife replied, her voice calm and cheerful. Aurelia rubbed her hands over the swelling, leaning over the chair to see between Cornelia's shaking legs.

The midwife held the baby's head in her hands, which were wrapped in coarse cloth to prevent slipping. The eyes were closed and the head appeared misshapen, distended, but the midwife seemed not to worry and urged them on as the next contraction hit and the rest of the baby slid into her hands. Cornelia sagged back into the chair, her legs feeling like water. Her breathing came in ragged gasps, and she could only nod her thanks as Aurelia wiped her brow with a cool cloth.

"We have a girl!" the midwife said as she took a small sharp knife to the cord. "Well done, ladies. Clodia, fetch me a hot coal to make a seal."

"Aren't you going to tie it?" Clodia asked as she stood.

The midwife shook her head, using her hands to clear the baby's skin of blood and membranes. "Burning's cleaner. Hurry up, my knees are aching."

Another heaving contraction brought a slithering mess of dark flesh out of Cornelia with a final cry of exhaustion. The midwife motioned to Aurelia to clear it away. Julius's mother attended to the afterbirth without a thought, now used to the woman's authority. She felt a glow of unaccustomed happiness as the new reality sank in. She had a granddaughter. Aurelia glanced at her hands covertly, relieved to see the shaking was absent for the moment.

A cry cut the air and suddenly the women were smiling. The midwife checked the limbs, her movements quick and practiced.

"She will be fine. A little blue, but turning pink already. She will have fair hair like her mother unless it darkens. A beautiful child. Have you the swaddling cloths?"

Aurelia handed them to her as Clodia returned, holding a tiny hot coal in iron tongs. The midwife pressed it to the tiny stump of cord with a sizzle, and the baby screamed with renewed vigor as the woman set about wrapping the child tightly, leaving only her head free.

"Have you thought of a name for her?" she asked Cornelia.

"If it was a boy, I was going to name him after his father, Julius. I always thought it . . . she . . . would be a boy."

The midwife stood with the baby in her arms, taking in Cornelia's pale skin and exhaustion.

"There's plenty of time to think of names. Help Cornelia onto the bed to rest, ladies, while I gather my things."

The sound of a fist striking the estate gates could be heard as a low booming in the birthing room.

"Tubruk usually opens the gate for visitors," Aurelia said, "but he has deserted us."

"Only for a few weeks, mistress," Clodia replied quickly, feeling guilty. "He said the business in the city would not take longer than that."

Aurelia seemed not to hear the reply as she left the room.

Julius's mother walked slowly and carefully out into the front yard, wincing at the bright sunlight after so long indoors. Two of her servants waited patiently by the gate, but knew better than to open it without her agreement, no matter who was standing there. It was a rule Tubruk had enforced ever since the riots years before. He seemed to care for the safety of the house, yet had left her alone as he had promised he would never do. She composed her expression, noticing a small drop of blood on her sleeve as she did so. Her right hand shook slightly and she gripped it in the other, willing the fit down.

"Open the gate!" came a man's voice from the other side, his fist banging on the wood yet again.

Aurelia signaled to the servants and they removed the

bracing beam, pulling the gate open for the visitor. Aurelia saw they were both armed, another rule of Tubruk's.

Three mounted soldiers entered, resplendent in gleaming armor and helmet plumes. They were dressed as if for a parade and the sight of them sent a chill through Aurelia.

Why wasn't Tubruk here? He would be able to handle this so much better than she could.

One of the men dismounted, his movements easy and assured. Holding the reins bunched in one hand, he handed Aurelia a roll of vellum sealed with thick wax. She took it and waited, watching him. The soldier shuffled his feet as he realized Aurelia was not going to speak.

"Orders, mistress. From our master the Dictator of Rome."

Still Aurelia was silent, gripping the hand that held the scroll with the other, her knuckles showing white.

"Your daughter by marriage is here and Sulla orders her presence before him in the city immediately," the man continued, realizing that unless he spoke, she might never open the scroll that confirmed the orders with Sulla's personal seal.

Aurelia found her voice as the shaking steadied in her for a moment. "She has just given birth. She cannot be moved. Return in three days and I will have her ready to travel."

The soldier's face hardened slightly, his patience unraveling. Who did this woman think she was? "Mistress, she will be made ready now. Sulla has ordered her to the city and she will be on the road immediately, willing or not. I will wait here, but I expect to see her in a few minutes at most. Do not make us come in to fetch her."

Aurelia paled slightly. "Wh...what about the child?"

The soldier blinked. There was no child mentioned in his orders, but careers were not made by disappointing the Dictator of Rome.

"The child too. Make them both ready." His expression softened a little. It would hurt nothing to be kind and the woman looked very fragile suddenly. "If you have a cart and horses that can be harnessed quickly, they can travel in that."

Aurelia turned without another word and disappeared into the building. The soldier looked up at his two companions, his eyebrows raised.

"I told you this would be easy. I wonder what he wants with the woman."

"Depends who the father is, I should think," one replied, winking lewdly.

*   *   *

Tubruk sat stiffly in the chair, nodding as he took the wine offered to him. The man he faced was his own age and they had been friends for the best part of thirty years.

"I still have difficulty recognizing I am not the young man I was," Fercus said, smiling ruefully. "I used to have mirrors all round my house, but every time I passed one, I would be surprised at the old man peering out at me. Still, the body fails, but the mind remains relatively sharp."

"I should hope so, you are not old," Tubruk replied, trying to relax and enjoy his friend's company as he had so many times over the years.

"You think not? Many of those we knew have gone on to cause mischief in the silent lands by now. Disease took Rapas and he was the strongest man I ever met. At the end, they say his son put him over his shoulder to carry him out into the sun. Can you imagine anyone putting that great ox over their shoulder? Even a son of his! It is a terrible thing to grow old."

"You have Ilita and your daughters. She hasn't left you yet?" Tubruk murmured.

Fercus snorted into his wine. "Not yet, though she still threatens to every year. In truth, you need a good, fat woman yourself. They hold off the old age wonderfully, you know. And keep your feet warm at night, as well."

"I am too set in my ways for new love," Tubruk replied.

"Where would I find a woman willing to put up with me? No, I've found a family of sorts at the estate. I can't imagine another."

Fercus nodded, his eyes missing nothing of the tension that filled the old gladiator's frame. He was prepared to wait until Tubruk felt ready to broach the reason for his sudden visit. He knew the man well enough not to hurry him, as much as he knew that he would help in any way he could. It wasn't just a matter of the debts he owed, though they were many; it was the fact that Tubruk was a man he respected and liked. There was no malice in him and he was strong in ways that Fercus had rarely seen.

Mentally, he tallied up his holdings and available gold. If it was a matter of money that was needed, there had been better times, but he had reserves and debts of his own that could be called in.

"How's business?" Tubruk asked, unconsciously matching Fercus's own thoughts.

Fercus shrugged, but stopped the light reply before it left his lips.

"I have funds," he said. "There is always a need for slaves in Rome, as you know."

Tubruk looked steadily at the man who had once sold him to be trained for combat in front of thousands. Even then, as a young quarry slave who knew nothing of the world or the training to come, he had seen that Fercus was never cruel to those who passed through his sales. He remembered despairing on the night before he was sent to the training pens, when his mind turned to ways of ending his life. Fercus had stopped by him as he walked his rounds and told him that if he had heart and strength, he could buy himself free and still have most of his life ahead of him.

"I will come back on that day and kill you," Tubruk had said to the man.

Fercus had held his gaze for a long time before replying.

"I hope not," he had said. "I hope you will ask me to share a cup of wine."

The younger Tubruk had been unable to reply, but later the words were a comfort to him, just to know that one day there could be the freedom to sit and drink in the sun, his own master. On the day he was free, he had walked through the city to Fercus's home and placed an amphora on the table. Fercus had set up two cups next to it, and their friendship had begun without bitterness.

If there was anyone in the world outside the estate that he could trust, then Fercus was the man, but still he was silent as he went over the plans he had made since Clodia had come to see him. Surely there was another way? The course he followed sickened him, but he knew if he would die to protect Cornelia, then he could surely do this.

Fercus stood and gripped Tubruk's arm.

"You are troubled, my old friend. Whatever it is, ask me." His eyes were steady as Tubruk looked up at him and held the gaze, the past open between them.

"Can I trust you with my life?" Tubruk asked.

Fercus gripped his arm all the tighter in response, then settled back into his seat.

"You don't have to ask. My daughter was dying before you found a midwife to save her. I would have died myself at the hands of those thieves if you had not fought them off. I owe such a debt to you that I thought I would never have the chance to repay it. Ask me."

Tubruk took a deep breath.

"I want you to sell me back into slavery—to the house of Sulla," he said quietly.

*　　　　　*　　　　　*

Julius barely felt Cabera's hands as they lifted his eyelids. The world seemed alternately dark and bright to him, and his head was filled with a red agony. He heard Cabera's voice from far away and tried to curse him for disturbing the darkness.

"His eyes are wrong," someone said. Gaditicus? The name meant nothing, though he knew the voice. Was his father there? Distant memories of lying in darkness on the estate came to him and merged with his thoughts. Was he still in bed after Renius had cut him in training? Were his friends out on the walls turning back the slave rebellion without him? He struggled slightly and felt hands pressing him down. He tried to speak, but his voice would not obey, though a mushy sound came out, like the moan of a dying bullock.

"That is not a good sign," Cabera's voice came. "The pupils are different sizes and he is not seeing me. His left eye has filled with blood, though that will pass in a few weeks. See how red it is. Can you hear me, Julius? Gaius?"

Julius could not answer even to his childhood name. A weight of blackness pressed them all away from him.

Cabera stood up and sighed.

"The helmet saved his life, at least, but the blood from his ears is not good. He may recover, or he may remain like this. I have seen it before with head wounds. The spirit can be crushed." The grief was clear in his voice and Gaditicus was reminded that the healer had come aboard with Julius and had a history that went back further than their time on *Accipiter*.

"Do what you can for him. There's a good chance we'll all see Rome again if they get the money they want. At least for a while, we're worth more alive than dead."

Gaditicus fought to keep the despair from his voice. A captain who had lost his ship was not likely to find another. Trussed helpless on the deck of the second trireme, he had watched his beloved *Accipiter* sink beneath the sea in a swirl of bubbles and driftwood. The slaves at the oars had not been released, and their screams had been desperate and hoarse until the waters took the ship. His career too had sunk with her, he knew.

The struggle had been brutal, but most of his men had finally been cut down, overwhelmed and attacked on two sides. Again and again, Gaditicus played over the short battle in his mind, looking for ways he could have won. Always he finished by shrugging, telling himself to forget the loss, but the humiliation stayed with him.

He had thought of taking his life to deny them his ransom and the shame it would cause his family. If they could even raise the money.

It would have been easier on them if he had gone down with *Accipiter* like so many of his men. Instead, he was left to sit in his own filth with the twelve surviving officers and Cabera, who had escaped by offering to use his skills as a healer for the pirates. There were always those with wounds that would not close and infections that clung to their genitals after whores in lonely ports. The old man had been busy since the battle and was only allowed to see them once a day to check their own wounds and dressings.

Gaditicus shifted slightly, scratching at the lice and fleas that had infested him since the first night in the cramped and filthy cell. Somewhere above, the men that held them captive swaggered about on the trireme's decks, rich with prisoners for ransom and the chests of silver stolen from *Accipiter*'s hold. It had been a profitable risk for them and he grimaced as he recalled their arrogance and triumph.

One of the men had spat in his face after his hands and feet were tied. Gaditicus flushed with anger as he thought of it. The man had been blind in one eye, his face a mass of old scars and stubbly bristle. The white eye had seemed to peer at the Roman captain, and the man's cackle almost made him show his anger and humiliate himself further by struggling. Instead, he had stared impassively, only grunting when the little man kicked him in the stomach and walked away.

"We should try to escape," Suetonius whispered, leaning in close enough for Gaditicus to smell his breath.

"Caesar can't be moved at the moment, so put it out of your mind. It will take a few months for the ransom messages to reach the city and a few more for the money to come back to us, if it comes at all. We will have more than enough time to plan."

Prax too had been spared by the pirates. Without his armor, he seemed much more ordinary. Even his belt had been taken in case the heavy buckle could be used as a weapon, and he constantly hitched up his bracae. Of all of them, he had taken the change in fortunes with the least obvious anger, his natural patience helping to keep them all steady.

"The lad's right, though, Captain. There's a good chance they'll just drop us all overboard when they get the silver from Rome. Or, the Senate could stop our families making the payment, preferring to forget us."

Gaditicus bristled. "You forget yourself, Prax. The senators are Romans as well, for all your poor opinions of them. They won't let us be forgotten."

Prax shrugged. "Still, we should make plans. If this trireme meets another Roman galley, we'll be sent over the side if they look like boarding us. A bit of chain around our feet would do the job nicely."

Gaditicus met the eyes of his optio for a few moments. "All right. We'll work out a few things, but if the chance comes, I'm not leaving anyone behind. Caesar has a broken arm as well as the head injury. It will be weeks before he can stand, even."

"If he survives," Suetonius put in.

Cabera looked at the young officer, his gaze sharp. "He is strong, this one, and he has an expert healer tending him."

Suetonius looked away from the old man's intense stare, suddenly embarrassed.

Gaditicus broke the silence. "Well, we have the time to consider all outcomes, gentlemen. We have plenty of that."

CHAPTER 6

Casaverius allowed himself a smile of self-congratulation as he surveyed the long kitchen hall. Everywhere, the bustle of the evening was coming to an end, with the last of the orders served hours before.

"Perfection is in the detail," he murmured to himself, as he had done every evening for the ten years he had been employed by Cornelius Sulla. Good years, though his once trim figure had swollen alarmingly in the time. Casaverius leaned back against the smooth plaster wall and continued grinding with his pestle and mortar, preparing a mustard seed paste that Sulla loved. He dipped a finger into the dark mixture and added a little oil and vinegar from the row of narrow-necked pots that hung along the walls. How could a good cook resist tasting his own meals? It was part of the process. His father had been even larger, and Casaverius took pride in his heaviness, knowing that only a fool would employ a thin cook.

The brick ovens had been closed to the air for long enough and should have cooled. Casa motioned to the slaves that they could be raked clean, ready for new charcoal in the morning. The air in the kitchen was still thickly sluggish with heat, and he pulled a rag from his belt to wipe his brow. With the weight, he seemed to sweat more, he admitted to himself, pressing the already damp cloth against his face.

He considered finishing the paste in one of the cool

rooms where iced dishes were prepared, but hated to leave the slaves unattended. He knew they stole food for their families, and in moderation he could forgive them. Left alone, though, they might grow incautious, and who knew what would disappear then? He remembered his father complaining about the same thing in the evenings and quickly whispered a prayer for the old man, wherever he was now.

There was a great peace at the end of a day that had gone well. Sulla's house was known for fine food, and when the call came for something special, he enjoyed the excitement and energy that stole over the staff, starting with the moment of anticipation as he opened his father's sheaf of recipes, untying the leather thongs that bound the valuable parchments and running his finger down the lettering, taking pleasure from the fact that only he could read them. His father had said that every cook should be an educated man, and Casaverius sighed for a moment, his thoughts turning to his own son. The lad spent mornings in the kitchens, but his studies seemed to fly from his mind whenever the day was fine. The boy was a disappointment and Casaverius had come to accept that he might never be able to run a grand kitchen on his own.

Still, there were years left before he would leave his plates and ovens for the last time, retiring to his small home in a good district of the city. Perhaps then he might find time to entertain the guests his wife wanted. Somehow, he never managed to bring his expertise into his own home, being satisfied with simple dishes of meat and vegetables. His stomach grumbled a little at the thought, and he saw the slaves were removing their own roasted packages of bread and meat from the ashes of the ovens, where they had been placed at the end. It was a small loss to the kitchen to be able to send them back to their quarters with a few hot mouthfuls, and it made a friendly atmosphere in the kitchens, he was sure.

The new slave, Dalcius, passed him, bearing a metal tray

of spice pots, ready to be placed back on their shelves. Casaverius smiled to him as he began unloading the tray.

He was a good worker and the broker at the sales had not lied when he said he knew his way round a kitchen. Casaverius considered that he might allow him to prepare a dish for the next banquet, under his watchful eye.

"Make sure the spices go in the right places, Dalcius," he said.

The big man nodded, smiling. He certainly wasn't a talker. That beard might have to be cut off, he thought. Casaverius's father had never let a beard into his kitchens, saying they made the place look untidy.

He tasted his mustard paste again and smacked his lips appreciatively, noting that Dalcius finished his task quickly and neatly. From his scars, he looked more like an old fighter, but there was nothing bullish about the man. If there had been, Casaverius couldn't have had him in the kitchens, where the endless rushing and carrying always meant a few would bump into each other. Bad tempers couldn't survive down below the rich houses, but Dalcius had proved amiable, if silent.

"I will need someone to help me tomorrow morning, to prepare the pastries. Would you like to do that?" Casaverius didn't realize he was speaking slowly, as if to a child, but Dalcius never seemed to mind and his silences invited the manner. There was no malice in the fat cook, and Casaverius was genuinely pleased when Dalcius nodded to him before going back into the stores. A cook had to have an eye for good workers, his father had always said. It was the difference between working yourself into an early grave and achieving perfection.

"And perfection is in the detail," he murmured again to himself.

At the end of the long kitchen hall, the door to the house above opened and a smartly dressed slave entered. Casaverius straightened, laying his mortar and pestle aside without thought.

"The master sends his apologies for the late hour and wonders if he may be sent something cold before he sleeps, an ice dish," the young man said, bowing.

Casaverius thanked him, pleased as always with the courtesy.

"For all his guests?" he asked quickly, thinking.

"No, sir, his guests have departed. Only the general remains."

"Wait here, then. I will have it ready in a few moments."

The kitchens went from end-of-evening stupor to alertness in the time it took Casaverius to issue new orders. Two of the kitchen runners were sent down the steps to the ice rooms, far below the kitchens. Casa strode under a low arch and through a short corridor to where the desserts were prepared.

"A lemon ice, I think," he muttered as he walked. "Beautiful bitter southern lemons, made sweet and cold."

Everything was in place as he entered the cool dessert room. Like the main kitchen, the walls were hung with dozens of amphorae filled with syrups and sauces, made and refilled whenever the kitchens were quiet. There was no hint of the oven heat in there, and he felt the sweat chill on his heavy body with a pleasurable shiver.

The ice blocks, wrapped in rough cloth, were brought up in minutes and crushed under his direction until the ice was a fine slurry. To this he added the bittersweet lemon and stirred it in, just enough to flavor without overpowering. His father had said the ice must not be yellow, and Casaverius smiled as he noted the color and fine texture, using a ladle to scoop the mixture into the glass bowls on a serving tray.

He worked quickly. Even in the cool room the ice was melting, and the journey through the kitchens would have to be fast. He hoped that one day Sulla would allow another passage to be cut in the rock under his luxurious home, so that the iced desserts could be brought straight up. Still, with care and speed, the dishes would reach his table almost intact.

After only a few minutes, the two bowls were full of the white ice and Casaverius sucked his fingers, groaning in exaggerated pleasure. How good it was to taste cold in the summer! He wondered briefly how much silver coin the two bowls represented, but it was an unimaginable sum. Drivers and carts transported huge blocks from the mountains, losing half in the journey. They were brought down to the dripping darkness of the ice rooms below him, there to melt slowly, but giving cool drinks and desserts for all the summer months. He reminded himself to check that supplies were adequate. It was almost time for a new order.

Dalcius entered the room behind him, still carrying his spice tray.

"May I watch you prepare the ices? My last master never had them."

Casaverius motioned him in, cheerfully. "The work is done. They must be rushed through the kitchens before they begin to melt."

Dalcius leaned over the table and his arm knocked over the jug of sticky syrup, which spread in a wide yellow stain. Casaverius's good humor vanished on the instant.

"Quick, you idiot, fetch cloths to clean it up. There is no time to waste."

The big slave looked terrified and he stammered, "I—I'm sorry. I have another tray here, master."

He held out the tray and Casaverius lifted the bowls, cleaning them quickly with his own sweat-soaked rag. No time to be sensitive, he thought. The ice was melting. He placed the bowls on the tray and wiped his fingers irritably.

"Don't just stand there, run! And if you trip over your own feet, I'll have you whipped." Dalcius moved quickly out of the room, and Casaverius began to wipe up the spilled mess. Perhaps the man was too clumsy for more difficult tasks.

Outside in the corridor, it was the work of a moment for Tubruk to empty the vial of poison into the bowls, stirring it in with a finger. That done, he raced through to the kitchen and handed the tray to the waiting slave.

The eyes that had seemed so nervous looked steadily at the retreating back as the door to the house above closed behind him. Now he must escape, but there was bloody work to do first. He sighed. Casaverius was not a bad man, but one day in the future, with the beard cut off and his hair grown back to its normal length, the cook might still be able to recognize him.

Feeling suddenly weary, he turned back toward the cool rooms, touching the bone-handled knife under his tunic as he walked. He would make sure it looked like a murder rather than suicide. That should keep Casaverius's family safe from revenge.

"Did you give him the tray?" Casa snapped as Tubruk reentered the small cool room.

"I did. I am sorry, Casaverius."

The cook looked up as Tubruk stepped quickly toward him. The man's voice had deepened slightly and the usual manner was missing. Casaverius saw the blade, and fear and confusion coursed through him.

"Dalcius! Put that down!" he said, but Tubruk shoved the dagger neatly into the fleshy chest, bursting the heart. Twice more he stabbed it home to be sure.

Casaverius fought for breath, but it would not come. His face purpled and his hands flailed, knocking the ladles and jugs off the tables with a crash.

Finally, Tubruk stood, feeling sick. In all his years as a gladiator and a legionary, he had never murdered an innocent and he felt stained by it. Casaverius had been a likable man and Tubruk knew the gods cried out against those that hurt the good. He steadied himself, trying to drag his gaze away from the fat man's body where it had slid onto the floor. He left quietly, his footsteps loud in the corridor that led back to the kitchen. Now he had to escape and reach Fercus before the alarm was sounded.

*　　　　　　　*　　　　　　　*

Sulla lolled on a couch, his thoughts drifting away from the conversation with his general, Antonidus. It had been a long day and the Senate seemed to be trying to block his nominations for new magistrates. He had been made Dictator with the mandate of restoring order to the Republic, and they had been eager enough to grant his every wish for the first few months. Recently, they had taken up *hours* of debate with long speeches on the powers and limitations of the office, and his advisers had said he should not impose on them too harshly for a while. They were small men, he thought. Small in deed and dreams. Marius would scorn them for fools, if he were still alive.

"... objections will be raised to the lictors, my friend," Antonidus was saying. Sulla snorted disdainfully.

"Objections or not, I will continue to have twenty-four of them with me. I have many enemies and I want them to be a reminder of my power as I walk between Capitoline hill and the Curia."

Antonidus shrugged. "In the past, there have been only twelve. Perhaps it is better to let the Senate have their way on this, to gain strength in more serious negotiation."

"They are a pack of toothless old men!" Sulla snapped. "Has not order returned to Rome in the last year? Could they have done it? No. Where was the Senate when I was fighting for my life? What help were they to me then? No. I am their master and they should be made to recognize that simple fact. I am tired of walking carefully around their sensibilities and pretending the Republic is still young and strong."

Antonidus said nothing, knowing that any objection he made would be met with wilder promises and threats. He had been honored at first to be taken on as military adviser, but the post had been a hollow one, with Sulla using him only as a puppet for his own orders. Even so, part of him agreed with Sulla's frustration. The Senate struggled to protect their dignity and old authority, while acknowledging the need for a Dictator to keep the peace in the city and Roman lands. It was farcical and Sulla was quickly tiring of the game.

A slave entered with the ices, placing them on a low table before bowing out of the room. Sulla sat up, his irritation forgotten for a moment.

"You will have to taste these. There is nothing like them for relief from the summer heat." He took a silver spoon and ladled the white ice into his mouth, shutting his eyes for a moment with pleasure. It was soon empty, and he considered calling for another bowl. His whole body seemed cooler after the ice, and his mind was calm. He saw Antonidus had not begun and urged him on.

"It must be eaten quickly, before it melts. Even then, it can be a wonderfully refreshing drink." He watched as the general sampled a spoonful and smiled with him.

Antonidus wanted to finish their business and go home to his family, but knew he could not rise until Sulla became tired. He wondered when that might be.

"Your new magistrates will be confirmed tomorrow at the Curia," he said.

Sulla lay back on his couch, his expression resuming its sulky lines. "They had better be. I owe those men favors. If there is another delay, the Senate will regret it, I swear before the gods. I will disband them and have the doors nailed shut!"

He winced slightly as he spoke and his hand drifted to his stomach, rubbing gently for a moment.

"If you choose to disband the Senate, there will be civil war again, with the city in flames once more," Antonidus said. "However, I suspect you would emerge triumphant at the end. You know you have unwavering support in the legions."

"That is the path of kings," Sulla replied. "It draws and repels me at the same time. I loved the Republic, would still love it now if it were run by the sort of men who ruled when I was a boy. They are all gone now, and when Rome calls, the little ones who are left can only run crying to me." He belched suddenly, wincing, and as he did so Antonidus felt a worm of pain begin in his own gut. A sudden fear brought him to his feet, his glance falling to the bowls, one empty, one barely touched.

"What is it?" Sulla demanded, pulling himself upright, his face twisting in the knowledge even as he spoke. The burning in his belly was spreading and he pressed his hand into himself as if to crush it.

"I feel it too," Antonidus said in panic. "It could be poison. Put your fingers down your throat, quickly!"

Sulla staggered slightly, going down onto one knee. He seemed about to pass out and Antonidus reached toward him, ignoring his own smaller pain even as it swelled.

He pushed a finger into the Dictator's limp mouth, grimacing as a flood of slippery pulp vomited out of him. Sulla moaned, his eyes rolling back in his head.

"Come on, come on, again," Antonidus insisted, pressing his fingertips into the soft flesh of the inner throat. The spasms came, ejecting dark bile and saliva from the lips until the Dictator heaved dryly. Then the wrenching chest sagged and the lungs ceased to draw, emptying in one last wheezing breath. Antonidus shouted for help and emptied his own stomach, hoping through his fear that he had not taken enough to kill him.

The guards were quick, but they found Sulla already pale and still and Antonidus semiconscious, spattered with a stinking broth of all they had eaten. He had barely enough strength to rise, but they were frozen, unsure without orders.

"Fetch doctors!" he croaked, his throat feeling raw and swollen. The pain in his stomach began to level off, and he took his hand away, trying to gather himself.

"Seal the house. The Dictator has been poisoned!" he shouted. "Send men to the kitchens. I want to know who brought this slop up here and the name of everyone who touched it. Move!" His strength seemed to leave him in that moment, and he let himself sag back onto the couch where he had been so peacefully discussing the Senate only minutes before. He knew he had to act quickly or Rome would erupt in chaos as soon as the news hit the streets. Once more he vomited, and when he was done he felt weak, but his mind began to clear.

When the doctors rushed in, they ignored the general to tend to Sulla. They touched him at the wrist and neck and looked at each other in horror.

"He is gone," one of them said, his face white.

"His killers will be found and torn apart. I swear it on my house and my gods," Antonidus whispered, his voice as bitter as the taste in his mouth.

*   *   *

Tubruk reached the small door that led out to the street just as shouts erupted in the main buildings of Sulla's city home. There was only one guard there, but the man was alert and ready, his face forbidding.

"Get back on your way, slave," he said firmly, his hand on his gladius. Tubruk growled at him and leapt forward, punching him off his feet with a sudden blow. The soldier fell awkwardly, knocked senseless. Tubruk paused, knowing he could step quickly over him, through the little trade entrance, and be gone. The man would recognize him and be able to give a description, though he could well be executed for failing to hold the gate. Tubruk took a grip on the despair that had filled him since killing Casaverius. His duty was to Cornelia and Julius—and to the memory of Julius's father, who had trusted him.

Grimly, he drew his small knife and cut the soldier's throat, standing clear so as to avoid getting blood on his clothes. The man gurgled with the cut, his eyes clearing for a moment before death took him. Tubruk dropped the knife and opened the gate, stepping out onto the city streets and into the thin crowd of people and food stalls, walking their peaceful journeys unknowing as the old wolf moved through them.

He had to reach Fercus to be safe, but there was more than a mile to go, and though he moved quickly he could not run for fear of someone spotting and chasing him. Behind, he could hear the familiar clatter of soldiers' sandals as they took up position and began halting the crowds, searching for weapons, looking for a guilty face.

More legionaries ran past him, their gazes sweeping the crowd as they tried to get ahead and close the road. Tubruk took a side street and then another, trying not to panic. They would not know yet whom they were looking for, but he had to shave the beard as soon as he was safe. Whatever happened, he knew they must not take him alive. At least then, with luck, they might never link him to the estate and Julius's family.

As the soldiers began to close the road, a man in the crowd suddenly ran, throwing aside a basket of vegetables he had been carrying. Tubruk thanked the gods for the man's guilty conscience and tried not to look back as the soldiers brought him down, squealing as they cracked his head onto the stone street. Tubruk walked through turning after turning with hurried steps, and the shouting was left behind at last. He slowed his pace in the darkening shadows as he reached the alley that Fercus had told him to make for. At first he thought it was deserted, but then he saw his friend step out from an unlit doorway and beckon to him. He went inside quickly, his nerves close to breaking, finally collapsing in the dirty little room that meant safety, at least for a while.

"Did you do it?" Fercus asked as he tried to get his breath back and his racing pulse to slow.

"I think so. We will know tomorrow. They have closed off the streets, but I made it clear. Gods, it was close!"

Fercus handed him a razor and motioned to a bowl of cold water.

"You still have to get clear of the city, my friend. And that will not be easy if Sulla is dead. If he is alive, it will be next to impossible."

"Are you ready to do what you have to?" Tubruk said quietly, rubbing the water into the bushy growth that covered his face.

"I am, though it hurts me to do it."

"Not as much as it will hurt me. Do it quickly once I have shaved."

He noticed his hand trembled as he used the narrow blade and cursed to himself as he cut the skin.

"Let me do it," Fercus said, taking the razor from him. For a few minutes there was silence between them, though their thoughts ran wildly.

"Did you get out without being seen?" Fercus asked as he worked at the stubborn bristle. Tubruk didn't answer for a long time.

"No. I had to kill two innocent men."

"The Republic can stand a little blood on its hem if Sulla's death restores equality to Rome. I cannot regret what you have done, Tubruk."

Tubruk remained silent as the blade cut away the last of his beard. He rubbed his face, his eyes sad.

"Do it now, while I feel numb."

Fercus took a deep breath, walking around to face the old

gladiator. There was nothing left of the shambling Dalcius in his strong face.

"Perhaps..." Fercus began hesitantly.

"It is the only way. We discussed this. Do it!" Tubruk gripped the arms of the chair as Fercus raised a fist and began to beat his face into an unrecognizable mess. He felt his nose break along old lines and spat onto the floor. Fercus breathed heavily and Tubruk coughed, wincing.

"Don't stop...yet," he whispered through the pain, wanting it to be over.

When they were finished, Fercus would return with him to his own home, leaving the rented room behind without a trace of them. Tubruk would be chained into a coffle of slaves leaving the city, his face swollen. His last act before the slave market had been to sign a chit of sale under his own name. Fercus would deliver one more anonymous slave to the estate outside the city, ready for a backbreaking life of work in the fields.

At last, Tubruk raised a hand and Fercus stopped, panting and amazed at how much effort the beating had taken to give. The man who sat in the chair bore only a small resemblance to the one who had come in from the streets. Fercus was satisfied.

"I never beat my slaves," he muttered.

Tubruk raised his head slowly. "You have not beaten one now," he said, swallowing blood.

*   *   *

Brutus ducked below a ridge of stone, panting. Their pursuers had brought bows and his quick glimpse had shown two archers hanging back while the others crept cautiously toward their position. As soon as he and Renius were forced to show themselves, the shafts would bite into them and it would be over.

Brutus pressed as closely as he could to the dark rock,

thinking furiously. He was sure he'd recognized Livia's husband as one of the archers, so it looked as if the man had been persuaded of her innocence while there was no one to argue with her. No doubt she would welcome him home as a hero if he dragged Brutus's body behind him.

The thought of her warmed Brutus for a moment. Her dull husband would probably never appreciate what he had.

Renius had given his dagger to the younger man, preferring the solid weight of his gladius. Brutus had his own sword sheathed and a small blade in each hand as he waited. He knew he could throw them well enough to kill, but he would hardly have a chance to aim before the archers sighted on him. It would be close.

He put his head over the ridge and took in the positions of the men climbing toward him. The archers shouted a warning to their companions, but Brutus was already out of sight and moving to a new position. This time, he rose fully and sent one knife flashing before he threw himself down.

A shaft buzzed overhead, but Brutus grinned as he heard the knife strike flesh. He moved again, farther along the ridge near to Renius, the second knife ready in his hand.

"I think you just scratched him," Renius muttered.

Brutus frowned at him for disturbing his concentration, flushing as a stream of raging oaths sounded over the crest.

"And annoyed him," Renius added.

Brutus tensed for another attempt. He would have loved to aim at one of the archers, but the bows could just be picked up by another and they stood farthest from the small ridge that hid the Romans.

He leapt up to find one of them almost on top of him. The man gaped at the sudden apparition and Brutus sank the blade into his exposed throat, dropping back and scrambling away on his stomach, raising dust.

Two more came at Brutus then, swinging blades. He rose

to meet them, trying to keep an eye on the archers behind and spoil their aim with sudden steps left and right.

A shaft creased the air by his legs as the first Greek was impaled on his gladius. Brutus hung on to the slumping body, using it as a shield. Though he was dying, the man shouted and swore at Brutus as the young man danced him to one side and then another. An arrow came from nowhere to spear into the man's back, and blood spilled out of his mouth onto Brutus's face. Brutus swore and heaved the body into the arms of his companion, then whipped his gladius up into the man's groin in the classic legion thrust. They fell away in silence onto the shrubs and flowers, and Brutus found himself looking at Livia's husband at the moment he released his arrow.

He began to move, but the blurring shaft reached him as he turned, knocking him onto his back. The armor had saved him and Brutus blessed his gods for luck as he rolled. He came up to see Renius punch Livia's husband flat before facing the last of them, who stood terrified, with his arms quivering under the strain of the bow.

"Easy, boy," Renius called to him. "Go down to your horse and go home. If you fire that thing, I'll bite your throat out."

Brutus took a pace toward Renius, but the old gladiator held out a hand to stop him.

"He knows what he has to do, Brutus. Just give him a little time," Renius said clearly. The young man holding the taut bow shook his head, looking pale with tension. Livia's husband writhed on the ground and Renius pressed a foot onto his neck to hold him.

"You've had your battle, boys, now go home and impress your wives with the story," Renius continued, gently increasing the pressure so that Livia's husband began to claw at his foot, choking.

The archer eased his grip and took two paces away. "Let him go," he said in a heavy accent.

Renius shrugged. "Throw your bow away first."

The young man hesitated long enough for Livia's husband to go purple, and then threw the bow over the rocks behind him with a clatter. Renius removed his foot, allowing Livia's husband to scramble up, wheezing. The old gladiator didn't make a move as the two young Greeks put distance between them.

"Wait!" Brutus called suddenly, freezing them all. "You have three horses you don't need down there. I want two of them."

*   *   *

Cornelia sat with her back straight, her eyes bright with worry as she faced Antonidus, the one they called Sulla's dog.

The man was merciless, she knew, and he watched every change in her face as he questioned her with a terrifying concentration. She had heard nothing good of Sulla's general, and she had to fight not to show fear or relief at the news he had brought. Her daughter was asleep in her arms. She had decided to call her Julia.

"Your father, Cinna, does he know you are here?" he asked, his voice clipped as his gaze bored into her.

She shook her head slightly. "I do not think so. Sulla called for me from my husband's home outside the city. I have been waiting in these rooms with my baby for days now, without seeing anyone except slaves."

The general frowned, as if something she had said didn't ring true, but his eyes never left hers. "Why did Sulla summon you?"

She swallowed nervously and knew he had seen it. What could she tell him? That Sulla had raped her with her daughter crying at her side? He might laugh or, worse, think she was trying to blacken the great man's name after his death and have her killed.

Antonidus watched her writhe in worry and fear and wanted to slap her. She was beautiful enough for it to be obvious why she had been summoned, though he wondered how Sulla could have been aroused by a body still loose from birth.

He wondered if her father had been behind the murder, and almost cursed as he realized there was yet another name to add to the list of enemies. His informants had told him Cinna was on business in the north of Italy, but assassins could have been sent from there. He stood suddenly. He prided himself on his ability to spot a liar, but she was either witless or knew nothing.

"Don't travel. Where will you be if I need to bring you back here?"

Cornelia thought for a moment, fighting the sudden elation. She was going to be released! Should she return to the town house or travel back to Julius's family estate?

Clodia was probably still there, she thought.

"I will be outside the city at the house where I was sought before."

Antonidus nodded, his thoughts already on the problems he faced.

"I am sorry for the tragedy," she forced herself to say.

"Those responsible will suffer greatly," he said, his voice hard. Again, she felt the intensity of his interest in her, making her own expression seem false under his scrutiny.

After a moment more, he stood and walked away across the marble floor. The baby awoke and began to whimper to be fed. Alone and deprived of a nurse, Cornelia bared her breast to the child's mouth and tried not to cry.

CHAPTER 7

Tubruk awoke, cramped and stiff with cold in the darkness of the slave house. He could hear other bodies move around him, but there was no sign of dawn in the chain room where they slept and were made ready for travel.

From the first hours with Fercus, working out the details, it was this part that he had barely allowed himself to consider. It seemed a small worry with the possibility of torture and death to come if the attempt on Sulla's life had failed, or if he was caught escaping. There were so many ways for him to suffer a disaster that the night and day he would spend as a slave had been pushed to the back of his mind, almost forgotten.

He looked around him, his eyes making out shapes even in the dark. He could feel the weight of the metal cuffs holding his hands to the smooth chain that clinked at the slightest movement. He tried not to remember what it had been like the first time, but his memory brought back those nights and days and years until they clustered and murmured within him and it was hard not to cry out. Some of the chained men wept softly, and Tubruk had never heard a more mournful sound.

They could have been taken from distant lands, or had slavery forced upon them for crime or debt. There were a hundred ways, but to be born to it was worse than all the rest, he knew. As small children, they could run and play in happy ignorance until they were old enough to understand they had no future but to be sold.

Tubruk breathed in the smells of a stable: oil and straw, sweat and leather, clean human animals who owned nothing and were owned themselves. He pulled himself upright against the weight of the chains. The other slaves thought he was one of them, guilty of something to have been beaten so badly. The guard had marked him as a troublemaker for the same reason. Only Fercus knew he was free.

The thought brought no comfort. It was not enough to tell himself that he was just a short journey from the estate and freedom. If you are thought a slave and if you are chained in darkness, unable even to rise, where then is precious liberty? If a free man is bound to a slave coffle, he is a slave, and Tubruk felt the old nameless fear he had felt in the same room decades before. To eat, sleep, stand, and die at another's whim—he had returned to that, and all his years of pride in winning his way to freedom seemed ashes.

"Such a fragile thing," he said, just to hear his voice aloud, and the man next to him grunted awake, almost pulling Tubruk over as he struggled up. Tubruk looked away, thankful for the darkness. He did not want the light to come through the high windows to reveal their faces. They were heading for short, brutal lives in fields, working until they fell and could not rise. And they were like him. Perhaps one or two of the men in this room would be picked out for their strength or speed and trained for the circus. Instead of ending their lives as crippled water carriers or taken by disease, they would bleed away their futures into the sand. One or two might have children of their own and see them taken for sale as soon as they had their growth.

The light came slowly, despite him, but the chained slaves were still, listless in their confinement. For many, the only sign of wakefulness was a slight noise of the chain as they stirred. With the light came food and they waited patiently.

Tubruk reached to his face and winced as he gauged the swelling from Fercus's blows the night before. The guard's surprise had been obvious when Tubruk was brought in. Fercus had never been a cruel man, and the guard knew Tubruk must have insulted him grievously to have such an obvious beating on the very night before being delivered to his new owners.

No questions had been asked, of course. Even though the slaves might pass only a few days in the house while Fercus took his profit, he owned them as utterly as the chair he sat in or the clothes he wore.

They were given wooden bowls filled with a slop of cooked vegetables and bread, and Tubruk was digging his fingers into his when the door opened again and three soldiers entered with Fercus. Tubruk kept his face down with the others, not daring to meet an eye, even by accident. A murmur of interest swept the room, but Tubruk did not add to it. He guessed why they were there and his belly seemed cold with tension. They would have spoken to all Sulla's kitchen staff by now and found that one called Dalcius was missing. Fercus had said he would be examined at the gates of the city before leaving, but had not expected them to be so thorough as to search his slave rooms even before setting off.

In the gray light of morning, Tubruk felt he would be spotted immediately, but the soldiers moved without hurry amongst the slaves as they ate, clearly intending to be thorough with the task they had been given. As well they might be, Tubruk thought sourly. If they missed him here and then he was identified at the gate, they would be severely punished. He wondered if Sulla had eaten the poison, and knew that he might not be sure for days or even weeks, if the Senate chose to delay the news. The people of Rome hardly ever saw the Dictator except from a distance over a crowd. They would continue with their lives unknowing, and if Sulla survived they might never learn of the attempt at all.

A rough hand reached under his chin as he chewed his food slowly. Tubruk allowed his head to be raised and found himself looking into the hard eyes of a young legionary. He swallowed the mouthful and tried to look unconcerned.

The soldier whistled softly. "This one's had a kicking," he said softly.

Tubruk blinked through his swollen eyes, nervously.

"He insulted my wife, officer," Fercus said. "I administered the punishment myself."

"Did you now?" the legionary continued.

Tubruk felt his heart pump powerfully in him as he looked away, remembering too late that he had been meeting the gaze where he should not.

"I'd have ripped his stomach out if he insulted mine," the legionary said, letting Tubruk's chin fall.

"And lose my profit?" Fercus replied quickly.

The officer sneered and spat one word: "Merchants."

He moved on to the next with Fercus, and Tubruk cleaned his bowl, gripping it hard to hide hands that shook with anger. Minutes later, the soldiers were gone and the guards entered to kick them to their feet, ready to be fastened into the cart that would carry them out of Rome and to their new homes and lives.

*   *   *

Julius pressed his head up to the bars of the little cell below the trireme deck, closing his left eye to see what was going on more clearly. With it open, the blur brought on his headaches and he wanted to delay that as long as possible each day. He pulled a deep breath into his lungs and turned back to the others.

"Definitely a port. Warm air, and I can smell fruit or spices. I'd say Africa."

After a month in the cramped semidarkness, the words caused a stir of interest in the Romans, who sat or lay against the wooden sides of their prison. He looked at them and sighed before shuffling back to his place, levering himself down carefully to avoid putting weight on the splinted arm.

The month had been hard on all of them. Denied razors and water to wash with, the usually fastidious soldiers were a ragged crew, filthy and dark-bearded. The bucket they had been given as their toilet was filled to overflowing and buzzed with flies. It had a corner to itself, but excrement had slimed the floor around it and they had no cloths to wipe themselves. In the heat of the day, the air had the stench of disease and two of the men had developed fevers that Cabera could barely control.

The old healer did what he could for them, but he was searched thoroughly every time he brought their food or tended their sick. The pirates still kept him busy with their own ailments, and Cabera said it was clear they had not had a healer on board for years.

Julius felt a headache beginning and stifled a groan. Ever since recovering consciousness the pains had been with him, sapping at his will and strength and making him snap at the others. They were all irritable and what discipline they had once had was being eroded in the darkness day by day, with Gaditicus having to step in more than once to stop blows as tempers frayed.

With his eyes closed, the headache remained quiescent, but Cabera had told him he must not stop using the blurred eye and to spend hours of each day focusing on the near and far or it would be lost to him when they were finally back in the sun. He had to believe it would end. He would return to Rome and Cornelia, and the misery would become memories. It helped a little to imagine it had already happened, that he was sitting in the sun on the estate wall, with his arm around Cornelia's slim waist and cool, clean air off the hills ruffling their hair. She would ask him how it had been in the filth and the stench of the cell, and he would make light of all of it. He wished he could remember her face more clearly.

Julius held his hand up and squinted at it, then the barred door, over and over until the headache began to throb in his left temple. He let his hand fall and closed his eyes to its wasted condition after a month on rations that kept them from death but did little more. What he wouldn't give for a cold oyster to slip down his throat! He knew it was stupid to torture himself, but his mind produced bright visions of the shells, as real as if they hung before him and as sharp as his sight had been before the fight on *Accipiter*.

He remembered nothing of that day. As far as his memory told the tale, he had gone from healthy and strong to broken and in pain in a moment, and for the first few days of consciousness he had been filled with rage at what had been taken from him. He had been blind in his left eye for long enough to believe he would never see again, and never be able to use a sword with any degree of skill.

Suetonius had told him that one-eyed men couldn't be good fighters, and he had already found he was missing things as he reached for them, his hand swiping the air as he failed to judge the distance properly. At least that had come back with his sight, though the shimmering outlines he could see with his left eye infuriated him, making him want to rub the eye clear. His hand rose to do just that again in habit, and he caught himself, knowing it would do no good.

The headache seemed to find another channel in his brain and worked its way into it until that spot throbbed in sympathy with the first. He hoped it would stay there and not go on. The thought of what had begun happening to him was a fear he had barely started to explore, but three times now the pain had swelled into flashing lights that consumed him and he had woken with his lips bitter from yellow bile, lying in his own filth, with Gaditicus holding him down grimly. In the first fit, he had bitten his tongue badly enough that his mouth filled with blood and choked him, but now they had a strip of grimy cloth torn from his tunic to shove between his teeth as he convulsed, blind.

All the red-eyed, stinking soldiers raised their heads at the tread of steps on the narrow rungs from the deck above. Anything unusual was seized upon to break the endless boredom, and even the two who were feverish tried to see, though one fell back, exhausted.

It was the captain, who seemed almost to glow with clean skin and health compared to the men of the *Accipiter*. He was tall enough to have to duck his head as he entered the cell, accompanied by another man, who carried a sword and a dagger ready to repel a sudden attack.

If his head hadn't been pulsing its sullen sickness, Julius might have laughed at the precaution. The Romans had lost their strength, unable to exercise. It still amazed him how fast the muscles became weak without use. Cabera had shown them how to keep themselves strong by pulling against each other, but it didn't seem to make much difference.

The captain breathed shallowly, his eyes taking in the full slop bucket. His face was tanned and creased from years of squinting against the glare of the sea. Even his clothes carried a fresh smell in with him, and Julius ached to be out in the air and the open spaces, so powerfully that his heart hammered with the need.

"We have reached a safe port. In six months, perhaps, you will be put down some lonely night, free and paid for." He paused to enjoy the effect of his words. Just the mention of an ending to their imprisonment had every man's gaze fastened to him.

"The amounts to ask for, now that is a delicate problem," he continued, his voice as pleasant as if he addressed a group of men he knew well instead of soldiers who would tear him apart with their teeth if they had the strength.

"It must not be so much that your loved ones cannot pay.

We have no use for those. Yet somehow I don't believe you will be truthful if I ask you to tell me how much your families will bear for you. Do you understand?"

"We understand you well enough," Gaditicus said.

"It is best if we reach a compromise, I think. You will each tell me your name, rank, and wealth, and I will decide you are lying and add whatever I think would be right. It is like a game, perhaps."

No one answered him, but silent vows were made to their gods and the hatred was clear enough in their expressions.

"Good. Let us start, then." He pointed to Suetonius, his gaze drawn as the young man scratched at the lice that left red sores on all their bodies.

"Suetonius Prandus. I am a watch officer, the lowest rank. My family have nothing to sell," Suetonius replied, his voice thick and hoarse with lack of use.

The captain squinted at him, weighing him up. Like the others, there was nothing to inspire dreams of wealth in his thin frame. Julius realized the captain was simply enjoying himself at their expense. Taking pleasure from having the arrogant officers of Rome reduced to bargaining with an enemy. Yet what choice did they have? If the pirate demanded too much and their families could not borrow the money, or worse, refused to, then a quick death would follow. It was hard not to play the game.

"I think, for the *lowest* rank, I will ask for two talents—five hundred in gold."

Suetonius spluttered, though Julius knew his family could pay that easily, or ten times that amount.

"Gods, man. They do not have the money!" Suetonius said, his unkempt body lending the feel of truth to the words.

The captain shrugged. "Pray to those gods that they can raise it, or over the side you go, with a bit of chain to hold you down."

Suetonius sank back in apparent despair, though Julius knew he would consider himself to have outwitted the pirate.

"You, Centurion? Are you from a rich family?" the captain asked.

Gaditicus glared at him for a moment before speaking. "I am not, but nothing I say will make any difference to you," he growled before looking away.

The captain frowned in thought. "I think...yes, for a centurion, a captain no less, like myself...it would be an insult if I asked less than twenty talents. That would be about five thousand in gold, I think. Yes."

Gaditicus ignored him, though he seemed to sag slightly in despair.

"What is your name?" the captain asked Julius.

For a moment, he too considered ignoring the man, but then his headache throbbed and a spike of anger rose in him.

"My name is Julius Caesar. I command a twenty. I am also the head of a wealthy house."

The captain's eyebrows rose and the others muttered amongst themselves in disbelief. Julius exchanged a glance with Gaditicus, who shook his head in a clear message.

"Head of a house! I am honored to meet you," the captain said with a sneer. "Perhaps twenty talents would be right for you as well."

"Fifty," Julius said, straightening his back as he spoke. The captain blinked, his easy manner vanishing.

"That is twelve thousand pieces of gold," he said, awed out of complacency.

"Make it fifty," Julius replied firmly. "When I have found you and killed you, I will need funds. I am far from home, after all." Despite the pain in his head, he mustered a savage grin.

The captain recovered quickly from his surprise. "You are the one that had his head broken. You must have left your wits on my decks. I will ask for fifty, but if it does not come, the sea is deep enough to hold you."

"It is not wide enough to hide you from me, whoreson," Julius replied. "I will nail your men to a line of crosses all along the coast. Your officers I may have strangled out of mercy. You have my word on it."

The soldiers erupted into a shout of cheers and laughter at the captain, who paled with anger. For a moment, it looked as if he would step farther into the cell to strike Julius, but he mastered himself and looked around scornfully at the baying men.

"I will set high prices on all of you. See if you cheer then!" he shouted over the jeers as he left with his crewman, who locked the door securely behind him, shaking his head in disbelief at Julius through the bars.

When they were sure there was no one to hear, Suetonius rounded on Julius.

"What did you do that for, you fool? He'll beggar our families for your stupid pride!"

Julius shrugged. "He'll set the prices at what he thinks he can get, just as he would have before coming down here, though he might ask fifty for me, out of spite."

"Caesar's right," Gaditicus said, "he was just playing with us." He chuckled suddenly. "Fifty! Did you see his face? That was Rome in you, lad." His laughter broke off into coughing, but he still smiled.

"I think you were wrong to bait him," Suetonius continued, and one or two of the others muttered agreement.

"He killed Romans and sank *Accipiter* and you think we should play his little games? I'd spit on you if I had any," Julius snapped. "I meant it too. Once I'm free, I will find him and cut him down. Even if it takes years, he will see my face before he dies."

Suetonius scrambled at him, raging, but was held by Pelitas as he tried to get past.

"Sit down, you idiot," Pelitas growled, shoving him back. "There's no point fighting amongst ourselves and he's barely recovered as it is."

Suetonius subsided with a scowl that Julius ignored, scratching idly under his splint as he thought. His eyes took in the sick men lying in damp, stinking straw.

"This place will kill us," he said.

Pelitas nodded. "We know they guard the top of the steps with two men. We'd have to get past them. Now we're docked, it might be worth a go?"

"Maybe," Julius said, "but they're careful. Even if we could dig the hinges out of the door, the deck hatch is bolted from above every time someone comes in here, even Cabera. I don't see how we could break it fast enough to get out before there's a crowd waiting for us."

"We could use Suetonius's head," Pelitas said. "A few sharp blows and one of them would give way. Either way, we win." Julius chuckled with him.

The following night, one of the sick men died. The captain allowed Cabera to drag out the body and dump it over the side without ceremony. The mood of those left sank toward complete despair.

CHAPTER 8

I am surrounded by women," Tubruk said cheerfully as they entered, bringing life and energy into the quiet *triclinium*. In the weeks that had followed Fercus's bringing him inside the gates and passing the bill of sale into his untied hands, Tubruk had regained much of the peace he had lost in the city. Coming together each morning to eat had become a ritual for them, and Tubruk had begun to look forward to the light breakfast. Aurelia was always at her best in the mornings, and if he was any judge, there was true friendship between Cornelia, Clodia, and herself. The house had not seen laughter since before the slave riots, and they lifted Tubruk's spirits.

His face had healed with time, though he bore a new scar over his left eye to remember the ordeal. He recalled the relief he'd felt when he first saw the legionaries dressed in black on the city streets, a uniform the city would see for a full year of mourning at the Dictator's death. Even then, the dark cloth had seemed inappropriate to the mood of Rome. Fercus had told him there was a fresh breeze blowing through the Senate, with Cinna and Pompey working to restore the old Republic and once again lay the ghosts of kings that Sulla had brought back to the streets.

The estate manager traveled only rarely into the city now, and always with caution. He thought the chances were good that he would never be linked with the poisoning of Rome's leader, but it took only one accusation and the Senate would tear the estate apart looking for evidence. If they found Fercus and tortured him, the broker would give Tubruk to them, he was sure. The man had a family he loved, and honor and friendship crumbled in the face of that. Still, it had been the right thing to do and they had won, even though he would never know a day of complete peace again while Sulla's friends and supporters searched for the assassin.

A month after his return to the estate, Tubruk had put on a heavy cloak and ridden to the city to make offerings at the temples of Mars and Vesta in thanks for the life of Cornelia. He had also prayed for the souls of Casaverius and the guard he had killed at the gate.

Cornelia had her daughter sitting on her lap, and Clodia was reaching out at intervals to tickle the baby under her armpits and make her laugh. Even Aurelia smiled at the childish giggles that came from Julia, and Tubruk spread honey on his bread with a mixture of emotions churning in him. It was good that Aurelia had found a little of the old happiness. She had been too long surrounded by stern men. When she had first held her granddaughter, she had cried without sobbing, tears falling from her.

Yet he was sure she was failing, and the thought brought him pain as he saw she had not eaten with the others. Gently, Tubruk pushed a plate of fresh, crusty bread over to her side of the low table, and their eyes met for a second. She took a piece and tore a sliver from it, chewing it slowly as he watched. She had said that eating brought on her fits and left her sick and vomiting. There was no appetite, and before he had watched her closely she had been losing weight alarmingly and hardly taking anything in.

She was wasting before him, and no matter what he said when they were alone, she would only weep and say she *could* not eat. There was no space in her for food.

Clodia tickled the child and was rewarded with a sudden belch of milky vomit. All three women rose as one to help clean it up, and Tubruk rose with them, feeling excluded and minding not a bit.

"I wish her father were here to her see her grow," Cornelia said wistfully.

"He will be, love," Tubruk said. "They have to keep those they ransom alive or the trade would stop. It's just a business deal to them. Julius will come home, and now Sulla is dead, he can start again."

She seemed to take more hope from his words than he felt himself. No matter what happened, Tubruk knew that even if Julius did make it back, he would not be the same after his experiences. The young lad who had taken ship to escape Sulla had died. Who would return was yet to be seen. Life would be harder for all of them after having to pay such a high ransom. Tubruk had sold some of the land of the estate to Suetonius's family, who had bargained cruelly over the price, knowing his need from their own demand. Tubruk sighed. At least Julius would be pleased to have a daughter, and a wife to love him. That was more than Tubruk had.

He glanced at Clodia and found her looking back at him, with something in her expression that brought the blood to his face like a boy's. She winked at him before turning back to help Cornelia, and he felt strangely uncomfortable. He knew he should be going out to see the workers who waited for his orders, but he sat and took another slice of bread and ate it slowly, hoping she would look his way again.

Aurelia swayed slightly and Tubruk moved quickly to her, taking her shoulder. She was incredibly pale and her skin looked waxen. He felt the lack of flesh under her *stola*, and the always present grief swelled in him.

"You should rest," he said quietly. "I will bring you more food later."

She did not reply and her eyes had taken on the lost gaze.

She moved with him as he walked her away from the table, her steps faltering and weak. He felt her frame shiver against him as the trembling began again, each time leaving her weaker than the last.

Cornelia and Clodia were left alone with the child, who pawed at Cornelia's dress to find a nipple.

"He is a good man," Clodia said, looking at the doorway they'd gone through.

"A shame he is too old to make a husband," Cornelia replied artlessly.

Clodia firmed her jaw. "Old? He is still strong where it matters," she said, her voice sharp. Then she saw Cornelia's bright eyes and blushed. "You see too much, my girl. Let the child feed."

"She is always hungry," Cornelia said, wincing as she allowed Julia to attach herself, pressing her little face deep into the breast.

"It helps you to love them," Clodia said, and when Cornelia looked up at her tone, Clodia's eyes were lined with tears.

*   *   *

In the cool dimness of the bedchamber, Tubruk held Aurelia tightly until the fit had finally passed from her. Her skin burned against him and he shook his head at her thinness. Finally, she knew him again and he lowered her back against soft cushions.

He had held her first on the night of her husband's funeral, and it had become a ritual between them. He knew she took comfort from his strength, and there were fewer bruises on her these days, with her thrashing limbs gripped tight in his arms. He found he was breathing heavily and wondered afresh how it was possible that she could have so much strength in such a wasted body.

"Thank you," she whispered, her eyes half open.

"It was nothing. I will bring you a cool drink and leave you to rest."

"I don't want you to leave me, Tubruk," she said.

"Didn't I say I'd care for you? I will be here for as long as you need me," he said, trying to force cheerfulness into his tone. She opened her eyes fully and turned her head to him.

"Julius said he would stay with me, but he left. Now my son has gone as well."

"Sometimes the gods make a mockery of our promises, love, though your husband was a decent man. Your son will come back safe, if I know him at all."

She closed her eyes again and Tubruk waited until natural sleep came before stealing out of the room.

*   *   *

As storms smashed the coast, the moored trireme pitched and rolled heavily despite the shelter of the tiny African bay, far from Roman lands. Several of the officers were retching, though there was no food to come up. Those who had water in their bellies from their meager ration struggled not to lose a drop, with their hands pressed tightly over their mouths. There was never enough and in the heavy heat their bodies craved moisture of any kind. Most of them cupped their hands as they urinated, gulping the warm liquid back as fast as they could before it was lost.

Julius remained unaffected by the rocking ship and took considerable pleasure from Suetonius's discomfort as he lay with his eyes shut, moaning softly with his hands on his stomach.

Despite the seasickness, there was a new mood of optimism in the tiny cell. The captain had sent a man to tell them the ransoms had all been paid, traveling by land and sea to a secret meeting spot where an agent for the pirates had completed the last leg of the long trip and brought the gold to this distant port. Julius had felt it was a small victory that the captain had not come down himself. They had not seen him for months since the day he had tried to torment them, and that pleased them all. Had he come, he might have been surprised at what he saw. They had come through the lowest point of the captivity and were growing stronger.

The desperate group of the first few months now waited patiently for their release. The fever had claimed two more, lessening the stifling crush a little. The new will to survive came partly from Cabera after that, who had finally managed to bargain for better rations for them. It had been a dangerous gamble, but the old man saw that little better than half of them would make it to freedom unless they were better fed and cleaned, so he had sat on deck and refused to heal another until they gave him something in return. The captain had been suffering at that time from a virulent rash he had picked up in the port, and hardly blustered at all before allowing it. With the food came hope and the men had started to believe they might see Rome and liberty again. Swollen, bleeding gums had begun to heal and Cabera had been allowed to give them a cup of white ship's tallow to rub on their sores.

Julius too had played his part. When his splint was removed, he was horrified to see the way his muscles had vanished, and immediately set about the exercises Cabera had suggested. It had been agony in the cramped space, but Julius had organized the officers into two groups of four and five. One would huddle together as close as possible for an hour and let the others have the space to wrestle and lift their comrades as deadweights, building back the muscles they had all lost, before changing over and letting the other group work and sweat. The slop bucket had been knocked over too many times to count, but the men grew stronger and no more succumbed to fevers.

The headaches came less often now, though the worst would leave him almost unable to speak with the pain.

The others had learned to leave him alone when he went pale and closed his eyes. The last fit had been two months before, and Cabera said that might well be the end of them. Julius prayed that was true. The memories of his mother's illness had given him a terrible fear of the weakness that threw him down and forced his mind into the dark.

With the news that the ship was ready to set sail and head for a lonely piece of coast to set them down, the officers of *Accipiter* were jubilant and Pelitas had even slapped Suetonius on the back in excitement. They were still bearded and wild-looking, but now they chattered with fantasies of bathhouses and being rubbed down with oil.

It was strange how things changed. Where once Julius dreamed of being a general like Marius, now he thought of being clean as a greater pleasure. It had not changed his desire to destroy the pirates, however. Some of the others talked of returning to the city, but he knew he could not while his family's money floated around in the hold of a pirate ship. His anger had pushed him to stand the sickness and pain that came from the hard exercise, and he had forced himself to do more and more each day, knowing he had to be strong if his word to the captain was not to be spit in the wind.

The motion of the trireme changed slowly, and the Romans gave a low cheer as the rolling steadied and they could hear the beat for the rowers as the ship moved into open sea.

"We're going home," Prax said wonderingly, with a catch in his voice. The word *home* had a strange power and one of the men began weeping. The others looked away from him, embarrassed, though they had seen worse in the months together. Many things had changed between them in that time, and Gaditicus sometimes wondered if they could work again as a crew even if *Accipiter* was produced whole and afloat for them. They had kept some semblance of discipline, with Gaditicus and Prax settling disputes and stopping fights, but the awareness of station had been slowly eroded as they judged each other by new rules and found different strengths and weaknesses.

Pelitas and Prax had become good friends, each seeing in the other something of the same phlegmatic outlook on life, despite the difference in ages. Prax had lost his swollen gut in the time in the cell, replacing it with hard muscle after weeks of pushing himself with the others in the daily exercises. Julius suspected that he would be pleased with the new lease on life when he was shaved and clean. He smiled at that thought, scratching a sore in his armpit.

Gaditicus had been one of those who suffered in the choppy waters of the dock, but he was gaining color as the ship cut through the waves instead of rocking in them. Julius had found a respect and liking for him that had been missing from his automatic obedience to the rank. The man had held the group together and seemed to appreciate what Julius and Cabera had done for them.

Suetonius had not flourished in the captivity. He had seen the bonds that had formed between Pelitas, Prax, Julius, and Gaditicus and resented bitterly Julius's being included. For a while, he had been friendly with the other four officers, and two camps had emerged. Julius had used those groups to compete against each other in the daily training, and eventually one of the officers had cuffed Suetonius as he complained to him in whispers.

Shortly after that, Cabera had been able to bring the first decent food they had seen since the beginning, and they had all cheered. Typical of the old man to have given the fruit to Julius to hand out. Suetonius couldn't wait for freedom and order to be restored, wanting to see the moment when Julius realized he was just a junior officer again.

Two weeks after leaving port, they were taken out of the cell in darkness and left on a strange coast, without weapons or supplies. The captain had bowed to them as they were taken to the small boat that would be rowed in to the beach beyond, where they could hear the crash of waves.

"Goodbye, Romans. I will think of you often as I spend your coin," he had called, laughing. They stayed silent, though Julius looked up at him steadily, as if noting every line of his face. He was furious that Cabera had not been allowed to leave with them, though he had known they might hold him. It was just one more reason to find the captain and rip his throat out.

On the beach, their bonds were cut and the sailors backed away carefully, daggers ready.

"Don't do anything stupid, now," one of them warned. "You can work your way home in time." Then they were in the boat and rowing hard for the trireme that was black against the moonlit sea.

Pelitas reached down and picked up a handful of the soft sand, rubbing it between his fingers.

"I don't know about you lads, but I'm going for a swim," he said, stripping off his infested clothes in a sudden rush. A minute later, only Suetonius stood on the shore, then he was dragged in by the shouting, laughing officers, clothes and all.

*   *   *

Brutus used his dagger to skin the hares they'd bought from a farmer, scooping out the guts into a slimy heap. Renius had found some wild onions, and with the crusty bread and a half-full wineskin, it would be a suitable feast for their last night in the open. Rome was less than a day's travel away, and with the sale of the horses, they were in profit.

Renius dropped a few heavy pieces of dead wood by the fire and lay down as close as he could, enjoying the warmth.

"Pass me the wineskin, lad," he said, his voice mellow.

Brutus pulled the stopper out and gave it to him, watching as Renius guided the spout to his mouth and gulped.

"I'd go easy if I were you," Brutus said. "You have no

head for wine and I don't want you picking a fight with me or weeping or something."

Renius ignored him, finally gasping as he lowered the skin.

"It's good to be home again," he said.

Brutus filled their small cooking pot to the brim and lay down on the other side of the fire.

"It is. I hadn't realized how much I'd missed it before the lookout sighted the coast. It brought everything back to me."

Shaking his head in memory, he stirred the stew with his dagger. Renius raised his head and rested it on his hand.

"You've come a long way from the boy I trained. I don't think I ever told you how proud I was when you made centurion for the Bronze Fist."

"You told everyone else. It got back to me in the end," Brutus replied, smiling.

"And now you'll be Julius's man?" Renius said, eyeing the bubbling stew.

"Why not? We walk the same path, remember? Cabera said that."

"He said the same to me," Renius muttered, testing the stew with a finger. Though it was clearly boiling, he didn't seem to feel the heat.

"I thought that was why you came back with me. You could have stayed on with the Fist if you'd wanted."

Renius shrugged. "I wanted to be at the heart of things again."

Brutus grinned at the big man. "I know. Now Sulla's dead, this is our time."

CHAPTER 9

I have no idea what you are talking about," Fercus said. He strained against the ropes that held him to the chair, but there was no give in them.

"I think you know exactly what I mean," Antonidus said, leaning in very close so that their faces almost touched. "I have a gift for knowing a lie when I am told one." He sniffed twice suddenly and Fercus remembered how they called him Sulla's dog.

"You reek of lies," Antonidus said, sneering. "I know you were involved, so simply tell me and I will not have to bring in the torturers. There is no escape from here, broker. No one saw you arrested and no one will know we have spoken. Just tell me who ordered the assassination and where the killer is and you will walk out unharmed."

"Take me to a court of law. I will find representation to prove my innocence!" Fercus said, his voice shaking.

"Oh, you would like that, wouldn't you? Days wasted in idle talk while the Senate tries to prove it has one law for all. There *is* no law down here, in this room. Down here, we still remember Sulla."

"I know nothing!" Fercus shouted, making Antonidus move back a few inches, to his relief. The general shook his head in regret.

"We know the killer went by the name of Dalcius. We

know he had been bought for kitchen work three weeks before. The record of the sale has vanished, of course, but there were witnesses. Did you think no one would notice Sulla's own agent at the market? Your name, Fercus, came up over and over again."

Fercus paled. He knew he would not be allowed to live. He would not see his daughters again. At least they were not in the city. He had sent his wife away when the soldiers came for the slave market records, understanding then what would happen and knowing he could not run with them if he wanted them to escape the wolves Sulla's friends would put on his trail.

He had accepted that there was a small risk, but after burning the sale papers, he had thought they would never make the link among so many thousands of others. His eyes filled with tears.

"Guilt overwhelms you? Or is it just that you have been found out?" Antonidus asked sharply.

Fercus said nothing and looked at the floor. He did not think he could stand torture.

The men who entered at Antonidus's order were old soldiers, calm and untroubled at what they were asked to do.

"I want names from him," Antonidus said to them. He turned back to Fercus and raised his head until their eyes met once more. "Once these men have started, it will take a tremendous effort to make them stop. They enjoy this sort of thing. Is there anything you want to say before it begins?"

"The Republic is worth a life," Fercus said, his eyes bright.

Antonidus smiled. "The Republic is dead, but I do love to meet a man of principle. Let's see how long it lasts."

Fercus tried to pull away as the first slivers of metal were pressed against his skin.

Antonidus watched in fascination for a while, then slowly grew pale, wincing at the muffled, heaving sounds

Fercus made as the two men bent over him. Nodding to them to continue, the general left, hurrying to be out in the cool night air.

*   *   *

It was worse than anything Fercus had ever known, an agony of humiliation and terror. He turned his head to one of the men and his lips twisted open to speak, though his blurring eyes could not see more than vague shapes of pain and light.

"If you love Rome, let me die. Let me die quickly."

The two men paused to exchange a glance, then resumed their work.

*   *   *

Julius sat in the sand with the others, shivering as dawn finally came to warm them. They had soaked the clothes in the sea, removing the worst of months of fetid darkness, but they had to let them dry on their bodies.

The sun rose swiftly and they were silent witnesses to the first glorious dawn they had seen since standing on the decks of *Accipiter*. With the light, they saw the beach was a thin strip of sand that ran along the alien coast. Thick foliage clustered right up to the edge of it as far as the eye could see, except for one wide path only half a mile away, found by Prax as they scouted the area. They had no idea where the captain had put them down, except that it was likely to be near a village. For the ransoms to be a regular source of funds, it was important that prisoners made it back to civilization, and they knew the coast would not be uninhabited. Prax was sure it was the north coast of Africa. He said he recognized some of the trees, and it was true that the birds that flew overhead were not those of home.

"We could be close to a Roman settlement," Gaditicus had said to them. "There are hundreds of them along the coast, and we can't be the first prisoners to be left here. We should be able to get on one of the merchant ships and be back in Rome before the end of summer."

"I'm not going back," Julius had said quietly. "Not like this, without money and in rags. I meant what I said to the captain."

"What choice do you have?" Gaditicus replied. "If you had a ship and a crew, you could still spend months searching for that one pirate out of many."

"I heard one of the guards call him Celsus. Even if it's not his real name, it's a start. We know his ship and someone will know him."

Gaditicus raised his eyebrows. "Look, Julius. I would like to see the bastard again as much as you, but it just isn't possible. I didn't mind you baiting the idiot on board, but the reality is we don't have a sword between us, nor coins to rub together."

Julius stood and looked steadily at the centurion. "Then we will start by getting those, then men to make a crew, then a ship to hunt in. One thing at a time."

Gaditicus returned the gaze, feeling the intensity behind it. "We?" he said quietly.

"I'd do it alone if I had to, though it would take longer. If we stay together, I have a few ideas for getting our money back so we can return to Rome with pride. I won't creep back home beaten."

"It's not a thought I enjoy," Gaditicus replied. "The gold my family sent will have pushed them all into poverty. They will be happy to see me safe, but I will have to see how their lives have changed every day. If you aren't just dreaming, I will listen to those ideas of yours. It can't hurt to talk it through."

Julius put out his hand and gripped the older man's shoulder, before turning to the others.

"What about the rest of you? Do you want to go back

like whipped dogs or take a few months more to try and win back what we have lost?"

"They will have more than just our gold on board," Pelitas said slowly. "They wouldn't be able to leave it anywhere and be safe, so there's a good chance the legion silver will be in the hold as well."

"Which belongs to the legion!" Gaditicus snapped with a trace of his old authority. "No, lads. I'll not be a thief. Legion silver is marked with the stamp of Rome. Any of that goes back to the men who earned their pay."

The others nodded at this, knowing it was fair.

Suetonius spoke suddenly in disbelief. "You are talking as if the gold is here, not on a distant ship we will never see again while we are lost and hungry!"

"You are right," Julius said. "We had better get started along that path. It's too wide to be just for animals, so there should be a village hereabouts. We'll talk it out when we have a chance to feel like Romans again, with good food in our bellies and these stinking beards cut off."

The group rose and walked toward the break in the foliage with him, leaving Suetonius alone, his mouth hanging open. After a few moments, he closed it and trotted after them.

*   *   *

The two torturers stood silently as Antonidus viewed the wreck that had been Fercus. The general winced in sympathy at the mangled carcass, glad that he had been able to enjoy a light sleep while it was going on.

"He said nothing?" Antonidus asked, shaking his head in amazement. "Jupiter's head—look what you've done to him. How could a man stand that?"

"Perhaps he knew nothing," one of the grim men replied.

Antonidus considered it for a moment. "Perhaps. I wish

we could have brought his daughters to him so I could be sure."

He seemed fascinated by the injuries and inspected the body closely, noting each cut and burn. He whistled softly through his teeth.

"Astonishing. I would not have believed he had such courage in him. He didn't even try to give false names?"

"Nothing, General. He didn't say a word to us."

The two men exchanged a glance again, hidden behind the general's back as he bent close to the bound corpse. It was a tiny moment of communication before they resumed their blank expressions.

*   *   *

Varro Aemilanus welcomed the ragged officers into his house with a beaming smile. Although he had been retired from legion life for fifteen years, it was always a pleasure to see the young men the pirates left on his small stretch of coast. It reminded him of the world outside his village, distant enough not to trouble his peaceful life.

"Sit down, gentlemen," he said, indicating couches that were thinly padded. They had been fine once, but time had taken the shine from the cloth, he noted with regret. Not that these soldiers would care, he thought as they took the places he indicated. Only two of them remained standing and he knew they would be the leaders. Such little tricks gave him pleasure.

"Judging by the look of you, I'd say you have been ransomed by the pirates that infest this coastline," he said, his voice drenched in sympathy. He wondered what they would say if they knew that the pirate Celsus often came to the village to talk to his old friend and give him the news and gossip of the cities.

"Yet this settlement is untouched," said the younger of the two.

Varro glanced sharply at him, noting the intense blue stare. One of the eyes had a wide, dark center that seemed to look through his cheerful manner to the real man. Despite the beards, they all stood straighter and stronger than the miserable groups Celsus would leave nearby every couple of years. He cautioned himself to be careful, not yet sure of the situation. At least he had his sons outside, well armed and ready for his call. It paid to be careful.

"Those they have ransomed are left along this coast. I'm sure they find it useful to have the men returned to civilization to keep the ransoms coming in. What would you have us do? We are farmers here. Rome gave us the land for a quiet retirement, not to fight the pirates. That is the job of our galleys, I believe." He said the last with a twinkle in his eye, expecting the young man to smile or look embarrassed at failing in that task. The steady gaze never faltered and Varro found his good humor evaporating.

"The settlement is too small for a bathhouse, but there are a few private homes that will take you in and lend you razors."

"What about clothes?" said the older of the two.

Varro realized he didn't know their names and blinked. This was not the usual way of such conversations. The last group had practically wept to find a Roman in such a strange land, sitting on couches in a well-built stone house.

"Are you the officer here?" Varro asked, glancing at the younger man as he spoke.

"I was the captain of *Accipiter*, but you have not answered my question," Gaditicus replied.

"We do not have garments for you, I am afraid..." Varro began.

The young man sprang at him, gripping his throat and pulling him out of his seat. He choked in horror and sudden fear as he was dragged over the table and pressed down onto it, looking up into those blue eyes that seemed to know all his secrets.

"You are living in a fine house for a farmer," the voice hissed at him. "Did you think we wouldn't notice? What rank were you? Who did you serve with?"

The grip lessened to let him speak and Varro thought of calling to his sons, but knew he didn't dare with the man's hand still on his throat.

"I was a centurion, with Marius," he said hoarsely. "How dare you..." The fingers tightened again and his voice was cut off. He could barely breathe.

"Rich family, was it? There are two men outside, hiding. Who are they?"

"My sons..."

"Call them in here. They will live, but I'll not be ambushed as we leave. You will die before they reach you if you warn them. My word on it."

Varro believed him and called to his sons as soon as he had the breath. He watched in horror as the strangers moved quickly to the door, grabbing the men as they entered and stripping their weapons from them. His sons tried to shout, but a flurry of blows knocked them down.

"You are wrong about us. We live a peaceful life here," Varro said, his voice almost crushed from him.

"You have sons. Why haven't they returned to Rome to join the armies like their father? What could hold them here but an alliance with Celsus and men like him?"

The young officer turned to the soldiers who held Varro's sons.

"Take them outside and cut their throats," he said.

"No! What do you want from me?" Varro said quickly.

The blue eyes fastened on his again.

"I want swords and whatever gold the pirates pay you to be a safe place for them. I want clothes for the men and armor if you have it."

Varro tried to nod, with the hand still on his neck.

"You will have it all, though there's not much coin," he said miserably. The grip tightened for a second.

"Don't play false with me," the young man said.

"Who are you?" Varro wheezed at him.

"I am the nephew of the man you swore to serve until death. My name is Julius Caesar," he said quietly.

Julius let the man rise, keeping his face stern and forbidding while his spirits leapt in him. How long ago had Marius told him a soldier had to follow his instincts at times? From the first instant of walking into the peaceful village, noting the well-kept main street and the neat houses, he had known that Celsus would not have left it untouched without some arrangement. He wondered if all the villages along the coast would be the same, and felt a touch of guilt for a moment. The city retired their legionaries to these distant coasts, giving them land and expecting them to fend for themselves, keeping peace with their presence alone. How else could they survive without bargaining with the pirates? Some of them might have fought at first, but they would have been killed and those that followed had no choice.

He looked over to Varro's sons and sighed. Those same retired legionaries had children who had never seen Rome, providing new men for the pirate ships when they came. He noted the dark skins of the pair, their features a mingling of Africa and Rome. How many of these would there be, knowing nothing of their fathers' loyalties? They could never be farmers any more than he could, with a world to see.

Varro rubbed his neck as he watched Julius and tried to guess at his thoughts, his spirits sinking as he saw the strange eyes come to rest on his beloved sons. He feared for them. He could feel the anger in the young officer even now.

"We never had a choice," he said. "Celsus would have killed us all."

"You should have sent messages to Rome, telling them

about the pirates," Julius replied distantly, his thoughts elsewhere.

Varro almost laughed. "Do you think the Republic cares
what happens to us? They make us believe in their dreams
while we are young and strong enough to fight for them, but
when that is all gone, they forget who we are and go back to
convincing another generation of fools, while the Senate
grow richer and fatter off the back of lands we have won for
them. We were on our own and I did what I had to."

There was truth in his anger and Julius looked at him,
taking in the straighter bearing.

"Corruption can be cut out," he said. "With Sulla in
control, the Senate is dying."

Varro shook his head slowly. "Son, the Republic was
dying long before Sulla came along, but you're too young to
see it."

Varro collapsed back into his seat, still rubbing his
throat. When Julius looked away from him, he found all the
officers of *Accipiter* watching him, waiting patiently.

"Well, Julius?" Pelitas said quietly. "What do we do
now?"

"We gather what we need and move on to the next village, then the next. These people owe us for letting the pirates
thrive in their midst. I do not doubt there are many more like
this one," he replied, indicating Varro.

"You think you can keep doing this?" Suetonius said,
horrified at what was happening.

"Of course. Next time, we will have swords and good
clothes. It will not be so hard."

CHAPTER 10

Tubruk swung the axe smoothly into the cut in the dying oak. A sliver of healthy wood jolted out under the blow, but the dead branches showed it was time for the old tree to come down. It wouldn't be long until he reached the heartwood, and he was sure the core was rotten. He had been working for more than an hour, and sweat plastered his linen bracae to him. He had removed his tunic after warming up and felt no need for it, despite the breeze that blew through the woods. The drying perspiration cooled him and he felt at peace. It was difficult not to think about the problems of running the estate after the ransom payment, but he pushed those thoughts aside, concentrating on the swing and strike of the heavy iron blade.

He paused, panting, and rested his hands on the long axe handle. There had been a time when he could have swung an axe all day, but now even the hairs on his chest had turned a winter gray. Foolish to keep pushing himself, perhaps, but old age came fastest to those who sat and waited for it, and at least the exercise kept his belly flat.

"I used to climb that tree," a voice sounded behind him. Tubruk jumped at the interruption to the quiet of the woods, turning with the axe in his hands.

Brutus was there, sitting on a stump with his arms folded and the old grin making his eyes bright. Tubruk laughed with the pleasure of seeing him and rested the axe against the wide trunk of the oak. For a moment, they didn't speak, then Tubruk crossed the space to him and gripped him in a great hug, lifting him off the stump.

"By all the gods, Marcus, it's good to see you, lad," Tubruk said as he let Brutus go. "You've changed. You're taller! Let me look at you."

The old gladiator stepped back and pulled on his tunic.

"That's a centurion's armor. You've prospered."

"Bronze Fist," Brutus replied. "Never lost a battle, though we came close once or twice when I was giving the orders."

"I doubt it. Gods, I'm proud of you. Are you back for good now, or on your way through?"

"My posting is over. There are a few things I want to do in the city before finding a new legion."

For the first time, Tubruk noticed how dusty the young man was.

"How far have you walked?"

"Halfway across the world, it feels like. Renius doesn't like to part with his money for horses, though we found a couple of nags for part of it."

Tubruk chuckled as he picked up the axe and rested it on his shoulder.

"He came back with you, then? I thought he'd given up on the city when they burned his house in the riots."

Brutus shrugged. "He's gone to sell the plot and find a place to rent."

Tubruk smiled in memory. "Rome is too quiet for him now. I should think he'd hate it." He clapped a hand on Brutus's shoulder. "Come down the hill with me. Your old room is just as it was and a good soak and rubdown will take the dust of the road out of your lungs."

"Is Julius back?" Brutus asked.

Tubruk seemed to slump a little as if the axe had suddenly become heavier.

"We had to raise a ransom for him when pirates took his galley. We're still waiting to hear if he's safe."

Brutus looked at him in amazement. "Gods, I haven't heard this! Was he wounded?"

"We know nothing. All I've had was the order for the money. I had to pay for guards to load it onto a merchant ship at the coast. Fifty talents, it was."

"I didn't think the family had that kind of money," Brutus said quietly.

"We don't now. All the businesses had to be sold, as well as some of the estate land. There's just the crop revenue left. The years will be hard for a while, but there is enough to live on."

"He's had his share of bad luck. Enough for a lifetime."

"I doubt he'll be down for long. Julius and you are the same. Money can always be made again, if you live long enough. Did you know Sulla was dead?"

"Even in Greece, we were told to wear black. Is it true he was poisoned?"

Tubruk frowned for a second, looking away before replying, "It's true. He made a lot of enemies in the Senate. His general, Antonidus, is still searching for the killers. I don't think he will ever give up."

As he spoke, he thought of Fercus and the terrible days that had followed after hearing he had been taken. Tubruk had never known fear like it, waiting for soldiers to march from the city and take him back for trial and execution. They had not come and Antonidus continued to question and search. Tubruk didn't even dare look for Fercus's family in case Antonidus was watching them, but he had sworn the debt would be repaid somehow. Fercus had been a true friend, but more than that, he had believed in the Republic with a passion that had surprised the old gladiator when he had first broached the plan for killing Sulla. Fercus had hardly needed to be persuaded.

"Tubruk?" Brutus broke into his thoughts, looking curious.

"I'm sorry. I was thinking of the past. They say the Republic has returned and Rome is once again a city of law, but it isn't true. They sink their teeth into each other to prevent anyone taking over from Sulla. Only recently, two senators were executed for treason on nothing more than the word of their accusers. They bribe and steal and give out free corn to the mob, who fill their bellies and go home satisfied. It is a strange city, Marcus."

Brutus put his hand on Tubruk's shoulder. "I did not know you cared so much about it," he said.

"I always did, but I trusted more when I was younger. I thought that men like Sulla and, yes, Marius could not harm her, but they can. They can kill her. Do you know that free corn wipes out small farmers? They cannot sell their crops. Their lands are put up for sale and added to the swollen holdings of the senators. Those farmers end up on the city streets being given the very corn that ruined them."

"There will be better men in the Senate in time. A new generation, like Julius."

Tubruk's expression eased a little, but Brutus was shocked at the depth of the bitterness and sadness he had seen revealed. Tubruk had always been a pillar of certainty in the lives of the boys. He struggled to find the right words to say.

"We will make a Rome that you can be proud of," he said. Tubruk reached up and gripped his outstretched arm.

"Oh, to be young again," he said, smiling. "Come on home, Aurelia will be thrilled to see you so tall and strong."

"Tubruk? I . . ." Brutus hesitated. "I won't stay for long. I have enough coin to get lodgings in the city."

Tubruk glanced at him, understanding. "This is your home. It always will be. You stay as long as you want."

The silence stretched again as they walked toward the estate buildings.

"Thank you. I wasn't sure if you'd expect me to make my own way now. I can, you know."

"I know, Marcus," Tubruk replied, smiling as he called out for the gates to be opened.

The young man felt a weight lift from him. "They call me Brutus now."

Tubruk put out his hand and Brutus took it in the legionary's grip.

"Welcome home, Brutus," Tubruk replied.

He led Brutus into the kitchens while the water was heated for his bath, motioning him to a chair while Tubruk cut meat and bread for him. He was hungry himself after the axe work, and they ate and talked with the ease and comfort of old friends.

*   *   *

The heat seemed to batter at his skin as Julius inspected the six new recruits. The African sun even made his armor painful to touch, and anywhere the metal made contact with his skin was an agony until he could shift it.

Nothing of his discomfort showed in his expression, though the first doubts tugged at his concentration as he looked at the men he'd found. They were strong and fit enough, but not one of them had been trained as a soldier. For his plan to work, he needed a force of fifty at least and had begun to believe that he would get them. The trouble was, they needed to take orders and make war with the sort of discipline the *Accipiter* officers took completely for granted. Somehow, he had to impress upon them the simple fact that they would die without it.

Physically, they were impressive enough, but only two of the six had volunteered and these from the last village. He expected there to be more as they came to resemble a proper

Roman half-century, but the first four had come because he had insisted on it, and they were still angry. The second village had seemed happy to be rid of the largest of them, and Julius guessed he was a troublemaker. His expression seemed set in a constant sneer that irritated Julius every time he saw it.

Renius would have beaten them into shape for him, he thought. That was a start. He had to think what Renius would do. Gaditicus and the others from *Accipiter* had followed him this far, hardly believing how easy it had been after the first settlement. Julius wondered how many Romans in all the hundreds of retirement farms had sons who could be taught to fight. There was an army out there and all that was needed was for someone to find them and remind them of the call of blood.

He stopped next to the troublemaker and saw how the eyes met his with polite inquiry and not a trace of fear or respect. He towered over most of them, his limbs long and lithely muscled, shining with sweat. The biting flies that tormented the officers of *Accipiter* seemed not to trouble him at all, and he stood like a statue in the heat. The man reminded him of Marcus to some extent. He looked every inch a Roman, but even the Latin he spoke was a corrupted mix of African dialect and phrases. Julius knew his father had died and left him a farm that he had neglected to the point of ruin. Left alone, he would have been killed in a fight or joined the pirates when the last of the money and wine ran out.

What was the man's name? Julius prided himself on learning them quickly, as he had once seen Marius do for every man under his command, yet under the cool stare, he couldn't think of it at first. Then it came to him. He had told them to call him Ciro, giving no other. He probably didn't even know it was a slave name. What would Renius do?

"I need men who can fight," he said, looking into the brown eyes that returned his glare so steadily.

"I can fight," Ciro replied, his confidence obvious.

"I need men who can keep their temper in a crisis," Julius continued.

"I can—" Ciro began.

Julius slapped him hard across the face. For a moment, anger flared in the dark eyes, but Ciro held himself still, the muscles of his bare chest twitching like a great cat's. Julius leaned close to him.

"Do you want to take up a sword? Cut me down?" he whispered harshly.

"No," Ciro replied, and the calm was back once more.

"Why not?" Julius asked, wondering how to reach him.

"My father . . . said a legionary had to have control."

Julius stayed where he was, though his thoughts spun wildly. There was a lever here.

"You didn't have control in the settlement where we found you, did you?" he said, hoping he had guessed correctly about Ciro's relationship with the villagers. The big man said nothing for a long time, and Julius waited patiently, knowing not to interrupt.

"I wasn't . . . a legionary then," Ciro said.

Julius eyed him, looking for the insolence he had come to expect. It was missing and silently he cursed the Senate for wasting men like these, who dreamed of being legionaries while wasting their lives in a strange land.

"You are not a legionary," Julius said slowly, and saw the mouth begin to twist in response to the rejection, "but I can make you one. You will learn brotherhood with me and from me, and you will walk the streets of the distant city with your head high. If anyone stops you, you will tell them you are a soldier of Caesar's."

"I will," Ciro said.

"Sir."

"I will, sir," he said, and stood tall.

Julius stood back to address the recruits, standing with the waiting officers of *Accipiter*.

"With men like you, what can't we achieve? You are the children of Rome and we will show you your history and your pride. We will teach you the gladius and battle formations, the laws, the customs, the life. There will be more to come and you will train them, showing what it means to be of *Rome*. Now we march. The next village will see legionaries when they see you."

The line of pairs was ragged and out of step, but Julius knew that would improve. He wondered if Renius would have seen the need in the new men, but dismissed the thought. Renius wasn't here. He was.

Gaditicus waited with him, falling in beside as they brought up the rear of the column.

"They follow you," he noted.

Julius turned quickly to him. "They must, if we are ever to crew a ship and take back our ransoms."

Gaditicus snorted softly, clapping his hand on Julius's armor.

Julius faltered and stopped. "Oh no," he whispered. "Tell them we'll catch them up. Quickly!"

Gaditicus gave the order and watched as the double file of Romans marched away along the path. They were quickly out of sight around a bend and Gaditicus turned to Julius enquiringly. He had gone pale and shut his eyes.

"Is it the sickness again?" Gaditicus asked.

Julius nodded weakly. "Before... the last fit, I tasted metal in my mouth. I can taste it now." He hawked and spat, his expression bitter. "Don't tell them. Don't..."

Gaditicus caught him as he fell, and held him down as his body jerked and twisted, his sandals cutting arcs in the undergrowth with the violence of their movement. The biting flies seemed to sense his weakness and swarmed around them. Gaditicus looked around for something to jam between

Julius's teeth, but the cloth they had used on *Accipiter* was long gone. He wrenched up a heavy leaf and managed to get the fibrous stalk across Julius's mouth, letting it fall in as the mouth champed. It held and Gaditicus bore down with all his weight until the fit was over.

Finally, Julius was able to sit up and spit out the stalk he'd almost bitten through. He felt as if he had been beaten unconscious. He grimaced as he saw his bladder had released, and thumped his fists into the earth in fury, scattering the flies before they darted back in at his exposed skin.

"I thought it was over."

"Perhaps that was the last one," Gaditicus replied. "Head wounds are always complicated. Cabera said it might go on for a while."

"Or for the rest of my life. I miss that old man," Julius said, his voice bleak. "My mother used to have shaking fits. I never really understood what it was like before. It feels like dying."

"Can you stand? I don't want to lose the men, and after your speech they could well march all morning."

Gaditicus helped the young officer to his feet and watched him take a few deep breaths to steady himself. He wanted to offer words of comfort, but the words didn't come easily.

"You will beat this," he said. "Cabera said you were strong and nothing I've seen makes me think differently."

"Maybe. Let's move on, then. I'd like to stay close to the sea, so I can wash."

"I could say I told you a joke and you pissed yourself laughing," Gaditicus said. Julius chuckled and Gaditicus smiled at him.

"There, you see? You are stronger than you realize. Alexander the Great had the shaking sickness, they say."

"Really?"

"Yes, and Hannibal. It is not the end, just a burden."

*   *   *

Brutus tried to hide his shock when he saw Aurelia the following morning. She was plaster-white and thin, with a web of wrinkles that had not been there when he'd left for Greece three years before.

Tubruk had seen his distress and filled the gaps in the conversation, telling Aurelia the answers to the questions she did not ask. The old gladiator was not sure she even recognized Brutus.

Aurelia's silence was covered by the laughter of Clodia and Cornelia as they tended Julius's baby at breakfast. Brutus smiled dutifully at the child and said she looked like her father, though in truth he could see no resemblance to anything human. He felt uncomfortable in the triclinium, aware that these people had formed bonds that excluded him. It was the first time he had ever felt like a stranger in that house, and it saddened him.

Tubruk left with Aurelia after she had eaten only a little food, and Brutus tried hard to take part in the conversation, telling the women about the blue-skinned tribe he had fought in his first few months with the Bronze Fist in Greece. Clodia laughed when he told them of the savage who had waved his genitals at the Romans, believing he was safe. Cornelia covered Julia's ears with her hands and Brutus blushed, embarrassed.

"I'm sorry. I am more used to the company of soldiers. It has been a while since I was in this house."

"Tubruk told us you grew up here," Clodia broke in to put him at his ease, knowing somehow that it was important she did so. "He said you always dreamed of being a great swordsman. Did you reach your dream?"

Shyly, Brutus told them of the sword tourney he had won, against the best of the legion centuries.

"They gave me a sword made with harder iron that keeps a better edge. It has gold in the hilt. I will show it to you."

"Will Julius be safe?" Cornelia asked without warning.

Brutus responded with a quick smile. "Of course. The ransom has been paid. There is no danger for him." The words came easily and she seemed reassured. His own worries were untouched.

*   *   *

That afternoon, he walked back up the hill to the oak with Tubruk, each of them carrying axes on their shoulders. They took up positions on each side of the trunk and began the slow rhythm of blows that ate a deeper and deeper gash into the wood as the day wore on.

"There is another reason for my coming back to Rome," Brutus said, wiping sweat from his forehead with his hand.

Tubruk laid down his axe and breathed heavily for a few moments before replying.

"What is it?" he asked.

"I want to find my mother. I am not a boy any longer and I want to know where I came from. I thought you might know where she was."

Tubruk blew air out of his lips, taking up the axe again.

"It will bring you grief, lad."

"I must. I have family."

Tubruk hammered his axe blade into the oak with enormous power, wedging it deeply.

"Your family is here," he said, levering it out.

"These are my blood. I never knew my father. I just want to know her. If she died without me seeing her, I know I would always regret it."

Tubruk paused again, then sighed before speaking.

"She has a place in the Via Festus, on the far side of the city, near the Quirinal hill. Think hard before you go there. It could disappoint you."

"No. She deserted me when I was only a few months old. Nothing she could do would disappoint me now," Brutus said softly, before taking up his axe again and continuing to cut at the old tree.

As the sun set, the oak fell, and they walked back to the estate house in the twilight. Renius was there, waiting in the shadow of the gate.

"They've built where my house stood," he said angrily to Brutus, "and some young legionaries marched me out of the city as a troublemaker. My own city!"

Tubruk let out an explosive shout of laughter.

"Did you tell them who you were?" Brutus asked, trying to remain serious.

Renius was clearly nettled by their amusement and practically snarled, "They didn't know my name. Pups, fresh from their mother's milk, every one of them."

"There is a room here, if you want it," Tubruk said.

Renius looked at his old pupil for the first time then. "How much are you asking?" he said.

"Just the pleasure of your company, old friend. Just that."

Renius snorted. "You're a fool, then. I'd have paid a fair rate."

At Tubruk's call, the gate was opened and Renius stalked in ahead of them. Brutus caught Tubruk's eye and grinned at the affection he saw there.

CHAPTER 11

Brutus stood at the crossroads at the base of the Quirinal hill and let the bustling crowd pass around him. He had risen early and checked his armor, thankful for the clean undertunic Tubruk had laid out. Some part of him knew it was ridiculous to care, but he had oiled each segment and polished the metal until it shone. He felt garish in the darker colors of the crowd, but he took comfort from the solid weight, as if it protected him from more than weapons.

The Bronze Fist had their own armorer, and like everyone else in the century, he had been the best. The greave Brutus wore on his right leg was skillfully shaped to follow the muscles. It was inscribed with a pattern of circles cut with acid, and Brutus had given a month's pay for it. Sweat trickled behind the metal sheath and he reached down to try to scratch the skin beneath without success. Practicality had made him leave the plume of his helmet back at the estate. It would not do to be catching it on lintels inside the house where his mother lived.

It was the sight of the building that had made him pause and take stock. He had been expecting a tenement of four or five stories, clean but small. Instead the front was covered in a façade of dark marble, almost like a temple. The main buildings were set back from the dust and ordure of the streets, visible only through a high gate. Brutus supposed Marius's house had been larger, but it was difficult to be sure.

Tubruk hadn't told him anything more than the address, but as he took in his surroundings Brutus saw it was a rich area, with a good part of the crowd made up of servants and slaves running errands and carrying goods for their masters. He had expected his mother to be impressed by the son who had become a centurion, but when he saw the house he realized she might think of him as just a common soldier, and hesitated.

He thought of going back to the estate. He knew Renius and Tubruk would welcome him without judging his failure, but hadn't he planned the meeting all the way from Greece? It would be ridiculous to turn back with the grand building in sight.

He took a deep breath and checked his armor one last time for imperfections. The leather laces were tied and there was not a blemish to be seen. It would do.

The crowd parted around him without jostling as he moved forward. Up close, the gate brought back memories of Marius's house on the other side of the city. He had barely reached it before it was swung open before him, a slave bowing and waving him in.

"This way, sir," the slave said, fastening the gate closed and walking before him down a narrow corridor. Brutus followed, his heart thumping. Was he expected?

He was taken into a room that was as lavish as any he had ever seen. Marble columns supported the ceiling and were gilded at the head and foot. White statues lined the walls, and couches were gathered around a pool in the center, where he caught a glimpse of heavy fish swimming almost motionless in the cool depths. His armor seemed clumsy and loud in the stillness, and Brutus wished he had unlaced the greave to have a good scratch before coming in.

The slave vanished through a doorway and he was alone

with only the soft rippling of the water to distract him. It was peaceful enough, and after a moment's thought he removed his helmet and ran his hands through his damp hair.

He felt the air move as another door opened behind him, and then stood abruptly in surprise as a beautiful woman walked toward him. She was painted like a doll and about his age, he judged. Her dress was of some fabric he had never seen, and through it he could see the outline of her breasts and nipples. Her skin was perfectly pale and the only ornament she wore was a heavy chain of gold that ran around her throat.

"Do sit," she said. "You should be comfortable." As she spoke she sat down on the couch he had leapt from and crossed her legs delicately, making the dress move and reveal enough to bring a flush to his cheeks. He sat down beside her, trying to find a scrap of the resolution he had summoned before.

"Do I please you?" she said softly.

"You are beautiful, but I am looking for . . . a woman I used to know."

She pouted and he wanted to kiss her with a terrible ache, to gather her into his arms and make her gasp. The image of it made his senses reel, and he realized the air had filled with a perfume that made him dizzy. Her hand reached out and touched him just at the top of the greave, where inches of his bare brown leg were revealed. He shivered slightly and then came to his senses in shock. He rose to his feet in a sudden movement.

"Are you expecting payment from me?"

The girl looked confused and younger than he had first thought. "I don't do it for love," she said, a good deal of the softness in her voice suddenly missing.

"Is Servilia here? She will want to see me."

The girl slumped into the couch, her flirtatious manner

gone in an instant. "She doesn't see centurions, you know. You have to be a consul to have a go with her."

Brutus stared at her in horror.

"Servilia!" he shouted, striding past the pool to the other side of the room. "Where are you?"

He heard a clatter of running feet approaching behind one door, so he quickly opened another and slipped through, closing it on the laughter of the girl on the couch. He found himself in a long corridor with a gaping slave looking at him, bearing a tray of drinks.

"You can't come through here!" the slave shouted, but Brutus pushed him aside, sending the drinks flying. The slave bolted away, then two men blocked the corridor at the end. Both held clubs and together they filled the narrow walkway, their shoulders brushing the walls as they strode toward him.

"Had a bit too much to drink, have you?" one of them grated as they closed.

Brutus drew his gladius in one smooth movement. It glittered, the blade etched like the greave with swirling designs that caught the light. Both men paused, suddenly uncertain.

"Servilia!" Brutus yelled at the top of his voice, keeping the sword leveled at the men. They drew daggers from their belt sheaths and advanced slowly.

"You cocky little bugger!" one said, waving his blade. "Think you can come in here and do what you like? I never got the chance to kill an officer before, but I'm going to enjoy this."

Brutus stiffened. "Stand to attention, you ignorant bastards," he snapped at them. "If I see a blade pointing my way, I will have you hanged."

The two men hesitated as he glared at them, responding to the tone almost as a reflex. Brutus took a furious step toward them.

"You tell me how men of your age have left their legion to guard a whorehouse. Deserters?"

"No . . . sir. We served with Primigenia."

Brutus held his face stiff to mask his surprise and delight. "Under Marius?" he demanded.

The older of the pair nodded. By now they were standing erect before him, and Brutus looked them up and down as if it were an inspection.

"If I had time, I would show you the letter he wrote to send me to my century in Greece. I marched with him to the steps of the Senate house to demand his Triumph. Do not shame his memory."

The two men blinked in discomfort as Brutus spoke. He let the silence stretch for a moment.

"Now, I have *business* with a woman named Servilia. You can fetch her to me, or take me to her, but you will act like soldiers while I'm here, understood?"

As the two men nodded, a door slammed open at the end of the corridor and a female voice snapped out.

"Stand away from him and give me a clear line of sight."

The two guards didn't move, their eyes locked on the young centurion. The tension showed in their shoulders, but they remained still.

Brutus spoke clearly to them. "Is this the one?"

The older man was sweating with strain. "She is the lady of the house," he confirmed.

"Then do as she tells you, gentlemen."

Without another word, the two guards stepped aside to reveal a woman sighting down the length of an arrow at Brutus.

"Are you Servilia?" he said, noting the slight shake of her arms as they began to tire.

"The name you have been yelling like a street brat selling fish? I own this house."

"I am no danger to you," Brutus replied. "And I'd ease off on that bow before you shoot someone by accident."

Servilia glanced at her guards and seemed to find comfort

in their presence. With a release of breath, she unbent the bow, though Brutus saw she held it so it could be quickly drawn and fired if he rushed at her. She had known the threats of soldiers before, he guessed.

The woman Brutus saw there was nothing like the one from the room of statues. She was as tall and slim as he was, with long dark hair that hung loose about her shoulders. Her skin glowed with sun and health and her face was not beautiful, in fact was almost ugly, but the wide mouth and dark eyes had a knowing sensuality that he thought would ensnare many men. Her hands were wide and strong on the bow, and gold bangles chimed on her wrists as she moved.

He took in every detail of her and felt pain as he recognized a touch of himself in the line of her perfect throat.

"You don't know me," he said quietly.

"What did you say?" she said, coming closer. "You disrupt my home and carry a blade into my rooms. I should have you whipped raw, and do not think your pretty rank will save you."

She walked superbly, he thought. He had seen that sort of sexual confidence in a woman only once before, at the temple of Vesta, where the virgins moved with insolence in every stride, knowing it was death to any man who touched them. She had something of that and he felt himself becoming aroused, sickened by it, but not knowing how to feel like a son. Blood rushed into his face and neck and she smiled sensually, showing sharp white teeth.

"I thought you would look older," he murmured, and a look of irritation came into her eyes.

"I look how I look. I still don't know you."

Brutus sheathed his sword. He wanted to say who he was and have shock break through her confidence, to see her eyes widen in amazement as she realized what an impressive young man he was.

Then it all seemed worthless. A long-suppressed memory

came to him of overhearing Julius's father talking about her, and he sighed to have it confirmed. He was in a whorehouse, no matter how rich it seemed. It didn't really matter what she thought of him.

"My name is Marcus. I am your son," he said, shrugging.

She froze as still as one of her statues. For a long moment she held his gaze, then her eyes filled with tears and she dropped the bow with a clatter and ran back down the corridor, slamming the door behind her with a force that shook the walls.

The guard was looking at Brutus with his mouth open.

"Is that true, sir?" he said gruffly. Brutus nodded and the man flushed with embarrassment. "We didn't know."

"I didn't tell you. Look, I'm going to leave now. Is anyone waiting to put a bolt in me as I go through the door?"

The guard relaxed slightly. "No," he said. "Me and the lad are the only guards. She doesn't need them, as a rule."

Brutus turned to leave and the guard spoke again.

"Sulla had Primigenia cut off the rolls in the Senate. We had to take what work we could find."

Brutus turned back to him, wishing he had more to offer.

"I know where you are now. I can find you again if I need you," he said. The guard stretched out his hand and Brutus took it in the legionary grip.

On his way out, Brutus passed through the room with the pool, thankful to find it empty. He paused only to collect his helmet and splash a little of the water on his face and neck. It didn't help cool his confusion. He felt dazed by events and desperately wanted to find somewhere quiet where he could think through what had happened. The thought of struggling in the busy crowds was an irritation, but he would have to get back to the estate. He had no other home.

At the gate, a slave came running toward him. He almost drew his sword again at the running footsteps, but the slave was another young girl, unarmed. She panted as she reached him and he noticed the rise and fall of her chest almost absently. Another beauty. It seemed the house was full of them.

"The mistress told me you should return here tomorrow morning. She will see you then."

Inexplicably, Brutus felt his spirits lift at the words.

"I will be here," he said.

*   *   *

The pattern along the coast suggested the next settlement would be farther than the soldiers could march in a day. They made better time when they crossed the tracks of heavy animals and could follow them until they turned away from the coast. Julius was unwilling to travel too far from the sound of crashing surf for fear of losing themselves completely. When they turned off a trail, it was hard, sweaty work to cut their way through stalks and thornbushes as high as a man's head and tipped with red thorns as if already marked in blood. Away from the sea, the air was thick with moisture, and stinging insects plagued them all, rising unseen from the heavy leaves as the Romans disturbed them.

As they made camp for the evening, Julius wondered if the isolation of the Roman settlements was evidence of some farsighted plan of the Senate's to prevent these disparate villages banding together as the generations passed, but guessed it was just to give them room to grow. He supposed he could have pushed the men on through the dark, but the officers from *Accipiter* were far less comfortable in the hot African night than those who had grown up on that coast. Strange animal calls and screams woke them and had hands reaching for their swords, while the recruits slept on, oblivious.

Julius had given Pelitas the task of selecting guards for the watches, matching new men with those he trusted, in pairs. He was well aware that every mile along the narrow game tracks was a chance for the young villagers to desert. With weapons scarce, they went unarmed during the day, but swords had to be given to those on watch, and one or two of them eyed the old iron blades with something like avarice. Julius hoped it was a greed for the things of their fathers, not a desire to steal what they could and run.

Gathering food had presented similar problems. It was crucial that the *Accipiter* men did not become dependent on their charges to eat. It would be a subtle but significant shift in the ladder of authority Julius had set up. He knew that those who dispense food are the masters, regardless of rank. That was a truth older than Rome herself.

He thanked the gods for Pelitas, who seemed able to trap small animals in these strange lands as once he had poached from the woodlands of Italy. Even the recruits had been impressed, watching him rejoin the group after only a few hours, bearing the limp bodies of four hares. With fifteen healthy men to feed, the evening hunt had become a vital skill, and Pelitas had helped to prevent them splitting into two camps of those who could stalk and those who had to wait to be fed.

Julius looked over to his friend, busy carving slices of pork from the side of a young pig he had caught earlier in the day, breaking its leg with a swiftly thrown rock as it rushed from cover almost on top of them. The mother had not been seen, though squeals had come to them from the distant shrubbery. Julius wished she had come closer so that they could be looking forward to a feast instead of a few hot mouthfuls. There was no spare fat on any of the men from *Accipiter,* and it would be a while before they lost their gaunt appearance completely. His mouth twitched as he supposed he had the same look. It had been such a long time since he had seen a mirror, and he wondered if his face had changed for better or worse. Would Cornelia be pleased if she saw him, or shocked and upset by the grim look he imagined in his eye, mute evidence to the horrors of imprisonment?

He chuckled to himself at the flight of fancy. He would be the same, no matter how his face had changed.

Suetonius looked up sharply at the laugh, always seeing insult where there was none. It was hard to resist baiting the young man, but in this Julius had set rigid restrictions on himself. He sensed the spite came from fear that Julius would use his new authority to strike back for old injuries. He could not afford to enjoy even a moment of that luxury, in case it broke up the unit he was trying to make. He knew he had to become the sort of leader who was above small grievances, to appear to them as Marius had once appeared to him—cut from better stone. He nodded to Suetonius briefly, then looked away at the rest.

Gaditicus and Prax supervised the camp, marking the perimeter with fallen branches, for want of anything better. Julius heard them go over the sentry rules with the men and smiled in a moment of nostalgia.

"How many times do you challenge?" Prax was saying to Ciro, as he had for all the men.

"Once, sir. They call to approach the camp and I say, 'Approach and be recognized.'"

"And if they don't call to approach the camp?" Prax said cheerfully.

"I wake someone else up, wait for them to get close, and chop their heads off."

"Good lad. Neck and groin, remember. Anywhere else and they can still have enough strength to take you with them. Neck and groin is fastest."

Ciro grinned, taking in every scrap of information Prax threw at him. Julius liked the big man's heart. He wanted to be a legionary, to know what his father had once loved. Prax too had discovered that he enjoyed teaching all the things he had learned in his decades of marching and sailing for Rome. Given time, the new men would be able to deceive anyone. They would look like legionaries and speak with the same casual slang and expressions.

Julius frowned to himself as he tried to find a comfortable position to lie down. Whether they would stand when all around them had been cut down and the enemy brought certain death to them with screaming triumph... that they couldn't know for sure until it happened. It didn't help that the men of *Accipiter* weren't even sure themselves where such wild courage came from. A man could spend a lifetime avoiding every conflict, then throw his life away to protect someone he loved. Julius closed his eyes. Perhaps that was the key, but not many men loved Rome. The city was too big, too impersonal. The legionaries Julius had known never thought of the republic of free voters, carved out on seven hills by a river. What they fought for was their general, their legion, even their century or their friends. A man standing next to his friends cannot run, for shame.

Suetonius yelped suddenly, leaping to his feet and beating at himself.

"Help! There's something on the ground here!" he shouted.

Julius jumped to his feet and the other men closed in on the fire, swords drawn. A part of Julius noted with pleasure that Ciro stayed at his post.

In the light of the fire, a black line of enormous ants moved like oil over the ground, disappearing back into the shadows beyond the light. Suetonius was becoming frantic and began to tear off his clothes.

"They're all over me!" he wailed.

Pelitas stepped forward to help him and as his foot stepped near the column, part of it slid toward him and he scrambled back with a shout, pulling at his legs with his bare fingers.

"Gods, get them off!" he cried.

The camp dissolved into chaos. Those who had been brought up on the coast were far calmer than the *Accipiter* officers. The ants bit as deeply as rats, and when the soldiers found them, their bodies broke away to leave the jaws still attached and tearing into the skin in death spasms. The grip was too strong to be pulled away with fingers, and Suetonius was soon covered in the dark heads, his hands bloody with tugging at them.

Julius called Ciro over and watched as he calmly checked the two Romans, breaking off the remaining bodies with his powerful hands.

"They're still in me! Can't you get the heads out?" Suetonius pleaded with him, shuddering in terror as he stood almost naked while the big man searched his skin for the last of them.

Ciro shrugged. "The jaws must be dug free with a knife, they can't be prized apart. The tribes use them to close wounds, like stitches."

"What are they?" Julius asked.

"Soldiers of the forest. They guard the column on the march. My father used to say they were like the outriders Rome uses. If you stay clear, they will not attack you, but if you are in their path, they'll make you jump like Suetonius."

Pelitas turned a baleful eye on the column that still streamed through the camp. "We could burn them," he said.

Ciro shook his head sharply. "The line is endless. Better just to move away from them."

"Right, you heard him," Julius said. "Pack up and get ready to move a mile down the coast. Suetonius, I want you clothed and ready to go. You and Pelitas can work the jaws out of your skin when we're settled again."

"It's agony," Suetonius whimpered.

Ciro looked at him and Julius felt a pang of shame and ir-ritation that the young officer was showing such a poor face to the recruits.

"Move, or I'll tie you down over the ants myself," he said.

The threat seemed to have an effect, and before the moon moved far in the sky, a new camp was set up, with Ciro and two others finishing their watch. They would all be tired from lack of sleep in the morning after the excitement.

Julius's head throbbed slowly, seeming to match the rhythms of the droning insects all around them. Every time he drifted into sleep, he'd feel the sting of an insect settling onto his exposed skin. They left smears of his own blood as he caught and cracked them, but there were always more waiting for him to lie still. He made a pillow of his kit and used a rag to cover his face, longing for the distant skies of Rome. For a moment, he could see Cornelia in his mind and he smiled. Exhaustion hit him moments later.

*   *   *

With itching red swellings on their skin and shadows under their eyes, they reached the next settlement before noon, less than a mile from the coast. Julius led the men into the square, taking in the sights and smells of a touch of civilization. He was struck again by the absence of fortifications of any kind. The old soldiers who had taken their lands on this coast must have little fear of attack, he thought. The farms were small, but there must be trade between these isolated places and native villages farther into the interior. He saw a number of black faces among the Romans who gathered to see his men. He wondered how long it would take for the Roman blood to mingle and be lost, so that distant generations would know nothing at all of their ancient fathers and their lives. The land would return to whatever state it had been in before they came, and even the stories around campfires would falter and be forgotten. He wondered if they remembered the empire of Carthage here, when thousands of ships had explored the world from ports along this very coastline. It was a chilling thought and he put it aside for later reflection, knowing he had to focus his mind if he was to come away from this place with more of what he needed.

As they had been told to do, his men stood to attention

in the double line, their expressions serious. With Julius's sword, only eight more of the men were armed and only three had proper armor. Spots of blood marked Suetonius's tunic and his fingers twitched to itch the scabs the ants had left all over him. Most of the *Accipiter* officers were raw from the sun and insects, and only the new recruits seemed unaffected.

Julius guessed they looked more like a troop of bandits or pirates than Roman legionaries, and saw more than a few of the people arm themselves surreptitiously, nervousness showing in all of them. A butcher paused in the process of cutting up what looked like a cousin of the young pig they had eaten the previous evening. He came out from behind his table with the cleaver resting on his arm, ready for a sudden attack. Julius let his gaze drift over the crowd, looking for whoever had the command. There was always someone, even in the wilderness.

After a tense wait, five men approached from the far end of the houses. Four were armed, three of them with long-handled wood axes and the last carrying a gladius that had snapped in some old battle, leaving him with little better than a heavy dagger.

The fifth man walked confidently to the newcomers. He had iron-gray hair and was thin as a stick. Julius guessed he was pushing sixty, but he had the upright bearing of an old soldier, and when he spoke, it was in the fluent Latin of the city.

"My name is Parrakis. This is a peaceful village. What do you want here?" he asked.

He addressed his question to Julius and seemed unafraid. In that moment, Julius changed his plan of browbeating the leader as he had the first. The village might have dealings with the pirates, but there was little evidence that they had profited from it. The houses and people were clean but unadorned.

"We are soldiers of Rome, lately of the galley *Accipiter*. We were ransomed by a pirate named Celsus. We mean to gather a crew and find him. This is a Roman settlement. I expect your aid."

Parrakis raised his eyebrows. "I am sorry, there is nothing here for you. I haven't seen Italy for twenty years or more. There is no debt to be paid by the families here. If you have silver, you may buy food, but then you must go."

Julius stepped a little closer, noting the way Parrakis's companions tensed while ignoring them conspicuously.

"These lands were given to legionaries, not to pirates. This coast is infested with them and you have a duty to help us."

Parrakis laughed. "Duty? I left all that behind a lifetime ago. I tell you again, Rome has no call on us here. We live and trade in peace, and if pirates come we sell our goods to them and they leave. I think you are looking for an army? You won't find it in this village. There's nothing of the city here, amongst farmers."

"Not all the men with me are from the ship. Some are from villages to the west. I need men who can be trained to fight. Men who are not willing to spend their lives hiding in this village as you do."

Parrakis flushed with anger. "Hiding? We work the land and struggle against pests and disease just to feed our families. The first ones came from legions that fought with honor in lands far from home and finally received the last gift of the Senate—peace. And you dare to say we are hiding? If I was younger, I would take a sword to you myself, you insolent whoreson!"

Julius wished he had just grabbed the man at the start. He opened his mouth to speak quickly, knowing he was losing the initiative. One of the men with axes broke in first.

"I'd like to go with them."

The older man whirled on him, spittle collecting whitely at the corners of his mouth. "To go and get yourself killed? What are you *thinking*?"

The axe carrier pursed his lips against the anger coming

from Parrakis. "You always said they were the best years of your life," he muttered. "When the old men get drunk, you always talk about those days like they were gold. All I have is the chance to break my back from dawn to dusk. What will I tell people when I am old and drunk? How good it was to slaughter a pig at festival? The time I broke a tooth on a piece of grit in the bread we make?"

Before the stupefied Parrakis could reply, Julius broke in, "All I ask is that you put it to the people of the village. I'd prefer volunteers, if there are more like this one."

The anger sagged from Parrakis, making him look exhausted.

"Young men," he said with a note of resignation. "Always looking for excitement. I suppose I was the same, once." He turned to the axe carrier. "Are you sure, lad?"

"You've got Deni and Cam to work the farm, you don't need me as well. I want to see Rome," the young man replied.

"All right, son, but what I said was true. There's no shame in making a life here."

"I know, Father. I'll come back to you all."

"Of course you will, boy. This is your home."

In all, eight from the village volunteered. Julius took six of them, turning down a pair who were little more than children, though one of them had rubbed soot onto his chin to make it look like the shadow of stubble. Two of the newcomers brought their own bows with them. It was beginning to feel like the army he needed to crew a ship and hunt the seas for Celsus. Julius tried to control his optimism as they marched out of the lush trees toward the coast for the first of the day's drills. He tallied what they needed in his head. Gold to hire a ship, twenty more men and thirty swords, enough food to keep them alive until they reached a major port. It could be done.

One of the bowmen tripped and fell flat, bringing most of the column to a staggering halt. Julius sighed. About three years to train them would be useful, as well.

CHAPTER 12

Servilia sat on the edge of the couch, her back straight. The tension was clear in every line of her, but Brutus felt he should not speak first. He had been awake for most of the night without resolving anything. Three times he had decided not to visit the house near Quirinal hill, but each time had been an empty gesture of defiance. There had never really been a moment when he wouldn't have come to her. He felt nothing like a son's love, yet some nebulous ideal made him return, with all the fascination of picking scabs and watching himself bleed for her.

He had wanted her to come for him when he was a child, when he was alone and frightened of the world. When Marius's wife had smothered him with her need for a son, he had recoiled from it, unnerved by emotions he didn't really understand. Still, the woman who faced him had a call on him that no one else had, not Tubruk, not even Julius.

In the unnatural stillness, he drank her in, looking for something he couldn't name or even try to understand. She wore a pure white stola against sun-dark skin without any jewelry. As it had been the day before, her long hair was un-bound, and when she moved, it was with a lithe grace that made it a pleasure just to watch her walk and sit, as much as he might admire the perfect gait of a leopard or deer. Her eyes were too large, he decided, and her chin too strong for classical beauty, yet he could not look away from her, noting the lines that marked her eyes and around her mouth. She seemed coiled and taut, ready to leap up and run from him as she had before. He waited and wondered how much of the tension showed in his own features.

"Why did you come?" she asked, breaking the awful silence. How many answers to that question had he thought through! Scene after scene had played in his imagination in the night: scorning her, offending her, embracing her. None of it had prepared him for the actual moment.

"When I was a child, I used to imagine what you were like. I wanted to see you, even once, just to know who you were. I wanted to know what you looked like." He heard his voice tremble and a spasm of anger rushed through him. He would *not* shame himself. He would *not* speak like a child to this woman, this whore.

"I have always thought of you, Marcus," she said. "I started many letters to you, but I never sent them."

Brutus took a grip on his thoughts. He had never heard his name from her mouth in all his years of being alive. It made him angry, and anger allowed him to speak calmly to her.

"What was my father like?" he asked.

She looked away at the walls of the simple room where they sat.

"He was a good man, very strong and as tall as you are. I only knew him for two years before he died, but I remember he was very pleased to have a son. He named you and took you to the temple of Mars to have you blessed by the priests. He became ill that year and was taken before winter. The doctors couldn't treat him, but there was very little pain at the end."

Brutus felt his eyes fill and brushed at them angrily as she continued.

"I...couldn't bring you up. I was a child myself and I

wasn't ready or able to be a mother. I left you with his friend and ran away." Her voice broke completely on the last phrase, and she opened her clenched hand to reveal a crumpled cloth that she used to wipe her eyes.

Brutus watched her with a peculiar sense of detachment, as if nothing she did or said could touch him. The anger had drained away and he felt almost light-headed. There was a question he had to ask, but it came easily now.

"Why didn't you come for me while I was growing up?"

She didn't answer for a long time, using the cloth to touch away the tears until her breathing had steadied and she was able to look at him again. She held her head with a fragile dignity.

"I did not want you to be ashamed."

His unnatural calm gave way to the emotions sweeping him, revealed as straw in a storm.

"I might have been," he whispered hoarsely. "I heard someone talking about you a long time ago and I tried to pretend it was a mistake, to put you out of my mind. It is true, then, that you ..."

He couldn't say the words to her, but she straightened still further, her eyes glittering.

"That I am a whore? Perhaps. I was once, though when the men you know are powerful enough, they call you a courtesan, or even a companion." She grimaced, her mouth twisting.

"I thought you might be ashamed of me, and I couldn't face seeing that in my son. Do not expect *me* to feel that shame. I lost that too long ago to even remember. I would live my life differently if I could go back, but I don't know anyone who hasn't the same useless, idle dream. I will not live my life now with my head bowed in guilt every day! Even for you."

"Why did you ask me to come back today?" Brutus asked, suddenly incredulous that he had answered the call so easily.

"I wanted to see if your father would still be proud of you. I wanted to see if *I* was proud of you! I have done many things in my life that I regret, but having you has comforted me whenever it was all too much to bear."

"You left me! Don't say it comforted you, you never even came to see me. I didn't even know where you were in the city! You might have gone anywhere."

Servilia held up four rigid fingers to him, folding her thumb under them.

"Four times I have moved house since you were a baby. Each time I sent a message to Tubruk to say where I was. He has always known how to contact me."

"I didn't know," he replied, struck by her intensity.

"You never asked him," she said, dropping her hand back into her lap.

The silence began again as if it had never been broken, suddenly swelling into the spaces between them. Brutus found himself looking for something he could say that would finally confound her, allowing him to walk out and away with dignity. Cutting remarks came and went in his thoughts until he finally saw that he was being a fool. Did he despise her, feel shame about her life or her past? He looked inside for an answer and found one. He felt not a scrap of shame. He knew in part it was because he had led men as an officer in a legion. If he had come to her when he had done nothing, he might hate her, but he had stood and measured his worth in the eyes of enemies and friends and was not afraid to measure it in hers.

"I ... don't care what you have done," he said slowly. "You are my mother."

She burst into a guffaw of laughter, rocking back into the couch. Once again he was lost in front of this strange woman, who was able to shatter every moment of calm he could summon.

"How nobly you say it!" she said through laughter. "Such a stern face to give me absolution. Did you not understand me at all? I know more about the way this city runs than any senator in his little robe and trim beard. I have more wealth than I could ever spend and more power in my word than you can imagine. You forgive me for my wicked life? My son, it breaks my heart to see how young you are. It reminds me of how young I was, once."

Her face became still and the laughter died from her lips.

"If I wanted you to forgive me anything, it would be for the years I could have had with you. Who I am, I would not change for anything, and the paths I have traveled to reach this day, this hour! They cannot be forgiven. You don't have the right or the privilege to do it."

"Then what do you want with me? I can't just shrug and tell you to forget that I grew to manhood without you. I needed you once, but those I trust and love are the ones who were with me then. You were not there."

He stood and looked down at her, confused and hurt. She stood with him.

"Will you leave me now?" she said quietly.

Brutus threw up his hands in despair.

"Do you want me to come back?" he asked.

"Very much," she said, reaching out to touch him on the arm. The contact made the room waver and blur.

"Good. Tomorrow?"

"Tomorrow," she confirmed, smiling through tears.

*   *   *

Lucius Auriga hawked and spat irritably. There was something about the air of central Greece that always dried his throat, especially when the sun was warm. He would much rather have been enjoying an afternoon sleep in the shade of his house than be summoned to this vast plain, where the constant breeze wore at his temper. It wasn't fitting for a Roman to be at the call of Greeks, no matter what their standing, he thought. It would no doubt be another complaint for him to deal with, as if he had nothing more to fill the days than to listen to their griping. He tugged his toga into position as they approached him. He must not seem discomfited by their choice of meeting place. After all, they were forbidden to ride, whereas he could simply mount up and be back inside the walls of Pharsalus before dark.

The man who had sent the summons walked unhurriedly toward them with two companions. His enormous shoulders and arms hung loosely, swinging slightly with his long stride. He looked as if he was fresh down from the mountains that broke the horizon all around them, and for a moment Lucius shivered delicately. At least they had not come armed, he thought. Mithridates was not usually a man who remembered to obey the laws of Rome. Lucius studied him as he walked over the scrub grass and wildflowers. He knew the locals still called him the king, and at least he walked like one, with his head unbowed, despite his disastrous rebellion.

All history now, Lucius thought, and before my time like everything else in this uncomfortable country. Even if the chance came to take the post of governor, he knew he would refuse it. They were such an unpleasant people. It baffled him how such coarse and vulgar farmers could have produced mathematics of such extraordinary complexity. If he hadn't studied Euclid and Aristotle, he would never have accepted the posting out of Italy, but the thought of meeting such minds had been intoxicating to the young commander. He sighed to himself. Not a Euclid to be found in a city of them.

Mithridates didn't smile as he halted before the small group of eight soldiers Lucius had brought with him. Turning on the spot, he gazed into the distance all around, then took a deep breath of air, filling his powerful chest and closing his eyes.

"Well? I have come here as you requested," Lucius said

loudly, forgetting for a moment that he must appear calm and unruffled. Mithridates opened his eyes.

"Do you know what this place is?" he said. Lucius shook his head. "This is the very spot where I was defeated by your people three years ago." He raised his thick arm with the fingers outstretched, pointing.

"That hill, can you see that? They had archers in the woods there, pouring down fire on us. We got to them in the end, though they had trapped and spiked the ground. A lot of men were lost in removing them, but we couldn't leave them at our back, you see? It destroys morale."

"Yes, but..." Lucius began. Mithridates raised his hand with the palm flat.

"Shhh," he said. "Let me tell the story." The man stood a foot higher than Lucius and seemed to carry a strength that forbade interruption. His bare arm reached out again, the corded muscles moving under the skin with his fingers.

"Where the land creases there, I had sling men, the best I have ever fought with. They brought down many of your people and then took up swords to join their brothers at the end. The main lines were behind you, and my men were astonished at the skill they saw. Such formations! I counted seven different calls in the battle, though there could have been more. The square, of course, and horns to encircle. The wedge—oh, it was something to see them form a wedge in the midst of my men. They used the shields so well. I think the men of Sparta would have held them, but on that day we were destroyed."

"I don't think..." Lucius tried again.

"Over there was my tent, not forty paces from where we stand today. The ground was mud then. Even now, these flowers and grasses look strange to me when I imagine that battle. My wife and daughters were there."

Mithridates the king smiled, his eyes distant. "I shouldn't have let them come, but I never thought the Romans would cover so much distance in a single night. As soon as we realized they were in the area, they were on us, attacking. My wife was killed at the end, and my daughters dragged out and murdered. My youngest girl was only fourteen and she had her back broken first before they cut her throat."

Lucius felt the blood draining from his face as he listened. There was such an intensity in the man's slow movements that he almost took a step back into the arms of his soldiers. He had heard the story when he first arrived, but there was something chilling in listening to the calm voice describe such horrors.

Mithridates looked at Lucius and his finger pointed at the younger man's chest.

"Where you are standing is where I knelt, tied and battered, surrounded by a ring of legionaries. I thought they would kill me then, and I invited it. I had heard my family screaming, you see, and I wanted to go with them. It started to rain, I remember, and the ground was sodden. Some of my people say rain is the tears of gods, have you ever heard that? I understood it then."

"Please..." Lucius whispered, just wanting to ride away and not hear any more.

Mithridates ignored him or didn't hear him through the memories. At times it seemed as if he had forgotten the Romans were there at all.

"I saw Sulla arrive and dismount. He wore the whitest toga I have ever seen. You have to remember that everything else was covered in blood and mud and filth. He looked... untouched by it all and that..." He shook his head slightly. "That was the strangest thing to see. He told me the men who had killed my wife and daughters had been executed, did you know that? He didn't have to hang them, and I didn't understand what he could want from me until he offered me a choice. Live and not raise arms again while he lived, or die at that moment, by his sword. I think if he hadn't said that about the men who killed my girls, I would have chosen death, but I took the chance he gave me. It was the right choice. I was able to see my sons again, at least."

Mithridates turned to the two men with him and smiled at them. "Hoca here is the eldest, but Thassus looks more like his mother, I think."

Lucius did take a step back as he realized what Mithridates was saying.

"No! Sulla didn't . . . you can't!" He broke off as men suddenly appeared from every direction. They came over the crest of every hill and walked from the woods where Mithridates had said the Roman archers had hidden. Horses thundered up to halt near the legionaries, who had all drawn their swords, waiting grimly and without panic for the end. Dozens of arrows pointed at them, waiting for the word.

Lucius grabbed Mithridates' arm in fear.

"That is past!" he shouted hopelessly. "Please!"

Mithridates took him by the shoulders and held him fast. His face was twisted in rage.

"I gave my word not to take arms while Cornelius Sulla lived. Now my wife and daughters are safely in the ground and I will have the blood owed to me!"

With one hand, he reached behind himself and withdrew a dagger from where it had been concealed. He pressed it against Lucius's throat and pulled the edge across quickly.

The legionaries died in seconds, impaled on shafts and unable even to return a blow.

The youngest of his sons nudged Lucius's body with his foot, his face thoughtful.

"That was a dangerous game, my king," Thassus said to his father. Mithridates shrugged, wiping blood from his face.

"There are spirits we love in this place. It was all I could do for them. Now give me a horse and a sword. Our people have been asleep for too long."

CHAPTER 13

Julius sat in the shadows of the drinking house and curled his fingers around the first cup of wine he had seen in nearly a year. The street noise of the Roman port drifted in from outside, and the murmur of conversation all around brought a feeling of home to him, especially if he closed his eyes.

Pelitas tipped his wine down his throat without ceremony, holding it high until he was sure every drop had come out before putting the vessel back on the wooden table. He sighed appreciatively.

"I think if I was here on my own, I would sell my armor and drink till I went blind," he said. "It's been a long time coming."

The others nodded, sipping or gulping at their own cups, bought with the last coins they had between them.

The rest of their men, new and old, were miles away up the coast, well hidden from casual patrols. Only the five of them had come into the port to decide where to go from there. It had been strange to be met and challenged by legionaries as they approached the first warehouses, but for most of the five officers the main feeling had been relief. The months along the coast were made into a distant adventure by the first clear order in Latin to identify themselves. At least the story of being taken by pirates had not caused more than a raised eyebrow as the soldiers took in the clean armor and serviceable weapons they wore. For that alone, their pride made the officers thankful. It would have been unpleasant to arrive as beggars.

"How long before the quaestor gets here?" Prax asked, looking at Gaditicus. As centurion, it was he who had spoken to the Roman officer in charge of the port, agreeing to meet later at the inn near the docks. It was a small point of tension that they all felt. The other officers had become so used to looking to Julius for the way forward that the reminder of their ranks sat awkwardly with them. Suetonius could barely keep himself from smiling.

Gaditicus sipped at his wine, grimacing slightly as it stung a sore on his gums.

"He said by the fourth hour, so we have a little time yet. He will have to send a report back to Rome that we are alive and well. No doubt he will offer us a berth on a merchant ship going that way."

He seemed lost in thought like the others, barely able to accept they had come back to civilization. Someone in the crowd brushed against him as he passed behind and Gaditicus stiffened. They had been away from the bustle of towns and ports for a long time.

"You can take a ship home if you want," Julius said quietly, looking around the table at the five men. "I'm going on, though."

For a moment, no one responded, then Prax spoke. "Including us, we have thirty-eight. How many of those have the skill and discipline to fight, Julius?"

"With the *Accipiter* officers, I would say no more than twenty. The rest are what we found, farmers with swords."

"Then it can't be done," Pelitas said gloomily. "Even if we could find Celsus, and the gods know that won't be easy, we don't have enough men to be sure of beating him."

Julius snorted angrily. "After everything we have achieved,

do you think I'm dropping it all now? Those are our men out in the woods, waiting for the word to start coming in. Do you think we should just leave them and take ship for Rome? No honor in that, Peli, none at all. You go home if you want. I'm not holding any of you here, but if you do go, I will share your ransoms out amongst them when we find and beat Celsus."

Pelitas chuckled at the angry words from the younger man. "You think we can do it? Honestly? You got us this far and I'd never have believed that if I hadn't been there to see you handle those settlements. If you say we go on, then I'll see it through."

"It can be done," Julius said firmly. "We need to get on board a merchant ship and take it out to sea. Away from the coast, we'll try to make ourselves as tempting as possible. We know the pirates work this coast; they'll take our bait. At least our men look like Roman legionaries, even if some are poor quality. We can put the good fighters in the front and bluff it through."

"I'm staying to the end," Prax said. "I need my ransom back to enjoy my retirement."

Gaditicus nodded in silence, lost in thought. Julius turned to the youngest of the officers and the one he had known the longest.

"What about you, Suetonius? Are you for home?"

Suetonius drummed his fingers on the wooden table. He had known this moment would come right from the start and had vowed then that he would take the first chance to go back. Of all of them, his family could easily stand the loss of his ransom, but the thought of returning in failure was a bitter draught. Rome had many young officers and the future did not look as bright as it had when he first stood on the decks of *Accipiter*. His father had expected quick promotion for his son, and when that hadn't happened, the senator had simply stopped asking. Now to have him back in the family estate with nothing but defeat in his record would be hard on all of them.

An idea formed in his mind as they watched him, and he struggled to keep any sign of it from showing. There was a way for him to return to the city in triumph if he was careful. Deliciously, it would involve the destruction of Julius, as well.

"Suetonius?" Julius repeated.

"I'm in," he replied firmly, already planning.

"Excellent. We need you, Tonius," Julius replied.

Suetonius kept his face still, though he seethed inwardly. None of them thought much of him, he knew, but his father would approve of what he was about to do, for the good of Rome.

"To business, gentlemen," Julius said, lowering his voice so that it wouldn't carry outside their small group. "One of us will have to go back to the men and tell them to come into the port. The soldiers here seemed to have no problem with the ransom story, so we will have them use that if they are questioned. We must be careful there. It will do us no good if a few are held for the quaestor to examine in the morning. I want to be at sea on the first dawn tide, with all of them on board."

"Can't we bring them in at night?" Pelitas asked.

"We can get past the few legionary guards, but a large group of soldiers boarding a merchant ship will be reported to the pirates. I've no doubt they have spies in this place, reporting which ships are carrying gold and cargoes they want. It's what I would do, and *Accipiter* put in here before we were attacked. They have the wealth to pay a few bribes, after all. The problem is getting nearly forty men aboard without making the trap obvious. We'll be better off with small groups of two or three at a time, over the whole night."

"If you're right, they will have watchers at the docks who will see us," Gaditicus said quietly.

Julius thought for a moment. "Then we will split the

men. Find out who can swim and have them reach the ship in the water, where we can bring them up on ropes. There is only a crescent moon tonight, so we should be able to do that without being spotted. The armor and swords will have to be carried on board like another package of goods to be sold. It has to be you, Pelitas. You swim like a fish. Can you bring them around the spit as soon as it gets dark?"

"It's a long swim, but without armor, yes. These boys grew up on the coast, after all. They should be able to make it," Pelitas replied.

Julius reached into his belt pouch and withdrew two silver coins.

"I thought you said the money was gone!" Prax said cheerfully. "I'll have another cup of the same, if you don't mind."

Julius shook his head, unsmiling. "Perhaps later. I kept these so a couple of you can come in here tonight and buy a few drinks. I want someone to play the part of a guard on his last night before sailing a valuable cargo—something that will be reported back to the pirates by their contacts. Whoever it is must not get drunk, or killed, so I need someone solid and dependable, perhaps with a few more years under his belt than most of us."

"All right, you don't have to beat the point to death," Prax said, smiling. "I could enjoy a job like that. You up for it, Gadi?"

The centurion shook his head slightly, looking at Julius. "Not this one. I want to stay with the men in case something goes wrong."

"I'll join you," Suetonius said suddenly.

Prax raised his eyebrows, then shrugged.

"If there's no one else," Suetonius continued, trying not to seem too eager. It would give him the chance he needed away from the others. Prax nodded reluctantly at him and Suetonius sat back, relaxing.

"I saw you watching the ships as we came in," Gaditicus prompted Julius. The younger man leaned closer and they all brought their heads forward to hear his words.

"There was one loading supplies," he muttered. "The *Ventulus*. Trireme and sail. A small crew we can take over without too much trouble."

"You realize," Suetonius said, "that if we steal a ship from a Roman port, that makes us pirates as well?" Even as he spoke, he realized it was a mistake to warn them, but part of him couldn't resist the little barb. They would remember later and know who had saved them from Julius's wild schemes. The others froze slightly as they considered the words, and Julius glared at the young watch officer.

"Only if we're seen. If it matters to you, then pay the captain for his losses out of your share," he said.

Gaditicus frowned. "No. He's right. I want it understood that none of the crew will be killed and the cargo will be left untouched. If we are successful, the captain must be paid for his time and lost profits."

He locked eyes with Julius and the rest of them could feel the tension between the two men making the silence uncomfortable. The issue of who commanded them had been ignored for so long that they had almost forgotten it, but it was still there and Gaditicus had ruled *Accipiter* with discipline once. Suetonius fought not to grin at the silent struggle he'd brought about.

At last, Julius nodded and the tension vanished.

"Right," he said. "But one way or another, I want control of that ship by nightfall."

A new voice spoke suddenly over them, making them all lean back.

"Who is the commanding officer here?" it said, unconsciously echoing much of their private thoughts. Julius examined his wine cup.

"I was the captain of *Accipiter*," Gaditicus said in reply, standing up to greet the newcomer. The man was a reminder of Rome even more than the legionaries that guarded the port. He wore a draped toga over bare skin, held by a silver brooch with an eagle etched in the metal. His hair was cut short and the hand he offered Gaditicus had a heavy gold ring on the fourth finger.

"You look healthier than most of the ransom men we get in this port. My name is Pravitas, the quaestor here. I see your cups are empty and I'm dry myself."

He signaled to a serving slave, who came quickly and filled their cups again with a better wine than the first. Obviously, the quaestor was well known in the port town. Julius noticed he had arrived without guards, another sign that the laws of Rome held firm there. He did have a long dagger in his belt, however, which he shifted slightly to allow himself to sit down on the bench with them.

When the wine was poured, the quaestor held up his cup for a toast. "To Rome, gentlemen."

They chorused the words and sipped the wine, unwilling to waste such quality in gulps without knowing if the man would order another.

"How long were you held?" he said as the cups were brought down again.

"Six months, we think, though it was hard to keep track of the time. What month is it now?" Gaditicus replied.

Pravitas raised his eyebrows. "A long time to be held prisoner. It is just after the Kalends of October."

Gaditicus worked it out quickly. "We were held for six, but it has taken three months to reach this port."

"You must have been dropped far away," Pravitas said with interest.

Gaditicus realized that he didn't want to explain how long they had spent training new soldiers to fight and respond to orders, so he just shrugged. "Some of us were injured. We had to take it slowly."

"The swords and armor, though? I am surprised the pirates didn't take those," Pravitas pressed.

Gaditicus thought of lying, but the quaestor could easily have had the five men locked up if he thought they were hiding something. He appeared to be suspicious already, despite his light tone, so Gaditicus tried to stay close to the truth.

"We picked these up at a Roman settlement, from an old armory. They made us work for them, but we needed to regain fitness, so it worked out well for us."

"Very generous. The swords alone must be worth a fair amount. Which settlement was it, do you know?"

"Look, sir. The old soldier who let us have them was helping Romans who had fallen on hard times. You should leave it at that."

Pravitas leaned back, his face still curious. It was a difficult situation and the five officers watched him closely. Although in theory all Roman citizens in the province were under his authority, he had limited power over soldiers. If he chose to have them arrested without evidence, the local legion commander would be furious.

"Very well. I will leave you your mystery. Perhaps I should make you prove your right to equipment worth a year's pay, but I imagine you will not be staying here long enough to make me investigate thoroughly?"

"We intend to take the first ship out," Gaditicus replied.

"Make sure you do, gentlemen. Do you need me to arrange passage, or did this 'old soldier' also give you money for the trip?"

"We will make our own arrangements, thank you," Gaditicus said tensely, barely managing to hide his irritation any longer.

"Then I will take your names for the report to Rome and leave you in peace," Pravitas replied. They gave them quickly and he repeated each one to fix them in his memory. He stood and inclined his head stiffly.

"Good luck on the return journey, gentlemen," he said, before making his way out through the busy inn onto the streets.

"Suspicious sod," Pelitas muttered when he had gone. The others murmured agreement.

"We have to move quickly now. I don't doubt the quaestor will have someone watching us until we are out of his province. It will be a little harder to make the plan work."

"Well, it was too easy before," Prax said. "We needed another challenge."

Julius smiled with the others. No matter what happened, they had developed a friendship that would never have come about if they were still on *Accipiter*.

"Go quickly back to the men, Peli. If you are followed, I expect you to lose them well before you get close. If you can't get clear, then have the men catch and tie the watchers until the night is over. It won't matter if they are missed tomorrow when we're gone."

Pelitas stood and drained his cup, belching softly. He left without another word and Julius looked around at the three men who were left.

"Now, *gentlemen*," he said, mimicking the quaestor's tone. "We have to get ourselves a merchant ship."

*   *   *

Captain Durus of the *Ventulus* was a contented man. He had a hold full of skins and exotic wood that would bring a small fortune back in Italy. The pride of the cargo were ten ivory tusks, each as long as a man. He had never seen the animals that died to provide them, but had bought them from a trader in the port, who in turn had bartered with hunters deeper inland. Durus knew he would triple his price on them at least and congratulated himself silently on the round of strong bargaining. Nearly two hours, it had taken, and he had been forced to take some worthless bolts of cloth as part of the sale. Even they would fetch a few bronze coins for slave clothing, he supposed, so he couldn't complain. It had been a successful trip, and even with the expenses of port fees and provisions for the crew and slaves, he should clear enough to buy his wife the pearls she wanted and perhaps a new horse for himself. A good stallion that would breed with his wife's mare, if he could get one for the right price.

His thoughts were interrupted by four soldiers walking along the dock to where *Ventulus* was tied up. He assumed they were from the meddling quaestor who controlled the port and sighed to himself, careful to smile as they drew close to him.

"Permission to come aboard?" one said.

"Of course," Durus replied, wondering if the man would try to squeeze yet another tax or bribe out of him. It really was too much.

"How can I help you?" he asked as they stepped onto the deck. He frowned as two of them ignored him, their eyes taking in every detail of the small merchant ship. Most of the men were enjoying shore leave, of course, so it was practically deserted, with only two others in sight on the deck where they stood.

"We need to ask you a few questions, in private," one of the soldiers said.

Durus struggled to look calm. Did they think he was a smuggler, a pirate? He tried not to look guilty, but there was always something to be found. There were so many regulations these days that it was impossible to remember them all.

"I have an excellent wine in my cabin. We can talk there," he said, forcing a smile.

They followed him without a word.

CHAPTER 14

Wait! Something's wrong," Suetonius hissed, holding Prax back as he was about to leave the shadow of the dock buildings. The optio shook off the restraining fingers in irritation.

"I can't hear anything. We need to get to Julius. Come on."

Suetonius shook his head, his gaze sweeping the empty dock. Where was the quaestor? Surely the man wouldn't have ignored the warning he'd sent? It had been so easy to whisper a message to a legionary as the man emptied his bladder in the dark outhouse of the inn. Before the soldier could finish and turn, Suetonius had vanished back into the press and lights of the crowd inside, his heart hammering with excitement. Had the man been too drunk to pass it on? As Suetonius recalled, he had been swaying slightly as he emptied the night's wine into the stone gutters.

The young Roman clenched his fists in frustration. The quaestor would reward a man who foiled piracy in the heart of a Roman port. Julius would be destroyed and Suetonius could return to Rome with his dignity intact, the humiliations he'd suffered behind him at last. Unless the drunken legionary had forgotten the message he'd whispered, or passed out on his way back to the barracks. He realized he should have made sure, but there had only been moments to pick his man before slipping away.

"What *is* it?" Prax said. "The ship is there. I'm going to run for it."

"It's a trap," Suetonius said quickly, stalling desperately. "There's something wrong, I can feel it." He dared not say more in case Prax began to suspect. His senses strained for some sign of the port soldiers, but he could hear nothing.

Prax squinted at the young man in the shadows.

"Well, I can't sense anything. If you've lost your nerve, then stay here, but I'm going."

The burly optio broke into a run toward the dim bulk of the merchant ship, skirting the flickering pools of light as he went. Suetonius watched him go, frowning. Better to be on his own, but if the quaestor didn't come, he would have to follow. He couldn't let them leave him behind to beg for a passage.

*   *   *

Tense and nervous as he gripped the railing, Julius peered out at the docks from the side of *Ventulus*. Where were Prax and Tonius? His eyes swept the open space between the ships and the warehouses, looking for his men, willing them to come quickly. The crescent moon had risen steadily and he was sure dawn could not be more than a few hours away.

He heard a slithering thump behind him and risked a glance to see another of the swimmers reach the shadows of the deck, lying on his back and blowing with exhaustion. Without lights to guide them, they had swum out into the deep waters along the spit of rock that formed the natural harbor, denied even a handhold on it by spined urchins and razor surfaces that skinned them at the slightest contact. Many had arrived with blood on their legs, the terror of sharks showing in their eyes. It had been hard on them, but Julius worried more for the others who couldn't swim, the giant Ciro among them. They had to make the run into port in darkness without alerting the quaestor's guards, and they were late.

There was only a glimmer of light from the cloud-covered moon, but there were torches at points all along the docks, flickers of dark yellow that moved and jumped in the breeze blowing away from the coast. The wind had changed an hour before and all Julius wanted to do was have the anchors pulled up, cut the holding ropes, and be gone. The captain was tied and bound in his cabin, his crew accepting the presence of a few extra soldiers without comment or alarm. It had gone almost better than Julius had hoped, but as he watched the torches snap and flutter, he felt a sudden fear that the quaestor had captured his men and it was all for nothing.

He wished he hadn't sent Prax and Suetonius to the inn. A fight could have started, or they could have raised suspicion with a clumsily told tale of riches on board. It had been too much of a risk, he admitted to himself, his knuckles white against the rail of *Ventulus*.

There! He recognized the figure of his old optio rushing toward the ship. Julius froze as he searched for Suetonius, but there was no sign. What had gone wrong?

Prax clambered on board, panting.

"Where is he?" Julius snapped at him.

"Behind me. I think his nerve went. We're better off leaving him," Prax replied, looking back to the dark port town.

In the distance, Julius heard a shout and leaned forward in that direction. Another came, but in the breeze he couldn't be sure what it was. He turned his head left and right, and then he heard the rhythmic beat of legionaries on the move, their iron-shod sandals making a noise on the cobbles that he would recognize anywhere. Ten, maybe twenty, men. Definitely not his. With Suetonius, there were only six others who were coming to the docks on foot. His mouth went dry. It had to be the quaestor, on his way to arrest them all. He *knew* the man had been suspicious.

Julius turned and looked at the narrow plank that shifted with *Ventulus,* anchoring the merchant ship to the dockside. Only a few damp sandbags held it steady. He could have the thing up in a second and order the ship under way. Gaditicus was guarding the captain. Pelitas would be with the slave master, ready for the signal to go. He felt terribly alone on the deserted deck and wished they were there to share the wait.

Julius shook his head in irritation. It was his decision and he would wait until he could see who was coming. He squinted at the dock buildings, praying his men would show, but there was nothing and he heard the unseen legionaries break into double time, the crash of their steps coming louder and louder.

When they came out of the dark alleys onto the torch-lit docks, Julius's heart sank. The quaestor was there himself and he led what looked like twenty of his men, armed and moving fast, straight for the line of dark ships and *Ventulus.*

*   *   *

Suetonius sagged in relief as he heard the clatter of soldiers. He would wait until they had captured the others and slip away at dawn. The quaestor would be pleased then to speak to the man who had given the warning. Suetonius smiled to himself. It would be tempting to stay for Julius's execution, just to catch his eye in the crowd. For a moment, Suetonius felt a pang of regret at the others, but shrugged unconsciously. They *were* pirates and not one of them had prevented Julius from destroying discipline with his obscene flattery and promises. Gaditicus wasn't fit to command and Pelitas ... he would enjoy seeing Pelitas brought down.

"Suetonius!" A voice shouted behind him, almost stopping his heart in shock. "Run, the quaestor's brought soldiers—go!"

Suetonius panicked as he felt his shoulder grabbed by the rush of men out of the shadows. A terrified glance showed him that the giant Ciro was bearing him along without slowing. Yanked out into the open, he could only gape as he saw the grim soldiers of the port streaming toward them, swords bared. He swallowed, staggering onward. There was no time to think. He could be cut down before they knew he had helped them. Swallowing his fear in fury, he ran with the others. There was no chance now for the private meeting between gentlemen he had imagined with the quaestor. He had to get through the chaos alive first. He clenched his jaw as he sprinted, passing Ciro in a few paces.

Julius almost cried out in relief as he saw the last of them running toward the ship. The quaestor's men spotted them immediately and bellowed out orders to halt.

"Come on!" Julius shouted to his men. He flicked his glance from one side of the dock to the other, groaning as he saw how close the quaestor's legionaries were to his own men. There wasn't enough time. Even if Ciro and the others made it onto the deck, they would be followed straight on by the first of the port soldiers.

Julius's heart hammered, making him feel light-headed as he watched both groups make for him. He held still, forcing himself not to move too soon, then turned and yelled over the decks.

"Now! Go, Peli! Now!"

Below him, deep in the body of the ship, he heard Pelitas answer with orders of his own. The *Ventulus* shuddered as the oars were shoved out of their resting blocks and pressed against the stones of the dock, starting the ship moving over the dark water. Julius sawed furiously at the rope that held them, cutting a gash in the rail as it parted. More shouts sounded below as the crew came awake with the movement, no doubt thinking they had come adrift. Julius knew they had expected another few days in the port, and he had only seconds before the deck would be filled with them. He ignored that problem as the plank to the docks shifted with the ship, the sandbags falling away.

Had he called too soon? The soldiers were less than fifty feet away from his men as the first ones leapt on, turning at bay then and unsheathing their swords. Suetonius moved like a ferret, his legs barely touching the plank as he threw himself onto the ship.

"Come on, Ciro. We're moving!" Julius shouted, waving his sword over his head. The big man was too slow. Without thinking, Julius started to move toward the plank, ready to jump onto the docks with him.

Drawing to a halt, Ciro unsheathed his gladius to meet the charge of the port soldiers.

"Ciro! There are too many!" Julius bawled at him, caught between his desire to help the last of his men and the knowledge that jumping down meant certain capture. The oars heaved out again and the plank fell.

Ciro took slow steps to the edge of the dock, not daring to turn his back. The quaestor's men rushed at him and Ciro lashed out with his fist at the first, a crunching blow that knocked the soldier over the edge and into the water. The legionary's armor dragged him down in a stream of silver bubbles. Ciro spun round then and gasped as a sword took him in the back. His arms flailed, but he roared and launched himself at the departing ship, catching the rail with one hand. Julius grabbed his wrist, looking down into dark eyes mad with pain and energy.

"Help me get him up!" Julius called as he struggled to keep his grip on the sweating skin. It took two more of them to heave Ciro up over the rail, and he gasped as his back tore and bled, leaving a dark smear on the wood where he lay.

"I didn't mean to kill him," Ciro said between rasping breaths.

Julius knelt by him and took his hand. "You had no choice."

Ciro's eyes were closed with the pain and he didn't see Julius's grim expression as he stood up and strode back to the rail. It began to swing away from the dock as the slaves found room to drop their oars into the water.

Not twenty feet away, the legionaries glared back, their hatred clear in their expressions. Despite being so close, it was a slowly widening gulf that they were powerless to cross, and as Julius watched them in silence, one of them spat on the stones in disgust.

The quaestor stood with them, his toga exchanged for a dark tunic and kilt of leather. His face was red with fury and exertion as he was forced to watch the ship move out of the harbor and finally be swallowed in the night. A couple of his men swore softly, as they too stared after *Ventulus*.

"Orders, sir?" one of them said, looking at the quaestor.

Pravitas did not reply until his breathing had settled and some of the redness was gone from his face.

"Run to the captain of the galley that put in yesterday. Tell him my orders are to set sail immediately to hunt the merchant ship *Ventulus*. I want him moving within the hour, on this tide."

The soldier saluted. "Yes, sir," he replied. "Should I give him an explanation?"

Pravitas nodded quickly. "Tell him a legionary has been murdered and the ship stolen by pirates."

*   *   *

Julius gathered his men in the darkness of the moving deck. Only Ciro was absent, left in a cabin to rest after his wound had been bound. The cut was deep under his shoulder blade, but it looked clean and with luck he would live.

The crew had been locked away below until their new situation could be explained to them. At least his officers could set sail and keep her moving without difficulty. Still, it rankled to have to keep innocent men prisoner. It was too close a reminder of their own captivity, and Julius sensed rather than saw the anger from the men of *Accipiter*.

"Things have changed," he said, trying to order his tumbling thoughts. "For those of you who haven't heard, one of the quaestor's soldiers drowned in the struggle to get ours on board. That means he will have every galley in the area looking out for us. We must stay as far from shore as we can and run from every sail for a while, until things settle down. I didn't plan for this, but there's no way back now. If we're caught, we're dead."

"I won't be a pirate," Gaditicus interrupted. "We started this to fight them, not to join the bastards."

"That quaestor has our names, remember?" Julius said. "The message he will send to Rome will describe how we stole a ship and drowned one of his men. Whether you like it or not, we *are* pirates until we can think of a way out of this mess. Our only hope is to follow through and capture Celsus. At least then we can show goodwill. It might stop them nailing us all up."

"Look where your ideas have brought us!" Suetonius snarled, shaking his fist. "This is disaster! There's no way back for any of us."

Arguments broke out from every side and Julius let them shout, fighting against his own despair. If only the quaestor had spent the night in bed, they would have been clear and away to find their captors.

Finally, he felt calm enough to interrupt.

"When you are finished arguing, you'll see we have no choices left. If we turn ourselves in, the quaestor will bring us to trial and execution. That is inescapable. I have one thing to add."

A hush fell and he felt sick as he saw the hope in their faces. They still thought he could bring about some change, and all he had left were promises he wasn't even sure he believed himself. He caught the eye of one after another of the officers from *Accipiter,* including them all.

"In that stinking prison, we would have thought it was a dream to be here with a ship, ready to take the battle back to our enemies. It has come at a price, but we'll deal with it when Celsus lies at our feet and his gold is ours. Straighten your backs."

"Rome has a long memory for her enemies," Gaditicus said, his voice bleak.

Julius forced himself to smile.

"But we are not the enemies of Rome. We know that. All we have to do is convince them as well."

Gaditicus shook his head slowly and turned his back on Julius, walking away across the deck. The first touch of dawn was in the sky, and gray dolphins played and leapt under the blunt bowsprit as *Ventulus* rode the waves, the oars cutting a fast stroke to take them away from land and retribution.

CHAPTER 15

Servilia walked slowly through the forum with her son, deep in thought. He seemed content with the gentle pace, his gaze lingering on the Senate house as they drew close to it. She barely noticed the great arches and domes, having seen them all a thousand times.

She glanced at Brutus without letting him see it. At her request, he had arrived for their meeting in the full polished uniform of a legion centurion. She knew the gossips would note him and ask his name, assuming the young man to be a lover. By now, more than a few would be able to confide in whispers that her son had returned to her, a mystery they would thrill to explore. He would not pass unnoticed through the heart of the city, she knew. There was something feral in the way he walked, his head bent to listen, a confidence that made the crowd part before him almost unconsciously.

They had met every day for a month, first in her house and then strolling together through the city. At first the journeys had been stiff and uncomfortable, but as the days passed they were able to converse without tension and even to laugh, though the moments were rare.

It had surprised her how much pleasure she took from being able to show him the shrines and tell the stories and legends that surrounded them all. Rome was full of legends and he took them all in with an avid interest that stimulated her own.

She ran a hand through her hair, pulling it back behind her head in a casual motion. A passing man stopped to stare at her, and Brutus frowned at him, making her want to giggle. At times, he tried to be protective, forgetting that she had survived in this city for all of his young life. Yet somehow she didn't mind it from him.

"The Senate is in session today," she said as she saw him looking through the bronze doors into the shadowed halls.

"Do you know what they are discussing?" he asked.

He had come to accept that there was little involving the Senate that she did not know. He hadn't asked if she had lovers in the *nobilitas*, but his suspicions were clear from the way he delicately skirted the subject. She smiled at him.

"Most of it is terribly dull: appointments, city ordinances, taxes. The dusty ones seem to enjoy it. I should think it will be dark before they are done."

"I would love to hear it," he said wistfully. "Dull or not, I would enjoy a day spent listening to those people. They reach so far across Roman lands, and all from that little place."

"You would be bored within an hour. Most of the real work is done in private. What you would see is the last stage as they draft the laws they have chewed over for weeks. It is not something a young man would enjoy."

"I would," he replied, and Servilia could hear the yearning in his voice. She wondered again what to do with him. He seemed content to spend each morning with her, but neither of them had discussed the future. Perhaps it was right to simply enjoy each other's company, but sometimes she saw his desire to move on, as yet without a place for which to aim. She knew he was drifting when he was with her, having stepped off the path of his life for a while. She could not regret a moment of it, but perhaps he would need a push to get him back to himself.

"In a week, they move on to the appointments of the highest posts," she said lightly. "Rome will have a new Pontifex Maximus and officials. Legion commands will be allocated over those days as well." She saw his head turn sharply toward her out of the corner of her eye as she spoke. There was still ambition there, then, underneath his relaxed exterior!

"I . . . should sign on with a new legion," he said slowly. "I can take a centurion post almost anywhere."

"Oh, I think I can manage something better than that for a son of mine," she said carelessly.

He stopped and took her arm gently. "What . . . How?" he began.

She laughed at his confusion, making him blush.

"Sometimes I forget how innocent you can be," she said, softening the words with her smile. "You have spent too long marching and fighting, I think. Yes, that's probably it. Mixing with savages and soldiers and not a breath of politics in your life."

She reached up to where he held her and pressed her hand over his with affection.

"The Senate are simply men, and men rarely do what is right. Most of the time, they do what they are persuaded, or ordered, or frightened into doing. Golden bribes will change hands, but the true currency of Rome is influence and favors. I have the first and I am owed many favors. Half those appointments will have been decided on already, in those private meetings. The rest can be bargained for or demanded."

She expected a smile at her words, but Brutus looked pained and she let her hand fall from his.

"I thought it was . . . different," he said quietly.

Servilia composed herself, caught between a desire not to shatter his illusions and an urgent need to wake the young soldier to reality before he got himself killed.

"Do you see that enclosure? You remember I told you it is

where the people of Rome come to vote for the appointments of the Senate, the tribunes, the quaestors, even the praetors? It is a secret vote and they take it seriously, yet time and again the same men are elected, the same families, with few changes. It seems fair, but the voters would not know an outsider. Only the Senate have fame enough and wealth enough to have their names in the mouths of the lowliest freemen of the city. It is all an illusion, but an elegant one. What is astonishing is that a few of the Senate do try to be just, earnestly improving the city and the welfare of her citizens." Servilia pointed over to the Senate house. "There are great men in that building, men who light up the city with their works. Most of the others, though, lack strength of any kind. They use the power of the Senate for riches and greater authority for themselves. That is the simple reality. The Senate is neither evil nor blessed, but a mixture, like everything else we set our hands to in this life."

Brutus studied her as he listened to her intensity. Whether she knew it or not, Servilia was not as detached and world-weary as she liked to appear. Her generally cynical air had vanished as she talked of the venal senators, the dislike obvious. She was not a simple woman, he thought to himself, not for the first time.

"I understand you. It's just that when I met Marius he was like a god. Small things were beneath him. I've met so many who couldn't see farther than their work or their rank, and when I look back he had a vision for the city and everything he did was to make it a reality, no matter what it cost him. He risked everything he owned to bring Sulla down, and he was right to! Sulla set himself up like a king in Rome the moment Marius was dead."

Servilia looked quickly around to see if anyone was close enough to overhear. She spoke softly.

"Don't say those names so loudly in public, Brutus. Those men may be dead, but the wounds are still fresh and they haven't found Sulla's killers yet. I'm glad you met Marius. He never came to my house, but even his enemies had respect for him, I know that. I wish there were more like him." Her tone lightened as she seemed to shrug away the seriousness of the subject. "Now let's walk on before the gossips start to wonder what we're talking about. I want to climb the hill up to the temple of Jupiter. Sulla had it rebuilt after the civil war, you know, shipping the pillars from the remains of the temple to Zeus in Greece. We will make an offering there."

"In his temple?" Brutus asked as they walked.

"The dead don't own temples. It belongs to Rome, or the god himself, if you want. Men try so hard to leave something behind. I think that's why I love them."

Brutus looked at her, struck again by the feeling that this woman had seen and lived lifetimes for his one.

"Do you want me to take a legion post?" he asked.

She smiled at the safer topic. "It would be the right thing to do. There is little point in me having favors owed if I never call them in, is there? You could spend your whole career as a centurion, overlooked by blind commanders, finishing your days with a little farm in a barely tamed new province, having to sleep with your sword. Take what I can give you. It pleases me to be able to help you after being gone from your life for so long. You understand? It is a debt I owe *you*, and I always pay my debts."

"What did you have in mind?" he asked.

"Ah, the interest sharpens, does it? Good. I would hate to think a son of mine lacked ambition. Let's see. You are barely nineteen years old, so religious posts are out for a few years. It should be military. Pompey will have his friends vote any way I want. He is an old companion. Crassus too will throw in with me for past favors. Cinna would clinch it. He is...a more current friend."

Brutus spluttered in amazement. "Cinna, Cornelia's father? I thought he was an old man!"

Servilia chuckled, the sound deep and sensual. "Sometimes he is, sometimes he's not."

Brutus went crimson with embarrassment. How could he look Cornelia in the eye the next time he met her?

Servilia continued, her mouth twitching upward as she ignored his confusion. "With their support, you could have command of a thousand men in any of the four legions they will review. What do you think?"

Brutus almost stumbled. What she offered was astonishing, but he realized he would have to stop being surprised at every revelation from Servilia. She was a very unusual woman in many ways, especially to have as a mother. A thought struck him and he stopped walking. She turned and looked at him with her eyebrows raised in enquiry.

"What about Marius's old legion?"

Servilia frowned. "Primigenia is finished. Even if the name were brought back, there can't be more than a handful of survivors. Use your head, Brutus. Every one of Sulla's friends would learn your name. You'd be lucky to survive a year."

Brutus hesitated. He had to ask or he would always wonder about not taking the chance.

"Is it possible, though? If I accept the risk, can those men you mentioned order it re-formed?"

Servilia shrugged and another passerby stared at her, captured for a moment. Brutus touched the hilt of his gladius and the man moved on.

"If I asked it, yes, but Primigenia was disgraced. Marius was declared an enemy of the state. Who would come to fight under that name? No, it's impossible."

"I want it. Just the name and the right to gather and train new soldiers. I can't think of anything I would want more."

Servilia looked into his eyes, searching them. "Are you sure?"

"Can Crassus, Cinna, and Pompey do it?" he said firmly.

Servilia smiled, still amazed at how this young man could send her emotions swinging from anger and amusement to pride in moments. She could not refuse him anything.

"It would take every favor I have, but they do owe me. For my own son, they would not deny me Primigenia."

Brutus wrapped his arms around her and she returned the embrace laughingly, swept up in his happiness.

"You will need to raise enormous capital if you are to bring a legion back from the dead," she said as he let her go. "I will introduce you to Crassus. I don't know anyone richer—I don't think there *is* anyone with more wealth—but he is not a fool. You will have to convince him of some return for his gold."

"I will give it some thought," Brutus said, looking back at the Senate building behind them.

*　　　　　*　　　　　*

Remembering his frustration on *Accipiter,* Julius never thought he would be thankful for the heavy weight and slow speed of a Roman galley. As dawn had arrived with the sudden glare of the tropical coast, his men had cried out in fear as the square Roman sail was first sighted. Julius had watched it for the first few hours of light, until he was certain the gap was closing. Grimly, he gave orders to send the cargo over the side.

At least the captain hadn't had to witness it, as he was still bound to a chair in his cabin. Julius knew the man would be raging when he found out, and more of Celsus's gold would have to be handed over to him if they were ever successful. There really wasn't a choice, though it had been an uncomfortable hour as his men brought out small groups of the crew to help them drop the valuable goods of a continent into their wake. Some of the rare woods bobbed in the waves where they fell, but the skins and bolts of cloth went quickly to the bottom. The last items to be thrown were enormous tusks of yellow ivory. Julius knew they were valuable and considered keeping them before his resolve firmed and he gave the reluctant signal to drop them overboard with the rest.

He had the men stand ready then, watching the sail on the horizon against the glare of the rising sun. If it still came closer, he knew the only thing left was to strip the ship of anything that could be torn out, but as the hours passed, the galley that followed them grew smaller and smaller until it was lost against the reflected light of the sea.

Julius turned to his men as they worked amongst the crew. He noticed Gaditicus was not with them, having stayed belowdecks when the call came to move the cargo. He frowned slightly, but decided not to go to him and force the situation. He would eventually see they had to continue with the original plan. It was their only hope. He would take *Ventulus* clear of the coast for a few weeks, continuing to train his recruits in sea warfare. He would have liked to have a corvus made, but they must look like any other merchant to tempt a pirate into an attack. Then he would see if he had managed to turn farmers into legionaries, or whether they would break and force him to see *Ventulus* sunk under him as *Accipiter* had been. He clenched his jaw and sent a short prayer to Mars. They must not waste this second chance.

CHAPTER 16

Alexandria looked around the small room she had been offered. It wasn't much, but at least it was clean, and it was hardly fair to take up space at Tabbic's tiny house now that her jewelry was bringing in a wage. She knew the old craftsman would let her stay longer, even accept a small rent if she insisted, but there was barely enough room for his own family in the tiny second-floor home.

She hadn't told them of her search, intending to surprise them with an invitation to dinner when she found a place. That was before almost a month of searching. They might have thought it strange that a woman who had been born a slave would turn anything down, but for the money she was willing to pay, the rooms offered had been dirty, damp, or infested with scurrying inhabitants she had not waited to examine closely.

She could have paid for more than one room, even a small house of her own. Her brooches were selling as fast as she could make them, and even with most of the profits going into new and finer metals, there was enough to add to her savings each month. Perhaps being a slave had taught her to value money when it came, as she begrudged every bronze coin that went on food or a roof over her head. Paying a high rent seemed like the ultimate idiocy, with nothing owned after years passing over hard-earned coin. Better to spend as little as possible and one day she could buy a house of her own, with a door to shut against the world.

"Do you want the room?" the owner asked.

Alexandria hesitated. She was tempted to try to bargain the price down still further, but the woman looked exhausted after a day working in the markets and it was an honest price. It wouldn't be fair to take advantage of the family's obvious poverty. Alexandria saw the woman's hands were sore and stained with color from the dye vats, leaving a faint blue mark over her eye as she brushed her hair back unconsciously.

"I have two more to see tomorrow. I will let you know then," Alexandria replied. "Shall I call here in the evening?"

The woman shrugged, her expression resigned. "Ask for Atia. I should be around. You won't find better for the price you want, you know. This is a clean house and the cat deals with any mice that get in. Up to you." She turned away to begin the evening's work preparing the food brought from the markets as part of her wage. Most of it would be near to spoiling, Alexandria knew, yet Atia seemed unbowed by the grind of her life.

It was a strange thing to see a freewoman on the edge of poverty. On the estate where Alexandria had worked, even the slaves were better fed and dressed than this woman's family. It was a view of life she had never explored before, and she had the oddest feeling of shame as she stood there in good clothes, wearing one of her own silver brooches as a pin for her cloak.

"I will see the others, then return to you," Alexandria said firmly.

Atia began to chop vegetables without comment, putting them into an iron pot over a clay stove built against the wall. Even the knife she held had a blade as thin as a fingernail, worn down but still used for want of anything better.

Outside in the street, a chorus of high-pitched yelling broke out and a grubby figure skidded through the open doorway, running straight into Alexandria.

"Whoa, lad! You almost had me over, then!" Alexandria said, smiling.

He looked at her with a quizzical expression in his blue eyes. His face was as dusty as the rest of him, but Alexandria could see his nose was dark and swollen, with a trace of blood at the end, smeared over his cheek as he wiped it, sniffing.

The woman threw down the knife and gathered him into her arms. "What have you been up to now?" she demanded, touching his nose.

The boy grinned and squirmed to get away from her embrace.

"Just a fight, Mam. The boys who work at the butcher's chased me all the way home. I tripped one of them when he went for me, and he landed one on my nose." The boy beamed at his mother and reached under his tunic, pulling out two bare chops, dripping blood. His mother groaned and snatched them with a quick dart of her hand.

"No, Mam. They're mine! I didn't steal them. They were just lying in the street."

His mother's face went white with anger, but he still clutched at her as she moved to the door, jumping as high as he could to retrieve his prizes from her grasp.

"I've told you not to steal and not to lie. Take your hands off me. These must go back to where they came from."

Alexandria was between Atia and the door, so she stepped out into the street to let her out. A group of boys stood around with a vaguely threatening air. They laughed to see the little boy jumping around his mother, and one of them held out a hand for the chops, which were slapped into his palm without a word.

"He's fast, missus. I'll give him that. Old Tedus told me to say he will summon the guard if your lad steals anything else."

"There's no call for that," Atia snapped in irritation, wiping the blood from her hands on a piece of cloth she pulled out of a sleeve. "Tell Tedus he's never lost anything he hasn't had back and I'll spread the word not to use his shop if he tries it. I will discipline my son, thank you."

"Fine job you're doing," the older boy sneered.

Atia raised her hand swiftly and he backed away, guffawing and pointing at the humiliated figure that still clung to her skirt.

"I'll give your little Thurinus a belting myself if I see him anywhere near the shop. See if I don't."

Atia flushed with anger and took a step forward, giving them the excuse they wanted to run off, calling back insults as they scattered.

Alexandria stood by the pair, wondering if she should just walk away. The scene she had witnessed was none of her business, but she was curious to see what would happen now the mother was alone with her rascal of a son.

The little boy sniveled and rubbed his nose gingerly. "I'm sorry, Mam. I just thought you would be pleased. I didn't think they would follow me all the way back here."

"You never think. If your father was alive, he'd be ashamed of you, boy. He would tell you we never steal and we never lie. Then he would warm your backside properly with his strap, which I should do myself."

The boy struggled to get away, kicking out at her as he found his arm held firmly.

"He was a money changer. You say they're all thieves, so he must have been too."

"Don't you dare say that!" Atia said through whitened lips. Without waiting for a response, she upended the boy on her knee and smacked him hard, six times. He struggled through the first three and lay silently still for the last. When she put him down, he skittered around the two women, pelting down the narrow street and disappearing around the nearest corner.

Atia sighed as she watched him run. Alexandria clasped

her hands together nervously, embarrassed to have witnessed such a private moment. Atia seemed to remember her suddenly and flushed as she met her eye.

"I'm sorry. He is always stealing and I can't seem to make him understand not to do it. He's always caught, but the next week he tries again."

"Is his name Thurinus?" Alexandria asked.

The woman shook her head. "No. They call him that because the family moved to the city from Thurin. It's an insulting nickname they have for him, but he seems to like it. His given name is Octavian, after his father. Little terror. Only nine years old, but more at home on the streets than in his own house. I do worry about him." She glanced at Alexandria, taking in the clothes and brooch properly.

"I shouldn't be bothering you with our troubles, miss. I don't mind admitting we could use the rent for the room. He wouldn't steal from you, and if he did I'd give it straight back, on my family's honor. You wouldn't know it, but there's good blood in his veins, Octavii and Caesar, if the little bugger would only realize it."

"Caesar?" Alexandria said sharply. The woman nodded.

"His grandmother was a Caesar, before she married into my family. No doubt she'd weep if she saw him steal meat from a butcher not three streets away. I mean, it's not as if they don't know his face! They'll break his arms if he does it again, and where will I be then?" Tears spilled from her eyes and, without thinking, Alexandria stepped forward to put an arm around her.

"Let's go inside. I think I will take that room of yours."

The woman straightened and glared at her. "I don't want charity. We get by and the boy will learn in time."

"It's not charity. Yours is the first clean room I have seen and I used to . . . work for a Caesar a few years ago. Could be the same family. We're almost relations."

The woman wiped her eyes with the cloth, producing it again from where it made a lump in her sleeve.

"Are you hungry?" she said, smiling.

Alexandria thought of the small pile of vegetables that waited to be chopped.

"I've already eaten. I'll pay you for the first month and then go back to where I'm staying and collect my things. It's not far off."

If she walked quickly and didn't dawdle at Tabbic's, Alexandria thought, she could make it back to her new home before dark. Perhaps by then they would have been able to buy a little meat with her rent.

*   *   *

The senators shifted uncomfortably in their seats. It had been a long session and many of them had reached the point where they were ignoring the complications of the arguments and simply voting whichever way they had agreed earlier.

With the evening shadows lengthening, torches were lit using tapers on long poles. The glow of the small flames was reflected in the polished white marble walls, and the air filled with the soft smell of scented oil. A large number of the three hundred senators who had gathered that morning had already left, letting the last few votes pass without their presence.

Crassus smiled to himself, having made sure his own supporters would remain until the torches were snuffed and the long day reached its official conclusion with the prayer for the safety of the city. He listened intently to the list of appointments, waiting for the one he and Pompey had included to be brought to the vote. Almost unwillingly, his eyes strayed to the legion list, cut into the white marble. Where Primigenia had been inscribed, there was now a blank space. It would be pleasing to undo another small piece of Sulla's legacy, even if he hadn't been asked to by his old friend.

At this thought, he looked across at Cinna and their eyes

met for a moment. Cinna nodded to the legion list and smiled. Crassus returned the smile, noting his friend's whitening hair. Surely Servilia could not favor such a winter father over himself? Just the thought of her stirred his blood, making him miss the end of a section in reminiscence. He watched the way Cinna voted and then raised his own hand with him.

More of the Senate rose, excusing themselves quietly, heading for homes and mistresses all over the city. Crassus watched Cato heave his bulk out of his seat. The man had been close to Sulla and it would sting him to miss the vote to come. Crassus tried not to let his face show his pleasure as they drew close and passed him, deep in discussion. It would be easier with them gone, but even with every Sullan in the building, he doubted if Cinna, Pompey, and himself could not force it through in their teeth. Restoring Primigenia would infuriate them. He reminded himself to thank Servilia for the idea when they next met. Perhaps a small gift to show his appreciation.

Pompey rose to answer a question concerning the new commander of a legion in Greece. He spoke with an engaging confidence of the new names, recommending them to the Senate. Crassus had heard there was another rebellion, and the losses meant chances for friends and relatives of the men in the Senate hall. He shook his head sadly, remembering the day when Marius had forced a vote that took Sulla away from Rome to put Mithridates down the first time. If Marius were here now, he would make them look up from their feet and do something about it! Instead, these fools argued and discussed the days away, when they should have been diverting a couple of the precious legions to shore up the Greek ones.

Crassus smiled wryly as he realized he was one of the fools he criticized. The last rebellion had led to civil war and a Dictator. Not one of the generals in the room dared put himself forward for fear of the others uniting against him. They did not want another Sulla and nothing was done as a result. Even Pompey waited and he was almost as impetuous as Marius himself. It would be suicidal to volunteer as Marius and Sulla had. There was too much spite and envy to let any one of their number have a victory over Mithridates. Sulla's fault, for letting him go free the first time. The man couldn't do anything right.

Pompey sat down and the vote was passed quickly, leaving only the last item of the day's business, proposed by Crassus and seconded by Pompey. They had kept Cinna's name out of the records at that point, as there were rumors he had been involved in Sulla's poisoning. Baseless, of course, but no one could stop the gossipmongers of Rome plying their trade.

For a moment, Crassus wondered if they *were* baseless, but then dismissed the thought. He was a practical man, and Sulla and the past were gone. If Cinna's daughter had avoided becoming Sulla's reluctant mistress, as he had heard whispered, that was surely proof that the gods looked with favor on Cinna's house—or the Caesars, perhaps. Definitely one of them.

He had heard some headway had been made finding the slave who carried the poison, but nothing yet was known about whoever ordered the death in the first place. Crassus looked around the half-empty room. It could have been almost any of them. Sulla had made enemies with a complete absence of caution. And caution should be the first rule of politics, Crassus thought. The second rule of politics should be to avoid attractive women needing favors, but a man didn't have too many chances for joy in his life and Servilia had provided some memories he cherished.

"Restoration of Primigenia to Legion Rolls," the Master of Debate announced, making Crassus sit up straight and concentrate.

"License to recruit, train, take oaths, and appoint officers under Senate authority to be given to Marcus Brutus of

Rome," the speaker continued in a drone that didn't match the murmur of excitement that swept through the remaining hundred senators in their seats. One of the Sullans left quickly, no doubt to bring his friends back for the vote. Pompey frowned as he saw Calpurnius Bibilus and two others stand to speak on the matter. The man had been a staunch supporter of Sulla's, and still swore his killers would be rooted out whenever he had the opportunity to do so.

It looked as if they had an old trick in mind. One after the other, they would speak to the Senate at great length until the session finished, or at the least until enough of their followers could be summoned to vote it down. If the proposal was pushed to the following session, it might not pass at all.

Crassus looked over to Cinna and caught his eye in commiseration. To his surprise, the older man flickered a wink in his direction. Crassus relaxed and settled back in his seat. Money was a powerful lever; he knew that as well as anyone. To hold up the vote, the Sullans had to be allowed to begin, and the Master of Debate recited the details of the proposal without once looking up at the benches where they stood, clearing throats noisily for his attention.

When the details had all been described, the Master of Debate called immediately for a vote. One of the Sullans swore loudly and walked out of the Senate hall, a gross breach of etiquette. The appointment passed easily and the session was declared closed. During the final prayer, Crassus sneaked a glance at Pompey and Cinna. He would have to choose his gift to Servilia with care. No doubt those two had similar ideas.

CHAPTER 17

Julius waited in the black hold, his sword drawn with the others around him. They were silent, waiting for the signal, and in that unnatural quiet, the creaking timbers of *Ventulus* seemed almost like muttered voices over the slap of waves against the hull.

Above them, the soldiers could hear the pirates laugh and swear as they tied their fast trireme to *Ventulus* and gathered on her decks without resistance. Julius strained to hear every sound. It was a tense time for them all, but most dangerous for those who remained above, where they could be cut down as an example or in simple cruelty. Julius had been surprised at first that any of the crew of *Ventulus* were willing to be on deck when the pirates boarded them. Their initial suspicion and anger at his men had vanished when he told them of the plan to attack pirates, and he believed in their enthusiasm. They had taken great pleasure in choosing those who would surrender on the decks, and Julius had realized that to these men a chance to strike back at the pirates they feared and hated would be the opportunity of a lifetime. Not for them the might of a legion galley. A merchant ship like the *Ventulus* always had to run for protection, and many of the crew had lost friends over the years to Celsus and his brother raiders.

Despite this, he had left Pelitas and Prax with them, dressed in rough clothes. It did not pay to trust strangers with their lives, and one of his officers would be able to shout the signal even if the crewmen betrayed them. He preferred not to leave anything to luck.

Voices sounded faintly through the hatches above their heads. His men shuffled, packed tightly, but not daring even to whisper. There was no way to be sure how many of the enemy stood on the deck. A pirate crew was usually smaller than the forces of a Roman galley and rarely more than thirty swords, but after witnessing the packed decks of the two ships that sank *Accipiter,* Julius knew he could not depend on superior numbers. He had to have surprise to be certain. With the remaining crew, a full fifty men waited with him. Julius had decided to allow the sailors their choice of weapons, reasoning that he could not spare men to guard them. The best he could manage was to have them mingle with his own soldiers, preventing a sudden attack on their rear as they rushed the deck.

One such stood close to him, carrying a rusting iron bar as a weapon. There was no hint of deception in the man, as far as Julius could see. Like the others, his gaze was fixed on the dark hatches, outlined with sunlight shining through the cracks in wide golden beams that swirled and glittered with dust. The beams moved almost hypnotically as *Ventulus* pitched and rolled in the swell. More voices spoke above and Julius tensed as he saw the light blocked by moving shadows, with the boards creaking under the weight. His own men would not stand on the hatches. It had to be the pirates, moving about their prize.

Julius had waited as long as he could before going below with the others, wanting to see how the pirates operated with his own eyes for the next time. To make it look real, he had to order the *Ventulus* rowers to a good stroke speed, but was ready to have some of the oars foul each other if the pirates couldn't close the gap. It hadn't been necessary. The enemy ship must have been stripped right down and drew steadily closer as the day wore on.

When they were close enough to count the oars, Julius had gone below to join his men. His greatest worry was that the enemy would employ a trained crew, as Celsus did. If they were wage-men, they might not be chained to the benches, and the thought of a hundred muscular rowers storming up to take on his men would mean disaster, armed or not. He'd seen the enemy ship carried a spiked ram that could anchor them if they smashed head-on into their prey, but guessed they wouldn't use it, preferring to come alongside and board. No doubt they felt secure so far from the coast and patrolling galleys, able to take their time off-loading cargo and possibly claiming *Ventulus* for their own rather than sinking her. Raiders didn't have shipyards, after all. He hoped they would have brought only a token force onto the decks of *Ventulus*. With the enemy tied securely, neither ship could escape, which was just as Julius wanted it. He sweated with anxiety as he waited for the signal. There were so many things that could go wrong.

Above, a strong wind was blowing, scattering tiny droplets of salt spray into the faces of the crew of *Ventulus* and their captors. Knowing the plan, they had surrendered without complaint, calling for the oars to be brought in and the sail dropped. *Ventulus* bobbed and rocked in the waves without wind and oars to make her move. A flight of arrows arced over as the pirates tied up, and Pelitas had to step aside not to be hit. He saw some of the crew sitting down on the deck, their hands in the air. No arrows were landing near them, so he copied the action, pulling Prax down with him. The shafts stopped flying as soon as they were all sitting. Pelitas heard laughter from the men waiting to board them, and he smiled grimly, waiting for the right moment. Julius had said to hold until the enemy had split their force between the two ships, but it was impossible to judge how many they had in reserve.

Pelitas decided he would shout when twenty men had crossed over their rail. More than that might not break in the first charge, and the last thing they wanted was a pitched battle on the decks. Too many of Julius's men were novices, and if the pirates didn't surrender quickly, the fight could turn and they would lose everything.

The first ten of the enemy reached the main deck of *Ventulus*. Though they were confident, Pelitas noted how they moved as a unit, protecting each other from a sudden lunge. They spread out slightly to the sitting crew, and he saw long leather cords hanging from their belts, ready for tying the prisoners. No doubt these ten were the best fighters, veterans who knew their business and could cut their way out of trouble. Pelitas wished Julius had let him bring a sword on deck. He felt naked without one.

The crew allowed themselves to be tied without a struggle, and Pelitas hesitated. With only ten on deck, it was too early to call, but they were working with efficiency, and if they trussed the rest as quickly, they could be no help at all when the fight started. He saw four more clamber over the rail to *Ventulus* and then looked into the serious face of the man who approached him, thongs ready in his hands. Fourteen would have to do.

As the man met Pelitas's eye, the Roman shouted loudly, making him jump and raise his sword.

"*Accipiter!*" Pelitas yelled, scrambling up. The pirate looked confused and snapped a response, but then the hatches banged open and Roman legionaries swarmed out amongst them, their armor gleaming in the sun.

The man by Pelitas swung to see them, his jaw dropping. Without hesitating, Pelitas leapt onto his back, pulling his forearm across the man's throat with all his strength. The man staggered forward a couple of steps, then reversed the sword in his hand and rammed it back into Pelitas's chest. He fell away in agony.

Julius led the charge. He killed the first man in front of him, swearing as he saw Pelitas had called it too soon. The archers were still on the other ship, and dark shafts struck the deck, killing one of the bound crew. There was no way to avoid them without shields, and Julius could only hope the charge wouldn't falter. His men had never been under fire and it was hard even for experienced soldiers, when every instinct said to dive and hide. His blade clanged against another and he punched around it, knocking his opponent flat. One quick shove into the exposed throat and he was over him.

In the space, Julius glanced left and right, taking in the scene. Most of the pirates on *Ventulus* were down. His men were fighting well, though one or two were struggling to pull arrows from their limbs, howling in pain.

A buzzing shaft struck Julius in the chest, knocking him back a step. He felt winded, but the vicious thing fell to the wooden deck with a clatter and he realized his armor had saved him.

"Board them!" he bellowed, and his men surged with him toward the pirate ship. More arrows cut through them with little damage, and Julius thanked the gods for the tough Roman plate. He jumped onto the rail of *Ventulus* and skidded, his iron-shod sandals slipping on the wood.

He landed at the feet of the enemy with a crash of metal and swearing. He batted away a jabbing sword with his forearm, taking a cut from the edge. His gladius was under him and he had to roll to free it. Another blade clanged against his shoulder, snapping off the plate.

The other Romans roared as they saw him fall, cutting wildly through the pirates who faced them. They threw themselves into the enemy ship without caution, pushing the line past Julius. Gaditicus grabbed his arm and heaved Julius to his feet.

"One more you owe me," Gaditicus growled as they rushed over the enemy deck together. Julius ran up to a pirate and lunged forward with his gladius, holding himself ready to avoid a counterthrust. Instead, the man lost his footing as he skipped back out of range and threw his sword out of his hand, sending it spinning over the planking. He looked terrified as Julius slowly lowered a heavy gladius to his throat.

"Please! Enough!" he shouted in terror. Julius paused, risking another flashing glance around him. The pirates were faltering. Many were dead and those remaining had their arms in the air, calling for peace. Swords clattered to the deck. The archers that still lived put their bows down, careful with them even as they surrendered.

Taking a step back, Julius looked behind him and his heart lifted in pride.

His recruits stood there in shining uniforms, swords drawn and held in first position. They looked every inch a legion: fifty, fresh and disciplined.

"Get up," he said to the fallen man. "I claim this ship for Rome."

The survivors were tied using the same cords brought for the crew of *Ventulus*. It was quickly done, though Julius had to order one of the crew restrained after he kicked his erstwhile captor in the head when the man had been bound.

"Ten lashes for that man," Julius said, his voice firm and strong. His men gripped the sailor firmly, while the rest of the crew of *Ventulus* exchanged glances. Julius stared them down, knowing it was important that they accept his orders. Left alone, they would probably have cut the prisoners to pieces, taking out years of hatred in an orgy of torture and violence. None of them met his eyes and instead they drifted apart from the congratulatory groups that had formed. Finally, Julius turned away to supervise the rest of the capture. The rowers he had feared could be heard belowdecks, yelling in terror at the sounds of the battle above. He would send men to quiet them.

"Sir, over here!" a voice called.

Prax held the body of Pelitas, his hand pressing against an open wound high in the chest. There was blood around his friend's mouth and Julius knew as he saw him that there was no hope. Cabera might have saved him, but nothing else could.

Pelitas was choking, his eyes open without focus. Each tearing breath brought more blood dribbling from his lips. Julius crouched by the pair and many of the others gathered around them, blocking the sun. In the silence as they watched, the passing seconds seemed to last a long time, but finally the labored breathing ceased and the bright gaze faded into glassy stillness.

Julius stood, looking down at the body of his friend. He signaled to two of the others.

"Help Prax take him below. I'm not putting one of ours into the sea with them." He walked away without another word and, of them all, only the officers from *Accipiter* understood why he had to show such a stern front. The commander would not reveal weakness in front of the men, and not a one of them doubted who led them anymore. Even Gaditicus kept his head bowed as Julius strode past him, walking alone.

When both of the ships were secure that night, Julius met with the other officers of *Accipiter* and they drank a toast to Pelitas, who had not made it to the end of his path.

Before sleep, Gaditicus walked on the moonlit deck of *Ventulus* with Julius. They were silent for a long time, lost in memories, but as they reached the head of the steps leading below, Gaditicus took his arm.

"You are in command here."

Julius turned to him and the older man could feel the force of his personality. "I know," he said simply.

Gaditicus formed a wry smile. "It was when you fell that I realized. All the men went after you without waiting for orders. I think they will follow you anywhere."

"I wish I knew where I was leading them," Julius said

quietly. "Perhaps one of the men we captured will know where Celsus is. We'll see in the morning." He looked away to the place on the deck where Pelitas had fallen. "Peli would have had a grand laugh about me slipping like that. It would have been a ridiculous way to die."

As he spoke, he chuckled without humor. The brave charge straight at the feet of the enemy. Gaditicus didn't laugh. He clapped his hand on Julius's shoulder, but the young man didn't seem to feel it.

"He wouldn't have died if I hadn't wanted to find Celsus. You all would be back in Rome by now, with your names clear from disgrace."

Gaditicus took the shoulder and turned it gently until Julius faced him once more.

"Weren't you the one who told us there was no point fretting over what might have been? We'd all like to go back and make better choices, but that just isn't the way it works. We have one chance, even if the world rests on it. I might not have sailed *Accipiter* down that piece of coast, but if I hadn't, who knows? I might have become ill or been stabbed in an inn, or fallen down steps and broken my head open. There just isn't any point in worrying about it. We take each day as it comes and make the best decisions we can."

"And if they turn out badly?" Julius muttered.

Gaditicus shrugged. "I usually blame the gods."

"Do you believe in them?" Julius asked.

"You can't sail a ship without knowing there's something more than men and stones. As for all the temples, I've always played it safe with my offerings. It doesn't hurt anyone and you never know."

Julius smiled slightly at the practical philosophy. "I hope . . . that I will see Pelitas again," he said.

Gaditicus nodded. "We all will, but not for a while yet," he replied. He dropped his hand from Julius's shoulder as he went below, leaving him there with his face turned into the sea breeze.

When he was alone, Julius closed his eyes and stood still for a long time.

*   *   *

The following morning, Julius split his men into two crews. He was tempted to take the captain's post in the faster pirate ship but, going on instinct, gave it to *Ventulus*'s captain-owner, Durus. The man had missed the fight completely, locked in his cabin, but when he understood the situation, he stopped shouting about the cargo they had thrown over-board. He hated the pirates as much as any of the crew and took great pleasure from seeing them bound as he had been only a few hours before.

When Julius made the offer, Durus took his hand to seal the bargain.

"Both ships are mine when you've found the man you want?"

"Unless one of them is sunk when we attack Celsus. My men will need a vessel to get back to Roman lands. I'd like it to be his, but he knows his business and taking it won't be easy, if we can find him at all," Julius replied, wondering how far he could trust the captain. To be certain of his loyalty, he would let only a few of the *Ventulus* crew go with him onto the other ship. His legionaries would keep the captain's nerve for him, if it faltered.

Durus looked pleased, as well he might. Selling the cap-tured ship would bring him far more than the value of the cargo he had lost, though he had groaned when he heard the ivory had been dropped overboard.

The main problem was what they were going to do with the pirates who had survived the fight. The wounded had been dispatched and dumped overboard with the others on Julius's orders. They had chosen their life and he had no sympathy for their cries. That still left seventeen to be guarded day and night. Julius set his jaw firmly. Their fate rested on his shoulders.

He had the pirates brought separately to the captain's cabin, where he sat calmly at the heavy table. Each one was tied and held tightly by two of his men. Julius wanted them to feel helpless, and the face he turned to them was as hard and cruel as he could make it. They had claimed their captain had been killed in the battle, which Julius wondered about. No doubt the man would prefer not to be known if he was amongst them.

"Two questions," he said to the first of them. "If you can answer them, you live. If not, you go over the side to the sharks. Who is your captain?"

The man spat on the floor by Julius's feet, looking away as if uninterested. Julius ignored it, though he felt warm specks of liquid touch his ankle underneath the table.

"Where is the man Celsus?" he continued.

There was no response, though Julius noted the prisoner had begun to sweat.

"Very well," he said quietly. "Let the sharks have him and bring me the next."

"Yes, sir," the soldiers said together.

The man seemed to come to life then, struggling and yelling madly all the way to the railing. They held him there for a few moments, while the younger of the pair took a knife from his belt. He cut the cords holding the pirate's hands just before heaving him over to hit the sea in a great splash, screaming.

Both soldiers leaned on the rail to watch the pirate's frantic struggles. He seemed to be trying to climb the side of the ship, but the slippery surfaces defeated him.

"I just thought he should have a chance," the younger man muttered as dark shadows in the water began to ease toward the thrashing figure. The sharks had been following the ships since the first bodies were thrown overboard and the pirate saw them coming for him almost as soon as the men above did. He went berserk in the water, beating it into foam around him. Then he was snatched from the surface and the two soldiers turned back to fetch the next man to be questioned.

The second one couldn't swim at all and just sank. The third cursed them all the way in, through the questions and out over the rail, right until he was taken under. More sharks had gathered in the water, sliding over each other in a bloody froth as they fought over the meat.

The fourth man spoke as soon as Julius asked the questions.

"You'll kill me anyway," he said.

"Not if you tell me what I want to know," Julius replied.

The man sagged in relief. "Then I am the captain. You won't kill me?"

"If you can tell me where Celsus is, you have my word," Julius said, leaning toward the man.

"In winter, he goes to Samos, in Asia. It's on the far side of the Greek sea."

"I don't know the name," Julius said, doubtfully.

"It's a big island off the coast—near Miletus. The Roman ships don't patrol near it, but I've been there before. I'm telling you the truth!"

Julius believed the man and nodded. "Excellent. Then that is where we will go. How far away is it?"

"A month straight, two at the most."

Julius frowned at the answer. They would need to stop for provisions and that meant more risk. He looked up at the two soldiers. "Throw the others to the sharks."

The pirate captain scowled at the order. "Not me, though. You said I wouldn't be killed."

Julius stood up slowly. "I have lost good friends to your people, as well as a year of my life."

"You gave your word! You need me to guide you there.

You couldn't find it without me," the man said quickly, his voice breaking in fear.

Julius ignored him, speaking to the soldiers holding his arms. "Lock him somewhere safe for the moment."

When they had gone, Julius sat alone in the cabin and listened as the remaining pirates were dragged out and over the side. He looked down at his hands as the noise finally came to an end and again he could hear the creaks and groans of a ship under sail. He expected to feel shame or remorse for what he had ordered, but surprisingly it did not come. Then he closed the door so he could weep for Pelitas.

CHAPTER 18

Alexandria sighed in irritation as she saw her brooch had been taken from the clothes she'd folded the night before. A quick look in the other rooms revealed that Octavian had left the house early, and she firmed her jaw as she closed the door behind her on her way to Tabbic's workshop. It wasn't just the valuable silver, or even the many hours she had put in shaping and polishing the brooch. It was the only one she had made for herself alone, and many of those who became buyers had seen and commented on it when they met her. The design was a simple eagle, which she wouldn't have chosen for her own shoulder if it hadn't become the symbol of all the legions and universally desirable. It was mainly officers who stopped her and asked about it, and to have it stolen by a grubby urchin made her clench and unclench her fists as she walked, her cloak falling loose around her shoulders and needing to be hitched up without the brooch.

Not only was he a thief but an idiot, she thought. How could he expect not to be caught? One worrying possibility was that the boy was so used to punishment that he had discounted it for the prize of her brooch, willing to take whatever came his way as long as he could keep it. Alexandria shook her head in irritation, muttering to herself what she would do when she saw him. He couldn't be shamed, even in front of his mother. She had seen that when the butcher's boys came for the meat he had taken.

Perhaps it would be better not to mention it to Atia. The thought of seeing the humiliation on her face was painful, and even after less than a week in her new room Alexandria had come to like the woman. She had pride and a sort of dignity. It was such a pity that none of it seemed to reach the son.

Tabbic's shop had been damaged toward the end of the riots two years before. Alexandria had helped him to rebuild, learning a little carpentry as he remade the door and workbenches. His livelihood had been saved by the timely removal of all the valuable metals to his own home above, well barricaded against the gangs of *raptores* that had run wild while the city was in chaos. As Alexandria approached the modest little premises, she resolved not to burden him with her irritation. She owed him a great deal, and not only for letting her stay safe with his family during the worst of it. It didn't seem to need saying, but there was a debt owed to Tabbic that she had vowed would be paid.

As she opened the oak door, the sound of high-pitched yelling filled the air. Her eyes glittered in satisfaction as she saw Tabbic was holding the struggling figure of Octavian in the air with one brawny arm. The metalworker looked up as the door opened, and turned the boy to face her when he saw it was Alexandria.

"You won't believe what this one just tried to sell me," he said.

Octavian struggled even more ferociously when he saw who had come in. He kicked at the arm that held him suspended apparently without effort. Tabbic ignored him.

Alexandria darted across the shop to the two of them.

"Where's my brooch, you little thief?" she demanded.

Tabbic opened his other hand and revealed the silver eagle, which she took and pinned back in place.

"Walked in as bold as anything and told me to make him

an offer!" Tabbic said angrily. Completely honest himself, he hated those who saw thieving as an easy life. He shook Octavian again, taking out his indignation on the boy, who whimpered and tried to kick him again, his eyes looking around for escape.

"What shall we do with him?" Tabbic asked her.

Alexandria thought for a few moments. As tempting as it might be to beat the boy all the way down the street, she knew her possessions could still be snatched up by his little fingers at any time. She needed a more permanent solution.

"I think I could persuade his mother to let him work for us," she said thoughtfully.

Tabbic lowered Octavian until his feet touched the floor. Immediately, the boy bit his hand and Tabbic hoisted him again with casual strength, leaving him to dangle in futile rage.

"You have to be joking. He's little better than an animal!" Tabbic said, wincing at the white tooth marks on his knuckles.

"You can teach him, Tabbic. There's no father to do it, and the way he's going, he won't live to grow up. You said you needed someone to work the bellows, and there's always sweeping up and carrying."

"Let me go! I'm not doing nothing!" Octavian yelled.

Tabbic looked him over. "The boy's skinny as a rat. No strength in those arms," he said slowly.

"He's *nine,* Tabbic. What do you expect?"

"He'll run as soon as the door opens, I'd say," Tabbic continued.

"If he does, I'll fetch him back. He'll have to come home sometime and I'll wait for him there, spank him, and turn him round. Being here will keep him out of trouble, and it'll be useful for both of us. You're not getting any younger and he could help me at the forge."

Tabbic let Octavian touch the floor again. This time he

did not bite, but watched the two adults warily as they discussed him as if he weren't in the shop.

"How much will you pay me?" he said, scrubbing angry tears out of his eyes with his dirty fingers, doing little more than smearing his face.

Tabbic laughed. "*Pay* you!" he said, his voice filled with scorn. "Boy, you'll be learning a *trade.* You should pay us."

Octavian spat a stream of oaths and tried to bite Tabbic once again. This time the metalworker cuffed him with the flat of his other hand without looking.

"What if he steals the goods?" he said.

Alexandria could see he was coming round to the idea. That was the problem, of course. If Octavian ran off with silver, or worse, the small store of gold that Tabbic kept locked away, it would hurt them all. She put on her sternest expression and took Octavian's chin in her hand, turning his face to her.

"If he does," she said, fixing the little boy with her gaze, "we will have a perfect right to demand he is sold as a slave to pay the debt. His mother too if it comes to it."

"You wouldn't!" Octavian said, shocked out of struggling by her words.

"My business is not a charity, lad. We *would,*" Tabbic replied firmly. Over Octavian's head, he winked at Alexandria.

"Debts are paid in this city—one way or another," she agreed.

*　　　　　　*　　　　　　*

Winter had arrived quickly and both Tubruk and Brutus were wearing heavy cloaks as they cut the old oak into firewood ready to be carted back to the estate stores. Renius didn't seem to feel the cold and had left his stump bare to the wind away from the sight of strangers. He had brought a young slave boy from the estate to place the branches steady for him to swing his axe. The boy hadn't spoken a word since his arrival at

Renius's heels, but he stood well clear when Renius swung, and his wind-reddened face fought to conceal a smile when the blade slipped and sent Renius staggering and swearing under his breath. Brutus knew the old gladiator well enough to wince in silent appreciation of what would follow if Renius saw the child's amusement. The work was making them all sweat and breathe frosty plumes in the winter air. Brutus watched critically as Renius swung, sending two smaller pieces spinning into the air. He raised his own axe again, looking over at Tubruk.

"What worries me most is the debt to Crassus. Just the quarters alone cost four thousand *aurei*." Brutus swung smoothly as he spoke, grunting as the stroke fell cleanly.

"What does he expect in return?" Tubruk said.

Brutus shrugged. "He just says not to worry, which means I can't sleep for thinking about it. The armorer he hired is turning out more sets than I have men for, even after scouring Rome. On my centurion's wage, I'd have to work for years just to pay him back for the swords alone."

"Amounts like that don't mean a great deal to Crassus. The gossip says he could buy half the Senate if he wanted to," Tubruk said, pausing to lean on his axe. The wind swirled leaves around them. The air they pulled in bit at their throats with cold that was almost a pleasure.

"I know. My mother says he already owns more of Rome than he knows what to do with. Everything he buys makes a profit, which is all the more reason to wonder where the profit is in buying Primigenia."

Tubruk shook his head as he raised his axe again. "He hasn't bought it, or you. Don't even say it. Primigenia is not a house or a brooch, and only the Senate can command it. If he thinks he is raising his own private legion, you should tell him to set a new standard on the rolls."

"He hasn't said that. All he does is sign the bills I send him. My mother thinks he is hoping to secure her approval with the money. I want to ask him, but what if it's true? I won't prostitute my own mother to that man or anyone, but I must have Primigenia."

"It wouldn't be the first time for Servilia," Tubruk remarked with a chuckle.

Brutus placed his axe carefully on a log. He faced Tubruk and the old gladiator paused as he saw his angry expression.

"You can say that once, Tubruk. Don't do it again," Brutus said. His voice was as cold as the wind that wrapped around them, and Tubruk rested again on his axe as he met the piercing eyes.

"You mention her a lot these days. I didn't teach you to drop your guard so easily with anyone. Neither did Renius."

Renius snorted softly in reply as he kicked a piece of branch from under his feet. His pile of split logs was barely half the size of the others, though it had cost him more.

Brutus shook his head. "She is my mother, Tubruk!"

The older man shrugged. "You don't know her, lad. I just want you to be careful until you do."

"I know enough," Brutus said, picking up his axe again.

For almost an hour, the three men worked in silence, cutting the wood and piling it onto the small handcart that stood nearby. Finally, seeing that Brutus wasn't going to speak, Tubruk swallowed his irritation.

"Will you go to the legion field with the others?" he asked without looking at Brutus. He knew the answer, but at least it was a safe topic to continue their conversation. Every year in winter, all the boys who had turned sixteen went to the Campus Martius, where new legions planted their standards. Only the lame and the blind would be turned away. Freshly restored to the rolls of the Senate, Primigenia qualified to plant their eagle with the others.

"I'll have to," Brutus replied, the words grudgingly wrung from him. His frowning expression eased as he talked. "With the ones from other cities, there could be as many as three thousand there. Some of them will contract with Primigenia. The gods know I need to raise the numbers, and quickly. Those barracks that Crassus bought are practically empty."

"How many do you have already?" Tubruk asked.

"With the seven that came in yesterday, nearly ninety. You should see them, Tubruk." The younger man looked into the distance as he saw their faces again in his mind. "I think every man who survived the battle against Sulla rejoined. Some had gone to other trades in the city, and they just threw down their tools and walked away when they heard Primigenia was being re-formed. Others we found guarding houses and temples, and they came without any argument. All for the memory of Marius."

He paused for a moment and his voice sharpened. "My *mother* had a guard who was an optio in Primigenia. He asked her if he could rejoin and she let him go. He'll help Renius to train the new ones as we get them."

Tubruk turned to Renius. "You'll be going with him?" he said.

Renius laid his axe down. "I've no future as a woodcutter, lad. I'll do my part."

Tubruk nodded. "Try not to kill anyone. You'll have a hard enough job getting them in as it is. The gods know Primigenia isn't one they dream of joining anymore."

"We have a history," Brutus replied. "The new legions they're raising won't be able to match that."

Tubruk looked sharply at him. "A shameful history, some think. Don't glare at me, that's what they'll say. They will have marked you as the legion that lost the city. You'll have a hard time of it." He looked around at the piles of wood and the full cart and nodded to himself.

"That's enough for today. The rest will keep. There's a hot cup of wine waiting for us back at the estate."

"Just one more then," Renius said, turning to the boy at his side without waiting for a response.

"I think my swing's a little smoother than when I started, don't you, boy?"

The slave rubbed his hand quickly under his nose, leaving a silvery smear along his cheek. He nodded, suddenly nervous. Renius smiled at him.

"One arm isn't as steady as two with an axe, mind. Bring up that branch and hold her still while I cut her."

The boy dragged a piece of oak to Renius's feet and began to stand away.

"No. Hold her steady. One hand on either side," Renius said, his voice hardening.

For a second, the boy hesitated, glancing at the other two, who were watching with silent interest. There was no help there. Wincing, the boy placed his hands against the rounded sides of the log and leaned back out of range, his face terrible in anticipation.

Renius took his time finding a grip he liked. "Hold her tight, now," he warned, beginning the swing as he spoke. The axe head came round in a blur and split the wood with a crack. The boy yanked his hands under his armpits, clenching his jaw against the sudden pain.

Renius sank into a crouch at the boy's side, resting the axe on the ground. He reached out and gently pulled one of the hands out to be inspected. The boy's cheeks were flushed with relief, and as Renius saw there was no wound, he grinned and ruffled his hair cheerfully.

"It didn't slip," the boy said.

"Not when it mattered," Renius agreed with him, laughing. "That was courage in you. It's worth a cup of hot wine, I'd say." The boy beamed at this, his stinging hands forgotten.

The three men met each other's eyes in memories and pleasure at the boy's pride as they took the handles of the cart and began walking back down the hill to the estate.

"By the time Julius gets back, I want Primigenia strong," Brutus said as they reached the gate.

*   *   *

Julius and Gaditicus peered through the bushes on the steep mountainside down at the distant, tiny ship moored below in the calm island bay. Both men were hungry and almost unbearably thirsty, but their waterskin was empty and they had agreed not to begin the trip back until it was dark.

It had taken longer than they expected to climb the gentler slope to the peak, where the ground fell away sharply. Each time the pair thought they had reached the summit, another was revealed, and in the end dawn had stopped them moving just after beginning the descent. By the time they caught their first view of the ship, Julius had been wondering if his pirate informer had been lying to save himself from the sharks. For the whole of the long journey to the island, the man had been chained at the oars of his own ship, and it looked as if he had earned his life with the details of Celsus's winter mooring.

Julius sketched what they could see in charcoal on parchment to have something to show the others when they were picked up. Gaditicus watched him in silence, his face sour.

"It can't be done, not with any certainty," Gaditicus muttered as he took another look through the low foliage. Julius stopped drawing from memory and rose up onto his knees to view the scene once more. Neither man wore armor, both for speed and to prevent the sun flashing off it and giving away their position. Julius settled back down again to finish his sketch, looking at it critically.

"Not by ship," he said after a while, disappointment etching his features. For two months of fast travel, the crews had drilled day and night, ready for the battle with Celsus. Julius would have bet his last coin on their ability to board and take him quickly with only a few casualties. Now, looking at the little bay that nestled between three mountains, all their planning seemed wasted.

The island had no central land, just three cold and ancient volcanic peaks that sheltered a tiny bay. From their high vantage point, they were able to see that deepwater channels ran between the mountains, so that whichever way Celsus was attacked, he could choose one of the others and disappear out to sea without hurry or danger. With three ships, they could have bottled him up neatly, but with only two it was a straight gamble.

Far below, Julius saw the dark shapes of dolphins swimming around the ship in the bay. It was a beautiful place and Julius thought he would like to return if he ever had the chance. From far away, the mountains looked grim and sharp, gray-green in the rays of the sun, but perched as high as they were, it was a glorious place. The air was so clear he could see details on the other two jagged peaks, which was why he and Gaditicus dared not move. If they could make out the movement of men on the deck of Celsus's ship, they could be seen in turn and their only chance for revenge would vanish.

"I would have expected him to winter in one of the big cities, far from Rome," Julius said thoughtfully. The island seemed uninhabited except for the moored ship, and he was surprised the hard-bitten crew of pirates didn't find it dull after months of preying on merchants.

"No doubt he visits the mainland, but you can see this place would be safer than anywhere for him. That lake in the foothills is probably freshwater, and I'd guess they could find enough birds and fish to have a feast or two. Who could he trust to look after his ship while he's away, though? All his men would have to do is pull up their anchors and he'd have lost it all."

Julius looked at Gaditicus with raised eyebrows. "The poor man," he said, rolling up his map.

Gaditicus grinned and looked up at the sun. "Gods. It'll

be hours before we can get back over the crest, and my throat is full of dust."

Julius stretched himself out with his arms behind his head.

"Rafts could get us close, with our ships following us in to block his escape. The next moonless night will give us enough time to lash a few together and plan. Now I'm going to get some sleep until it's dark enough to go back," he murmured, closing his eyes. Within a few minutes, he was snoring softly, and Gaditicus looked at him in amusement.

The older man was too tense to sleep, so he carried on watching the movements of the men on board the ship in the bay far below. He wondered how many would die if Celsus had the sense to post good lookouts each night, and wished he had the young man's confidence in the future.

CHAPTER 19

The black water was bitterly cold, soaking into the Romans as they lay completely flat on the rafts and paddled slowly toward the dark hulk of Celsus's ship. Though they ached for speed, each man held himself steady, moving numb hands through the still water with gentle ripples. Julius's crew had worked feverishly to lash rafts together, stripping away boards and ropes from the two ships that sheltered on the seacoast outside the bay. When they were done, five platforms moved slowly through the deep channels toward the beach where Celsus was moored, swords bundled together in cloth to balance the weight. They had no armor with them. For all the advantage it would give them, Julius guessed there would be no time to tie it all in place, and instead his men shivered in wet tunics and leggings, hardly protected from the night breeze.

*   *   *

Celsus awoke suddenly in his cabin and listened for whatever sound had wakened him. Had the wind turned? The bay was a perfect shelter, but a storm could send a surge down the channels that might weaken his anchors' grip on the clay bottom. For a moment, he thought of turning over in his narrow bunk and letting sleep come again. He had drunk too much with the others that evening, and the slippery grease of roasted meat had hardened into wax spatters on his skin. He rubbed idly at a spot, scratching off the residue of the feast with a fingernail. No doubt his officers were sleeping off the drunk, and someone had to patrol the ship each hour. He sighed and reached around him in the dark for his clothes, wrinkling his nose at the smell of stale wine and food that wafted from them.

"Should know better," he muttered to himself, wincing as a flare of bitter acid made its presence felt up his throat. He wondered if it was worth waking Cabera to make him mix some of the chalky gruel that seemed to help.

There was a sudden scuffling outside his door and the sound of a body striking the deck. Celsus frowned, taking his dagger from the hook out of habit rather than alarm as he opened the door and looked out.

There was a shadow there, featureless and dark against the starlight above.

"Where's my money?" Julius whispered.

Celsus shouted in shock, barging forward and hammering his arm against the figure as he went. He felt hard fingers grab his hair as he came out onto the deck, and his head was jerked back for a moment before they slipped. He scrambled away, bellowing, wary of the blade he imagined coming for his unprotected back.

The main deck was a confused mass of struggling figures, but no one answered him. Celsus saw that his men were down, too sodden with drink and sleep to put up much of a fight. He skirted the knots of men and raced aft to his armory. They would make a stand there. It wasn't lost yet.

Something heavy thumped into his neck and he staggered. His feet tangled in a roped figure and he fell with a crash. The silence was eerie. There were no shouts or orders in the dark, just the grunts and breathing of men who fought for their lives without mercy, using anything that came to their hands. Celsus had a glimpse of one of his men struggling with a thick rope around his neck, clawing at it, then he was up and moving again in the blackness, shaking his head to clear it of panic, his heart racing with wasted strength.

The armory was surrounded by strangers, their wet skins catching glimmers of starlight as they turned to him. He couldn't see their eyes and raised his dagger to stab as they slid toward him.

An arm circled his throat from behind and Celsus slashed at it madly, making it fall away with a moan. He spun wildly, waving the blade before him, then the shadows parted and a spark lit the scene like a stroke of lightning, showing him their gleaming eyes for a moment before the dark returned, worse than before.

Julius struck again to light the oil lamp he had taken from Celsus's own cabin, and Celsus cried out in horror as he recognized the young Roman.

"Justice for the dead, Celsus," Julius said as he played the light over the man's stricken features. "We have almost all your men, though some have barricaded themselves in down below. They'll keep."

His eyes glittered in the lamplight and Celsus felt his arms gripped with awful finality as the others moved in on him, yanking the dagger from his fingers. Julius leaned in close until they were almost touching.

"The oarsmen are being chained to their benches. Your crew will hang from crosses, as I promised you. I claim this ship for Rome and for the house of Caesar."

Celsus gazed at him in stupefied fascination. His mouth hung loosely as he tried to understand what had happened, but the effort was beyond him.

Without warning, Julius punched him hard in the belly. Celsus could feel the acid leap in his stomach and choked for a second as his throat filled with bitterness. He sagged in the arms of his captors and Julius stood back. Celsus lunged at him suddenly, breaking the relaxed grip of the men behind.

He crashed into Julius and they both went down, the lamp spilling its oil over the deck. In the confusion, the Romans moved to put out the fire with the instinctive fear of those who sailed wooden ships. Celsus landed a blow on the struggling figure beneath him and then leapt for the side of his ship, desperate to get away.

The giant figure of Ciro blocked him and he never saw the blade he ran onto. In agony, he looked up at the face of his killer and saw nothing there, only blankness. Then he was gone, sliding off the sword onto the deck.

Julius sat up, panting. He could hear the crack of timbers nearby as his men forced their way into barricaded cabins. It was nearly over and he smiled, wincing as his lips bled from some blow he'd taken in the struggle.

Cabera walked toward him over the wooden deck. He looked a little thinner, if that was possible, and the wide smile had at least one more tooth missing from the one Julius remembered. Still, it was the same face.

"I told them over and over you would come, but they didn't believe me," Cabera said cheerfully.

Julius stood and embraced him, overwhelmed by relief at seeing the old man safe. There were no words that needed to be said.

"Let's go and see how much of our ransoms Celsus managed to spend," he said at last. "Lamps! Lamps over here! Bring them down to the hold."

Cabera and the others followed him quickly down a flight of steps so steep as to be almost a ladder. Every jostling man there was as interested as he was in what they might find. The guards had been drunk and easily taken in the first attack, but the barred door was still closed, as Julius had ordered. He paused with his hand on it, breathless with anticipation. The hold could be empty, he knew. On the other hand, it could be full.

The door gave easily to axes and as Julius was followed in,

the oil lamps lit the hollow space below the oar decks just above them. The angry muttering of the rowers sounded as ghostly echoes in the confined space. Their reward for allegiance to Celsus would be slavery, the only trained crew in Rome's service.

Julius took a sharp breath. The hold was lined with great shelves of thick oak, running all the way around its walls from the floor to the high ceiling. Each shelf held riches. There were crates of gold coins and small silver bars in stacks, placed carefully so as not to affect the balance of the ship. Julius shook his head in disbelief. What he saw in front of him was enough to buy a small kingdom in some parts of the world. Celsus must have been driven mad with worry over such treasures. Julius doubted he ever left his ship, with so much to lose. The only thing he couldn't see was the packet of drafts that Marius had given him before his death. He'd always known they would be worthless to Celsus, who could never have drawn the large sums from the city treasury without his background becoming known. Part of Julius had hoped they hadn't gone down with *Accipiter*, but the money lost was nothing compared to the gold they had won in return.

The men who entered with him were struck dumb at what they saw. Only Cabera and Gaditicus moved farther into the hold, checking and appraising the contents of each shelf. Gaditicus paused suddenly and pulled a crate out with a grunt. It had an eagle burned into the wood, and he broke the lid with his sword hilt with all the enthusiasm of a child.

His fist came out holding bright silver coins, freshly minted. Each was marked with the characters of Rome and the head of Cornelius Sulla.

"We can clear our names returning these," he said with satisfaction, looking at Julius.

Julius chuckled at the older man's sense of priorities. "With this ship to replace *Accipiter*, they should welcome us as long-lost sons. We know she's faster than most of them,"

Julius replied. He saw that Cabera was slipping a number of valuable items into the folds of his robe, held from falling by the tight belt that cinched his waist. Julius raised his eyes in amusement.

Gaditicus began to laugh as he let the coins trickle back through his fingers into the crate.

"We can go home," he said. "Finally, we can go home."

*   *   *

Julius refused to allow Captain Durus to take the two triremes he'd been promised in exchange for his lost cargo, knowing it would be foolish to strip their defenses until they were safe in a Roman port. While Durus raged at this decision, Gaditicus visited Julius in the cabin that had belonged to Celsus, now scrubbed clean and bare. The younger man paced up and down its length as they talked, unable to relax.

Gaditicus sipped at a cup of wine, savoring Celsus's choice.

"We could land at the legion port at Thessalonica, Julius, and hand over the legion silver and the ship. When we're cleared, we could sail round the coast, or even march west to Dyrrhachium and take ship for Rome. We're so close now. Durus says he'll swear we had a business arrangement, so any charges for piracy won't run."

"There's still that soldier Ciro killed on the docks," Julius said slowly, deep in thought.

Gaditicus shrugged. "Soldiers die and it's not as if he butchered him. The man was just unlucky. They won't be able to make anything stick now. We're free to return."

"What will you do? You have enough to retire on, I should think."

"Perhaps. I was thinking of using my share to pay the Senate for the slaves that went down with *Accipiter*. If I do that, they might even send me back to sea as captain. We've taken two pirate ships, after all, which they can't overlook."

Julius rose and took the other man's arm. "I owe you a great deal more than that, you know."

Gaditicus gripped the arm that held him. "There's no debt to me, lad. When we were in that stinking cell...and friends died, my will went with them for a while."

"You were the captain, though, Gadi. You could have stood on your authority."

Gaditicus smiled a little ruefully. "A man who needs to do that may find he isn't standing very high after all."

"You're a good man, you know—and a fine captain," Julius said, wishing he had better words for his friend. He knew it had taken a rare strength for Gaditicus to swallow his pride, but without that they would never have been able to take back their lives and honor.

"Come on, then," he said. "If it's what you want, we'll cross to Greece and rejoin civilization."

Gaditicus smiled with him. "What will you do with your share of the gold?" he asked, a little warily.

Only Suetonius had complained when Julius had claimed half for himself, with the rest to be shared equally. After taking out the Roman silver and the ransoms for the *Accipiter* officers, the shares they would get were still more money than they would ever have expected to see. Suetonius had not spoken a word to Julius since being given his allotted sum, but his was the only sullen face on the three ships. The rest of them looked on Julius with something like awe.

"I don't know what I'll do, yet," Julius said, his smile fading. "I can't go back to Rome, you remember?"

"Sulla?" Gaditicus said, recalling the young man who had joined his galley just before the tide at Ostia, his face soot-streaked from the burning city behind him.

Julius nodded grimly. "I can't return while he lives," he muttered, his mood darkening as quickly as it had lifted.

"You're young to be worrying about that, you know.

Some enemies can be beaten, but some you just have to out-
live. Safer too."

*   *   *

Julius thought about the conversation as they slipped through
the deepwater channel that sheltered Thessalonica from the
storms of the Aegean Sea. The three ships ran abreast before
the gusting wind with their sails cracking and every spare
hand on the decks to clean and polish. He had ordered three
flags of the Republic made for the masts, and when they
rounded the last bay to the port, it would be a sight to lift
Roman hearts. He sighed to himself. Rome was everything he
knew. Tubruk, Cornelia, and Marcus, when they met again.
His mother. For the first time he could remember, he wanted
to see her, just to say that he understood her illness and that
he was sorry. A life in exile was not to be borne. He shivered
slightly as the wind cut at his skin.

Gaditicus came up to the rail by his elbow. "Something's
not right, lad. Where are the trading ships? The galleys? This
should be a busy port."

Julius strained his eyes to see the land they approached.
Thin streams of smoke lifted into the air, too many to be
cooking fires. As they came close enough to dock, he could
see that the only other ships in the port were listing badly,
bearing signs of fire. One was little better than a gutted shell.
The water was covered in a scum of sodden ashes and broken
wood.

The rest of the men came to stand at the rail and watched
the unfolding scene of desolation in stricken silence. They
could see bodies rotting on shore in the weak sunlight. Small
dogs tugged at them, making the splayed limbs twitch and
jump in a vulgar parody of life.

The three ships moored and the soldiers disembarked
without breaking the unnatural stillness, hands ready on their
swords without having to be ordered. Julius went with them,

after telling Gaditicus to stay ready for a fast retreat. The Roman captain accepted the order with a nod, quickly assembling a small group to stay with him to handle the rowers.

On the faded brown stone of the docks, women and children lay together, great wounds in their flesh filled with clouds of buzzing flies that rose humming at the approach of the soldiers. The smell was appalling, even with the chill breeze coming off the sea. Most of the bodies were Roman legionaries, their armor still bright over black tunics.

Julius walked past the clumps of them with the others, re-creating the action in his mind. He saw many bloodstains around each group of the dead, no doubt where the enemy had fallen and been dragged away for burial. To leave the Roman bodies where they lay was a deliberate insult, an act of contempt that began to kindle a rage in Julius that he saw reflected in the eyes of those around him. They walked with swords held ready, stalking the streets in growing anger and chasing rats and dogs away from the corpses. But there was no enemy to challenge. The port was deserted.

Julius stood breathing heavily through his mouth, looking at the broken body of a small girl in the arms of a soldier who had been stabbed in the back as he ran with her. Their skin had blackened from exposure, the hardening flesh creeping back to reveal their teeth and dark tongues.

"Gods, who could have done this?" Prax whispered to himself.

Julius turned to him with his face a bitter mask. "We'll find out. These are my people. They cry out to us, Prax, and I will answer them."

Prax glanced at him and felt the manic energy pouring off the younger man. When Julius turned to face him, he looked away, unable to meet his eyes.

"Form a burial crew. Gaditicus can say the prayers over them when they are in the ground." Julius paused and looked at the horizon, where the sun burned a dull winter copper.

"And get the rest of them out cutting down trees. We'll do the crucifixions here, along this coast. It will serve as a warning to whoever is responsible for this."

Prax saluted and ran back to the mooring point, pleased to get away from the stench of death and the young officer whose words frightened him, for all he thought he'd known the man before.

*   *   *

Julius stood impassively while the first five men were nailed to the rough-cut trunks. Each cross was raised with ropes until the upright slid into the holes to hold them, made steady with hammered wooden wedges. The pirates screamed until their throats were raw and no more sound came but the whistle of air. From one of them, bloody sweat dribbled from his armpits and groin, thin crimson lines that wrote ugly patterns on his skin.

The third man spasmed in agony as the iron spike was thumped through his wrist into the soft wood of the cross-beam. He wept and pleaded like a child, pulling his other arm away with all his strength until it was gripped and held for the blows of the hammer and the nail that speared him through.

Before his men completed the brutal task with his shuddering legs, Julius walked forward as if in a daze, drawing his sword slowly. His men froze at his approach and he ignored them, seeming to speak his thoughts aloud.

"No more of this," he muttered, thrusting his sword into the man's throat. There was a look of relief in the eyes as they glazed, and Julius looked away as he wiped his sword, hating his own weakness, but unable to stand watching any longer.

"Kill the rest quickly," he ordered, before walking alone back to the ship. His thoughts ran wildly as he strode across the dock stones, sheathing his sword without being aware of it. He'd promised to put them all on crosses, but the reality was an ugliness he could not bear. The screaming had cut through his nerves and made him ashamed. It had taken all his will to see the first few nailed after the horror of the first.

He grimaced in anger at himself. His father would not have weakened. Renius would have nailed them himself and not lost sleep. He felt his cheeks burn with shame and spat on the dock as he reached the edge. Still, he could not have stood with his men and watched any longer, and walking away from them alone would have damaged him in their eyes, after his own orders began the cruel deaths.

Cabera had refused to join the legionaries on the dock for the executions. He stood at the rail of the ship with his head on one side in unspoken question. Julius looked at him and shrugged. The old healer patted him on the arm and produced an amphora of wine in his other hand.

"Good idea," Julius said distantly, his thoughts elsewhere. "Fetch a second, though, would you? I don't want dreams tonight."

CHAPTER 20

Only a few of the port buildings had roofs and walls secure enough to be used by Julius's men. Too many of
the others had been torched, with just their stone walls standing as empty shells. Alternating between the warehouses and
the three ships, Julius sent his men scouring the local area for
supplies. Though Celsus had laid in enough to last him most
of a winter, it would hardly serve to feed so many active soldiers for long.

The legionaries walked warily as they searched, never
alone and always with an eye for a surprise attack. Even with
the bodies cleared and in the earth, the port was a silent,
brooding place, and they lived with the thought that whoever
had destroyed the peaceful Roman settlement could still be
close, or coming back.

They found only one man alive. His leg had been gashed
and infection had set in quickly. They found him when they
heard him move to kill a rat that came too close to the smell
of blood. He smashed its head with a stone and then yelled in
terror as Julius's men took him by the arms and brought him
out into the light. After days in darkness, the man could
hardly bear even the weak morning sun, and he babbled
crazily at them as they dragged him back to the ships.

Julius summoned Cabera as soon as he saw the swollen
leg, though he guessed it was useless. The man's lips were

rimed dry crusts and he wept without tears as they tipped a bowl of water into his mouth. Cabera probed the puffy flesh of the leg with his long fingers, finally shaking his head. He stood to one side with Julius.

"It has turned poisonous and reached right up to his groin. It's too late to take it off. I can try to ease the pain of it, but he hasn't much time left."

"Can't you . . . put your hands on him?" Julius asked the old man.

"He's gone too far, Julius. He should be dead already."

Julius nodded with bitter resignation, taking the bowl from his men and helping the man to hold it to his lips. The skeletal fingers shook too much to keep it still, and as Julius held one of them, he almost recoiled from the fever heat that burned through the taut skin.

"Can you understand me?" he asked.

The man tried to nod as he sipped, and choked horribly, turning bright red with the efforts that tore at his remaining strength.

"Can you tell me what happened?" Julius pressed, willing the man to breathe. Finally the spasms died and the man let his head fall onto his chest, exhausted.

"They killed everyone. The whole country's in flames," he whispered.

"A rebellion?" Julius asked quickly. He had expected some foreign invader, rampaging through a few coastal towns and back to ships. It was a common enough tale in that part of the world. The man nodded, motioning with his quivering fingers for the water bowl. Julius passed it to him, watching as he emptied it.

"It was Mithridates," the man said, his voice hoarse and raw. "When Sulla died, he called them . . ." He coughed again and Julius stood in shock, walking out onto the deck and away from the ripe smell of sickness that had filled the room. *Sulla was dead?* He gripped the rail of Celsus's ship until his hands cramped. He hoped it had been a slow agony for the man who had taken Marius from him.

Some part of him had imagined scenes where he would return to Rome with his new men, rich and growing in power, to battle Sulla and revenge Marius. In his quieter moments he knew it for a child's fantasy, but it had sustained him for a long time, a dream that made the months in the cell, the fits, all of it, bearable.

As the day wore on, Julius threw himself into the thousand tasks that needed to be organized as they secured the port area. The orders he gave and the men he spoke to seemed distant, as he tried to think his way through the news he had heard from the dying man. At least organizing the provisions and billets gave him something to occupy him. Sulla's death left a hole in his future, an emptiness that mocked his efforts.

The merchant Durus found him clearing poison from a well with three of the legionaries. It was common enough for an invading force to sour local water with rotting animals, and Julius was working numbly with the others, pulling up slimy dead chickens and trying not to gag at the smell as they were thrown aside.

"I need to have a word with you, sir," Durus said.

At first Julius didn't seem to hear him, and he repeated it more loudly. Julius sighed and crossed over to him, leaving the other soldiers to drop the hooked ropes for another try. Julius wiped his stinking hands on his tunic as he walked, and Durus saw that he was exhausted, suddenly realizing how young the man was. With tiredness banking the fires in him, he looked almost lost. The merchant cleared his throat.

"I'd like to leave with my two triremes, sir. I've put my name to a letter saying you hired *Ventulus* to hunt pirates. It's time for me to get back to my family and my life."

Julius looked steadily at him without replying. After a

pause, Durus started again. "We did agree that when you found Celsus I would have my ship and the other trireme to make up for the lost cargo. I don't have any complaints, but I need you to give the order to have your men leave my ships so I can sail home. They won't take orders from me, sir."

Julius felt torn and angry. He had never realized how hard it could be to keep some semblance of honor alive. He had promised Durus the two ships, but that was before he found the Greek port ravaged by a war. What did the man expect? Every martial instinct drummed into Julius said to refuse flatly. How could he think of giving up two of his most valuable assets with Mithridates cutting everything Roman from the flesh of Greece?

"Walk with me," he said to Durus, striding past him so that the captain had to break into a trot to keep up. Julius walked quickly back to the docks where the three ships were moving gently in the swell. His guards saluted him as he approached, and Julius returned the gestures, halting suddenly at the edge, where the galleys loomed over them both.

"I don't want you to go home," he said curtly.

Durus colored with surprise. "You gave me your word I could leave when you had taken Celsus's ship," he snapped.

Julius turned to him and the captain gulped silently at his expression.

"I do not need to be reminded, Captain. I will not stop you leaving. However, Rome needs these ships." He thought for a long time, his eyes dark as he watched the ships rise and settle in the dirty waters.

"I want you to take them round the coast as fast as you can and find whichever port Rome is using to land the legions in the west. Hand over the legion silver in my name . . . and in the name of Captain Gaditicus of *Accipiter*. They will put you on the run back to Rome for more soldiers, I should think. There's no profit for you in that, but both ships are fast and they'll need anything that can float."

Durus shifted his weight from one foot to another, astonished. "I am months overdue. My family and creditors will think I'm dead as it is," he said, playing for time.

"Romans *have* died, did you not see the bodies? Gods, I'm asking you for a service to the city that bore and raised you. You've never fought for her or bled for her. I'm giving you a chance to pay back a little of what you owe."

Durus almost smiled at the words, but stopped himself as he realized the young man was completely serious. He wondered what his city friends would make of this soldier. He seemed to have a view of the city that had nothing to do with beggars and rats and disease. He realized that Julius saw the city as something greater than he did, and for a moment, he felt a touch of shame in the face of that belief.

"How do you know I won't take the money and head straight for northern Italy and home?" he asked.

Julius frowned slightly, turning his cold eyes on the merchant. "Because if you do, I will be your enemy and you know well enough that I will find you eventually and destroy you." The words were casually spoken, but after watching the executions and hearing how Celsus had been thrown over the side of his own ship, Durus wrapped his robe tightly around himself against the chill wind.

"Very well. I will do as you say, though I curse the day you first stepped onto *Ventulus*," he replied through gritted teeth.

Julius called up to the guards at the prows of Durus's ships. "My men to disembark!"

The soldiers in sight saluted and disappeared to fetch the others. Durus felt a wave of relief leave him giddy.

"Thank you," he said.

Julius paused as he began to walk back to the storehouses. Behind him, where the stone docks faded into soil, five figures hung from crosses.

"Don't forget," he said, then turned his back on the captain and strode away.

Durus doubted that was possible.

*   *   *

As night fell, the men gathered in the best of the storehouses. One of the walls was scorched, but the fire hadn't taken. Apart from the acrid smell in the air, it was warm and dry. Outside, it had begun to rain, a low drumming on the thin wooden roof.

The oil lamps came from Celsus's ship, and once they were gone, the men would be reduced to finding private supplies in the abandoned houses of the port. As if to prepare the soldiers for that moment, the flames guttered low, barely lighting the empty space of the store. Corn kernels spilled by looters littered the floor, and the soldiers sat on torn sacking, making themselves comfortable as best they could.

Gaditicus rose to speak to the huddled men. Most had been working all day either repairing the roof or shifting supplies to and from the ships that would leave on the dawn tide.

"It is time to consider the future, gentlemen. I'd wanted to rest for a while in a solid Roman port before contacting home. Instead, a Greek king has butchered our soldiers. It must not go unpunished."

A mutter ran through the men, though whether in agreement or frustration it was difficult to tell. Julius looked over them as he sat by Gaditicus. They were his men. He had spent so long with the simple goal of finding and killing Celsus that he had never given much thought to what would come afterward, barring the distant dream of one day confronting the Dictator of Rome. If he brought a new century into a legion, the Senate would have to recognize his authority with an official post.

He grimaced silently in the shadows. Or they might not, putting Gaditicus in charge and reducing Julius back to commanding only twenty of them. The Senate were not the sort to recognize the unusual authority he possessed over the motley group, though his new wealth could give him influence if he used it wisely. He wondered if he could be satisfied with such a position and smiled to himself, unnoticed by the men watching Gaditicus. There was a simple answer. He'd learned there was nothing finer than leading and nothing more of a challenge than having no one to ask for help. At the worst times, they had looked to him to know the way forward, to see the next step. The gods knew it was far easier to follow, without thought, but not half so satisfying. Part of him longed for the security, the simple pleasure in being part of a unit. But in his heart he wanted the heady mixture of fear and danger that came only with command.

How could Sulla be dead? The thought returned again and again to nag at him. The wounded man on board Celsus's ship had known nothing of it, just that the soldiers had been told to wear black for a whole year. When the man had fallen unconscious, Julius had left him in Cabera's hands, and as the sun sank, the man died, his heart failing at last. Julius had ordered him buried with the other Roman corpses, and it shamed him when he thought he had never even asked the man's name.

"Julius? Do you want to speak to them?" Gaditicus said, breaking into his thoughts and making him jump. Guiltily, he realized he hadn't heard anything the older officer had said. He stood slowly, marshaling his thoughts.

"I know most of you hoped to see Rome, and you will. My city is a strange place: marble and dreams, borne up with the strength of the legions. Every legionary is bound by oath to protect our people anywhere you find them. All a Roman has to do is say 'I am a Roman citizen' and be guaranteed our shelter and authority." He paused and every eye in the storehouse was on him.

"But you have not taken that oath and I cannot compel

you to fight for a city you have never seen. You have more wealth than most soldiers would see in ten years. You must make a free choice—to serve under oath, or to leave. If you leave us, you will go as friends. We have fought together and some have not made it this far. For others of you, it may be far enough. If you stay, I will give Celsus's treasure into the care of Captain Durus, who will meet us on the west coast when Mithridates is beaten."

Another low rumble of voices filled the room as he paused again.

"Can you trust Durus?" Gaditicus asked him. Julius thought for a moment, then shook his head.

"Not with so much gold. I will leave Prax to keep him honest." He searched out his old optio and was pleased to see him signal consent. With that settled, Julius took a deep breath as he looked over the seated men. He could name them all.

"Will you take the legion oath and be sworn to my command?"

They roared their agreement at him. Gaditicus whispered harshly, leaning close to Julius's ear.

"Gods, man. The Senate will have my balls if I do!"

"You should leave, then, Gadi, join Suetonius back at the ship while I give them the oath," Julius replied.

Gaditicus looked at him coolly, weighing him up. "I wondered why you left him there," he said. "Have you thought where you will lead them?"

"I have. I'm going to raise an army and lead them straight down Mithridates' throat."

He held out his hand and Gaditicus hesitated, then took it in a brief grip that was almost painful.

"Then our path is the same," he said, and Julius nodded his understanding.

Julius raised his arms for quiet, smiling as it came. His voice carried clearly in the sudden silence. "I never doubted you," he said to the men. "Not for a moment. Now stand and repeat these words."

They rose as one and stood to attention, with heads raised and backs straight.

Julius looked round at them and knew he was committed to his course. There was nothing in him to say turn back, but with the oath, his life would change until Mithridates was dead.

He spoke the words his father had taught him when the world was simple.

"Jupiter Victor, hear this oath. We pledge our strength, our blood, our lives to Rome. We will not turn. We will not break. We will not mind suffering or pain.

"While there is light, from here until the end of the world, we stand for Rome and the command of Caesar."

They chanted the words after him, their voices clear and firm.

CHAPTER 21

Alexandria tried to watch without being obvious as Tabbic explained a technique to Octavian, his voice a constant low murmur accompanying each movement of his powerful hands. On the workbench in front of them, Tabbic had laid a thick piece of gold wire on a square of leather. Both ends of the wire were trapped in tiny wooden clamps, and Tabbic was gesturing to show how Octavian should move a narrow wooden block over the wire.

"Gold is the softest metal, boy. To make a pattern in the wire, all you have to do is press the marking block gently against it and run it back and forth, keeping your arm very straight, as I showed you. Try it."

Octavian brought the block down slowly, letting the ridged teeth of the underside rest on the fragile-looking line of precious metal.

"That's the way, now use a little more pressure. That's it, back and forth. Good. Let's see it, then," Tabbic continued. Octavian lifted the block clear and beamed as he saw the regular series of beads that had been formed by the pressure. Tabbic peered at it, nodding.

"You have a light touch. Too much pressure will snap the wire and you have to go back to the beginning. Now I'll free the clamps and turn it over for you to finish the beading. Line the block up carefully and be as gentle as you can this time; the joints will be thin as the hairs of your head."

Tabbic caught Alexandria's eye as he stretched his back, aching after bending so long at the low bench he had made for Octavian. She winked at him and he blushed slightly, clearing his throat gruffly to hide a smile. She knew he had begun to enjoy the lessons with Octavian. It had taken a long time for him to lose a portion of his mistrust for the little thief, but she had known from his work with her how much he enjoyed teaching his skill.

Octavian cursed as the narrow wire gave under his hand. Ruefully, he lifted the block to reveal three cut pieces. Tabbic brought his heavy eyebrows together and shook his head, gathering the broken pieces up carefully to be melted and rolled once more.

"We'll try again later, or tomorrow. You nearly had it that time. When you can mark the full wire neatly, I'll show you how to fix it as a rim for one of the ladies' brooches."

Octavian looked downcast, and Alexandria held her breath as she waited to see if he would throw one of the violent tantrums with which he'd plagued them for the first few weeks. When it didn't come, she let the air out of her lungs with a slow rush of relief.

"All right. I'd like that," he said slowly.

Tabbic turned away from him, searching through the packages of finished work that had to be taken back to their owners.

"I have another job for you," he said, handing over a tiny pouch of leather, folded and tied. "This is a silver ring I repaired. I want you to run over to the cattle market and ask for Master Gethus. He runs the sales, so he won't be hard to find. He should give you a sestertius for the work. You take the coin and run straight back here, stopping for nothing. Understand? I'm trusting you. If you lose the ring or the coin, you and I are finished."

Alexandria could have laughed out loud at the little boy's earnest expression. Such a threat would have been worthless for the first weeks of the apprenticeship. Octavian wouldn't have minded being left alone. He had struggled mightily against the combined efforts of his mother, Tabbic, and Alexandria. Twice she'd had to search the local markets for him, and the second time she'd dragged him to the slave blocks to have him valued. He hadn't run again after that, instead adopting a sullenness Alexandria thought might be permanent.

The change had come midway through the fourth week of work, when Tabbic showed him how to make a pattern on a sheet of silver with tiny droplets of the molten metal. Though the little boy had burned his thumb when he tried to touch it, the process had fascinated him and he'd missed his dinner that night, staying to watch the final piece being polished. His mother, Atia, had arrived at the shop with her tired face full of apology. Seeing the tiny figure still working with the graded polishing cloths had left her speechless, but Alexandria woke the next morning to find her clothes had been cleaned and mended neatly in the night. No other thanks were necessary between them. Though the two women saw each other only an hour or two each day before sleep, they had both found friendship of the kind that can surprise two reserved and private people, working so hard that they never realized they were lonely.

*   *   *

Octavian whistled as he trotted through the crowds at the cattle market. When the farmers brought their animals into the city for bidding and slaughter, it was a busy place, rich with the warm scents of manure and blood. Everyone seemed to be shouting to each other, making complicated gestures with their hands to bid when they couldn't be heard.

Octavian looked for one of the sellers, to ask for Gethus.

He wanted to pass over the mended ring and get back to Tabbic's shop faster than the adults would believe.

As he wove around the shifting mass of people, he entertained himself by imagining Tabbic's surprise at his speedy return.

A hand grabbed suddenly at his neck and the little boy was lifted off his feet with a lurch, his feet slipping. He let out a blast of shocked wind at the interruption to his thoughts, struggling wildly in instinct against his attacker.

"Trying to steal someone's cow, are you?" a hard, nasal voice sounded by his ear.

He jerked his head around, groaning as he saw the heavy features of the butcher's boy he'd crossed before. What had he been thinking? Like a fool, he'd dropped his usual guard for predators and they'd caught him without the slightest effort.

"Let me go! Help!" he yelled.

The older boy smacked him hard across the nose, making it bleed.

"Shut up, you. I owe you a beating anyway, in return for the one I got for not stopping you last time." The burly arm was wrapped around Octavian's neck, squeezing his throat as he was dragged backward into an alleyway. He strained to get away, but it was hopeless and the rushing crowd didn't even look in his direction.

There were three other boys with the butcher's apprentice. All of them had the long-armed rangy growth of children used to hard physical work. They wore aprons stained with fresh blood from their labors at the market, and Octavian panicked, almost fainting with terror at their cruel expressions. The boys jeered and punched at him as they turned a corner in the alley. There, the din of the market was cut off by the high walls of tenements that leaned out above, almost meeting the ones opposite and creating an unnatural darkness.

The butcher's boy threw Octavian into the sluggish filth

that was ankle deep in the alleyway, a combination of years of refuse and human waste thrown from the narrow windows above. Octavian scrambled to one side to escape, but one of them kicked him hard enough to shove him back into place, lifting the small body and grunting with the impact. Octavian screamed with pain and fear as the other two joined the first, kicking with hard feet at whatever part of him they could reach.

After a minute, the three boys rested with their hands on their knees, panting from effort. Octavian was barely conscious, his body curled into a tight ball of misery, barely distinguishable from the dirt he lay in.

The butcher's boy pulled back his lips into a sneer, raising his fist and laughing coarsely as Octavian flinched from him.

"Serves you right, you little Thurin bastard. You'll think twice before stealing from my master next time, won't you?" He took careful aim and kicked Octavian in the face, whooping as the small head was rocked back. Octavian lay senseless with his eyes open and his face half submerged. Some dirty water flowed between his lips and, even unconscious, he began to cough and choke weakly. He didn't feel the fingers that searched him or hear the pleased shout when the older boys found the silver ring in its protective pouch.

The butcher's boy whistled softly as he tried on the metal band. The stone was a simple dome of heavy jade, held to the metal with tiny silver claws.

"I wonder who you stole this from?" he said, glancing at the prone figure. Each of them kicked the boy once more on behalf of the owner of the ring, then they walked back to the market, thoroughly pleased with the upturn in their fortunes.

Octavian woke hours later, sitting up slowly and retching for minutes as he tested his legs to see if they could hold him. He felt weak and too sore to move for a long time, crouched over and spitting elastic strands of dark blood onto the ground. When his head cleared enough, he searched his pocket for the ring, then the ground all around him. Finally, he was forced to admit that he had lost it, and fresh tears cut through the dirt and crusted blood on his face. He staggered back to the main road and sheltered his eyes against the painful sunlight. Still crying, on unsteady feet, he made his way back to Tabbic's shop, his mind blank with despair.

*   *   *

Tabbic tapped his foot on the wood of the shop floor, anger in every line of his frowning face.

"By hell, I'm going to kill the brat for this. He should have been back ages ago."

"So you've been saying for the last hour, Tabbic. Perhaps he was delayed or couldn't find Master Gethus," Alexandria replied, keeping her voice neutral.

Tabbic thumped a fist on the worktop. "Or perhaps he's sold the ring and run away, more likely!" he growled. "I'll have to make it good, you know. Jade stone, as well. It'll cost me a day of work and most of an aureus in materials to make Gethus a new one. No doubt he'll claim his dying mother gave it to him and want compensation on top of that. Where *is* that boy?"

The thick wooden door to the shop creaked open, letting in a swirl of dust from the street. Octavian stood there. Tabbic took one look at his bruises and torn tunic and crossed over to him, his anger vanishing.

"I'm sorry," the little boy cried as Tabbic guided him deeper into the shop. "I tried to fight them, but there was three and no one came to help me." He yelped as Tabbic probed his heaving chest, looking for broken bones. The metalsmith grunted, whistling air through his closed teeth.

"They did a fair job on you, right enough. How's your breathing?"

Octavian wiped his running nose gingerly with the back of a hand.

"It's all right. I came back as quick as I could. I didn't see them in the crowd. Usually I keep a lookout for them, but I was hurrying and..." He broke off into sobs and Alexandria put her arm around him, waving Tabbic away.

"Go on with you, Tabbic. He doesn't want an examination. He's had a bad time and he needs care and rest."

Tabbic stood clear as she took the boy into the back room and up the stairs to his home above the shop. Alone, he sighed and rubbed his grizzled face with a hand, scratching at the gray stubble that had come through since his morning shave. Shaking his head, he turned to his bench and began selecting the tools he would need to remake the ring for Gethus.

He worked in silence for a few minutes, then paused and looked back at the narrow stairs as a thought struck him.

"I'll have to make you a decent knife, my lad," he muttered to himself, before taking up the tools once more. After a while, as he was sketching the setting with chalk, he murmured, "And teach you to use the thing, as well."

*   *   *

Brutus stood on the Campus Martius, with the eagle standard of Primigenia in the ground at his side. He had been pleased to see that some of the other recruiting legions had to use banners of woven cloth, whereas the old standard Marius had made had been found for him. Hammered gold over copper, it caught the morning sun and he hoped it would catch the eye of more than a few of the crowd of boys who had been gathering since before dawn. Not all of them would be signing on with a legion. Some had come just to watch, and for those the food-sellers had set up stalls before first light. The smells of grilled meat and vegetables made him hungry, and he thought of getting an early lunch, jingling the coins in his pouch as he eyed the crowd around the line of standards.

He'd expected it to be easier. Renius looked every inch a lion of the old Rome, and the ten men they'd brought with them were impressive in new armor, polished to a high sheen for the admiration of the crowd. Yet Brutus had been forced to watch as all along the line, hundreds of young Romans signed up to be legionaries without one of them coming near his post. A few times, smaller groups had gathered, pointing and whispering, then moved on. He'd been tempted to grab a couple of the lads and find out what they'd said, but he held his temper. With noon close, the crowd had halved and, as far as he could see, Primigenia was the only standard not to be surrounded by windfalls from the new generation.

He gritted his teeth. The ones who had already joined would attract more to those eagles. By now, he imagined people asking what was wrong with Primigenia that no one wanted to join it. Hands would cover mouths and they would whisper with puerile excitement of the traitor legion. He cleared his throat and spat on the sandy soil. The testing finished at sundown and there was nothing to do but stand and wait for it to end, hoping perhaps to pick up a few stragglers as the light faded. The thought made him burn with embarrassment. He knew if Marius were there, he would have been walking amongst the young men, cajoling, joking, and persuading them to join his legion. Of course, back then there had been a legion to join.

Brutus resumed his sullen appraisal of the crowd, wishing he could make them understand. Three young men wandered toward his standard and he smiled at them as welcomingly as he could.

"Primigenia, is it?" one of them said.

Brutus watched as one of them hid a smile. They were here for sport, he guessed. For a fleeting instant, he considered knocking their heads together, but he controlled himself, sensing the eyes of his ten men on him. He could feel Renius bristle at his side, but the older man kept his peace.

"We were the legion of Marius, consul of Rome," he said, "victors in Africa and all over Roman lands. There is a glorious history here, for the right men who join us."

"What's the pay like then?" the tallest said, with a mock-serious tone.

Brutus took a slow breath. They knew the Senate set the pay for all legions. With Crassus to back him, he would have loved to offer more, but the limit was there to prevent wealthy sponsors undermining the whole system.

"Seventy-five denarii, same as the others," he replied quickly.

"Hold on, Primi*genia*? Weren't they the ones who smashed the city up?" the tall boy asked as if he had been given a sudden revelation. He turned to his grinning friends, who were happy to let him give the show.

"It is!" he said, delighted. "Sulla broke them, didn't he? They were led by some traitor or other."

The tall one paused as he caught the change in his friends' expressions, realizing he had gone too far. As he turned back, Brutus swung his fist, but Renius blocked the blow with an outstretched arm. The three young men all flinched at the threat, but their leader quickly recovered his confidence, his mouth twisting into a sneer.

Before he could speak, Renius stepped in close to him. "What's your name?"

"Germinius Cato," he replied haughtily. "You will have heard of my father."

Renius turned to the soldiers behind him. "Put his name down. He's in."

The arrogance faded into amazement as Germinius watched his name inked onto the bare scroll.

"You can't do that! My father will have your—"

"You're *in*, boy. In front of witnesses," Renius replied.

"These men will swear it was voluntary. When we dismiss you, you'll be free to run and tell your father how proud you are."

Cato's son glared at the older men, his confidence surging back. "My name will be off that scroll before sundown," he said.

Renius stepped close to him again. "Tell him Renius took the name. He'll know me. Tell him you'll always be known as the boy who tried to back out of serving the city in the legions. He'll be destroyed if something like that gets out, wouldn't you say? You think you'll follow in his footsteps after shame like that? The Senate doesn't like cowards, boy."

The young man paled with anger and frustration. "I will . . ." He paused and a terrible doubt crept into his face.

"What you'll do is stand by this eagle until we're ready to give you the oath. Until I'm told different, you're the first recruit of the day."

"You can't stop me leaving!" Germinius replied, his voice cracking.

"Disobeying a lawful order? I'll have you whipped if you take another step away from me. Stand to attention before I lose my patience!"

The bark of an order held Germinius in impotent rage. Under Renius's eye, he drew himself straight. At his side, his friends began to edge away.

"Your names!" Renius snapped, freezing them. They looked mutely at him and he shrugged.

"Mark them down as legionaries two and three of the day. That will serve, now I know your faces. Stand straight for the crowd, boys." He turned to the soldiers of Primigenia behind him for a moment, ignoring their amazement.

"If they run," he said clearly, "I want them dragged back and flogged on the field: It'll cost us a few recruits, but the others might as well see there's a hard side to all that glory."

The three young Romans faced the crowd stiffly, and

Renius looked surprised as Brutus drew him a few steps out of their hearing.

"Cato will go berserk," Brutus muttered. "Of all legions, he won't want his son in this one."

Renius cleared his throat and spat on the dusty grass of the field. "He won't want him branded a coward, either. It's your choice, but you'll gain nothing by letting them go now. He may try to buy you off or he may endure it. We'll know in a day or two."

Brutus looked closely at the old gladiator and shook his head in disbelief. "You've forced this on me now, so I'll see it through."

Renius glanced at him. "If you'd hit him, his father would have killed you."

"You didn't know who he was when you stopped me!" Brutus retorted.

Renius sighed. "I taught you better, lad, I really did. What else should I think when a boy wears his father's crest on a gold ring big enough to buy a house with?"

Brutus blinked at him, then walked over to the three new recruits and examined Germinius's hand for a moment without speaking. He was about to return to Renius when three more boys detached from the crowd and approached the Primigenia eagle.

"Sign your names on the scroll there and stand with the others, lads," Renius told them. "We'll give you the oath when there's enough of a crowd." A smile tugged at the corners of his mouth as he waved them over.

CHAPTER 22

Between the heat of Greece and the excuses, Julius was finding it hard to keep his temper. He was desperate for recruits, but the walled Roman city had forgotten its founding duty and every demand was met with delay and discussion.

"I have the young men. Now bring out the veterans," Julius said to the city elder.

"What? Would you leave us defenseless?" the man spluttered in indignation.

Julius remained silent, waiting a few moments before replying, as Renius used to. He'd found the small pauses gave weight to his words like nothing else.

"My men are going directly from here to attack Mithridates. There is no one else for you to defend against. I do not have time to train more farmers to be legionaries, and from what you say, there is no other Roman force within a hundred miles of here.

"Every man within these walls who has ever held a sword in service of Rome, I want out here, armed and armored as best you can."

The besieged elder began to speak again and Julius interrupted him, raising his voice slightly. "I do not expect to have to mention the conditions of their retirement. It would be an attack on their honor for me to remind them that they were given land on the understanding that if Rome called them, they would answer. She calls. Fetch them out."

The elder turned away, almost running back to the council hall. Julius waited with his men standing to attention at his back. He had suffered enough of the council's delays, and part of him had no sympathy at all. They were in a conquered land and the constant worry of rebellion had occurred. Did they expect to sit it out behind their fine walls? He wondered what might have happened if Mithridates had reached them first. Hardly worth betting that they would have declared loyalty to him out of fear for their families, throwing open the gates and kneeling in the dust.

"Someone's coming up the main street," Gaditicus said behind him.

Julius turned to his left and listened to the measured step of at least a century of legionaries. He swore under his breath. The last thing he needed at that moment was to come face-to-face with another officer from the regular legions.

As they came into sight, Julius's spirits leaped.

"Legionaries . . . halt!" came a graveled voice, its bark echoing back from the walls of the small square.

One of Julius's men whistled softly in surprise at what they saw. The men were old. They wore armor that dated back almost fifty years in some cases, with simpler designs of plate and mail. Their bodies showed the results of decades of war. Some lacked an eye or a hand. Others showed ancient puckered scars on their faces and limbs, poorly stitched, seaming their skins in long crescents.

The commander was a burly man with a shaven head and a powerful set of shoulders. His face was deeply wrinkled, but he still gave an impression of strength that reminded Julius vaguely of Renius as he saluted, judging Julius's command instinctively by the distance he kept from the others.

"Quertorus Far reporting, sir. We thought the council

would talk all day, so we sent out the call without them. The veterans are ready to be inspected, sir."

Julius nodded and followed the man, watching as more and more of them entered the square and lined up in neat formation.

"How many are there?" he asked, trying to judge the worth of the whitebeards he saw standing straight in the winter sun.

"Altogether, nearly four hundred, sir, though some are still making their way in from outlying farms. We should be all in by dark tonight."

"And the average age?" Julius continued.

Quertorus stopped and turned to face the young officer before him. "They're veterans, sir. That means old. But they're all volunteers and they're as hard and tough as you're going to need to smoke out Mithridates. They need a few days to drill together, but remember, they've all been tested and they've all come through. A lot of men have died for Rome over the years. These are the ones that won."

The man had an insolent expression, but Julius could hear the belief in his words as he tried to reassure the stern young officer who had come to their city for an army.

"And you, Quertorus? Do you command them?"

The bald man laughed, a short chop of sound, quickly cut off. "Not me, sir. The council thinks it does, I suppose, but these men go their own way and have done for a long time, most of them. Mind you, when Mithridates took the port, they began polishing their swords again, if you understand me."

"You don't talk as if you were one of them," Julius said, turning it into a question.

Quertorus raised his eyebrows. "Didn't mean to, sir. I did my twenty years with the First Cyrenaica, ten of them as optio."

Some instinct prompted Julius to ask, "The last ten?"

Quertorus cleared his throat and looked away for a moment. "More like ten in the middle, sir. Lost my rank toward the end for excessive gambling."

"I see. Well, Quertorus. It seems we're gambling again, you and I," Julius said quietly.

Quertorus beamed at him, revealing missing teeth in his lower jaw. "I wouldn't bet against them, sir, not if you knew them."

Julius eyed the massed ranks with less confidence than he showed. "I hope you're right. Now step into rank yourself and I'll address them."

For a second, he thought Quertorus might refuse and he wondered if the man had lost his rank for more than just gambling, a fairly common occupation of legionaries not on duty. Then the bald man stepped into the ranks and came to attention, his eyes on Julius with interest. Julius filled his lungs with air.

"Veterans of Rome!" he bellowed, making those closest to him jump. He'd always had a powerful voice, but part of him wondered if it would be enough if some of them were deaf.

"My men and I passed two villages to the south before we came here, collecting recruits. The news we heard is that Mithridates is camped about a hundred miles to the west. You can be sure that fresh Roman legions will be on the march as I speak, coming east from the coast ports at Dyrrhachium and Apollonia. I intend to force him toward them; to be the hammer for the Roman anvil."

He had their interest, all right. Every eye was on him, from his own men and the grizzled veterans. He thanked his gods for the decision to march ten miles north to recruit at the city.

"With you, I have a thousand at my command to attack Mithridates. Some from this city and the villages are untrained. Others I have brought with me are used only to fighting at sea in Roman galleys. You were the land legions and you must be the backbone as we march. I will give each of you a sword brother from my men to train."

He paused, but there was silence and he knew then that the veterans still remembered the old discipline. He wondered how many would last the miles before they even saw action. With young, fresh soldiers, he could cover the distance in less than three or four days, but with these? There was no way of knowing.

"I need one of you to be quartermaster, preparing packs, equipment, and food from what you can find within the city walls."

Quertorus stepped forward, his eyes glinting with pleasure.

"Quertorus?" Julius said to him.

"Quartermaster, sir, with your permission. I've been wanting a chance to poke the eye of the council for a long time."

"Very well, but their complaints will come to me and I will treat them seriously. Take three of my men and start readying the supplies. We need a shield for every man and any spears or bows you can find. I want a field kitchen outside the walls with a meal ready for all of them before dark. There's still light enough for drill and I want to see how well these men can move. They will be hungry when we're done."

Quertorus saluted and marched smartly over to Gaditicus, who remained at attention where Julius had left him with the others. Julius watched as three were selected to go with him, and tried to ignore forebodings that he had just let the wolf loose amongst the geese. As they hurried away, Julius saw the city elder come rushing out of the council hall, making his way directly to the assembled veterans. Julius turned away from him without interest. Whatever the council had decided was no longer of importance.

"I've seen you can stand and I know from your scars that

you can fight," he shouted along the ranks. "Now I need to see if you can remember your formations."

At his order, they turned and marched along the main street to the gate that led out of the small city. Those who had waited in the side roads filed in behind the others with precision, and Julius signaled Gaditicus to bring up the rear. The two men exchanged glances as they joined the column marching out, leaving the council elder calling behind them, his voice fading as he finally realized they would not listen to him any longer.

*   *   *

It took a while for the legionaries to form four equal lines, the veterans mixed with the younger men. Julius walked stiffly up and down the rows, judging the quality of the men who had gathered in his name. As he frowned at them, he fought to remember the lessons on field tactics and routines that Renius had drummed into him so many years ago. None of them had dealt with starting a legion from scratch, but some of it came easily to him as soon as he thought about the practical problems of having the large group move and respond to orders. The worry that would not leave him was that one of the veterans would realize he had never commanded infantry before. He deepened his frown. He would just have to bluff it through.

Beginning with the corner men, he set up a simple square, working through the figures in his head while they waited. He separated the others into thirty numbered rows, then directed the corner men to take their positions. When they were ready, Julius shouted the order, "Slow march to square formation!"

It was ragged, but the men moved with solemn concentration until they stood again in silence.

"Now look around you, gentlemen. I want a veteran next

to a younger man wherever possible. We will mix speed with experience. Move!"

Once more, they changed position, the shuffle of feet eerie without accompanying chatter. Julius saw that his men were taking the lead from the veterans in manner and smiled slightly, even as he remembered Renius telling him that the man who led should be respected but cold. He must not smile. He could not be liked. They had loved Marius, but they had fought for him for years and Julius didn't have that kind of time.

"We have two cohorts of four hundred and eighty. Split at the fifteenth line and leave a row between you." Once again they moved and a long avenue opened up in the dusty earth.

"The first cohort will be named Accipiter, the hawk. The other will be Ventulus, the breeze. Accipiter will be commanded by my second, Gaditicus; Ventulus, by myself. Say the names to yourselves. When you hear them in battle, I want you to react without thought." He decided not to mention that one was a merchant ship and the other lay at the bottom of the sea. He wiped sweat from his forehead.

"Before we begin the formation drills, we must have a name."

He paused, thinking desperately as his mind went blank. The veterans watched him impassively, perhaps guessing at his sudden lack of confidence. The right name would lift them as they charged, and Julius began to panic as nothing came to him, overwhelmed by the importance of getting it absolutely right the first time.

Come on! he urged himself. Speak the name and give them an identity. His eyes raked them, angry with his sudden indecision. They were Romans, young and old. He had it.

"You are the Wolves of Rome," he said. His voice was quiet, yet it carried to the farthest of them. One or two of the veterans stood straighter as he spoke, and he knew he had chosen well.

"Now. Ventulus cohort form up in four maniples to my right. Accipiter break to the left. We have three hours before dark. Position drill until you drop."

He could not resist clenching a fist in fierce satisfaction as they moved smoothly apart. He called Gaditicus from the ranks of Accipiter and returned his salute.

"I want you to run through every formation you know until dark. Don't give them a moment to think. I will do the same with mine. Change your unit commanders if they are obviously unfit or to reinforce your discipline, but with care. I want them working well by the time we eat."

"Are you thinking of marching tomorrow?" Gaditicus asked, keeping his voice too low to carry to the men nearby.

Julius shook his head. "Tomorrow we will run battle games, yours against mine. I want the old ones to remember and the young ones to get used to following orders in the field, under pressure. See me tonight and we'll work out the details. Oh, and Gaditicus..."

"Yes, sir?"

"Work yours hard, because tomorrow Ventulus will take them to pieces and make you start again."

"I look forward to seeing you try, sir," Gaditicus retorted with a small smile, saluting once more before returning to his new command.

*   *   *

As Julius gave the order to march two days later, he felt a surge of pride, making his feet light on the foreign earth. His right eye was almost closed where one of Gaditicus's men had caught him with an axe handle, but he knew the pain would pass.

More than a few of both cohorts limped with the battering they had taken at each other's hands in the mock battles, but they had changed from strangers into Wolves, and Julius knew they would be hard to kill, harder still to break.

They would cross the eighty miles of wood and plain and Mithridates would need a lot of his rebellious farmers to withstand what would be thrown at him, Julius was certain. He felt as if there was good wine in his stomach, making him want to laugh with excitement.

Alongside him, Gaditicus sensed his mood and chuckled, wincing as he cracked his swollen mouth once again.

"One thing about the galleys. You didn't have to carry this much metal and kit on your back," he complained in an undertone.

Julius clapped him on the shoulder, chuckling. "Think yourself lucky. They used to call my uncle's men 'Marius's mules' for the weight they could bear."

Gaditicus grunted in reply, shifting his heavy pack to ease his muscles. The legs had the worst of it. Many of the veterans had huge calves, showing a strength built over years of marching. Gaditicus made a silent oath that he would not call his cohort to rest until Julius did or one of his veterans dropped. He wasn't sure which was more likely.

Julius began lengthening his stride through the ranks up to the front. He felt as if he could march all day and night and the Romans at his back would follow him. Behind, the city dwindled into the distance.

CHAPTER 23

A lifetime of fighting in foreign lands did not make for soft men, Julius reflected as he marched on toward the end of the second day, half blinded with dust and sweat. If the veterans had let themselves go in their retirement, he doubted they could have matched the eager pace of the younger men. It looked as if the hard labor of clearing land for farming had kept them strong, though some of them seemed made of sinew and skin under their old armor. Their leather tunics were cracked and brittle after so long lying in chests, but the iron straps and plates of their armor gleamed with oil and polish. They could call themselves farmers, but the speed with which they had responded to his summons showed their true natures. They had once been the most disciplined killers in the world, and every stride of the long march brought back something of their old fire. It showed in their posture and their eyes as the enthusiasm for war was rekindled. They were men for whom retirement was the death, who felt most alive in the camaraderie of soldiers, when they could spend their fading energies in sudden blows and the dry-mouthed terror of meeting the enemy charge.

Julius carried an old shield on his back, torn from its hangings over someone's door by Quertorus. It was prevented from chafing against his shoulder blades by a heavy waterskin that gurgled musically with every step. Like the others from the galleys, he felt the lack of fitness that comes from having your movements restricted to a deck, but his lungs were clear and there was no trace of the shuddering fits that had plagued him since the head wound. He didn't dare to dwell on them, but he still worried at what would become of his authority if they started again. There was nowhere private on a forced march.

For most of the first day, Julius had set a comfortable pace. They had too few men to risk losing more of the veterans than was inevitable, and they had all made it to the first camp. Julius had used the younger men for sentry duty, and none of them had complained, though Suetonius had clearly bitten back a comment before taking his post with surly obedience. There were times when Julius would have been happy to have him flogged and left on the trail, but he held his temper. He knew he had to form bonds with the men. Bonds that would be strong enough to withstand the first hectic moments of battle. They had to see him as he had once seen Marius—a man to follow into hell.

On the second day, Julius had matched pace with Gaditicus at the front of the two cohorts for most of the morning. They had little breath for discussion, but they agreed to take turns at the head, allowing the other to drift back among the units, assessing weaknesses and strengths. For Julius, the trips back were valuable, and it was during them that he had begun to see the light of excitement even in the expressions of the weakest of his men. They had shrugged off the petty laws and restrictions of city life, returning to the simplest world they had ever known.

Julius had marched abreast of a line about halfway back in Ventulus cohort for the best part of an hour. One of the veterans had caught his attention, the only one he passed not to meet his eye. The man had to have been one of the oldest there, hidden from easy sight by the bulk of the soldiers around him, which Julius guessed could be deliberate. Instead of a helmet, he wore the ragged skin of an old lion that covered his entire head and ended in a neatly sliced line at his shoulders. The dead cat's eyes were dark, sunken holes, and like its owner, the headgear looked too far gone to be useful. The old man marched while staring straight ahead, his eyes screwed up to wrinkled slits against the dust. Julius examined him with interest, taking in the hard lines of sinew that stood out in his neck and the swollen knuckles of his hands that looked more like clubs of bone than fingers. Though the veteran kept his mouth pursed shut, it was obvious from his sunken cheeks that there were few teeth left in the old jaw. Julius wondered what spirit could keep such an ancient marching through the miles, always staring toward a destination neither of them could see.

As noon approached and Julius was ready to call a halt for food and an hour of blessed rest, he saw the man develop a limp in his left leg and noted the knee had swollen in the short time he had been with him. He bellowed the halt and the Wolves crashed to a stop in two paces, together.

As Quertorus collected the cooking equipment, Julius found the old man sitting with his back to a stunted tree. His seamed face tightened as he bound the weak knee in a strip of cloth, winding on so many layers that it could hardly bend at all. He had removed the lion-head skin, placing it carefully to one side. His hair was wispy and gray, sticking to him in sweaty strands.

"What's your name?" Julius asked him.

The old man spoke as he wound the cloth, testing the movement and grunting in discomfort with each try. "Most of them call me Cornix, the old crow. I'm a hunter, a trapper in the forests."

"I have a friend who could ease that knee for you. A healer. He's probably older than you are," Julius said quietly.

Cornix shook his head. "Don't need him. This knee's taken me on a lot of campaigns. It will last one more."

Julius didn't insist, impressed by the stubbornness of the man. Without another word, he fetched some of the warm bread and bean stew that Quertorus had heated through. It would be their last hot meal as they drew within scouting range of Mithridates and couldn't risk smoke being seen. Cornix took it, nodding his thanks.

"Strange sort of commander, you are," he said through mouthfuls, "bringing me food."

Julius watched him eat without replying for a moment.

"I'd have thought you would have left soldiering behind you. It must be, what, twenty years since you were with a legion?"

"More like thirty, and you know it," the man replied, smiling to reveal a mash of unchewed bread. "Still miss it sometimes."

"Do you have a family?" Julius asked, still wondering why the man wasn't safe in the hills instead of breaking the last of his strength with the others.

"They moved north and my wife died. Just me now."

Julius stood and looked down at the placidly chewing figure, watching him wince as he flexed the bound knee. Julius's gaze strayed to where Cornix had rested his shield and sword against the tree, and the old man followed his eyes, choosing to answer the unspoken question.

"I can still use it, don't you worry."

"You'll need to. They say Mithridates has a great host of an army."

Cornix sniffed disdainfully. "Yes, they always say that." He finished a mouthful of the stew and took a long pull from his waterskin. "Are you going to ask me, then?"

"Ask you what?" Julius replied.

"I could see it was eating you up all the time you was marching near me. What's a man of my age doing going to war? That was it, wasn't it? You were wondering if I could even lift that old sword of mine, I'd guess."

"It crossed my mind." Julius chuckled, responding to the gleam of humor in the dark eyes.

Cornix laughed with him, a long wheezing series of hard sounds. Then he fell silent and looked straight at the tall young commander with all the confidence of youth and all his life in front of him.

"Just to pay my debts, lad. That old city gave me a lot more than I gave back. I should think this last one'll make us even at the end."

He winked as he finished speaking and Julius smiled faintly, realizing suddenly that Cornix had come with him to die, perhaps preferring a quick end to a lonely, drawn-out agony in some desolate hunter's cabin. He wondered how many of the others wanted to throw their lives away with the last of their courage, rather than wait for a death that crept up on them in the night. Julius shivered slightly as he walked back to the campfires, though the day was not cold.

*   *   *

There was no way to be sure where Mithridates camped with his irregulars. The reports Julius had from Roman survivors behind them could be mistaken, or the Greek king could have moved many miles while the Wolves were marching into the area. The biggest worry was that the two forces would stumble on each other's scouts and be forced into action before Julius was ready. His own scouts understood that all their lives depended on not being spotted, and Julius had the fastest and fittest of them traveling out for miles looking for fresh signs of the enemy while the bulk of the Wolves concealed themselves in the scrub woodland. It was a frustrating time. Forbidden fire and unable to hunt widely, they were cold and damp each night and barely warmed by the weak sun that came to them through the trees during the day.

After four days of inaction, Julius was practically ready to order the men into the open and take the consequences. All but three of his scouts had come in past the outer line of guards and were eating cold food with the others in miserable silence.

Julius chafed as he waited for the last three. He knew they were in the right area, having found a slaughtered Roman century stripped of armor and weapons only five miles to the east, caught unawares as they guarded a lonely fort. The bodies looked pitiful in death and no words Julius might have said could have fired his men's determination so thoroughly.

The scouts came in together, thudding through the wet leaves with the slow trot they used to cover miles without a rest. Ignoring the cold stew that waited for them, they came straight to Julius, their faces tired but animated with excitement. All three had been out for the whole four days, and Julius knew immediately that they had found the enemy at last.

"Where are they?" he asked, standing quickly.

"Thirty miles further west," one replied, eager to get the news out. "It's a heavy camp. It looks as if they're preparing to defend against the legions coming from Oricum. They've dug in at a narrow point between two sharp slopes." He paused for breath and one of the others took up the report without a pause.

"They've spiked the slopes and the ground to the west. They had a wide line of scouts and guards out, so we couldn't get too close, but it looked good enough to stop cavalry. We saw archers practicing and I think we saw Mithridates himself. There was a big man giving orders to his units. He looked like the one in command."

"How many were there?" Julius snapped, wanting this detail more than all the rest.

The scouts glanced at each other and then the first spoke again.

"We think about ten thousand, at a rough guess. None of

us could get close enough to be sure, but he had the whole valley between the hills covered in leather tents—maybe a thousand of them. We guessed at eight or ten men to each one. . . ."
The other two nodded, watching him to see how he took the
news. Julius kept his face carefully blank, though he was disappointed. No wonder Mithridates felt confident enough to
stand against the legionaries on their way to him. The Senate
had sent only Sulla before against a smaller rebellion. If they
sent one legion again, Mithridates could well be victorious,
gaining himself another year before the Senate heard the news
and dragged back every spare man from the other territories.
Even then, they might be reluctant to leave the rest of Roman
lands exposed. Surely they would not dare to lose Greece?
Every Roman-held city that hid from the king behind high
walls could be destroyed before the Senate finally gathered a
crushing force. The rivers would run red before the last of
Rome was cut from Mithridates' lands, and if he could unite
all the cities, it could mean war for a generation.

Julius dismissed the scouts to fetch food and get some
well-deserved rest. It would be little enough, he knew.

Gaditicus came to his side, his eyebrows raised in interest
as the scouts left.

"We've found him," Julius confirmed. "Ten thousand of
them at the highest estimate. I'm thinking of moving ten
miles tonight and then the last twenty or so when it gets dark
tomorrow. Our archers will drop the sentries and we'll hit the
main force before dawn."

Gaditicus looked worried. "The veterans will be close to
exhaustion if you push them that far in darkness. We could be
slaughtered."

"They're a great deal fitter than when we left their city. It
will be hard and we'll lose a few, I have no doubt, but we have
surprise with us. And they have marched all their lives. I will
want you to organize a fast retreat after that first attack. I
don't want them to think about a death struggle against so

many. Pitch it to them as a running blow—straight in, kill as many as we can, and away. We get as far away as possible before dawn, and, well, I'll see what shape we're in then." He looked up through the mossy trunks at the sky above.

"Not long till darkness, Gadi. Make your men ready to move. I'll halt them as close as I can for tomorrow night, but we must not be seen. We'll work on the tactics when we're closer. There's no point planning the details until I can see how they have set themselves. We don't need to beat them, just force them to break camp and move west toward the legions coming from the coast."

"If they are coming," Gaditicus replied quietly.

"They will be. No matter what happened after Sulla's death, the Senate can't afford to let Greece go without a fight. Form the ranks, Gadi."

Gaditicus saluted, his features smoothing. He was aware that any attack would be risky against such numbers, but he thought the night strike Julius suggested was the best choice, given the men they had available. In addition, Mithridates had assembled an army from untrained irregulars who were about to meet a force that included some of the most experienced gladius fighters alive. Against ten thousand, it wasn't much of an edge, but it would make a difference.

As he gave Accipiter cohort the orders to break camp, he watched how the younger men and veterans worked together, quickly and quietly assembling in loose formation until they cleared the woods. Wolves indeed, some of them.

CHAPTER **24**

Mithridates had lost his perimeter guards and didn't yet know it. Julius had watched his outer ring for almost an hour, smiling at last when he saw the simple system the Greek king used. Each of his guards stood next to a burning torch set atop a wooden pole. At random intervals, they would detach it and wave the flame above their heads, answered by the inner ring and the others spaced around them.

Mithridates may have been a king, but he was no tactician, Julius had realized. The Wolves had broken the defense with pairs of archers, one to down the sentry as soon as he had signaled, the other to collect the torch and replace it in the bracket. It was quickly done and they were able to draw in to the inner circle. Those men were closer to each other, and replacing them took almost an hour. Julius had urged caution, but even he was growing tense as the time wore on waiting for the last to make his signal, the man completely unaware that only Romans could answer him.

Cabera loosed the final silent arrow and the enemy soldier fell in a shadowy heap without a sound. Moments later, the spot of light illuminated another dark figure who stood calmly as if all was well. There was no alarm and Julius clenched a fist in excitement.

The camp at the foot of the hills was lit by pole torches like the ones the sentries used. Seen from afar, the dark winter night was broken by a sea of golden spots, unwinking eyes that glowed at them as they waited for Julius's signal. For the young commander, the whole world seemed to be hanging on his word. He approached the nearest of his false sentries and nodded to Cabera, who lit an oil-soaked arrow from the torch, firing it quickly as the flames spread toward his fingers.

Gaditicus saw the splinter of flame launch upward and pointed his sword at the camp before them. His men moved in from their staggered position without a single shout or battle cry. They ran in eerie silence toward the pools of light that marked the camp, converging with Ventulus on two sides to cause maximum panic and disruption.

The Greek army had retired with the coming of night, depending on their far-flung rings of guards to warn them of an attack. The first many of them knew of danger was when their leather tents were ripped open and unseen swords stabbed through at their sleeping bodies, killing dozens in the first few seconds. Shouts mingled with screams and the sleeping camp began to wake and take up weapons.

"Wolves!" Julius bellowed, judging the time for silence was over. The excitement swept him as he and his men ran through the camp, killing anyone who stumbled out of their tents. He had told his men to kill two each of the enemy and then fight their way out, but three had fallen to his own blade and he was barely at the end of the first rush. He could feel the panic of Mithridates' men. Their officers were slow to respond to the attack, and without orders, a hundred individuals tried to take the battle to the shadowed attackers, dying in scores on veteran blades. Julius's cry was echoed by Gaditicus's cohort, hundreds of voices adding to the confusion and fear of the enemy. Cabera fired his remaining arrows into dark tents, and Julius cut a naked man down as he tried to bring his sword to bear. It was chaos and in the confusion Julius almost missed the moment he'd sworn he would not ignore.

It came after many minutes, when horns sounded and

the running Greeks began to gather in their units. In the tents the Roman forces had missed, the enemy had armed themselves and now began to fight back, orders in Greek heard over the hack and thump of blows.

Julius spun round to take off a man's hand at the wrist as he leapt at him. Every cut with the heavy blade caused awful damage, but his next blow was blocked neatly and he found two men against him and more running in from all sides. They had recovered and it was time to retreat before his Wolves were cut to pieces.

"Disengage!" he bellowed, even as he swung low with the gladius, cutting deeply into an ankle of the closest man to him. The second sprawled over the body as he rushed in, and Julius stepped clear, turning in the space and suddenly sprinting away, his sandals skidding in the bloody dust. His men came with him on the instant, turning and running as soon as they could get free of the press.

Outside the torches of the camp, the night was a black hiding place. As Julius called the disengage, all the sentry torches had been extinguished and the Romans scattered invisibly, disappearing rapidly from the edge of the camp, leaving wreckage and bodies behind them.

The Greek units halted at the edge of the camp lights, unwilling to run into a darkness that seemed to contain thousands of the enemy—a foe they had been told was more than a week of marching away in a different direction. Confused orders were shouted back and forth as they hesitated and the Wolves ran clear.

*　　　　　*　　　　　*

Mithridates raged. He had been torn from sleep by screams at the farthest end of his camp. His own tent was in the mouth of the narrow pass, and as his sleepy mind cleared, he realized they were under attack from the safe side, where he knew his men had cleared out Roman settlements all the way from the encampment to the frightened cities along the eastern coast.

His ten thousand men covered a vast stretch of the valley, and by the time he had brought his captains to the scene of the attack and begun restoring order, the Romans were gone.

Grimly, they tallied the dead. The officers who survived estimated a full five thousand had come against them, leaving more than a thousand Greek dead on the ground. Mithridates roared in frustration as he saw the bodies piled in tents, killed before they even had a chance to face the enemy. It was carnage and he knew again the frustration he had felt when Sulla had come for him years before.

How could they have got behind him? he wondered silently as he walked amongst the ungainly dead. He looked into the dark scrub and was overcome with anger, throwing his sword into the night. The darkness swallowed it almost as soon as it left his hand.

"The sentries are dead, sir," an officer reported.

Mithridates looked at him with eyes made red from smoke and interrupted sleep.

"Post more and break the camp ready for a dawn march. I want them hunted down." As the man ran to fulfill his orders, Mithridates looked again at the desolation around him. A thousand men had been lost and he had seen only a few of the Romans on the ground amongst them. Why did they retreat? Whichever legion it was, it looked as if they could have run right over the camp before light came, such had been the panic and disarray of his men. Where would they be safe, if not in the heart of their own land, their own camp?

When he had retired that night, it had been with the confidence of leading the biggest army he had ever gathered, ever seen. Now he knew he would not sleep again without fear that their strength would be mocked, their lives cut from them with savage ease. He watched the faces around him, seeing the fading shock and terror, and doubt crept into him.

He'd thought himself surrounded by lions, but found they were lambs.

He tried to shrug off despair, but it pressed heavily on him. How could he hope to take on Rome? These men had come to his banner after a few quick victories against the hated Romans, but they were young men filled with dreams of Sparta, Thebes, and Athens. Dreams of Alexander that he might not be able to bring about. His head bowed and his heavy fists clenched as the men scurried around him, not daring to speak to the furious king.

$$* \qquad * \qquad *$$

"We should go back," Suetonius said. "One more attack while they are breaking camp. They'd never expect it."

"And how would we escape again, with dawn coming?" Julius replied irritably. "No. We march until we find cover." He turned his face away so as not to see the sullen expression that he knew would follow his words. Even that was slightly more bearable than the vicious pleasure that had gripped the young officer since the raid. It sickened him. For Julius, the short battle had been without honor, a simple practical business of reducing the enemy numbers. The hot rush of excitement that had filled his veins in the fighting had faded as soon as he was clear, but Suetonius had been almost sexually aroused by the easy killing.

The veterans too, Julius noted, had moved away from the Greek camp as fast as they were able, without cheers or care for minor wounds. They kept a professional silence, as he had ordered. Only Suetonius had chattered as they marched, seemingly unable to stop himself spilling over with self-congratulation.

"We could send in our archers and fire from cover before retiring," he said, his mouth opening wetly at the prospect. "Did you see the sentry I shot? Straight through his throat, perfect, it was."

"Be silent!" Julius snapped at him. "Fall back in the ranks and keep your mouth shut." He'd had enough of the man and there was something deeply unpleasant in his enjoyment of the slaughter. It hadn't seemed to surface in the sea battles, but somehow, killing men as they slept had awakened something ugly in the young officer, and Julius wanted to push it as far from him as he could. A thought of the crucifixions flashed into his mind and he shuddered, wondering if Suetonius would have shown mercy or gone on to the very end of them. He suspected it would have been slow if Suetonius had been giving the orders.

The young watch officer didn't drop back immediately, and Julius nearly struck him. He seemed to think they shared some private relationship that sprang from the memories in common, right back to the cell on Celsus's ship. Julius looked him in the face and saw that it was twisted in spite, the mouth working as he thought of a reply to the order.

"Get back, or I'll kill you here," Julius snarled at him, and the lean figure trotted away at last into the darkness of the marching men behind.

One of the veterans stumbled with a curse. It was easy enough to do without a moon to see the ground. They had set a hard pace from the first, with no complaints. Every man there knew Mithridates would be out looking for them as soon as it was light enough to see. They had less than two hours to dawn, and at full speed they could cover nearly ten miles in that time.

With the wounded, it would be less. Without having to ask, those men who had trouble walking were supported by two others, but most of the wounds were minor. The nature of the fighting had left the Romans either dead or untouched for the most part. Julius hadn't had time to judge their losses, but he guessed they had done well, far better than he had hoped.

As he marched, he worked through how he would have

defended the Greek army if he had had charge of them. A better sentry system for a start. It was that weakness that had let them run straight into the heart of the camp without an alarm. The Wolves had been lucky, it seemed, but for all his faults, Mithridates was not a fool. It would be harder the next time, with more Roman dead. Unseen at the head of the long column, Julius was finally able to take a moment in the silence of the night march to examine the success. For all Suetonius's debased enjoyment, he was right. It had been perfect.

As dawn came, most of the men were exhausted. Grimly, Julius forced them to stagger on, keeping up a string of orders and threats. A few miles more brought them to a series of sharp wooded hills that would hide them from the day and discovery. They would sleep and eat there, but as he listened to the groans of the veterans as even their iron will faded under the endless march, he guessed they would have to stay hidden for a while longer, to recover their strength.

*   *   *

At dawn, Mithridates sent out all his small store of horses in groups of twenty, with orders to report back the moment they sighted the enemy. His original plan of uprooting the entire camp for the search had worried him. Perhaps that was what they intended him to do, to leave the apparent shelter of the small valley and march out onto the plains where the hidden legion could take them apart. He paced his tent in an agony of frustration, cursing his indecision. Should he retreat to a city? They were all Roman and would defend their walls against him to the last man. But where was safe on the plains? He knew it was possible that more legions would be coming from the west to crush the rebellion, and played with the idea of disbanding his men, sending them back to their farms and valleys. No, he couldn't do that. The Romans could well take them one by one as they looked for rebels, and he would have gained nothing.

He grated his teeth in the same impotent anger that had coursed through him ever since he had seen the bodies of his men the night before. Would Alexander allow himself to be trapped between legions?

He stopped his pacing suddenly. No, Alexander would not. Alexander would carry the fight to them. But in which direction? If he moved his army back into the east, he could still be caught by those coming up behind. If he moved west toward the Roman ports, he would have these night killers to harry his rear guard. The gods forgive him, what would *Sulla* do? If the scouts came back with no news, and he didn't act, he would begin losing men to desertion, he was sure.

Sighing, he poured himself a third cup of wine, despite the acid feeling in his empty stomach as it rebelled at such punishment so early in the day. He ignored the discomfort irritably as he tipped it back. In a little while, he would have to tell his sons that they had cost lives by not moving fast enough during the night.

He drank more and more as the day wore on and the scouts returned on lathered mounts with nothing to report. Of all the camp, only Mithridates the king had drunk himself to sleep as night fell.

*   *   *

Julius knew the estimates of the short night raid were going to be vague or exaggerated. It was the nature of soldiers to claim greater success than they had achieved. Yet even allowing for that, he thought they had reduced Mithridates' force by between eight hundred and a thousand, losing only eleven of their own. Those men would not be buried under the eyes of Roman gods. There had been no time to collect the bodies, but it was still a thorn under the skin of the veterans, who had never liked to leave their own in enemy hands.

The younger men had released some of the night's tension as soon as they reached the safety of the tree line in the hills and Julius had given permission to stand down. They had whooped and cheered until they were hoarse, while the veterans looked on smiling, more concerned with cleaning and oiling their equipment than celebrating.

Quertorus had sent out fifty of their best hunters to bring back meat, and by mid-morning had a steaming meal ready, roasting hares and deer together on small fires. Any flame was a risk, but the trees would break up the smoke and Julius knew they needed the rejuvenation and warmth of hot meat, and only insisted the fires be scattered as soon as the last of the hunters' kills were cooked.

The difference that age makes was clear that afternoon. The young recruits were fully recovered, moving energetically about the camp in small groups, chatting and laughing. The veterans lay like the dead, without even turning in sleep, so they woke stiff and cramped. Bruises spread under their skins, appearing where there had been no mark the night before. The younger ones shrugged off their wounds, but didn't mock the veterans for their stiffness. They had seen their skill and not their age.

Julius had found Cornix chewing amiably as he sat close to the cooking fires, obviously enjoying the warmth in his old bones.

"You survived, then," Julius said, genuinely pleased the old man had lived through the chaos of the attack. The knee was still heavily wrapped and flat against the ground to rest.

Cornix gestured in welcome, waving a piece of meat vaguely. "They couldn't kill me, right enough," he agreed, sucking dry the meat he held before pressing it into his cheek to soften enough for chewing. "There were a lot of them, I noticed." His eyes searched out Julius's, full of interest in the young man.

"Eight or nine thousand left, we think," Julius said.

Cornix frowned. "It'll take forever to kill that many," he

observed seriously as he worked the piece of meat around his mouth, ruminating.

Julius grinned at the old man. "Yes, well. Craftsmen take time over their work," he said.

Cornix nodded in agreement, a smile breaking over his wrinkled face despite himself.

Julius left him with his meal and found Gaditicus. Touring the camp together, they visited each of the sentries, who stood in threes so that there would always be one to give warning of an attack. Each group was in clear sight of the next all the way around the camp. It used a lot of men, but Julius had ordered short watches of only two hours, so the changes came quickly and the night passed without alarm.

The following day, as darkness fell early in the winter evening, they marched out of the woods and once again attacked the camp of Mithridates.

CHAPTER 25

Antonidus paced up and down the lushly furnished room, his skin mottled with anger. The only other occupant, lounging on a soft purple couch, was the corpulent figure of the senator, Cato. The eyes that watched Antonidus seemed small, lost in the fleshy expanse of the sweating face. They gleamed with intrigue as they followed the steps of Sulla's erstwhile general, tracking up and down the marble. Cato grimaced slightly as he saw the road dust that clung to Antonidus. The man should have known better than to demand a meeting before he had even washed himself.

"I have no new information, Senator. Not a scrap of it," Antonidus said.

Cato sighed theatrically, reaching out a pudgy hand to the arm of his couch and pulling himself upright. The fingers that gripped the wood were slick and sticky with sugary residues from the dinner Antonidus had interrupted. Idly, Cato sucked them clean as he waited for the irritable man to find calm. Sulla's dog had never been a patient man, he knew. Even when the Dictator had been alive, Antonidus had conspired and wheedled for more authority and action where none was needed. After the rather sordid assassination, Antonidus had acted outrageously, far exceeding his authority as he searched for the killers. Cato had been forced to throw his support behind the man when his activities were discussed in Senate, or see him brought down by those he had offended. It was a fragile protection even then and Cato wondered if the pacing general knew how close he was to destruction. Antonidus had offended almost everyone that mattered in the city in the previous months, questioning even those who were above suspicion.

Cato wondered to himself how Sulla had been able to stand the grim company of his general. He soon tired of it himself.

"Have you considered that you may not find whoever ordered the assassination?" he asked.

Antonidus stopped his pacing as he spoke, spinning to face the senator.

"I will not fail in this. It has taken longer than I thought, but eventually someone will talk or some evidence will be found that will point a bloody finger, and I will have my man."

Cato watched him carefully, noting the manic glitter of his eyes. Dangerously obsessive, he thought, considering having the man quietly removed before he caused any more trouble. The public efforts had been made, and if Sulla was not avenged, well, the city would continue regardless, whether Antonidus was successful or not.

"It could take years, you know," Cato continued. "Or you could die without finding your culprit. It would not be so strange. If anyone was going to reveal themselves or be betrayed, I did think it would happen soon after the deed, but nothing points that bloody finger of yours and may never do so. It may be time to give up the chase, Antonidus."

The black eyes bored into him, but Cato was unaffected. He cared nothing at all for the man's obsession, for all he had been content to let him run wild around the houses of Rome for a while. Sulla was dead and ashes. Maybe it was time to bring the dog to heel.

Antonidus seemed to sense the thoughts in the flat, bored expression with which Cato returned his glare.

"Give me a little longer, Senator," he asked, his angry looks replaced by a sudden wariness.

Perhaps after all, he did know how Cato protected him from the outrage of the other senators, the fat man mused. Dismissively, he looked away and Antonidus spoke hurriedly.

"I am almost sure the killing was at the order of one of three men. Any one of them could have arranged it, and they were all supporters of Marius before the war."

"Who are these dangerous men?" Cato inquired archly, though he could have reeled off the names as easily as the general. The informers reported to him before Antonidus, after all, as well they should have, with Cato's money in their purses.

"Pompey and Cinna are most likely, I think. Perhaps Cinna most of all, as Sulla was . . . interested in his daughter. And Crassus, the last of them. Those three had the money and influence to buy a murder, and they were no friends to Sulla. Or they could have acted together, with Crassus providing the money and Pompey the contacts, for example."

"You have named some powerful men, Antonidus. I trust you have not mentioned your suspicions to anyone else? I would hate to lose you," Cato said with mockery in his tone.

Antonidus seemed not to notice. "I will keep my thoughts to myself until I have proof to accuse them. They have profited by Sulla's death and openly vote against his supporters in Senate. My instinct tells me it was one of them, or they were consulted. If I could only question them to be sure!" He was practically grinding his teeth in anger, and Cato had to wait as the general's skin lost its mottling and the spasm of rage faded.

"You may not approach them, Antonidus. Those three are well protected by Senate tradition and their guards. Even if you are correct, they may yet escape you."

He said this mainly to see if Antonidus could be taunted into a complete loss of control and was gratified to see the purpling veins in the man's forehead and neck. Cato laughed and the general snapped out of his anger, bewildered by the sudden sound. How had Sulla been able to bear him? Cato wondered. The man was as open as a child and as easy to manipulate.

"The solution is an easy one, Antonidus. You hire your own assassins, being careful not to let them know you." He had his complete attention now, he noted with satisfaction. Cato felt the beginnings of a wine headache and wanted the angry little fellow to leave him.

"Send your killers to the families, Antonidus. Choose a loved wife, a daughter, a son. Leave a mark on them to show it was done for Sulla's memory. One of your arrows will hit home, and the others...? Well, they were never friends of mine. There will be advantages in having them made vulnerable for a time. Then let it be finished and imagine Sulla is at rest in a sensible fashion, as good ghosts should be."

He smiled as Antonidus mulled over the idea, the thin face lighting with bright cruelty. The lines of worry eased from the general's forehead where they had been carved over the months since the poisoning. Cato nodded, knowing he had reached his man. His thoughts turned to the possibility of a little cold meat before he slept, and he barely noticed as Antonidus bowed out of the room, moving with quick, excited steps.

Later, as he pressed food into his slowly chewing mouth, Cato sighed with irritation as his thoughts turned to the problem of his idiot son and Renius. He remembered watching the man fight in the arena and shivered deliciously as he pictured a controlled savagery that had shocked even the baying crowd of Rome to silence. A man who risked his life so cheaply would not be easy to turn. What could he offer for his son? The boy general, Brutus, was heavily in debt. Perhaps gold would sway him. Power was such a fickle thing, and where money and influence failed, as he thought they must, he would need such useful tools as Antonidus. It would have been a shame to lose him.

* * *

Alexandria paused before knocking on the gate of the estate she had known so well. The five miles from the city had been a little like turning back time for herself. She had last stood there as a slave, and memories flooded her. Being whipped by Renius, kissing Gaius in the stables, working until she dropped in wind and rain, killing men with a kitchen knife in the darkness under the walls at the height of the riots. If Julius hadn't taken her into the city, she could be working there still, broken by the years.

Old faces came back to her and the intervening time seemed to vanish, so that it took every bit of her courage to raise her hand and thump it into the heavy wood.

"Who is there?" a strange voice called, accompanied by quick footsteps to the top of the wall within. A face she did not know looked down at her, carefully blank as the slave took in her appearance and the little boy who held her hand. She raised her head defiantly under this scrutiny, looking back as confidently as she could despite her racing heartbeat.

"Alexandria. I have come to see Tubruk. Is he here?"

"Please wait for a moment, madam," the slave replied, disappearing.

Alexandria took a quick breath. He had judged her as a freewoman. She straightened her shoulders further, her confidence growing. It would be hard to face Tubruk, and she had to force herself to be calm as she waited. Octavian remained silent, still angry at the decision they had made for him.

When Tubruk pushed open the gate and came out to her, she almost wilted, gripping Octavian's hand hard enough to make him yelp. The man seemed unchanged, still the same as the rest of the world swept wildly onward. His smile was genuinely friendly and she felt some of her tension ease.

"I heard you were doing well," he said. "I can have some food brought if you're hungry."

"Thirsty, after the walk, Tubruk. This is Octavian." Tubruk bent down to look at the small boy as he edged behind Alexandria, looking worried.

"Good morning, lad. I expect you are hungry?" Octavian nodded convulsively and Tubruk chuckled. "I never knew a boy who wasn't. Come inside, I'll have refreshments brought to us."

Tubruk paused in thought for a moment.

"Marcus Brutus is here," he said, "and Renius with him."

Alexandria stiffened slightly. The name of Renius carried bitter memories. Brutus, too, was a name from her forgotten past; sweetness mixed with pain. She gripped Octavian tightly as they passed through the gate, more for her own comfort than his.

The courtyard brought bright memories back to her with a small shudder. She had stood . . . there, to stab a man who grabbed at her, and Susanna had died over by the gate. She shook her head and took a deep breath. It was too easy to become lost in the past, here of all places.

"Is the mistress at home?" she asked.

Tubruk's expression changed slightly as he replied, making him look older. "Aurelia is very unwell. You won't be able to see her, if that's what you want."

"I'm sorry to hear that, but it was you I came to see."

He led them into a quiet room that she had rarely entered in her time as a slave. The floor was warm and the room felt comfortable and lived in. Tubruk left them to arrange a meal and she began to relax even further as they waited alone. Octavian fidgeted irritably, scuffing his sandals on the rug until Alexandria stopped his swinging feet with a firm grip on his knee.

When Tubruk returned, he put down a tray with a jug and bowls of freshly sliced fruit. Octavian fell on it with delight, and Tubruk smiled at the boy's enthusiasm as he sat down and waited for Alexandria to speak.

"It's about Octavian that I want to speak to you," she said after a pause.

"Would you like me to have someone show him the stables?" Tubruk replied quickly.

She shrugged. "He knows what I'm going to say."

Tubruk filled a cup with cool apple juice for her, and she sipped at it as she collected her thoughts.

"I own a part share in a metalsmith's in the city, and we took Octavian on as an apprentice. I won't lie to you and say he was perfect. He was almost wild for a while, but he's a different boy now." She was interrupted by the sight of Octavian trying to cram melon slices into his mouth. Tubruk saw her look and stood suddenly.

"That's enough for now, lad. Go and find the stables. Take a couple of the apple pieces for the horses."

Octavian looked at Alexandria, and when she nodded, he grinned and scooped up a handful of the fruit, disappearing out of the room without another word. His footsteps echoed for a moment, then all was still again.

"He doesn't remember his father, and he was a street urchin when we took him in. You should see how he's changed, Tubruk! The boy is fascinated by the skills Tabbic teaches him. He's good with his hands and in time I think he could make a fair craftsman."

"So why have you brought him to me?" Tubruk prompted gently.

"We haven't been able to let him out onto the street for nearly a month now. Tabbic has to walk him home each evening and then come back alone in the dark. The streets aren't safe even for him these days, but Octavian has been badly beaten three times since we took him on. The first time, he had a silver ring stolen, and we think they look for him in case he is carrying something else. There's a gang of boys involved. Tabbic has complained to their masters when he knows who they are, but the third beating came right after that. It's breaking the lad, Tubruk. Tabbic made him a knife but he wouldn't take it. He said they'd kill him with it if he pulled a blade on the gang, and I think he's probably right." She took a deep breath to continue.

"His mother is desperate and I said I would ask you if you'd take him and teach him a trade. We hoped you could have him work around the estate for a year or two, then when he's older, we could take him back to the shop and he could continue with the apprenticeship." She felt she was babbling and came to a halt. Tubruk looked down at his hands and she went on hurriedly, unwilling to let him speak and refuse.

"His family are related to Julius distantly. Their grandfathers were brothers or something, or brothers-in-law. You're the only one I know who can get him away from the street gangs, Tubruk. It will save his life. I wouldn't ask if there was anyone else, but..."

"I'll take him," Tubruk said suddenly. Alexandria blinked in surprise and he chuckled. "Did you think I wouldn't? I remember when you risked your life for this house. You could have run away and hidden in the stables, but you didn't. That is enough for me. There's always work around an estate like this, even though we've lost a bit of land since you were last here. He'll earn his food, don't worry. Will you leave him here today?"

Alexandria felt like throwing her arms around the old gladiator. "Yes, if you like. I knew I could depend on you. Thank you. Will you let his mother visit him from time to time?"

"I will have to ask Aurelia, but it should be possible as long as it isn't too frequent. I'll tell her about the family link. She'll probably love the idea."

Alexandria sighed with relief. "Thank you," she said again.

They both turned their heads as quick footsteps approached from outside. Octavian came running in, his face flushed and excited.

"There are horses in the stables!" he announced, making them both smile.

"It's been a long time since there were boys in this old place. It will be good to have him here."

Octavian looked from one to another, shifting his feet nervously. "I'm staying, then?" he asked quietly.

Tubruk nodded. "Lots of hard work waiting for you, lad."

The little boy leapt in pleasure. "It's beautiful here!" he said.

"He hasn't been outside the city since he was a baby," Alexandria said, embarrassed. She took Octavian's hands in hers and held him still, her expression serious.

"Now, you do as you're told. Your mother will come out to see you as soon as you're settled. Work hard here and learn all the skills you can. Understand?"

Octavian nodded, beaming at her. She let him go.

"Thank you, Tubruk. I can't tell you how much this means to me."

"Look, lass," he said gruffly. "You are a freewoman now. You've walked the same path that I have. Even if you hadn't fought in the riot, I'd help if I could. We look out for each other now and then."

She looked at him with sudden understanding. For most of her young life, he had been the estate manager. She had forgotten he knew as much about slavery as she did, that they shared a bond she had never realized. She walked with him to the gate, the tension vanishing from her.

Brutus and Renius were there, leading two young mares and talking in low tones. Brutus looked sharply at Alexandria as he caught sight of her. Without a word, he handed the reins to Renius and rushed over to her, lifting her off the ground in a great hug.

"Gods, girl, it's been years since I saw you last."

"Put me *down*," she replied furiously, and Brutus almost dropped her at the icy tone.

"What's wrong? I thought you'd be pleased to see me after—"

"I won't be handled like one of your slave girls," she snapped. Her cheeks burned. Part of her wanted to laugh at her sudden attack of dignity, but everything was happening too quickly. Mute with embarrassment, she held up her hand, bare of the iron finger ring that marked a slave.

Brutus laughed at her. "I didn't mean to offend, mistress," he said, bowing low.

She was tempted to kick him, but with Octavian and Tubruk looking on, she had to bear his cheerful mockery. Insufferable, as he always had been. A memory of something Julius had said flashed into her mind, and as Brutus rose she swung to slap his face.

He began to move to hold her wrist, then clearly thought better of it and let her connect. His smile never faded.

"Whatever that was for, I hope it's over now," he said. "I—"

"Julius told me what you boasted about me," she broke in. This was all wrong. She wanted to sit and laugh with this young wolf of a man that she'd known, but every expression and word he spoke seemed to enrage her.

Brutus's face cleared in sudden understanding, "He said I boasted...? Oh. The clever bastard. No, I never did. He thinks ahead, does Julius. When we see him, I'll have to let him know how well it came out. He'll love this. Slapping me in front of Renius! Beautiful."

Renius cleared his throat. "I'll take your horse to the stables until you've finished playing," he muttered, leading the mares away into the gathering gloom.

Alexandria frowned after him, noting the way he

wrapped both sets of reins around his wrist with the ease of practice. No welcome from him.

Without warning, tears pricked into her eyes. Except for Octavian, nothing seemed to have changed since the night of the attack on the estate. They were all there and she was the only one who seemed to feel the years behind them.

Tubruk shifted from one foot to the other, looking down at Octavian's fascinated expression.

"Close your mouth, boy. There's work to be done before you sleep tonight." He nodded to Alexandria. "I'll leave you two alone to talk while I show Octavian his duties." He shook his head at Brutus, then led Octavian away with a firm grip.

Left alone in the darkening courtyard, Brutus and Alexandria spoke at the same time, broke off, and started to speak again.

"Sorry," Brutus tried again.

"No, I acted a fool. It's been such a long time since I was here and with Tubruk and you ... and Renius; it all came back."

"I never told Julius we'd slept together," he continued, stepping closer. She was very beautiful, he noted, one of those women who looked best in the twilight. Her eyes were large and dark and the way her head tilted up at him made him want to kiss her. He remembered how they had, once, before Marius had given him his papers for the legion post in Greece.

"Tubruk didn't say Julius was here," she said.

He shook his head. "We're still waiting for news. He was ransomed in Africa, but he should be on his way back by now. Nothing is really the same as it was, you know. You're a free-woman, I've been a centurion, and Renius has lost the ability to juggle."

She giggled suddenly at the image and he took the moment to gather her in once more. This time, she returned the embrace, though when he tried to kiss her, she turned her head slightly away.

"I can't even give you a proper welcome?" he said in astonishment.

"You are a terrible man, Marcus Brutus. I haven't been pining away waiting for you, you know," she replied.

"I have. I'm half the man I used to be," he replied with a sad shake of his head. "I want your permission to see you, and if I don't get it, I may waste away altogether."

He sighed like a broken bellows and they laughed together easily, without embarrassment.

Before she could answer, a call sounded from the lookout on the gate, making Alexandria jump.

"Riders and cart approaching," the slave called down.

"How many?" Brutus responded, stepping away from her. All trace of his flirtation vanished, and if anything, Alexandria preferred his new manner to the old.

"Three men on horses—one cart pulled by oxen. The men are armed."

"Tubruk! Renius! Primigenia to the gate," Brutus ordered. Soldiers came out of the estate buildings, a file of twenty men in armor that made Alexandria gasp.

"So Marius's old legion is with you now," she said, wonderingly.

Brutus flashed a glance at her. "Those who survived. Julius will need a general when he returns," he said. "Best if you don't go near the gate until we know what this is about, all right?"

As she nodded he left her, and away from him, she felt suddenly alone. Memories of blood came back to her and she shuddered delicately, moving toward the light of the buildings.

Tubruk came out from the stables with Octavian beside him, forgotten. Leaving the boy to wander around the stone courtyard, the estate manager climbed the gate steps and looked down at the clatter of arriving soldiers.

"Late for a visit, isn't it?" he called down. "What is your business here?"

"We come from Cato to see Marcus Brutus and the gladiator Renius," a deep voice rumbled back.

Tubruk looked down, nodding in satisfaction as he saw his archers were in position around the courtyard. They were well drilled and anyone who tried to assault the house would be destroyed in seconds. Brutus had his soldiers in a defensive ring as Tubruk signaled to him to open the gate.

"Move slowly now, if you value life and health," he warned Cato's men.

The gate opened and closed quickly as the cart and riders came in. Covered by drawn bows, the riders dismounted slowly, tension showing. Renius and Brutus approached them, and the leader nodded as he recognized the one-armed gladiator.

"My master, Cato, believes a mistake has been made. His son was wrongly sworn to Primigenia when in fact he was promised to another legion. My master understands how youthful enthusiasm could have carried him away in the Campus Martius, but regrets that he cannot serve with you. The cart is full of gold in compensation for the loss."

Brutus moved around the sweating oxen and threw back the covering on the cart, revealing two heavy chests. He opened one and whistled softly at the gold coins within.

"Your master places a high value on his son's worth to Primigenia," he said.

The soldier looked impassively at the vast wealth he had revealed. "The blood of Cato is without price. This is just a token. Is Germinius here?"

"You know he is," Brutus replied, tearing his gaze away from the gold. It would be quickly swallowed by what he owed to Crassus, but it was a huge amount to turn down, nonetheless. He looked at Renius, who shrugged, knowing it had to be Brutus's decision. It would be easy to unlock the door of Germinius's room and hand him over. Rome would appreciate the beauty of such a move, and Brutus would be known as an astute bargainer to have brought Cato to this position. He sighed. Legionaries were not the property of their commanders, to be bought and sold.

"Take it back," he said, taking a last, wistful look at the gold. "Thank your master for the gesture and tell him his son will be well treated. There should be no enemies here, but Germinius took the oath and it cannot be broken except by death."

The soldier inclined his head stiffly. "I will bear the message, but my master will be most displeased that you cannot see a way to end this unfortunate mistake. Good night, gentlemen."

The gates were opened again and without another word the small party of guards trundled out into the darkness, the cattle lowing mournfully as their driver poked and prodded them to turn their backs on the estate.

"I would have taken the gold," Renius said as the gates closed.

"No, you wouldn't, old friend. And neither could I," Brutus replied. In silence, he wondered what Cato would do when he heard.

*   *   *

Pompey called for his daughters as he walked into his home on Aventinus hill. The house was filled with the scent of hot bread, and he took a deep appreciative breath as he went through into the gardens, looking for them. After a long day of reports on the continuing offensive against Mithridates, he was exhausted. If it hadn't been so desperately important, the situation would have been almost farcical. After weeks of debate, the Senate had finally allowed two generals to take their legions to Greece. As far as Pompey could see, they had chosen the least able and least ambitious of any of the men under Senate command. The reasoning was all too clear, but such cautious generals had advanced slowly into the mainland, unwilling to take even the smallest risk. Painstakingly, they had encircled small settlements, laid siege if necessary, and moved on. It made Pompey want to spit.

He had wanted the command of a legion himself, but that desire instantly raised the hackles of the Sullans and they had voted down his appointment in a block the moment his name had appeared on the lists. The struggle to protect their careers at the expense of the city was an obscene display, as far as Pompey was concerned, yet they had forced him into line. If he raised a force of "volunteers" himself, with Crassus making the purse, he knew they'd declare him an enemy of the Republic before he'd reached the ships. Daily, the frustration grew as the reports revealed an almost complete lack of achievement. They hadn't even found the main army yet.

He rubbed the bridge of his nose to relieve some of the pressure. It was cool in the gardens, at least, though the breezes failed to calm his temper. To have the robe of the Senate gripped by such small dogs! Angry little terriers with no imagination and no sense of glory. Shopkeepers, and Rome was run by them.

Pompey walked slowly through the gardens, his hands clasped tightly behind his back, lost in thought. Gradually, he felt the tensions of the day disperse. For years, it had been his habit to break the working day from his home life with a short stroll in the peaceful gardens. Refreshed, he could join his family at the evening meal and laugh and play with his daughters, the miserable Senate forgotten until the new dawn.

He almost missed the body of his youngest girl, lying facedown in the bushes near the outer wall. When his eyes glanced that way, he began a smile of recognition, expecting her to leap up and embrace him. She loved to surprise him as he came home, dissolving into fits of laughter as he jumped in shock.

He saw blood on her dress in dark brown stains and his face went slowly slack, drooping in a grief he couldn't begin to resist.

"Laura? Come on, girl, get up now."

Her skin was very white and he could see a butcher's cut where her neck met the patterned cloth of her child's dress.

"Come on, darling, up you get," he whispered.

Someone crossed to her and sat down in the damp leaves by her small limbs.

He stroked her hair for a long time as the sun set and the shadows lengthened slowly around them. He knew vaguely that he should be calling for help, shouting, crying, but he didn't want to leave her, even for the time it would take to summon his wife. He remembered carrying her on his shoulders in the summer and the way she would copy everything he said in her high, clear voice. He had sat with her through teething fevers and sickness and now he was with her for the last of it, gently murmuring to her, tugging the collar of the dress higher to cover the red-lipped wound that was the only bright color of her.

After a time, he stood and walked stiffly into his house. Time passed and a woman screamed in grief.

CHAPTER 26

Mithridates looked out into the dawn mists, wondering if another attack would come. He pulled his heavy cloak around his shoulders and shivered, telling himself it was just the morning cold. It was hard not to feel despair.

The night attacks had grown in daring and hardly anyone slept easily in the sprawling camp anymore. Each evening, they would decide the sentries with lots, and those who were chosen would turn their red-rimmed eyes to each other and shrug, already expecting death. If it did not come, they would walk back into the protection of the main camp with a return of confidence that would last until they next took the wrong token from the pot as it was passed around.

Too often they did not return. Hundreds of sentries missed the roll call each dawn. Mithridates was sure more than half were quietly deserting him, but it looked as if the camp was surrounded by an invisible enemy who could pick and choose each kill at a whim. Some of the sentries were found with arrow wounds, the barbs carefully taken from their flesh to be used again. It did not seem to matter how many men stood watch together, or where he placed them, each day brought fewer men back into the camp.

The king glared into the damp mist that seemed to clog his lungs with winter cold. Some of his men believed they were being attacked by the ghosts of old battles, spreading tales of ancient white-bearded warriors glimpsed for a moment before they disappeared, silently. Always in silence.

Mithridates began to pace along the line of his men. As exhausted as their king, they nonetheless had their weapons ready and stood alertly waiting for the mist to lift. He tried to smile at them and lift their morale, but it was hard. The impotence of having lives whittled away for week after week had taken the heart out of too many of his men. He shuddered again and cursed the white mist that seemed to linger over the tents while the rest of the world woke. Sometimes he thought if he could just find a horse and ride quickly away, he would break into sunshine and look back to see only the valley covered in the shroud.

A body lay untouched between tents. The king paused and looked down at it, angry and ashamed that the young warrior had not been buried. That, even more than the listless stares of his men, told him how far things had gone since they first staked the hills and toasted success and the destruction of Rome. How he *hated* that name.

Perhaps he should have marched his army away, but always came the nagging thought that moving them onto the plains was what the enemy hoped for most of all. Somewhere, hidden from his scouts, was a legion of men with a commander who was like no one Mithridates had ever met. He seemed to want to destroy them in pieces. Sudden flights of arrows would spit the bodies of anyone wearing an officer's helmet or carrying a standard. It had reached the point where men had refused to take up the flags and bore the punishment whipping rather than invite a death they saw as inevitable.

It was an evil thing to watch the morale fall from such heights. He'd given orders to the groups of sentries to kill any man who tried to desert, but even more had disappeared the night after, and he still didn't know if they were dead or had run away. Sometimes he would see just a pile of their armor, as if they had shrugged off the metal with their honor, but occasionally the piles were spattered with blood.

Mithridates the king rubbed his tired face roughly, bringing color to his cheeks. He couldn't remember the last time he had slept, not daring drunkenness now, with the chance of attack at any time in the night. They *were* like ghosts, he thought leadenly. Deadly, quick-moving spirits that left white flesh on the grass behind them.

His sons had worked out units of reinforcement, so that there were always fresh fighters in support, but it hadn't worked. Mithridates wondered if his men were hanging back, unwilling to be the first to reach the enemy and be killed. When the Romans had vanished, the reinforcements would arrive with a great roaring and crashing of shields and swords, forming rings around the wounded and shouting insults into the night, but it seemed like a futile kind of spite, a coward's final blow or sneer when safe.

The mist began to thin and Mithridates pinched his cheeks with his powerful thumbs to ward off the cold. Soon he would receive the night's report of sentries lost, and he hoped it would be one of those times when every man arrived back dazed at their good fortune, staggering from the relief after hours of tension and fear. Those were rare nights now.

On one occasion, he had tried to ambush the enemy with a force of a hundred hidden near two of the sentry positions. Every one of them had been found long dead and cold the following day. After that, he hadn't tried again. Ghosts.

A breeze lifted around him and he pulled his cloak even tighter. The mist swirled and boiled away in minutes, revealing the dark plain. Mithridates froze in fear as he saw the lines of soldiers waiting in silence. Perfect ranks of legionaries, their armor glittering painfully in a silver blur. Two cohorts. A thousand men. Two thousand feet away, waiting for him.

His heart thudded painfully under the wide muscles of his chest, making him feel light-headed. He heard the shout go through the camp as his surviving officers roused the men to stand and run to their positions. Panic touched him then. A thousand men on one side. Where were the rest?

"Send out the scouts!" he bellowed. Runners raced to the backs of horses, galloping through the lines of the camp.

"Archers to me!" he continued, his order passed down the line. Hundreds of bowmen began to converge on the cloaked figure. He gathered their officers around him.

"It'll be a ruse, a trick. I want you to protect this side of the camp. Send every shaft you have at them to keep them away. Kill them all if you can. I will guard the head, where the main attack must come. Spend every arrow without stinting. They must not hit our rear as the others attack. Morale would not survive it."

The officers nodded and bowed, stringing their bows expertly even as they straightened up. Their faces showed the first touches of excitement, the joy of power that comes from sending death in stinging swarms while your own men stand safe.

Mithridates left their units to form and took his horse from the groom that held it, cantering through the camp to the head. The despair lifted from him and he sat straighter in the saddle as he saw his men standing ready all around. It was day and even ghosts could be killed in the day.

*   *   *

Julius stood in the right flank of the veterans, at the head of Ventulus cohort. Three lines of one hundred and sixty men stood with him; six centuries of eighty, with the veterans in the first and third and the weakest fighters in the second rank, where they could not waver or run. With Gaditicus and the men of Accipiter, they covered nearly a mile of land, silent and still. There were no more games to be played. Every one of the Wolves knew they could be dead before the sun was high, but they stood without fear. Their prayers were all said and now there was only the killing to come.

It was bitterly cold and some of the men shivered as they waited for the mist to lift. They did not speak and it was not even necessary for the newly appointed optios to crack their staffs into any of the younger men to keep them quiet. They all seemed to sense the moment, as the mist finally moved on a freshening breeze. Their heads came up almost like dogs with a scent, knowing the effect the sight of them would have.

Some of the veterans had wanted to charge while the morning mist was still thick, but Julius had told them he wanted the enemy to know fear before the final attack, and they had accepted his orders without question. After three weeks of destructive attacks on the camp, they looked with something like awe on the young commander as he marched alongside them. He seemed to be able to guess every move that Mithridates would make and counter them brutally. If Julius said it was time for one last open blow to break the Greeks, they would march where he marched, without complaint.

Julius surveyed the tent lines with curiosity, savoring the moment. He wondered which of the scurrying figures was the king, but he couldn't be sure. As the sunlight lit the valley, doubt clawed at him for a moment. Even with the losses and desertions by the hundreds over the last few nights, it was still a huge expanse that made his own force look small in comparison. He bared his teeth slightly in anticipation, pressing his doubts aside and knowing he had their measure. Many of those tents were empty.

Every day of waiting had been an agony of indecision for Julius. Captured deserters told stories of plummeting morale and poor organization. He knew everything of their officers, their equipment, and their appetite for a battle. At first, he had been content with the idea of night attacks and tearing pieces from the army until Mithridates lost his nerve and ran straight into the legions coming from the coast. But the weeks had passed without a sign of the Greeks breaking camp or Roman support appearing on the horizon.

Around the beginning of the third week, Julius had faced the possibility that legions might not come before Mithridates snapped out of his defensive lethargy and began to think like a real commander. On that night, with the Greek sentries deserting in dozens and passing only feet from his own men unknowing, Julius started to make plans for a full attack.

Now the bulk of the Greek army were forming into wide blocks of ten deep, and Julius nodded grimly, remembering lessons from his old tutor. They would not be able to bring as many swords to bear as his own wide line, but the ten ranks would prevent a rout as the enemy that had been killing them forever in the dark faced them at last on the plain. He swallowed painfully as he scrutinized the terrain, waiting for the perfect moment to give the order. He saw a tall man leap astride a horse and gallop away and then hundreds of archers form into units. They would make the air black with arrows.

"A thousand of them," he whispered to himself. His men had shields now, many of them stolen from the Greeks they had killed night after night. Even so, each successful flight would bring down a few, even as they linked the shields and sheltered under them.

"Sound the advance—quickly!" he snapped at the *cornicen,* who raised an old battered horn and blew the double note. The two cohorts stepped forward as one, thumping the Greek earth together. Julius glanced right and left and grinned savagely as he saw the veterans dress the line as they moved, almost without noticing it. No one lagged behind. The old men had hungered for the sort of attack they understood almost as much as Julius, and now their impatience could finally be released.

At first they closed slowly. Julius waited for the archers to fire and almost froze as thousands of long black splinters hummed into the air at him. The aim was good, but the veterans had faced archers all around the Roman lands. They moved without haste, crouching low and pulling in limbs, each man's shield touching his brother's beside him. It formed an impenetrable wall and the arrows thumped uselessly into the laminated wood and brass.

For a moment, there was silence, then the veterans rose as one, shouting wildly. The shields were bristling with spent shafts, but they hadn't lost a man. They moved forward twenty quick paces and then the air hummed again and they ducked down under the shields. Somewhere, a Roman cried out in pain, but they moved on three more times, losing only a few pale bodies on the field behind them.

They were close enough to charge. Julius gave the order and the triple note sounded along the line. The Wolves broke into a fast run and suddenly they were only a few hundred feet from the archers and the black cloud was passing over them.

The Greek archers held their position too long, desperate to kill the ones who had hurt them so badly. Their front rank tried to turn away from the charging Romans, but there was no order to it and the Wolves roared into their confusion, turning it into terror as they fought to get away.

Julius exulted as the Roman line went through them, cutting their way into the squares with bloody skill. The ranks of Greeks dissolved into screaming chaos after only seconds. Julius ordered Ventulus to press them and Gaditicus moved his men out slightly to the left to widen the angle of the rout.

The panic spread like a gale through the Greek ranks. With their own men yelling in terror and sprinting away from the front line and the air filled with the screams of the dying, they began to edge away from the line of Wolves, peeling off from their units and throwing their weapons away as their officers shouted helplessly at them.

More and more began to run and then suddenly there were enough of them fleeing for even the bravest to turn and join the rushing throng.

The Wolves attacked in a frenzy, the veterans cutting through the enemy with all the skill and experience of a hundred battles and the younger men with raw energy and the coursing joy that made their hands shiver and their eyes wild as they cut the Greeks down, red-limbed and terrible in their killing.

The enemy streamed away in all directions. Twice, officers tried to rally them and Julius was forced to support Accipiter to break the largest gathering of men. The knot of frightened soldiers held for less than a minute and then broke again.

The camp became a carnage of trampled bodies and broken equipment, and the veterans began to tire, arms aching after hundreds of blows.

Julius ordered the saw formation for Ventulus, where the middle rank moved right and left against the others to block gaps and support the weakest places. His cohort swept through the camp and they seemed to have been killing all day.

Gaditicus had advanced farther and it was his men who came on Mithridates and his sons, surrounded by nearly a thousand men. They seemed to act as an anchor on the deserters who ran around them, slowing their headlong flight and pulling them back to join the last stand. Julius ordered the wedge to break the line, and his men shrugged off their tiredness one last time. Julius took the second row himself, behind Cornix on point. They had to break the last stand quickly. These men had not run and they stood under the eyes of their king, fresh and waiting.

Ventulus formed the wedge as if they had fought together

all their lives. The shields came up to protect the edges of the arrowhead, and they crashed into the Greek lines, sending them reeling back into each other. Only the man at the head was unprotected, and Cornix fell in the first flurry of strikes. He rose lathered in blood and holding his stomach in with one hand while the other struck and struck until he fell again, this time not to rise. Julius took the point position, the giant Ciro moving to his side.

Julius could see Mithridates moving through his own men toward the Romans, his expression manic. As Julius felt rather than saw the forward thrust begin to falter, he could have cheered as the king shoved his own men aside to reach them. He knew the Greek king should have hung back and the Romans would not have reached him. Instead, Mithridates was roaring orders and those closest stepped back to allow him the kill.

He was a huge man, wrapped in a heavy purple cloak. He made no attempt at defense, but brought his sword down from above his head with terrible force. Julius ducked away and his answering blow was blocked with a clang that numbed his arm. The man was strong and fast. More Greeks fell all around them as the veterans roared once more and moved on, pushing the guards back and cutting them down with scores of blows. Mithridates seemed unaware as the line pressed past him, and he bellowed as he brought his sword round again in a vicious sweep at Julius's chest, sending the young man staggering back, his armor dented in a line. Both men were blowing air raggedly with exertion and anger. Julius thought one of his ribs had cracked, but now Mithridates was deep behind the front rank and Julius knew he had only to call and the king would be cut down from all sides.

With their king alone and embattled, the guards were struggling desperately to reach him. The veterans tired and fell against them, their strength faltering. Mithridates seemed to sense it.

"To me, my sons!" he shouted. "Come to me!" And their efforts doubled into a frenzy.

Julius leaned back around the outside of a blow and then cut in fast, tearing his jagged blade through the shoulder. Mithridates stumbled as Ciro stabbed him in his powerful chest, shouldering into him with an explosion of strength. The king's blood poured out and he dropped his sword from limp fingers. His eyes met Julius's for a moment, then he slipped down into the press of mud and bodies. Julius raised a red sword in triumph and Accipiter hit the Greek flank, breaking them utterly and sending them running with the last of their brothers.

*   *   *

They had no oil to burn the bodies, so Julius ordered great pits to be dug at the rear of the camp. It took a week to make them deep enough to hold Mithridates' dead. Julius had forbidden celebration with so many of the broken army still alive. The irony of having to set up an armed perimeter of the very camp he had attacked for so long did not escape him, but he knew that with the charismatic king dead, there was little chance of the survivors gathering for another attack. He hoped the nerve had been cut out of them, but though Mithridates' sons had been killed at the end, Gaditicus thought more than four thousand others had escaped, and Julius wanted to get away from the valley as soon as the last of his wounded had recovered or died.

Less than five hundred of the Wolves had survived the attack on the camp, most of their number lost in the last battle around the Greek king. Julius had them buried separately and no one complained about the work. They gave them a full funeral that lasted most of a day, and the funeral torches gave off a stinking black smoke that seemed fitting for their sacrifice.

When all the dead were in the ground and the camp was clear of wreckage, Julius gathered his officers to him. From the veterans, he chose the ten most senior centurions to represent their voice and was sad that Cornix had not survived the fight to join them, though he knew the ancient warrior had chosen the manner of his death without regret. Quertorus came with the others and it was only as they sat down together that Julius noticed Suetonius too had joined them, though he held no command. The young man's arm was heavily bound where it had been cut, and the sight of it prevented Julius from sending him away. He had earned his place, perhaps, though Julius wondered if he had enjoyed it half so much as the night attacks he seemed to relish.

"I want to move on to the coast and rejoin Durus and Prax. Somewhere between here and the sea must be a legion, unless the Senate has lost its mind completely. We will deliver Mithridates' body to them and set sail for home. There's nothing more to hold us here."

"Will you disband the men?" Quertorus asked.

Julius looked at him and smiled. "I will, but at the coast. There are too many survivors from the Greek army for me to be sending ours away now. As well as that, a number of the men I brought to your city died in the fighting, and I have gold to share out amongst the survivors. I think it would be fair to give shares to all those who survived."

"Will you take the shares from your half, then?" Suetonius said quickly.

"No, I will not. The ransoms will all be given back to their rightful owners as I promised. Whatever remains from the half will be shared out amongst the Wolves. If you don't like that, I suggest you put it to them. Tell them how they don't deserve a little gold to take back to their city and villages for what they have done here."

Suetonius subsided with a frown and the veterans watched him with interest. He didn't meet their eyes.

"How much gold are we talking about?" Quertorus asked interestedly.

Julius shrugged. "Twenty, maybe thirty aurei per man. I will have to work it out when we meet Durus."

"This man has all that gold in his ship," one of the others broke in, "and you expect him to be there?"

"He gave his word. And I gave mine to find and kill him if he broke it. He'll be there. Now, I want everyone ready to march within the hour. I've had enough of this camp. I've had enough of Greece."

He turned to Gaditicus with a wistful expression. "*Now* we can go home," he said.

*   *   *

They found the first of two legions only eighty miles inland under the command of Severus Lepidus. In the heavily fortified camp, Julius and Ciro presented the body of Mithridates to Lepidus on a bier of cut wood. Ciro remained silent as they laid the body on a low table in an empty tent, but Julius saw that his lips were moving in silent prayer, showing respect for a vanquished enemy. As Ciro finished, he felt Julius's gaze on him and returned the look without embarrassment.

"He was a brave man," Ciro said simply, and Julius was struck at the change in him since they had first met in a tiny village on the African coast.

"Did you pray to Roman gods?" Julius asked him.

The big man shrugged. "They do not know me yet. When I reach Rome, I will speak to them."

The Roman legate sent an escort of soldiers to guide the Wolves to the sea. Julius did not protest the decision, though the escort felt more like a prisoner detail than a guarantee of their own safe passage.

Durus was aboard his ship when they finally arrived at the docks and called him out. He didn't seem overjoyed that they had survived, but quickly mellowed when Julius told him he would be paid for his time as well as the passage back to Brundisium, the closest port on the Roman mainland.

It was strange to be back on a ship again and Julius spent some of his new wealth in buying every barrel of wine in the port for a final celebration. Despite Suetonius's objections, the wealth of Celsus was shared out amongst the surviving Wolves and many would return home rich by their previous standards, even after an expensive trip in the comfort of a caravan ride or on horseback.

The veterans had asked to see Julius privately one last time before they left for home in the east. He had offered them ranks with him back in Rome, but they had only chuckled and looked at each other. It was difficult to tempt men of their age who had gold in their pouches, and he hadn't really expected them to come. Quertorus had thanked him for all of them, and they had cheered him, filling the ship with the noise. Then they had gone.

Durus caught the dawn tide out without fanfare or announcement. The young survivors of the Wolves had all stayed on, and they relished the short experience as sailors, with the easy enthusiasm of the young. The seas were calm and it was only a few short weeks before they tied up at the Brundisium port and stepped down onto the land.

Those who had been there from the beginning looked at each other dazedly for long moments as three centuries of his Wolves formed into a column for the march to Rome. Freshly promoted to command a fifty, Ciro dressed the line and stood in wonder as he considered finally seeing the city that had called him. He shivered, rolling his shoulders. It was colder than his tiny farm on the African coast, but still he felt a rightness to the land. He sensed the ghosts of his line had come out to greet their son, and was proud.

Julius went down on his knees and kissed the dusty ground with tears in his eyes, too overwhelmed to speak. He had lost friends and suffered injuries he would carry for the rest of his life, but Sulla was dead and he was home.

PART TWO

CHAPTER 27

Cato wiped a pudgy hand across his brow. Even with the chill of winter still gripping Rome, the Senate building was full and the air heavy with the heat of three hundred of the nobilitas packed into the small space. Cato held up his hands for silence and waited patiently as the babble of noise slowly stilled.

"This Caesar, this *reckless* young man, has shown nothing but disdain for Senate will. Acting alone, he has caused the deaths of hundreds of Roman citizens, many of them veterans of our legions. As I understand it, he assumed an authority he was never granted and behaved throughout as I would expect a nephew of Marius to behave. I call on the body of the Senate to censure this little cockerel—to show our repugnance at his waste of Roman lives and his disregard of our authority over him."

He resumed his seat with a satisfied grunt, and the Master of Debate stood, looking relaxed. He was a large, florid man with little patience for fools. Though his authority was nominal, he seemed to enjoy controlling the more powerful men of the Senate.

Cinna had risen at Cato's words, his face flushed in anger. The Master of Debate nodded for him to speak, and Cinna swept the rows with his gaze, holding their attention.

"As many of you know, I am related to Caesar through

my daughter's marriage," he began. "I came here not to speak in his defense, but to take part in what I expected to be our just and proper congratulation." A wave of muttering from Cato's supporters prevented him from carrying on for a moment, but he waited with icy patience until they subsided.

"Should we not congratulate a man who broke one of the enemies of Rome? Mithridates lies dead, his army dispersed, and some of you speak of *censure*? It is beyond belief. Instead of counting the lives of his men lost in a battle against a larger force, think instead of those innocents who live because Mithridates was crushed. How many more of our people would have died by the time our cautious legions finally edged close enough to engage the enemy? By the reports, it seems as if they might never have reached the Greek forces at all!"

Another storm of muttering broke out, with jeers and shouts rising over the rest. Many of the senators on both sides rose to speak and fidgeted as they waited. The Master of Debate caught Cinna's eye and raised his eyebrows in question. Cinna gave way with ill grace and resumed his seat.

Senator Prandus stood at Cato's side. He was a tall, spare figure next to the bulk of his patron, and he cleared his throat slightly as he was signaled to speak.

"My son Suetonius was one of those taken by pirates with this Caesar. I have his reports on which to base my opinions, and they point to the danger of this Roman to everything we stand for. He acts without consultation of any kind. He rushes into conflict without a thought for other methods to solve a problem. His first and last answer to everything is blind attack. I have details of executions and torture carried out in his name, unsanctioned by the Senate. He compelled old soldiers into battle for little more than personal glory. I must agree with the honorable Cato that this Caesar should be called here for a just punishment for his actions. We should not forget the allegations of piracy that have been leveled against him by Quaestor Pravitas. If he is commended, as some seem to think would be correct, we may well create another Marius and come to regret our generosity in time."

Cato pushed a nervous-looking man to his feet. Senator Bibilus almost stumbled as he rose under the pressure of the heavy hands. His face was pale and beads of nervous sweat stood out on his brow. Breaking custom, he began to speak before he had received permission, and his first words were lost in the hoots of derision that followed.

"... should consider the withdrawal of Senate membership," he said, and gulped saliva from his throat. "Or possibly a ban on holding army rank. Let him be a merchant with the looted gold he has brought back with him."

As he spoke, the Master of Debate glared stonily at him, and a brief gesture sent Bibilus back to his seat, his face burning with embarrassment. The Master of Debate looked grim and turned to face the opposing benches, clearly determined to redress the balance with his choices. Crassus was given leave to speak. He nodded thanks and stared calmly around the packed rows until there was a proper stillness once more.

"How you do reveal your secret fears!" he snapped. "Another Marius, you say. His nephew! How we must tremble! It sickens me. Did you think our precious Republic could survive without military power? How many of you here have commanded men in successful battles?" His gaze swept the rows, knowing that Cato had served only the two-year minimum to see him up the political ladder. Other heads nodded while Cato stifled a yawn and looked away.

"We have a young man who knows how to lead soldiers," Crassus continued. "He gathered a small army and routed a force eight or nine times their size. True, he acted without first seeking our approval, but he could hardly have waited a year or two until we had finished discussing it!"

The Master of Debate caught his eye, but Crassus ignored him.

"No, what causes such poisonous spite in some of us is the shameful fact that this young man has shown our choice of legion commanders to be wrong. His success is proof that we did not act with enough energy and speed to defend our possessions in Greece. *That* is what rankles with these gentlemen. That is the only reason for their anger against him. Let me remind you that he won the oak wreath for his bravery at Mytilene. He is a gifted, loyal soldier of Rome, and it would shame us not to recognize that publicly. I hear Bibilus murmuring about having him stripped of legion rank, and I ask myself, what victories has Bibilus brought to us? Or Cato? And there is Prandus hinting at piracy when he knows the charges were proven idiocy when the full facts came to light. No wonder he skirts such a difficult issue when his own son was one of those accused! We should laud Caesar with honors for what he has done."

"Enough, Crassus," the Master of Debate said sternly, satisfied he had allowed enough time to repair the outburst by Bibilus. "Both sides of the debate have spoken. We can move on to a vote."

Those still standing sat down reluctantly, looking around the hall and trying to gauge the result before it had started. Before the vote could begin, the massive bronze doors to the chamber swung open and Pompey entered, causing a new stir of interest. Since the death of his daughter a week before, he had not been seen anywhere near the forum or the Senate, and there were many whispered questions about his tragedy and what would come of it.

The Master of Debate motioned to Pompey, indicating a seat for him in the rows. Instead of sitting, Pompey walked to his place and stood waiting to be recognized.

Sighing, the Master of Debate raised his hand toward him. All noise ceased as every eye fastened on the new arrival.

Cato in particular watched him with glittering intensity, taking in every detail. The daughter's ashes could not have been long in the ground, but no signs of that grief showed on the man's face. He seemed calm as he looked around at the packed benches.

"Forgive my absences and my lateness, Senators. I have buried my daughter," he said quietly, without a trace of infirmity in his voice. "I make a vow before you that those responsible will regret using the innocent in games of power, but that is a problem for another day." He spoke reasonably, but those close to him could see every muscle in his shoulders was rigid, as if he held a great rage barely in check.

"Tell me, what is the vote this morning?" he asked the Master of Debate.

"It is to decide censure or approval for the actions of Julius Caesar in Greece," the man replied.

"I see. How does Cato stand on the issue?" Pompey asked without looking over to the sprawling figure that straightened suddenly in his seat.

The Master of Debate risked a glance at Cato. "He has argued for censure," he replied, bewildered.

Pompey joined his hands behind his back and those near him could see the whiteness of the knuckles as he spoke. "Then I shall vote against him."

For a long moment, he held Cato's gaze in the stillness until everyone there was aware of the new enmity between them. Whispers began as the older ones sat up with fresh interest.

"Furthermore, I call on my supporters to vote against him. I call on every vote owed me in debt. Discharge them here and clear your slate with me."

The Senate erupted into chatter as they discussed the implications of such a move. It was practically a declaration of war, and Cato set his fleshy mouth in a thin line of irritation as the Master of Debate announced the vote. By calling in all his favors at the same time, Pompey was throwing away years of careful arrangements and alliances, simply to show his contempt in public.

Crassus paled slightly. It was a foolhardy thing for Pompey to do, though he thought he understood it. No one there could doubt that Pompey had subtly identified the man responsible for his daughter's murder. Cato would lose a lot of his power while those around him weighed up this new threat and decided whether to distance themselves. He sighed. At least the vote would be won and Cato damaged by the decision. Though the numbers reflected many long-held obligations to Pompey, it was still difficult for the fat senator to stand almost alone with hundreds of his colleagues ranged against him.

The vote passed quickly and Pompey resumed his seat to engage in the discussion for the legion rank Julius would be given on his return to Senate. With most of the senators wanting to get out of the building into the cool fresh air, it was surprisingly quick and Cato hardly took part, stunned into immobility by the humiliation forced on him.

As they filed out through the bronze doors, Cato grimaced and inclined his head in Pompey's direction, acknowledging the victory. Pompey ignored him and left quickly for home without speaking to anyone.

*　　　　　*　　　　　*

Tubruk climbed the inner steps up the wall of the estate, thankful for the early warning brought in by the field slaves. He strained to see details of the marching column coming along the road toward them.

"Two or three centuries, it looks like," he called down to Cornelia, who had come out from the buildings at the summons. "I can't see standards, but they're in full armor. It could be part of the Roman garrison."

"Will you turn out the men?" Cornelia asked nervously.

Tubruk didn't reply at first, intent on his scrutiny of the

approaching force. They were well disciplined and armored, but the absence of standards worried him immensely. The death of Pompey's daughter had brought a tension back to the old families of Rome that had been missing since the death of Sulla. If such a powerful senator could suffer an attack in his own home, then no one was safe. Tubruk hesitated. If he summoned Brutus and his soldiers to guard the gate, it could be seen as provocation, or an insult to a legitimate force. He gripped the hard stone of the wall as he came to a decision. He would rather offend someone than be found vulnerable, and the approaching centuries could be assassins with all legion marks removed.

"Call Brutus. Tell him I need his men out here now!" Tubruk shouted down to Cornelia. She abandoned dignity to run back into the estate buildings.

By the time the approaching column was less than a thousand paces away, Brutus had his men in formation by the gate, ready to rush out into the attack. There were only twenty with him and Tubruk wished they'd had room for more, though he'd laughed at the young commander traveling with even that many at first.

Brutus felt the old anticipation tighten his stomach. For a moment, the child in him wished he hadn't left Renius in the city barracks, but it was a momentary weakness. As he bared his gladius, his confidence swelled and his men responded, their tension giving way to tight smiles. They could all hear the tramp of soldiers moving closer to the estate, but there was not a trace of fear in them.

A small figure ran out of the stables and skidded to a stop almost at Brutus's feet.

"You're not coming with us," Brutus snapped to forestall the request. He knew very little about the urchin Tubruk had rescued, and at that moment he lacked the patience for an argument. Octavian opened his mouth and Brutus barked an order at him, made angry by the sight of a glinting dagger in the boy's hand.

"Get away from here!"

Octavian froze, his eyes wide, then turned on his heel and stalked away without a word. Brutus ignored him, instead watching Tubruk for news of what was happening outside. It was frustrating to be waiting blind, but Brutus understood that soldiers sent by the Senate should not be met with drawn swords. Bloodshed would certainly follow, even if the original errand was an innocent one.

On the top of the wall, Tubruk squinted as the approaching army came closer, marching steadily along the road to the estate. With a deep expulsion of breath, all the tension went out of him in an instant, unseen by those below.

"Marcus Brutus," he called down, "I request that you have your men open the gate and go out to meet them."

Brutus looked up at him quizzically. "Are you sure? If they're hostile, we can defend better from within the walls."

"Open the gates," Tubruk replied quietly, with a peculiar expression on his face.

Brutus shrugged and gave the order to the men of Primigenia, who drew their swords as they moved forward. His heart pounded and he felt the wild joy that came from his certainty. There was no one alive who could beat him with a blade, not since a day with Renius in the same yard, many years before.

"All right, you old devil, but if I get killed, I'll be waiting for you when it's your time!"

        *   *   *

Julius saw the armed men come out of the gates and stiffened. What had happened?

"Ready weapons!" he snapped suddenly and his men lost their cheerful expressions on the instant. What had seemed a victorious return had suddenly become edged with danger.

Cabera jumped at the order, scanning the unknown force with a squint. He reached out a hand to catch Julius's attention, but thought better of it and grinned to himself, raising his dagger and gesticulating furiously with it. He was enjoying himself tremendously, but his mood wasn't shared by the soldiers around him. They had been expecting a hero's welcome after too many hard months of travel and killing. Their expressions were savage as their swords came out one more time.

"Line formation!" Julius ordered, seething. If his house had been taken, he would destroy them, leaving nothing alive. His heart twinged for his mother and Tubruk.

He ran a professional eye over the soldiers deploying before the walls. No more than twenty, though they could have others hidden inside. Legionaries. They moved well, but he would trust his Wolves against any other soldiers anywhere, and they had the numbers. He put all thoughts of his family aside and prepared to give the order to charge.

*   *   *

"Sweet Mars! They're going to attack!" Brutus exclaimed as he saw the column swing out into an offensive formation. As he saw the numbers against him, he was tempted to order his men back into safety, but there wouldn't be time to close the gates and the enemy would cut them to pieces as they retreated.

"Secure the gates, Tubruk!" he bellowed. The old fool had completely misjudged the threat and now there was a price to be paid.

To Brutus's pride, the men of Primigenia didn't falter as they understood the fact of their inevitable destruction. They took their positions close to the estate wall and readied weapons, unstrapping javelins to throw as the charge came. Each man carried four of the long spears, and many of the enemy would fall to them before they were close enough for swords.

"Steady . . ." Brutus called over the heads of his men. Just a few more paces and the advancing lines would be in range.

Without warning, the order to halt rang out and the opposing ranks shuddered to a disciplined stop. Brutus raised his eyebrows in surprise, scanning the faces of the enemy. He caught sight of Julius and suddenly laughed out loud, to the bemusement of those around him.

"Stand down!" he ordered his twenty and watched as they restrapped their javelins and sheathed their swords. When everything was back in place, he marched them toward the halted soldiers, chuckling.

Julius spoke first.

"Have you *any* idea how close I just came to carving you up?" he asked, grinning.

"I was thinking much the same thing. My men would have dropped a couple of spears through you before you came ten paces closer. Still lucky, I see."

"*I* recognized you," Cabera interjected smugly.

Brutus whooped to see the old man still alive. All three embraced, to the complete confusion of the battle lines surrounding them. Julius broke away first and noticed the three linked arrows on Brutus's breastplate.

"Gods! That's Primigenia, isn't it?"

Brutus nodded, his eyes bright. "I have command, though we're a little understrength at present."

"How much understrength?"

"By about four thousand men, as it happens, but I am working on it."

Julius whistled softly. "We have a lot to talk about. Does Tubruk know I'm back?"

Brutus looked over his shoulder at the white walls of the estate. The figure of the estate manager raised an arm in greeting from the top. Cabera waved back enthusiastically.

"Yes, he knows," Brutus replied, smiling wryly.

"I'm going to have to find barracks in the city for my men," Julius said. "They can set up tents on the estate while I see to a few matters, but I need somewhere permanent for them as well as training facilities."

"I know just the place and the man to train them," Brutus responded. "Renius came back with me."

"I'll need him, and you," Julius replied, already planning.

Brutus smiled. His heart felt light as he looked on his old friend. There were new scars on his face that gave him a harsher look than he remembered, but it was still the same man. On impulse, he put out his arm and Julius gripped it firmly, caught up in the same emotion.

"Is my wife safe?" Julius asked, searching Brutus's face for news.

"She's here, with your daughter."

"I have a daughter?" Julius's smile stretched right across his face in a foolish beam. "Why are we standing here? A daughter! Come on!"

He called a quick order to set up camp around the walls and rushed off, with Brutus marching his twenty behind, his mind whirling. There was so much to tell Julius. About Sulla's murder, and Pompey's daughter, the Senate gossip his mother told him. Julius would have to meet Servilia! With Julius back, it seemed as if the world was steady again, and Brutus felt his worries lift away. With his old friend there to help him, he would remake Primigenia back to its old strength, beginning with the men Julius had brought with him. Julius made problems seem easy and he of all people would understand why the "Traitor's Legion" had to be reborn.

Brutus laughed as he came face-to-face with Tubruk, who had waited for him inside the gate with a wry expression of amusement.

"Good eyes for a man of your age," he said to the old gladiator.

Tubruk chuckled. "A soldier pays attention to details, like who the commander is," he said cheerfully.

Brutus shrugged off his embarrassment. "Where's Julius rushed off to?"

"He's with his wife and daughter, lad. Give him a little time alone with them."

Brutus frowned slightly. "Of course. I'll take my men back to the city barracks and stay the night there. Let him know where I am."

"I didn't mean . . . you don't have to leave, lad," Tubruk said quickly.

Brutus shook his head. "No. You're right. This is a time for him to be with his family. I'll see him tomorrow." He turned stiffly and ordered his men into a marching column outside the gates.

Cabera wandered into the estate yard, beaming at everything. "Tubruk!" he called. "You are going to feed us well, yes? It's been such a long time since I had good wine and those civilized little dishes you Romans are so proud of. Do you want me to see the cook? I liked that man, he was a fine singer. Are you well?"

Tubruk lost the frown that had creased his forehead as Brutus marched away. It was impossible not to be touched by the wave of enthusiasm Cabera seemed to bring with him wherever he went. He had missed the old man as much as anyone and came down the steps to greet him.

Cabera saw the old gladiator glance after Brutus and patted his shoulder.

"Let the boy go. He always was a prickly one, remember? They will be like brothers again tomorrow, but Julius has a lot of catching up to do first."

Tubruk blew air out of his cheeks and gripped the slender shoulders of the healer with rekindling enthusiasm. "The cook will despair when he sees how many he has to feed, but I promise you, it will be better than the rations you're used to."

"Aim much higher than that," Cabera replied seriously.

*   *   *

Cornelia turned quickly when she heard running footsteps. For a second, she didn't recognize the officer standing there, tanned and thin from his travels. Then his face lit with pleasure and he stepped forward to wrap his arms around her. She held him tightly, breathing in the smell of his skin and laughing as he lifted her to the points of her feet.

"It's been such a long time without you," he said, his eyes sparkling over her shoulder as he pressed the air out of her. Her ribs ached by the time he let go, but she didn't care at all.

For a long time, Julius was able to forget everything but the beautiful woman in his arms. At last he put her down and stepped back, holding her hand as if unwilling to let her stray from him again.

"You're still gorgeous, wife," he said. "And I hear we have a daughter."

Cornelia pursed her lips in irritation. "I wanted to tell you myself. Clodia, bring her in now," she called, and her nurse entered quickly enough to make it obvious that she had been standing outside waiting for them to finish.

The little girl looked around with interest as she was brought to her parents in Clodia's arms. Her eyes were the same soft brown as her mother's, but her hair was as dark as Julius's own. He smiled at the child and she beamed back at him, her cheeks dimpling.

"She's almost two now and a terror round the house. She knows a lot of words already when she's not too shy," Cornelia said proudly, taking her from Clodia.

Julius wrapped his arms around both of them and applied a gentle pressure.

"I used to dream of seeing you again at the worst times. I didn't even know you were pregnant when I left," he said as he released them. "Does she walk yet?"

Both Clodia and Cornelia nodded and smiled at each

other. Cornelia set her daughter down and they watched as she trotted around the room, stopping to examine everything she came across.

"I called her Julia, after you. I wasn't sure if you were coming back and..." Cornelia's eyes filled with tears and Julius held her tightly again.

"All right, wife, I made it home. That's an end to it."

"Things were...difficult for a while. Tubruk had to sell some of the land to pay the ransom."

She hesitated before telling him everything. Sulla was dead, thank all the merciful gods. It would only hurt Julius to know what she had suffered at his hands. She would warn Tubruk to say nothing.

"Tubruk sold some of the land?" Julius said in surprise. "I had hoped...no, it doesn't matter. I'll get it back. I want to hear everything that has happened in the city since I left, but it will have to wait until I have had a long bath and changed my clothes. We came straight here from the coast without entering the city." He raised a hand to stroke her hair and she shivered slightly at the touch. "I have a surprise for you," he said, calling in his men.

Cornelia waited patiently with Clodia and her daughter while Julius's men brought in their packs, piling them in the center of the room. Her husband was still the same whirlwind of energy she remembered. He called for servants to show the men the way to the wine stores with orders to take as much as they needed. More were dispatched on a dozen errands and the house came to scurrying life around him. Finally, he closed the door and beckoned Cornelia over to the leather packs.

She and Clodia let out unwilling gasps as they saw the shine of gold coins inside as he undid one flap. He laughed with pleasure and showed them more and more of them, full of bars or coin in silver and gold.

"All the ransom and four times as much again," he said cheerfully as he retied the packs. "We will buy our land back."

Cornelia wanted to ask where he had found such wealth, but as her eyes traveled over the white scars on his dark arms and the deep one on his brow, she stayed silent. He had paid heavily for it.

"Tata?" came a little voice, and Julius laughed as he looked down and found the small figure with her hands upraised to be held.

"Yes, my darling girl. I am your father, come home from the ships. Now I am for a good soak and a fine meal before sleep. The thought of being in my own bed is a pleasure I can hardly describe."

His daughter laughed at his words and he hugged her.

"Gently! She's not one of your soldiers, you know," Clodia said, reaching up to take her.

Julius felt a pang as the child left his arms and he sighed with satisfaction as he looked at them all.

"There's so much to do, my darling," he said to his wife.

*　　　　　*　　　　　*

Too impatient in the end to wait, Julius had called for Tubruk to report to him while he bathed the dust and filth of the journey from his body. The hot water turned a dark gray after moments of scrubbing, and the heat made his heart thump away some of the weariness.

Tubruk stood at the end of the narrow pool and recited the financial dealings of the estate over the previous three years, as once he had for Julius's father. When Julius was finally clean, he seemed younger than the dark warrior who had first come into sight at the head of a column. His eyes were a washed-out blue, and when the rush of energy from the hot water faded, Julius could barely stay awake to listen.

Before the young man could fall asleep in the pool, Tubruk handed him a soft robe and towels and left him. His step was light as he walked down the corridors of the estate, listening to the songs of the drunken soldiers outside. For the first time since the event, the guilt that had plagued him over his part in the death of Sulla lifted as if it had never existed. He thought he would tell him when all the business of his return to Rome was settled and things were quiet again. The murder had been done in his name after all, and if Julius knew, Tubruk would be able to send anonymous gifts to the families of Casaverius, Fercus, and the parents of the young soldier who had stood against him at the gate. Especially Fercus, whose family were almost destitute without him. Tubruk owed them everything for their father's courage, and he knew Julius would feel the same.

He passed Aurelia's door and heard a low keening from the room inside. Tubruk hesitated. Julius was too tired to rouse and he hadn't yet asked after his mother. Tubruk wanted nothing more than to go to his own bed after a long day, but then he sighed and went in.

CHAPTER 28

The messenger from the Senate arrived the following dawn. It took Tubruk some time to rouse Julius, and when he finally greeted the Senate runner, he was still less than fully alert. After so many months of tension, the one night in his own home had done little to remove the bone-deep exhaustion.

Yawning, Julius rubbed a hand through his hair and smiled blearily at the young man from the city. "I am Julius Caesar. Deliver your message."

"The Senate requires you to attend a full council at noon today, master," the messenger said quickly.

Julius blinked. "That's all?" he asked flatly.

The messenger shifted slightly. "That is the official message, master. I do know a little more, from the gossip amongst the runners."

"Tubruk?" Julius said, and watched as the estate manager passed over a silver coin to the man.

"Well?" Julius asked when the coin had disappeared into a hidden pouch. The messenger smiled.

"They say you are to be given the rank of tribune for your work in Greece."

"Tribune?" Julius looked at Tubruk, who shrugged as he spoke.

"It's a step on the ladder," the estate manager replied

calmly, indicating the messenger with his eyes. Julius understood and dismissed the runner back to the city.

When they were alone, Tubruk clapped him on the back. "Congratulations. Now are you going to tell me how you earned it? Unlike the Senate, I don't have messengers to run all over the place for me. All I have heard is that you beat Mithridates and overran an army twenty times your size."

Julius barked a surprised laugh. "Next week it will be thirty times the size, as the Roman gossips tell the story. Perhaps I shouldn't correct them," he said wryly. "Come for a walk with me and I'll tell you all the details. I want to see where this new boundary is."

He saw Tubruk's sudden frown and smiled to ease the man's worry.

"I was surprised when Cornelia told me. I never thought you of all people would sell land."

"It was that or send the ransom short, lad, and there's only one son of the house."

Julius gripped his shoulder in sudden affection. "I know, I'm only teasing you. It was the right thing to do and I have the funds to buy it back."

"I sold it to Suetonius's father," Tubruk said grimly.

Julius paused as he took this in. "He would have known it was for the ransom. He had to raise one for his son, after all. Did you get a good price?"

Tubruk replied with a pained expression. "Not really. He drove a very hard bargain and I had to let more of it go than I wanted. I'm sure he saw it as good business, but it was"—he screwed his face up as if something bitter had entered his mouth—"shameful."

Julius took a deep breath. "Show me how much we've lost and then we'll work out how to get the old man to return it to me. If he's anything like his son, it won't be easy. I want to be back for when my mother wakes, Tubruk. I have a ... great deal to tell her."

Something stopped Julius telling Tubruk about the head wound and the fits that came after it. In part, it was shame at the lack of understanding he had shown his mother over the years, which he knew he had to put right. More than that, though, he didn't want to see pity in the old gladiator's eyes. He didn't think he could bear it.

Together, they walked out of the estate and up the hill to the woods that Julius had run through as a boy, Tubruk listening as Julius told him everything that had happened in the years he had been away from the city.

The new boundary was a solid wooden fence right across the path where Julius remembered digging a wolf trap for Suetonius years before. The sight of it on land that had been in his family for generations made him want to break it down, but instead he leaned on it, deep in thought.

"I have enough gold to offer him far more than the land is worth, but that sticks in my throat, Tubruk. I don't like to be cheated."

"He'll be at the Senate meeting at noon. You could sound him out there. We may be misjudging the man. Perhaps he will offer to return the land for what he paid for it," Tubruk said, his doubts showing clearly.

Julius knocked his knuckles on the solid fence and sighed. "Somehow I doubt that. Suetonius must be home by now and we fell out about a few things on the ships and in Greece. He won't be wanting to do me any favors, but I am getting my father's land back. I'll see what Marcus thinks."

"Brutus now, you realize? Did you know he made centurion with the Bronze Fist? He'll be wanting your advice about Primigenia as well."

Julius nodded and smiled at the thought of being able to talk again with his old friend. "He must be the youngest general Rome has ever had," he said, chuckling.

Tubruk snorted. "A legate without a legion, then." He sobered suddenly, his eyes becoming cold with memory.

"Sulla had the name struck from the legion rolls after Marius's death. It was awful in Rome for a while. Nobody was safe, not even the Senate. Anyone Sulla named as enemy of the state was dragged out of their home and executed without trial. I thought of taking Cornelia and the baby away, but..." He caught himself, remembering what Cornelia had said to him as he returned to his own room from Aurelia's the night before, while Julius lay deeply asleep.

The old gladiator felt torn between his loyalties to Julius and to Cornelia. His relationship with both of them was far closer to fatherly love than the professional duty of an estate manager. He hated to keep secrets, but he knew that what had happened with Sulla should be hers to tell first.

Julius didn't seem to notice his preoccupation, lost in thought himself.

"Thank the Furies that bastard's dead, Tubruk. I don't know what I'd have done if he'd lived. I suppose I could have written to you to take my family out of the country, but a life in exile would have been the end of me. I can't describe what it felt like to touch my feet on Roman soil again after so long. I hadn't really known the strength of it until I left, you understand?"

"You know I do, lad. I don't know how Cabera can stand to wander as he does. A rootless life is beyond me, but then perhaps we have deeper roots than most, here."

Julius let his gaze pass over the green-shadowed woods that held so many memories, and his resolve firmed. He would have back what had been taken.

Another thought struck him. "What of Marius's house in the city?"

"It is lost," Tubruk said without looking at him. "Sold at auction when Sulla was declared Dictator. A great deal of property changed hands by his order. Crassus bought some of it, but for the most part the bidding was a farce, with Sulla's supporters taking the best."

"Do you know who lives there now?" Julius asked, his voice tight with anger.

Tubruk shrugged. "It was given to Antonidus, Sulla's general, or rather he paid a tiny amount of its worth. They called him Sulla's dog for his loyalty, but he gained a great deal from his master."

Julius clenched a fist slowly. "That is a problem I can settle today, after the Senate meeting. Does he have many soldiers at his command, this Antonidus?"

Tubruk frowned as he understood, then a smile tugged at his mouth. "A few house guards. He has a nominal rank, which no one has thought to take from him, but he is not linked to a particular legion. You have the men to turn him out if you do it quickly."

"Then I shall do it quickly," Julius replied, turning away from the fence and looking back toward the estate. "Will my mother be awake by now?"

"She usually is. She doesn't sleep much these days," Tubruk replied. "Her illness is the same, but you should know she grows weaker."

Julius looked with affection on the old gladiator, whose emotions were always closer to the surface than he pretended. "She would be lost without you," he said.

Tubruk looked away and cleared his throat as they began to walk back to the estate. His continuing duty to Aurelia was not open for discussion, despite the fact that it had been more and more in his thoughts over the previous few months. He thought of her when he looked at Clodia and admitted the affection that had sprung out of nothing to surprise him. Cornelia's nurse was a gentlewoman and she had made it clear that she shared the quiet love he felt for her. Yet there was Aurelia to care for and he knew he could never retire to a small house in the city while there was still that obligation in his life, even if they could buy Clodia free of slavery as she seemed so sure they could. There was little to be gained in worrying about the future, he reflected as they neared the estate. It made a mockery of planning, every time. All they could ever do was be ready for the swift turns and changes it would bring.

Octavian was waiting for them at the gate. Julius looked at him blankly as they drew abreast, pausing in surprise as the small boy bowed deeply to him.

"And who is this?" he said, turning to Tubruk, amazed to see him blushing in embarrassment.

"His name is Octavian, master. I did tell him I would present him to you when there was time, but he has lost his patience *yet* again, I see."

Octavian paled slightly at the criticism. It was true that he hadn't been able to wait, but he hadn't disobeyed so much as assumed Tubruk would have changed his mind, which was entirely different, he thought.

"Tubruk is looking after me for my mother," he said brightly to Julius. "I am learning how to fight with a gladius and ride horses and—"

Tubruk cuffed him gently to stop the recitation, his embarrassment growing. He had meant to explain the situation to Julius, and was mortified to have it thrust on him without a moment to prepare.

"Alexandria brought him," he said, sending Octavian tottering away with a push in the direction of the stables. "He is a distant relative of yours, from your grandfather's sister. Aurelia seems to like him, but he's still learning his manners."

"And how to fight with a gladius and ride horses?" Julius asked, enjoying Tubruk's confusion with gentle amusement. Seeing the estate manager flustered was a new experience for him, and he was quite happy to allow it to run for a while.

Tubruk scratched the back of his ear with a grimace and looked after Octavian as the little boy finally took the hint and trotted out of sight.

"That was my idea. He was being hurt by apprentices in

the city, and I thought I could show him how to take care of himself. I was going to clear it with you, but . . ."

Julius cracked with laughter, made worse by Tubruk's stunned expression.

"I've never seen you so nervous before," Julius said. "I think you have taken a liking to the little puppy?"

Tubruk shrugged, irritated by the change in mood. Typical of Octavian to ignore his orders yet again. Each day seemed to start afresh for him, with his lessons or punishments completely forgotten.

"He has a hardy spirit for a lad so young. He reminds me of you sometimes, now we've cleaned him up a little."

"I won't question anything you have done in my absence, Tubruk. If your judgment was good enough for my father, it will always be good enough for me. I'll see the lad properly when I return this evening or tomorrow. He was a bit small to be fighting on the backstreets of the city, wasn't he?"

Tubruk nodded, pleased Julius hadn't objected. He wondered if it was the right moment to mention that the boy had his own room in the house and his own pony in the stables. Probably not.

Still smiling, Julius went into the main buildings, and Tubruk was left alone in the yard. A flicker of movement from the stables registered in his vision and he sighed. The boy was spying again, probably worried that his pony would be taken away, the only threat that had any effect on him.

*   *   *

Julius sat silently in his mother's dressing room and watched while a slave applied the oils and paints that went some way toward hiding her wasted condition. The fact that she had allowed him to see her without the aids worried him as much as the actual shock of how thin and ill looking she had become. For so long, he had promised himself that he would reveal his understanding of her sickness and achieve a companionship of sorts from the rubble of his childhood. As the moment had come, he couldn't think how to begin. The woman sitting in front of the mirror was almost a stranger to him. Her cheeks had sunk into darkened hollows that resisted the paints the slave applied, showing through the lighter colors like a shadow of death that hung over her. Her dark eyes were listless and weary and her arms were so pitifully thin it made him wince to look at them.

Aurelia had known him, at least. She had greeted him with tears and a delicate embrace that he returned with infinite care, feeling as if he could break the fragile thing she had become. Even then, she gasped slightly as he held her, and guilt swept over him.

When the slave had packed her materials into an elegantly veneered case and bowed out of the room, Aurelia turned to her son and essayed a smile, though her skin crinkled like parchment under the applications of false colors.

Julius struggled with his emotions. Cabera had said his condition was different from his mother's, and he knew she had never suffered a wound like the one that had nearly killed him. Even so, they had something in common at last, though the gulf seemed unbridgeable.

"I . . . thought of you a great deal while I was away," he began.

She didn't reply, seemingly transfixed by the examination of her face in the polished bronze. Her long, thin fingers rose to touch her throat and hair as she turned this way and that, frowning at herself.

"I was injured in a battle and ill for a long time," Julius struggled on, "and afterward a strange fit would come over me. It . . . reminded me of your sickness and I thought I should tell you. I wish I had been a better son to you. I never understood what you were going through before, but when it happened to me it was like a window opening. I'm sorry."

He watched her shaking hands smooth and caress her

face as he spoke, their movements becoming more and more agitated. Worried for her, he half rose out of his seat and the movement distracted her so that she turned her face to him.

"Julius?" she whispered. Her pupils had widened darkly and her eyes seemed unfocused as they passed over him.

"I am here," he said sadly, wondering if she had heard him at all.

"I thought you had left me," she went on, her voice sending a shudder through him.

"No, I came back," he said, feeling his eyes prickle with grief.

"Is Gaius all right? He's such a willful boy," she said, closing her eyes and lowering her head as if to shut out the world.

"He is . . . well. He loves you very much," Julius replied softly, bringing up his hand to clear the tears that stung him.

Aurelia nodded and turned back to her mirror and her contemplation. "I am glad. Would you send in the slave to tend me, dear? I will need a little makeup to face the house today, I think."

Julius nodded and stood looking at her for a moment.

"I'll fetch her for you," he said, and left the room.

*   *   *

As the noon shadow marked the sundial of the forum, Julius entered the great expanse with his guards, taking a direct route to the Senate building. As he crossed the open space, he was struck by the changes in the city since he'd left. The fortifications Marius had raised along the walls had been dismantled, and there were only a few legionaries to be seen. Even they were relaxed, walking with their mistresses or standing in small groups chatting, without a sign of the tension he had expected. It was a city at peace again and a shudder passed through him as he walked over the flat gray stones. He had brought ten soldiers of his command into the city, wanting them close while he was out of armor and in his formal robe.

Such a precaution seemed unnecessary and he didn't know if he was pleased or sorry. The battle for the walls was as fresh in his mind as if he had never left, but the people enjoying the spring sunshine laughed and joked with each other, blind to the scenes that flashed into his mind. He saw Marius fallen again and the clash of dark figures as Sulla's forces cut down the defenders around their general.

His mouth twisted in bitterness as he considered how young and full of joy he had been that night. Fresh from the marriage bed, he had seen all their dreams and planning crushed and his own future altered forever. If they had beaten Sulla, if they had only beaten Sulla, Rome would have been spared years of brutality and the Republic might have regained some of its former dignity.

He halted his men at the bottom of the wide marble steps, and despite the contented mood in the forum, he told them to remain alert. After the death of Marius, he had learned it was ultimately safer to expect trouble, even by the Senate building.

Leaving his men to stand in the sun, Julius looked up at the studded bronze doors that had been unbarred for the assembly. Senators stood in pairs and threes, discussing the issues of the day as they waited for the gathering to be called. Julius saw his father-in-law, Cinna, with Crassus and walked up the steps to greet them. They had their heads close together as they talked, and Julius saw anger and frustration on their faces. Crassus was still the thin brown stick of a man Julius remembered, disdaining any sign of his wealth in his simple white robe and sandals. He had seen Cinna last at his wedding to Cornelia, and of the pair of senators, he had changed the most in the intervening years. As he turned to greet Julius, the younger man was struck by the wrinkles that had cut into his face, the visible effects of his worries. Cinna smiled tiredly at him and Julius returned it uncomfortably, never having got to know the man properly.

"'The wanderer returns to us, his sword and bow at rest,'" Crassus quoted. "Your uncle would be proud of you if he were here."

"Thank you. I was just thinking of him," Julius replied. "Seeing the city again is hard after so long, especially here. I keep expecting to hear his voice."

"It was forbidden even to mention his name while Sulla was alive, did you know?" Crassus asked, watching him for a reaction.

Only a slight tightening of the mouth betrayed the young man's feelings. "Sulla's desires meant little to me while he lived; less so now," he said flatly. "I would like to visit the tomb of Marius after the Senate meeting, to pay my respects."

Crassus and Cinna exchanged glances and Crassus touched him on the arm in sympathy.

"I'm sorry, his remains were taken and scattered. It was some of Sulla's soldiers, though he denied it. I think that was why he left instructions to be cremated himself, though friends of Marius wouldn't stoop so low."

He dropped his hand as Julius tensed with anger, visibly struggling to remain controlled. Crassus spoke calmly, giving him time to compose himself.

"The Dictator's legacy still plagues us in the form of his followers in Senate. Cato is first amongst them, and Catalus and Bibilus seem content to follow his lead in everything. I believe you know Senator Prandus, whose son you were captured with?"

Julius nodded. "I have some business to discuss with him after the meeting today," he replied, once again giving the outward appearance of calm. Surreptitiously, he held his right hand in his left, suddenly worried that the emotions that swelled in him would begin a fit on the very steps of the Senate and disgrace him forever. Crassus affected not to notice anything was wrong, for which Julius was grateful.

"Have a care with Prandus, Julius," Crassus said sternly,

leaning in close so that the senators entering the building couldn't overhear them. "He has powerful connections with the Sullans now, and Cato counts him as a friend."

Julius inclined his head even closer to Crassus and whispered harshly, "Those who were friends to Sulla are enemies of mine."

Without another word, he turned from the pair to ascend the final steps to the doors and disappear into the shadowed hall within.

Crassus and Cinna looked at each other with guarded surmise as they followed at a slower pace.

"Our aims converge, it seems," Cinna said quietly.

Crassus nodded curtly, unwilling to discuss it further as they moved amongst their colleagues to their seats, passing enemies and friends alike.

Julius felt the vibrant energy of the gathering as soon as he entered it. There were few vacant places and he had to take a position in the third row back from the speaker's rostrum. He took in the sights and sounds with satisfaction, knowing he had finally returned to the heart of power. Seeing so many strangers, he wished for a moment that he had stayed with Crassus and his father-in-law for them to name the new faces. For the moment, however, he was content just to watch and learn, overlooked by the predators until he had better defenses. He smiled tightly to himself at the vision of battle that the Senate represented to him. It was a false one, he knew. Here, the enemies could be the ones who greeted him most fondly, then set assassins on him as soon as they turned away. His father had always been disparaging of the bulk of the nobilitas, though he'd admitted a grudging respect for the few that held honor above politics.

The assembly became quiet and an elderly consul Julius did not know began the day's oath. As one, they stood for the solemn words: "We who are Rome pledge our lives for her peace, our strength for her own, and our honor for her citizens."

Julius repeated the chanted words with the others and felt the beginnings of excitement. The heart of the world was beating still. He listened with utter concentration to the agenda of discussions they would undertake, and managed to remain outwardly unaffected as the consul came to "the post of tribune to be awarded to Gaius Julius Caesar for his actions in Greece." A few of those who knew him turned to watch his reaction, but he showed them nothing, pleased for the warning he had bought from the messenger. He resolved to hire advisers there and then to help him understand every one of the issues of the day. He would need expert jurists to prepare the law cases he would undertake as soon as he was awarded the first post of his political career. He was grimly certain that the first trial before magistrates would be against Antonidus after he took back his uncle's house. That the arguments would have to involve a public defense of Marius gave him a great deal of satisfaction.

Cato was easy to recognize by his bulk, though Julius didn't remember seeing him on his only other visit to the Senate house, years before. The senator was obscenely large and his features almost seemed to have been smothered in the billowing folds of flesh, so that the real man looked out from somewhere deep within the face. He had a coterie of friends and supporters around him, and Julius could see from the deference shown that he was a man of influence, even as Crassus had warned. Suetonius's father was there and their eyes met momentarily before the older man looked away, pretending he hadn't seen. A moment later the man whispered something in Cato's ear, and Julius found himself the subject of a stare that seemed amused rather than worried. With an impassive expression, Julius marked the man in his mind as an enemy. He noted with interest the way Cato's eyes flickered to fasten on Pompey as he entered and took a seat his own supporters had held for him.

Julius too watched Pompey, judging the changes in the man. The tendency toward softness of flesh had gone from Pompey's figure. He looked trim and hard-muscled as a soldier should, a greyhound compared to Cato. His skin was burned dark and Julius remembered he had spent time in Spain overseeing the legions there. No doubt the task of dealing with the rebellious tribes of the provinces had melted the fat from him.

Pompey rose smoothly for the first item and spoke on the need for a force to be sent against the sea pirates, estimating they had a thousand ships and two thousand villages and towns in their control. Given his own bitter experiences, Julius listened with interest, a little shocked that the situation had been allowed to get so far out of hand. He was amazed when others stood to refute Pompey's figures and argue against stretching their forces further.

"I could clear the seas in forty days if I had ships and men," Pompey snapped in return, but the vote passed against him and he took his seat again, his brows knotted in frustration.

Julius voted in three other matters, noticing Pompey, Crassus, and Cinna matched his views on each occasion. On all three they were defeated and Julius felt his own frustration rise. A slave revolt near Vesuvius had proved difficult to put down, but instead of sending a crushing force, the Senate gave permission for only one legion to deal with them. Julius shook his head in disbelief. He hadn't realized at first how cautious the Senate had become. From his experiences with Marius and his own battles, Julius knew an empire had to be strong to survive, yet many of the senators were blind to the problems facing their commanders around the Mare Internum. At the end of an hour of speeches, Julius had a far better understanding of the annoyance felt by men like Prax and Gaditicus at the ditherers of the Senate. He had expected to see a nobility of action and aspect to match the oath they had taken, not petty bickering and factions opposing each other.

Lost in these thoughts, he missed hearing the next item and only the sound of his own name broke his reverie.

"... Caesar, who shall be awarded the post of military tribune with all rights and honors in our thanks for the defeat of Mithridates in Greece, and the taking of two pirate vessels."

All the senators stood, with even Cato levering himself ponderously onto his feet.

Julius grinned boyishly as they cheered him and pretended not to notice the ones who stood in silence, though he marked every face as his gaze swept round the packed rows.

He sat down with his heart beating in excitement. A tribune could levy troops and he knew three hundred not far away who would be the first to join his command. Cato caught his eye and nodded to him, testing. Julius returned the gesture with an open smile. It would not do to warn the man he had a new enemy.

*   *   *

As the bronze doors were once again thrown open to admit daylight into the Senate house, Julius moved quickly to intercept Suetonius's father as he made his way out.

"I would like a word, Senator," he said, interrupting a conversation.

Senator Prandus turned to him, raising his eyebrow in surprise. "I can't imagine that we have anything to discuss, Caesar," he replied.

Julius ignored the cold tone and went on as if the matter were between friends. "It's the land my estate manager sold you to pay my ransom. You know I was successful in getting the gold back, including your own son's. I would like to meet with you to discuss the price to return it to my family."

The senator shook his head slightly. "I'm afraid you will be disappointed. I have wanted to expand my holdings for some time, and I have plans to build another house there for my son once those woods have been cleared. I'm sorry I can't help you."

He smiled tightly at Julius and would have turned back to his companions. Julius reached out and took his arm, only to have his grip shaken off with a quick jerk. Senator Prandus's face flushed with anger at the touch.

"Have a care, young man. You are in the Senate house, not some distant village. If you touch me again, I will have you arrested. From what my son has told me, you are not the sort of person I want to do business with."

"He may also have mentioned that I am not a good person to have as an enemy," Julius murmured, keeping his voice low so that it would not be overheard.

The senator froze for a moment as he considered the threat, then turned away stiff-necked to catch up with Cato as he passed through the doors.

Thoughtfully, Julius watched him go. He had expected something similar from the man, though the news of a house to be built on his old land was a blow. At the peak of the hill, it would look down on his estate, a position of superiority that would no doubt give Suetonius enormous satisfaction. He looked around for Crassus and Cinna, wanting to speak to them before they left for their homes. In a way, what Suetonius's father had said was true. Using force in Rome would lead quickly to disaster. He would have to be subtle.

"First is Antonidus, though," he muttered under his breath. Force would do very well there.

CHAPTER 29

Walking through the city at the head of his ten soldiers sparked painful memories as Julius made his way to the street of Marius's old home. He remembered the excitement he'd felt as the storm of energy around the general had caught him up in its wake. Each street and turning reminded him of that first clattering journey to the Senate, surrounded by the hardest men of Primigenia. How old had he been then, fourteen? Old enough to understand the lesson that the law would bend for strength. Even Sulla had quailed before the soldiers in the forum, on stones made wet with the blood of the heaving crowds. Marius had been granted the Triumph he wanted and the consulship that followed, though Sulla had brought him down at the end. Grief sat heavily on Julius as he wished for just one more moment with the golden general.

None of Julius's men had ever seen Rome before, and four of them were from small villages along the African coast. They struggled not to stare, but it was a losing battle as they saw the mythical city made real before their eyes.

Ciro seemed awed simply by the numbers of people they passed in the bustling streets, and Julius saw the city with fresh eyes through the big man's reactions. There was nowhere like it in the world. The smells of food and spices blended with shouts and hammering, and woven through the crowds were tunics and togas of blue and red and gold. It was a feast of the senses and Julius enjoyed their wonder, remembering how he had ridden at Marius's shoulder on a gilded chariot, every street filled with cheering people. The sweet glory of it was mixed in memory with the pain of what came after, but still, he had been there, on that day.

Even with only the largest roads named, Julius remembered the way without difficulty, almost unconsciously taking the exact route he had taken on his first visit after passing through the forum. Gradually, the streets became less crowded and cleaner as they rose above the valley of winding tenements and climbed the paved hill road that was lined with modest doors and gates, each hiding splendor within.

Julius halted his men a few hundred feet from the gate he remembered, and approached alone. As he drew up to it, a small, stocky figure dressed in a simple slave tunic and sandals came up to the bars to greet him. Although the man smiled politely, Julius noticed his eyes flicked up and down the road with automatic caution.

"I have come to speak to the owner of the house," Julius said, smiling and relaxed.

"General Antonidus is not here," the gatekeeper replied warily.

Julius nodded as if he had expected the news. "I will have to wait for him then. He must have the news I carry."

"You can't come in while—" the man began.

With a jerk of his arm, Julius reached through the bars as he had once seen Renius do. The gatekeeper pulled back as he moved and almost made it, but Julius's fingers found a grip in the tunic and yanked him hard into the bars.

"Open the gate," Julius said into the man's ear as he struggled.

"I won't! If you knew the man this house belongs to, you wouldn't dare. You will be dead before sunset unless you let me go!"

Julius heaved with his whole weight to jam the man

against the bars. "I do know him. *I* own this house. Now open the door or I will kill you."

"Kill me then—you won't get in, even so," the man snapped, still struggling wildly.

He filled his lungs to call for help and Julius grinned suddenly at his courage. Without another word, he reached through the bars with his other hand and took the key to the gate from the man's belt. The gatekeeper gasped in outrage and Julius gave a low whistle for his men to approach.

"Hold this one and keep him quiet. I need both hands to work the lock and bar," Julius ordered. "Don't hurt him. He's a brave man."

"Help!" the gatekeeper managed before Ciro's heavy hands clamped his mouth.

Julius fiddled the key into the hole in the plate and smiled as it clicked. He raised the bar and the gate swung open as two guards clattered into the courtyard beyond, their swords raised.

Julius's men moved in quickly to disarm them. Against so many, the two guards dropped their swords as they were surrounded, though the gatekeeper went crimson with rage as he watched. He tried to bite Ciro's hand and was cuffed roughly in response.

"Tie them up and search the house. Do not spill blood," Julius ordered, watching coolly as his men broke into pairs to search the house he knew so well.

It had hardly changed. The fountain was still there and Antonidus had left the gardens as he had found them. Julius could see the spot where he had kissed Alexandria and could have traced his way to her room in the slave quarters without a guide. It was easy to imagine Marius bellowing laughter somewhere out of sight, and Julius would have given a great deal at that moment to see the big man once again. The sudden sadness of memory weighed him down.

He didn't recognize any of the slaves or servants that were

brought out and tied in the courtyard by his men, working with cheerful efficiency. One or two of his legionaries bore scratches on their faces from a struggle, but Julius was pleased to see that none of the prisoners had been harmed even so. If he was to be successful in appealing a law case and reestablish his right to the house as surviving heir, he knew it was important that it was achieved peacefully. The magistrates would be members of the nobilitas, and any stories of bloodshed in the middle of the city would prejudice them against him from the start.

It was quickly done and, without any further discussion, his men lifted the captive bundles out onto the street, the gatekeeper last of all. He had been gagged to stop his shouting, but still champed in anger as Ciro deposited him on the road. Julius closed the gate himself and locked it with the key he had taken from him, winking at the furious figure before he turned away.

His men were in two ranks of five before him. It was not enough to hold the house against a determined assault, and the first thing he had to do was send a couple as runners back to the estate to fetch a full fifty of his best fighters. It was all very well to plan for a court case, but whoever actually held the house in his possession would have a clear advantage and Julius was determined not to lose it when Antonidus returned.

In the end, he sent three of the fastest runners wearing messenger tunics taken from the house stores. His main worry was that they would become lost in the unfamiliar city, and he cursed himself for not bringing someone from the estate to help them find their way back to the Tiber bridge.

When they had gone, he turned to his men, a slow smile spreading on his face.

"I told you I would find you quarters in Rome," he said.

They chuckled, looking about them appreciatively.

"I need three of you to stay on guard by the gate. The others will relieve them in two hours. Stay alert. Antonidus will come back before the day is much older, I'm sure. Summon me when he arrives."

The thought of that conversation cheered him immensely as the guards took up their positions. The house would be secure by evening and then he could turn his attention to rebuilding Marius's name in the city, if he had to fight the whole of the Senate to do it.

*　　　　　*　　　　　*

Brutus and Cabera were at the estate when two of the messengers arrived from Julius, the third some miles behind. Well used to command, Brutus quickly organized a fifty and began the fast march back to the city. Julius couldn't have known that so many soldiers would have been stopped from entering, so Brutus had them remove their armor and swords. He sent them into the city in pairs or threes to gather again out of sight of city guards, who were the eyes of the Senate in Rome. Last to come through was the cart full of their weapons, and Brutus stayed with that to bribe the gate captain. Cabera pulled a bottle of wine from under the coverings to press into the man's hand with coins, and with a conspiratorial wink, they were let through.

"I don't know whether to be pleased or appalled at how easy that was," Brutus muttered as Cabera whipped the reins on the pair of oxen that pulled the heavy cart. "When this is over, I'll be tempted to go back to that guard and have a word with him. It wasn't even a large bribe."

Cabera cackled as he made the reins crack in the air. "He would have been too suspicious if it was. No, we paid just enough to make him think of us as wine dealers avoiding the city tariff. You look like a guard and he probably thought of me as the wealthy owner."

Brutus snorted. "He thought you were a cart driver. That tatty old robe of yours doesn't look much like a wealthy owner to me," he replied as they wound on through the streets. Cabera snapped the leather reins again in irritation as a response.

The cart blocked the road neatly, with its wheels fitting between the stepping-stones used by the walking crowds. There was nowhere to pass or turn and their progress toward Marius's house was slow, though Cabera enjoyed shouting at the other drivers and shaking his fist at anyone who dared to cross in front of them. Four of Julius's men fell in behind them, obviously pleased to have the cart to follow through the tortuous maze of streets. Neither Brutus nor Cabera dared look back at them, though Brutus wondered how many would still be wandering through the markets at sunset. His directions had been simple enough, he was sure, but then after months of working with Primigenia at their barracks as well as his trips to see his mother, he knew Rome as well as anybody. Pretending to check the wheels under them, Brutus looked around and was relieved to see the number of followers had grown to nine of the men Julius had wanted. He hoped they wouldn't make it too obvious, or the curious people of Rome would quickly be joining them and an impromptu procession would arrive at Marius's old house, with the cart at the head and any attempt at stealth ruined.

As they turned in to the hill that led up to the great house he remembered so vividly, Brutus saw a gesticulating figure shouting at someone inside the gate. At least the road was wide enough so that stopping on it would not bring all the traffic in the area to a shuddering halt, he thought gratefully.

"Get out and check the wheels or something," he hissed to Cabera, who clambered down with an ill grace and walked around the cart, pronouncing "Wheel" as he came to each one. The shouting man at the gate didn't seem to notice the laden cart that had stopped just down from him, and Brutus risked another glance back, blinking in surprise at the group of men who had assembled behind him. Even worse, they had fallen into ranks and, despite their clothing, looked exactly what they were—a group of legionaries pretending to be citizens. Brutus leapt out of the cart and ran over to them.

"Don't stand to attention, you fools. You'll have every house in the area sending guards out to see what you're doing!"

The men shuffled around uncertainly and Brutus raised his eyes in exasperation. There was no help for it. Already the servants and guards at nearby gates had come right up to the bars for a look at the milling group of soldiers. Distantly, he could hear cries of alarm sounding around them.

"Right. We can forget secrecy. Get your swords and armor from the cart and follow me to the gate. Quickly! The Senate will have a fit when they find we have an army in the city."

All uncertainty banished, the relieved soldiers grabbed their equipment and laced it tight without any fuss. It took only a few minutes and then Brutus told Cabera to stop the inspection of the cart that had continued without pause, his announcement of each wheel growing increasingly weary.

"Now forward," Brutus growled, his cheeks flushing at the gathering number of onlookers. They marched toward the gate in perfect ranks, and for a second, he was distracted from his embarrassment by a quick professional assessment of the men following him. They would do very well for Primigenia.

*   *   *

Antonidus was pale with anger by the time Julius had finished explaining his position.

"You dare!" he bellowed. "I will appeal to the Senate. This house is mine by right of purchase, and I will see you dead before you steal it from me."

"I have stolen it from no one. You had no right to offer money for property that was my uncle's," Julius replied calmly, rather enjoying the man's fury.

"An enemy of the state, his lands and wealth confiscated. A traitor!" Antonidus shouted. He would have liked nothing better than to reach through the bars and grab the insolent young man's throat, but the guards that watched him within had their swords drawn and his own two were badly outnumbered. He thought through what Julius might find in the rooms of the house. Was there any evidence linking him to Pompey's daughter? He didn't think so, but the thought nagged at him, lending a wild edge of panic to his outrage.

"A traitor named by Sulla, who attacked his own city?" Julius replied, his eyes narrowing. "Wrongly named, then. Marius defended the Senate from a man who would set himself up as Dictator. He was a man of honor."

Antonidus spat in disgust on the ground, his spittle almost touching the hem of the still-bound gatekeeper.

"*That* for his honor," he roared, taking the gate bars in his hands.

Julius motioned one of his men forward and Antonidus was forced to drop his hands away.

"Do not think to put your hands on anything I own," Julius said.

Antonidus would have replied, but a sudden clatter of legion sandals from down the hill made him pause. He glanced at the sound and a leer stole over his features.

"Now you will see, you criminal. The Senate has sent men to restore order. I will have you beaten and leave you on the street as you have left my men."

He stepped away from the gate to greet the newcomers. "This man has broken into my house and abused my servants. I want him arrested," he said to the nearest soldier, flecks of white gathering at the corners of his mouth from his exertions.

"Well, he has a friendly face. Let him keep it," Brutus replied, grinning.

For a few seconds, Antonidus did not understand, then slowly he took in the numbers of armed men who stood against him and noted their lack of legion insignia.

He backed away slowly, his head coming up in defiance. Brutus laughed at him.

Antonidus went to stand between his two guards, who shifted nervously at being identified as his before so many possible enemies.

"The Senate will hear me," Antonidus rasped, his voice hoarse from shouting.

"Tell your masters to set a date for a hearing. I will defend my actions within the law," Julius replied, finally unlocking the gate for Brutus to bring the men in off the street.

Antonidus glared at him, then turned on his heel and strode away, his pair of guards following.

Julius stopped Brutus with a touch on his arm as he passed.

"Hardly the quiet gathering I envisaged, Brutus."

His friend pursed his mouth, unable for a moment to meet his eyes. "I got them here, didn't I? You have no idea how hard it is to bring armed men into this city. The days of Marius slipping in a fifty here and there are gone."

Cabera joined them, strolling through the open gate with the last of the soldiers.

"The guards at the city gate thought I was a prosperous merchant," he said lightly.

Both Julius and Brutus ignored him, their eyes locked together. Finally, Brutus bowed his head slightly.

"All right, it could have gone more smoothly."

The tension between them disappeared as he spoke and Julius grinned.

"I did enjoy it when he thought you were from the Senate, though," he said, chuckling. "Just that moment was probably worth the public arrival of the men, I think."

Brutus still looked rueful, but a smile stole slowly over his face in response. "Perhaps. Look, the Senate will hear from him about you having this many men. They won't allow it. You should think about moving some out to the Primigenia barracks."

"In a while, I will, but we need to make a few plans first.

My other centuries at the estate should be brought in as well."
A thought struck Julius. "How is it that the Senate doesn't object to Primigenia in the city?"

Brutus shrugged. "They're on the legion rolls, don't forget, but the barracks are actually outside the walls on the north side, near the Quirinal gate. I have one of the best training grounds in Rome, *and* Renius as sword master. You should see it."

"You've done so much, Brutus," Julius said, gripping his shoulder. "Rome will not be the same now we're back. I'll bring my men to you as soon as I'm sure Antonidus won't try again."

Brutus held the arm, his enthusiasm spilling over. "We do need your men. Primigenia has to grow. I won't rest until it's back to the old strength. Marius—"

"No, Brutus." Julius dropped his arm. "You have misunderstood me. My men are sworn to me alone. They cannot be under your command." He didn't want to be hard on his friend, but it was better to be clear from the start.

"What?" Brutus replied, surprised. "Look, they aren't part of any legion and Primigenia has less than a thousand men. All you have to do—"

Julius shook his head firmly. "I will help you with recruiting, as I promised, but not with these. I'm sorry."

Brutus looked at him in disbelief. "But I am rebuilding Primigenia for *you*. I would be your sword in Rome, remember?"

"I remember," Julius replied, taking his arm again. "Your friendship means more to me than anything except for the lives of my wife and daughter. Your blood is in my veins, do you remember *that*? Mine is in yours." He paused and gripped the held arm tightly. "These men are my Wolves. They cannot be under your command. Let this go."

Brutus pulled his arm away with a jerk, his face hardening. "All right. You keep your Wolves while I struggle for every new recruit. I will return to my barracks and my own men. See me there when you want to bring your soldiers in. Perhaps we can discuss the fees for their lodging then."

He turned away and twisted the key in the gate to open it.

"Marcus!" Julius called to his back.

Brutus froze for a moment, then opened the gate and walked away, leaving it swinging behind him.

*   *   *

Even in the company of his two remaining guards, Antonidus kept his hand on the dagger in his belt as he made his way through the dark alleys. Narrow as they were, at night there were too many places for the raptores to lie in wait for him to relax. He breathed through his mouth as he walked, trying to ignore the pools of foul water that had ruined his sandals in the first few steps away from the main streets. One of his men stifled a curse as his foot skidded through a heap that was fresh enough not to be completely cold.

Daylight rarely reached this part of Rome, but at night the shadows took on a fearful aspect. There was no law there, no soldiers who could come, and no citizens who would dare answer a call. Antonidus gripped his dagger even more tightly, starting as something scrambled away from their footsteps as they passed. He didn't investigate, but stumbled on almost blind, counting the corners by feeling them out with his hands. Three corners from the entrance, then four more down to the left.

Even in the night, the alleys carried the foot traffic that the bulk of Rome would never see. There was little conversation between the people they saw, and that muted. Hurrying figures passed the three men without acknowledgment, skirting the filthy pools with their heads down. Where single torches lit the path for a few paces, the people stepped around the light, as if to fall within its scope was to invite disaster.

Only his fury made Antonidus push on, and even then it was not without fear. The man he had met had told him never to come uninvited into these streets, but losing his home gave him a courage born in anger. Even that was fading in the dark and the rising discomfort.

At last he reached the point he had found before, a cross path between mildewed walls, somewhere deep in the heart of the warren. He paused to look for his man, his eyes straining in the darkness. Water dripped slowly onto stone nearby and a sudden scuffle of feet made his men spin round nervously, flourishing their own daggers before them, as if to ward off spirits.

"You were told not to seek me out until the last night of the month," a sibilant voice said by the general's ear.

Antonidus almost fell in panic, his feet slipping on the wet stones as he jumped in horror at the closeness. His dagger cleared his belt in reaction, but his wrist was clamped in a grip that held him helpless.

The man who faced him wore a cloak and hood of dark rough cloth, his features covered, though it was hardly necessary in the inky blackness of the alleyways. Antonidus almost gagged at the strange sweet scent coming from him. It was the smell of disease, of soft corruption masked with perfumed oil, and he wondered afresh whether the cloak hid more than just identity. The dark man leaned so close as to almost touch his ear with the hidden lips.

"Why have you come clattering in here, disturbing half my watchers with your noisy fumbling?"

The voice was a hiss of anger and so close that it carried the sweetness in a rush of warm breath that made Antonidus want to gag. He shuddered in reaction as the hood touched his cheek lightly.

"I had to come. I have more work for you and I want it done quickly."

The grip strengthened on his wrist, almost to the point

of pain. Antonidus could not turn his face to look directly at the man, for fear that their faces would touch. Instead, he looked away, trying not to grimace as the sickly odor seemed to taint every breath he took.

The dark figure tutted, a series of tiny clicks. "I have not yet found a way to Crassus's wife. It is too soon for another. In haste, my brothers die. You have not paid enough for me to lose men for you, only for the service."

"Forget Crassus. He is nothing to me now. I want you to seek out the daughter of Cinna and kill her. She must be your target now. Leave a token with Sulla's name as you did with Pompey's bitch."

Gently, he felt his wrist guided back toward his belt and, understanding, sheathed his dagger as the pressure was released. He held himself steady as he waited, not daring to show his revulsion openly by moving away. He knew that if an insult was perceived, neither he nor his men would live to see the open streets again.

"She will be well guarded. You will have to pay for the lives of those I will lose in reaching her. Ten thousand sesterces is the price."

Antonidus clamped his jaw shut over his intake of breath. Cato would cover the debt, he was sure. Was it not his idea to hire these men? He nodded convulsively.

"Good. It will be paid. I will have my guards bring the gold here on the day we discussed, as before."

"You will have to find other guards. Do not come here uninvited again or the cost will be higher," the voice whispered, moving swiftly away from him.

Quick footsteps followed and in only a moment Antonidus could feel he was alone. Gingerly, he stepped over to where his men had stood, reaching down with his hands and recoiling as he felt the wetness of their opened throats. He shuddered and walked quickly back the way he had come.

CHAPTER 30

Julius brought his men into the Primigenia barracks an hour before dawn. As Brutus had said, the buildings and training yard were impressive and Julius whistled softly under his breath as he marched in under the outer arch of the main gate, noting the well-spaced sentries and fortified positions within.

The gate guards must have been told to expect them and waved the soldiers through without a halt. Once inside, though, with the heavy gate closed behind them, Julius found himself in a killing ground similar to the one between the walls at Mytilene. Any one of the buildings that faced the main yard could have been lined with archers, and with no way to retreat, the only forward path was a narrow one that was itself interrupted with wall slits for more. Julius shrugged as his centuries halted in order, dressing their ranks until they filled the yard in a perfect square.

Julius wondered how long Brutus would keep him waiting. It was a difficult thing to predict after so long away from his oldest friend. The boy he had known would have been there already, but the man who led the remnants of Primigenia had changed a great deal in their time apart—perhaps enough to bury the boy; he didn't yet know.

With no outward sign of his impatience, Julius stood impassively with his men as the minutes stretched. He did need the barracks, and from what Tubruk had said, they were as good as Brutus claimed. With Crassus behind the purchase, the purse was heavy enough to buy the best in the city, after all. While he waited, Julius considered buying part of the barracks out of Crassus's hands. Privately, he agreed with Tubruk that the relationship the rich senator was fostering could be a thorn for the future, no matter how friendly he appeared at present.

Brutus strode out of the main building with Renius at his side. With interest, Julius saw the capped stump of Renius's left arm, though he kept his face still. Brutus looked furious and Julius's hopes died in him.

As Brutus reached him, he halted stiffly, giving the salute from one equal to another. Julius returned it without hesitation. For a second, Julius felt pain at the space that separated them before his resolve firmed. He would not give way. Brutus wasn't someone he wanted to use his wits to flatter and control. That sort of manipulation was for enemies or formal allies, not for the boy he'd caught a raven with, so many years before.

"Welcome to Primigenia barracks, Tribune," Brutus said.

Julius shook his head at the formal tone. A touch of irritation spiked in him and he spoke to Renius, ignoring Brutus. "It is good to see you, old friend. Can't you make him understand these men are not Primigenia?"

Renius looked impassively back at him for a moment before replying.

"This is not a time to split your strength, lad. The choosing day on the Campus is over this year—there'll be no extra men for another legion. You two should stop puffing your chests at each other and make peace."

Julius snorted in irritation. "By the gods, Brutus, what would you have me do? Primigenia can't have two commanders and my men are sworn to me alone. I found them in villages and made them into legionaries from scratch. You can't expect me to hand them over to another commander after everything they've been through with me."

"I thought...you of all people would want to see Primigenia strong again."

"As a tribune, I can levy troops for you. I'll send around the country for them. I swear we'll remake Primigenia. I owe Marius as much as you, and more."

Brutus's eyes searched his own, judging his words. "But will you be building your own legion as well? Will you apply for a new name to be added to the rolls?" he asked, his voice tight with tension.

Julius hesitated and Renius cleared his throat to speak. The habit of years of obedience made them wait for him. He looked Julius in the eye, holding him.

"Loyalty is a rare thing, boy, but Brutus risked his life for you when he had Primigenia put back on the rolls. Men like Cato stand against him now and he did it for you. There's no conflict. Primigenia is your legion, can't you see that? Your men can swear to service under a new oath and still be yours."

Julius looked at the two men and it was like looking back into his childhood. Reluctantly, he shook his head. "There cannot be two commanders," he said.

Brutus stared at him. "Are you asking me to take the oath to you? To hand over command?"

"How else could you be my sword, Brutus? But I can't ask you to lay down the rank you always dreamed of having. It is too much." Julius took his arm gently.

"No," Brutus murmured, suddenly firming his resolve. "It is not too much. We have older oaths between us and I always swore I would be there when you called. Are you calling now?"

Julius took a long, slow breath, weighing his friend and feeling his heart thud in his chest with a sudden burst of speed.

"I call," he said quietly.

Brutus nodded firmly, the decision made. "Then I will take the vow with these Wolves of yours, and we will begin this day with Primigenia reborn."

*   *   *

Keeping a guard of only five of his men, Julius strode through the busy city streets following the directions Tubruk had supplied. His spirits were light as he moved through the crowds. He had his uncle's house safe in his possession and well guarded by twenty soldiers. Even more important, the problem of what to do with Primigenia had been resolved. Silently, he blessed Brutus and Renius for their loyalty to him. Even in his pride, part of him whispered that in the end he had manipulated their love for him as coldly as any enemy. There had been no other way, he told himself, but the inner voice would not be still.

Not far from Marius's house, Julius found Tabbic's shop easily. As he came close to it, excitement filled him. He hadn't seen Alexandria since his wedding day and at first had been frightened to ask Tubruk if she'd survived the vicious fighting that followed his own flight from the city. As he put his hand to the door, he hesitated, experiencing a touch of the old nervousness that had plagued him in her presence. He shook his head in amusement as he recognized the feeling, then went in, his men blocking the narrow walkway outside.

Alexandria was standing only a few paces from the door, and she turned to greet whoever had entered. She laughed at seeing him, with the simple pleasure of meeting an old friend. She was standing with a gold necklace around her throat, with Tabbic working on the catch behind her.

Julius drank in the sight of her. The gold lit her throat with its reflection, and she seemed to have found a poise or a confidence that had been missing when he knew her before.

"You look beautiful," he said, closing the shop door behind him.

"That's because I'm standing next to Tabbic here," she said lightly.

Tabbic grunted, looking up from his work. The jeweler took in the man who had entered the shop, and straightened with a hand pressed into the small of his back.

"Are you buying or selling?" he asked, removing the necklace from Alexandria's neck as he spoke. Julius was sorry to see it go.

"Neither, Tabbic. Julius is an old friend," Alexandria replied.

Tabbic nodded in guarded welcome. "The one who's looking after Octavian?"

"He's doing well," Julius said.

Tabbic sniffed, quite failing to hide a brief smile of affection. "I'm glad of it," he said quietly, before going into the back of the shop with the necklace, leaving them alone.

"You are looking thin, Julius. Is that beautiful wife of yours not feeding you?" Alexandria asked artlessly.

Julius laughed. "I've only been back a couple of days. I have Marius's old place as a town house."

Alexandria blinked in surprise. "Quick work," she said. "I thought Sulla's general was living there."

"He was. I'll have to go to the forum court to keep it, but it will give me a chance to clear Marius's name in this city."

Her smile disappeared at this reminder of harder times, and she busied her hands with removing an apron, cursing as the knot resisted her fingers. Julius wanted to step forward and help her, but resisted with an effort of will. He had been shocked to feel a surge of the old attraction to her as he came into the shop. It worried him enough to stand well clear until she had finished untying the strings herself.

You are a married man, he told himself firmly, yet he found himself blushing as she looked at him again.

"So why have you come to our humble little shop? I doubt it's just to look me up, Julius."

"It could be. I was pleased when Tubruk said you had survived. I heard about Metella taking her life." As he always had with her, he found himself fumbling for words, annoyed by his own lack of fluency.

Alexandria turned to him, her eyes glittering. "I wouldn't have left her if I'd known what she was going to do. Gods, I would have taken her with me to Tabbic's place. She was a victim, as much as the men that bastard Sulla killed on the streets. I'm only sorry he died quickly, so they say. I would have wanted it slow, for him."

"I haven't forgotten, for all the Senate seems to want to," Julius agreed, his voice bitter. A look of silent communication passed between them, a memory of those they had lost and an intimacy between them that was fresher than they could have guessed.

"You'll make them pay, Julius? I hate the thought of the gutter filth I saw then still roaming free. Rome's a dirtier place than you can see from the forum, I know."

"I'll do what I can. I'll start by making them honor Marius, which should stick hard in a few throats," he replied seriously.

She smiled again at him. "Gods, I am glad to see your face after so long. It brings the past back to me," she said, and his blush returned, making her chuckle with memory. Her confidence as a freewoman had made her almost unrecognizable, but still he felt that she was someone he could trust simply because she had been part of the old times. The more cynical voice in him suspected he was being hopelessly naive. They had all changed and Brutus should have been enough of a reminder of that already.

"I never thanked you for the money you left with Metella for when I was free," she said. "I bought a part share in this shop with it. It meant a lot to me."

He waved her thanks away with his hand. "I wanted to help you," he replied, shifting his feet.

"Did you come to the shop to see how I'd spent it?"

"No, I know I said I could have come to see you just for friendship, but as it happens..." he began.

"I knew it! You want a pendant for your wife, or a beautiful brooch? I'll make you something special to match her eyes." Her cheerfulness contrasted his more serious mood, so different from the stumbling boy she'd known.

"No, it's for the trial and after. I want to commission bronze shields to honor Marius; his likeness, his battles, even his death when the city fell. I want them to tell the story of his life."

Alexandria rubbed a hand over her bound hair, leaving a tiny smudge of gold filings on the edge. The flecks caught the light as she moved, and despite himself, Julius would have liked nothing more than to rub his thumb gently against her skin to remove them. He concentrated, irritated with himself.

She frowned in thought, taking a stylus and wax slate from a shelf.

"They should be large, maybe three feet across to be clear at a distance."

She began to scratch sketches into the pane of wax, squinting one eye almost closed. Julius watched as she brushed back a loose tendril of hair from her forehead. Tubruk had said she was good and the man's judgment was usually to be trusted.

"The first one should be a likeness. What do you think of this?"

She turned the slate around and Julius relaxed as he saw a face he recognized. The features had something of the strength he remembered, though the simple lines could never be more than an echo of the life that had filled Marius.

"It's him. I didn't know you could do that sort of thing."

"Tabbic loves to teach. I can make your shields for you, but the metal alone will be expensive. I don't want to bargain with you, Julius, but you are talking about months of work. This is the sort of thing that could make my name in the city."

"The cost isn't important. I'll trust you to set a fair price, but I'll need them in weeks, not months. The Senate won't let the trial wait for long, with Antonidus raging about his lost house. I need the best you can make as fast as you can produce them."

"Tabbic?" Alexandria called.

The grizzled metalsmith strolled out from the back room, still holding tools. She explained quickly and Julius smiled as the man's face lit with interest. Finally, he nodded.

"I can take the normal work of the shop, but the brooches on order will have to be put off. Mind you"—he rubbed his chin thoughtfully—"it might raise the price of the ones you've finished, which couldn't hurt. We'll have to hire bigger premises and a much larger forge. Let's see..." He took another slate from the shelf and together the two of them wrote and talked in low voices for a long time while Julius watched in exasperation. Finally they reached agreement and Alexandria turned back to him, the gold in her hair still bright against her skin.

"I'll take the work. The price will depend on how many failures we have to recast. I'll have to discuss which scenes you want when you have a couple of hours free."

"You know where I am," he said. "You can always come out there if you need to see me."

Alexandria fiddled idly with her stylus, suddenly uncomfortable. "I'd prefer it if you came to me," she said, unwilling to explain how the old estate had tested her strength the last time she'd passed through the gate. Julius understood what she didn't say.

"I'll do that. I might even bring that boy in when I come. Tubruk says he's always talking of you and, er... Tabbic."

"You must. We both miss him around here. His mother

goes when she can, but it must be hard on him to be away from her," she replied.

"He's a terror around the estate. Tubruk caught him riding my horse in the fields a few days ago."

"He didn't beat him?" Alexandria asked too quickly.

Julius shook his head, smiling. "He wouldn't. Luckily Renius didn't find the boy, though how he could thrash him with only one hand, I don't know. Tell his mother not to worry about him. He's my blood, I'll look after him."

"He never had a father, Julius. A boy needs one more than a girl."

Julius hesitated, not wanting the responsibility. "Between Renius and Tubruk, I daresay he'll grow straight."

"They are not his blood, Julius," she replied, holding his gaze until he looked away.

"All *right*! I'll keep him with me, though I haven't had a moment's peace since coming back to the city. I'll look after him."

She grinned impishly at him. " 'There is no greater exercise to a man's talents than the upbringing of his son,' " she quoted.

Julius sighed. "My father used to say that," he said.

"I know. And he was right. There's no future for that boy running on the streets of this city. None at all. Where would Brutus be if your family hadn't taken him in?"

"I have agreed, Alexandria. You don't need to beat it to death."

Without warning, she raised her hand to touch the white scar that crossed his forehead. "Let me look at you," she said, standing closer and whistling softly. "You're lucky to be alive. Is that why your eye is different?"

He shrugged, ready to turn the conversation away. Then the story spilled out of him, the fight on *Accipiter,* the head wound that took months to heal, the fits that remained with him.

"Nothing is the same since I left," he said. "Or everything is and I have changed too much to see it. Cabera says the fits could be with me for the rest of my life, or stop tomorrow. There is no way of telling." He held up his left hand and squinted at it, but it was steady.

"I sometimes think life is nothing more than pain with moments of joy," she replied. "You are stronger than before, Julius, even with the wound. I've found the trick is to wait through the pain and take the moments of happiness without worrying about the future."

He dropped his hand, suddenly ashamed that he had talked so intimately of his fears. It was not a burden for her, or anyone except himself. He was the head of a family, a tribune of Rome, and the general of Primigenia. Strange how he couldn't muster the sort of pleasure he knew such a dream would once have given him.

"Have you...seen Brutus?" Julius asked after a pause. She turned away and busied her hands with clearing up the tools on Tabbic's workbench.

"We are seeing each other," she said.

"Oh. I haven't told him we...um..."

Alexandria laughed suddenly, looking at him over her shoulder. "You'd better not. There's enough competition between you two without putting me in the middle."

To his astonishment, Julius recognized a spike of jealousy enter his thoughts. He struggled with it. She was not his and, except for a frozen perfect moment years before, never had been. She didn't seem to sense the private whirl of his memories as he looked at her.

"Keep him close to you, Julius. Rome is more dangerous than you know," she said.

Julius almost grinned at the thought of what he had survived just to return to it, but the fact that his life mattered to her at all sobered him.

"I'll keep him close," he said.

*   *   *

Julius dismounted from his horse to walk the last two miles to the estate outside the city. Plans swirled around his head as he strolled along with the reins wrapped around his arm. Since his return, events had moved too quickly to grasp. Gaining the tribune post, taking Marius's house and command of Primigenia, meeting Alexandria again. Julia. Octavian. Cornelia. She was like a stranger to him. He frowned as he walked along, lulled by the clicking of hooves in the dust at his side. Her memory had helped him through the worst of the captivity. The desire to return to her was a secret strength in him that overcame injury, sickness, and pain. Yet when he had finally held her, it was as if she were someone else. He hoped it would ease with time, but part of him still yearned for the wife he loved, though she was only a mile away and waiting for him.

The law case to come worried him not at all. He'd had more than six months of monotony in a ship cell to hone a defense of Marius, and if Antonidus hadn't given him the chance, he knew he would have forced the issue in some other way. Having his uncle continue as a figure of shame in the city was not something he could stand.

Cornelia came to the gate to meet him and he kissed her. Belatedly, it occurred to him that there were other things between husband and wife that he had neglected in the two nights since his return. Intimacy would restore his love for her, he was sure. With the exhaustion of his travels fast disappearing, he kissed her again, lingeringly, and preoccupied with his thoughts, he didn't notice her stiffen in sudden panic against him. He passed the horse into the care of the slave who waited in attendance.

"Are you all right?" he whispered, close to her ear. The smell of her perfume filled his lungs with coolness.

She nodded silently.

"Is the baby asleep, wife?"

She pulled her head back to look at him. "What do you have in mind?" she asked, fighting to remain calm.

"I'll show you, if you want," he said, kissing her again. Her skin was pale and beautiful as they walked together into the privacy of the house.

He felt clumsy inside the bedroom, covering his nervousness with kisses between flinging his garments onto the floor. There was something wrong in her responses, but he couldn't be sure it wasn't just the long separation. They had known each other for such a little time, all in all, that he knew he shouldn't expect an easy intimacy and coaxed her to relax by stroking her neck and running his hands lightly down her back as they sat naked together, with only a single dim lamp to make the room gold.

Cornelia bore his kisses and wanted to sob out her grief for what had been hurt in her. She had told no one about what Sulla had done, not even Clodia. It was a shame she had hoped to forget, something she had successfully pressed deep away inside her until it almost hadn't happened. She moved with Julius as he became aroused, but felt nothing except fear as the memories of the final visit of the Dictator flashed into her mind unbidden. She heard again the cry of her daughter in the cot at her bedside as Sulla pressed on her, and tears seeped slowly from her eyes as the cruelty surfaced in her memories with appalling force.

"I don't think I can, Gaius," she said, her voice breaking.

"What is it?" Julius replied, shocked at her tears.

Cornelia curled against him and he wrapped his arms around her body, resting his head on hers as sobs convulsed her.

"Has someone hurt you?" he whispered, and a great emptiness stole into his chest as he voiced the terrible thought.

She could not answer him at first, but then she began to whisper, her eyes tightly closed. Not the worst of it, but the beginning, the terror of her pregnancy, the helpless anger at knowing there was no one to stop Sulla in all Rome.

Julius felt a great sadness weight him down as he listened. Without warning, tears of rage and frustration came from him at what she had gone through. He controlled himself, viciously biting his lip against the questions he wanted to ask, the pointless stupid questions that would serve nothing except to wound both of them even further. None of it mattered, except for him to hold her and hold her until the sobbing slowly died away into tiny aching shivers.

"He is dead now, Lia. He cannot hurt you or frighten you anymore," he said.

He told her how her love had kept him strong when he thought he would go insane in the dark cell, how proud he had been at the wedding, how much she meant to his life. His tears dried with hers, and as the moon sank toward dawn, they slept, slipping away from each other.

CHAPTER 31

With the sun only two spans above the horizon, Tubruk found Julius leaning against the outer wall of the estate, a blanket over his bare chest against the morning cold.

"You look ill," the old gladiator told him. To his surprise, Julius didn't reply and hardly seemed to notice his approach. The young man's eyes were red from too little sleep, and the chill breeze sent shivers over his skin that he ignored. Tubruk could see the white traces of scars against the darker tan, a written script for old pain and struggle.

"Julius?" Tubruk asked gently. There was no response, but Julius let the blanket fall, standing only in his sandals and short bracae leggings that reached halfway down his thighs.

"I need to run for a while," Julius said, looking up at the woods on the hill above them. His voice was as cold as the breeze and Tubruk narrowed his eyes in worry.

"I'll come with you, lad, if you don't mind waiting for me," he replied, and when Julius shrugged, Tubruk returned to the house to strip off his heavy tunic and leggings.

When he returned, Julius was stretching his leg muscles slowly, and the estate manager joined him, lacing the leather ankle strips of his sandals high up on his calf.

When they were both ready, they set off together up the hill, Julius making the pace.

Tubruk ran easily for the first mile through the woods,

thankful he had not neglected his fitness. Then, when his chest began to burn with the exertion, he glanced over at Julius. He ran lightly over the broken trail, his lungs expanding his chest in long, slow breaths. Tubruk matched him, staying at his shoulder for short bursts of speed, then back to the slower pace over and over. Julius didn't speak as he pushed himself on, the sweat pouring from him in spattering droplets that stung his eyes.

After another mile, they turned out of the cool green dark of the woods and ran along the estate perimeter. Tubruk began to puff out short, painful breaths, his legs protesting. As fit as he was, no man of his age could have matched the punishing pace for long, and Julius showed not a sign of distress as he ran, as if his body's discomfort was ignored or even forgotten. His eyes were fixed in inward concentration and he didn't see Tubruk begin to hurt. The old gladiator understood somehow that it was important to be there when Julius finally ran himself out, but the effort was making flashing lights appear in his vision and his heart pounded painfully along his pulse points, creating waves of heat that added to his growing dizziness.

Julius halted without warning, resting his hands on his knees and breathing heavily. Tubruk stopped instantly, grateful for the respite. He inched over to block the path that Julius followed, hoping he wouldn't just start again after a few seconds' pause.

"Did you know about what happened to Cornelia?" Julius asked him.

Tubruk felt cold, his exhaustion irrelevant. "I knew," he said grimly. "Clodia told me."

Julius suddenly swore in violent rage, clenching his fists, his face flushing further in uncontrolled emotion. Tubruk almost took a step away from him and wondered at himself. The young man paced back and forth, his fury making his hands grasp the air for something to hold and kill. His eyes fixed on the estate manager and it took all of Tubruk's will to return the gaze.

"You told me you would protect her," Julius snarled at him, taking a step toward Tubruk that brought him only inches from the older man's face. "I trusted you to keep her safe!"

Julius raised his fist in sudden spasm and Tubruk held still, accepting the blow to come. Instead, Julius snorted and whirled away.

Tubruk spoke quietly, knowing something of the surging emotions that had stolen Julius's control.

"When Clodia told me, I acted," he said.

Julius didn't seem to hear him. "That bastard Sulla terrified her, Tubruk. He put his *filthy* hands on her," Julius said, and broke into sobs. He went slowly down onto his knees in the scrub grass, one hand covering his eyes. Tubruk crouched and put his arms around the young man, pulling him into his chest with a great heave of strength. Julius didn't resist, his voice a muffled croak.

"She thought I would hate her, Tubruk, can you believe that?"

Tubruk held him tightly, letting the sorrow work its way through. When Julius quieted at last, Tubruk let him go and looked into his face, pale with grief.

"I killed him, Julius. I killed Sulla when I heard," he said. Julius opened his eyes wide in shock and Tubruk continued, relieved to be able to say it at last, "I took a post as a slave in his kitchens and dressed his food with aconite."

Julius unfroze as he realized the danger they faced. He grabbed Tubruk's arms in a powerful grip. "Who else knows?"

"Only Clodia. I didn't tell Cornelia, to protect her," Tubruk replied, resisting the urge to break the hold on him.

"No one else? Are you certain? Could you be recognized?"

Finally angry, Tubruk reached up with his hands and

removed Julius's stiff fingers with a grunt. "Everyone who could mark me is dead. My friend of thirty years who sold me into Sulla's household died under torture without giving me up. Except for Clodia and us, there is no one else to make the link, I swear it." He looked into Julius's hard eyes and spoke slowly and with force through his teeth, guessing at his thoughts. "You will *not* touch Clodia, Julius. Do not think of it."

"While she lives, my wife and daughter are in danger," Julius replied, unabashed.

"While *I* live as well. Will you kill me too? You will have to if you hurt Clodia, on my word you will, or I will come for you myself."

The two men stood close, both of them rigid with tension. The silence between them grew, but neither one looked away. Then Julius shuddered and the manic quality went from his eyes. Tubruk remained, glaring at him, needing him to concede the point. Finally, the young man spoke.

"All right, Tubruk. But if the Sullans ever come for her, or for you, there must be no link back to my family."

"Do not ask me for that!" Tubruk replied, furious. "I have served your family for decades. I will not give my blood and hers as well! I love her, Julius, and she loves me. My duty, my love for you, will not stretch to hurting her. It will not happen.

"In any case, I know there is no path from Sulla to me, or to you. I have blood on my hands to prove it."

When Julius spoke again, his voice was heavy with weariness. "Then you must leave. I have funds enough to set you up somewhere far from Rome. I can free Clodia and you can take her with you."

Tubruk clenched his jaw. "And your mother? Who will look after her?"

All the passion faded from the younger man, leaving him exhausted and empty. "There is Cornelia, and I can hire another nurse. What other choice is there, Tubruk? Do you think I want this? You have been with me all my life. I can barely imagine not having you to run the estate, but the Sullans are still searching for the assassins, you know that. Oh gods, Pompey's daughter!"

He froze in horror as the implications of the death hit home. His voice was a hoarse whisper.

"They struck blind. Cornelia is already in danger!" he said. Without another word, he scrambled into a run back toward the estate, cutting left to the narrow bridge across the stream. Tubruk swore and raced after him, unable to close the gap on his tired legs. As soon as it had been said, the old gladiator knew Julius was right and panic touched him then. To lose Cornelia after all he had done to protect her made him want to cry out in anger as he forced a faster pace, ignoring the pain.

*   *   *

Cornelia had slept as lightly as her husband, and when the two men arrived panting back at the estate, she was with Clodia and Julia, discussing a trip into the city. She heard Julius calling for his soldiers and rose from the couch, her nervousness evident. Despite the moments of tenderness he'd shown her, he was not the man who'd left Rome in flames behind him years before. His innocence had gone from him, perhaps with the scars that he wouldn't talk about. There were times when she thought there were no more tears inside her for what Sulla had taken from both of them.

When he came storming into the room, her eyes widened nervously.

"What is it?" she asked.

Julius frowned at Clodia in response, knowing as Tubruk had that making Cornelia part of the secret would only increase her risk. Tubruk followed him in and shared a glance with the old nurse, nodding his head a fraction to confirm what she had guessed. Julius spoke urgently, relieved to find her safe. The run home had been an agony for him as he tormented himself with images of assassins creeping through the house to hurt her.

"I think you could be in danger from the friends of Sulla. Pompey lost his daughter and he was close to Marius. I should have thought of it before! It could be that those who seek to avenge the Dictator are striking at his enemies even now, hoping to catch the real assassin in their nets. I will have to send for some of Primigenia to guard you here and get messengers to Crassus. He could be another target. Gods, and Brutus even! Though he's well protected, at least."

He paced around the room, his bare chest still heaving from the sprint home.

"I will have to use guile against them, but I cannot leave those men alive. One way or another, I will have to break the back of their alliance in Sulla's name. We cannot live expecting the assassin's knife." He turned suddenly and pointed at the estate manager, standing bathed in sweat by the door.

"Tubruk, I want you to keep my family safe until this is over. If I have to be in Rome, I need someone I can trust to look after my family here."

The older man straightened with dignity. He would not mention the wild threats Julius had made on the run, but trying to guess the way Julius's constantly spinning mind would change next was beyond him.

"You want me here?" he said, the words carrying a meaning that made Julius stop his pacing.

"Yes. I was wrong. My mother needs you. *I* need you more than ever. Who else can I trust?"

Tubruk nodded his understanding, knowing the conversation on the hill would not be mentioned again. The young man who paced like a leopard was not one to dwell on the mistakes of the past.

"Who is the threat?" Cornelia asked, holding her head high against the fear that had swelled in her.

"Cato leads them, with his followers. Antonidus perhaps. Even Suetonius's father may be part of it. They will be behind it, or know of it," Julius replied. Cornelia shuddered at the name of the general she remembered. Her husband swore as a thought struck him.

"I should have killed Sulla's dog when I had the chance. He was just a few feet from me outside Marius's gate. If he had a hand in the murder of Pompey's daughter, he is more of a danger than I realized. Gods, I have been blind!"

"You must see Pompey, then. He is your ally, whether he realizes it or not," Tubruk said quickly.

"And Crassus, and your father Cinna too," Julius replied, motioning to Cornelia. "I must meet with all of them."

As Cornelia sank back onto the couch, Julius went down on one knee and took her hand in his.

"I will not let anything harm you, I promise. I can make this place a fortress with fifty men."

She saw his need to protect her in his eyes. Not love, but the duty of a husband. She'd thought she had grown numb to loss, but to see his face so cold and earnest was worse than anything.

Forcing a smile, Cornelia pressed a hand to his cheek, still warm from the run. A fortress, or a prison? she thought.

*　　　　　*　　　　　*

When riders were sighted on the road from the city two days later, Julius and Brutus roused the estate in minutes. Renius had brought fifty of Primigenia from their barracks, and by the time the riders approached the gates, it would have taken an army to breach their defenses. There were archers on every wall and Cornelia was hidden with the others in a new suite of rooms Julius had designated for exactly this purpose. Clodia had taken Julia down without an argument, but precious time had been lost moving Aurelia, who understood nothing of what was happening.

Julius stood alone in the courtyard, watching as Tubruk and Renius took their final positions. Octavian had been sent down with the women, over his furious protests. Everything became still and Julius nodded to himself. The estate was secure.

With his sword sheathed, he climbed the steps to the ledge above the gate and watched as the riders halted at a distance, made wary by the sudden show of force on the walls. A carriage moved up between them, drawn by twin horses who pranced forward a last few reluctant steps, sensing the tension. Julius watched without speaking as one of the riders dismounted and laid a cloth of silk in the dust.

Cato stepped ponderously out onto it, adjusting the folds of his toga with delicate attention. The dust of the road had not touched him, and he looked up into Julius's eyes without expression before motioning to his men to dismount and approach the gate.

Behind his back, Julius raised his fingers to signal the number of strangers. There were too few for an open attack, but Julius was uncomfortable having such a man anywhere near those he loved. He tensed his jaw as they walked into the shadow of the gate. Brutus had told him about Cato's son, but there was nothing he could do to change what had happened. Like Brutus, he would just have to see it through.

A fist thumped against the heavy beams of the gate.

"Who calls on my house?" Julius said, looking Cato in the eye below. The man stared back impassively, content to wait through the formalities. He would know better than anyone what turmoil was going on in Julius's mind. A senator could not be refused.

A soldier at Cato's side spoke loudly enough for his voice to carry into the house. "Senator Cato desires entrance on a private matter. Dismiss your men and open this gate."

Julius did not reply, instead descending into the yard and conferring quickly with Brutus and Tubruk. The defenders on the walls were brought down and sent into the buildings to await a call to arms. The others were given tasks that allowed them to remain close. It was farcical to see armed men taking horses from the stable and grooming them in the open, but Julius was not in the mood for risk and as he opened the gate himself, he wondered if blood would be spilled in the next hour.

Cato passed through the gate, smiling slightly as he saw the numbers of armed men in the area.

"Expecting a war, Caesar?" he said.

"A legion must drill, Senator. I would not like to be caught unprepared," Julius replied. He frowned as Cato's men entered behind their master. He had to allow it, but he thanked his house gods for his foresight in bringing so many of Primigenia out of the city barracks. Cato's men would be dead in seconds if he gave the order. Their faces showed they understood this as well as anyone as their horses were led away, leaving them exposed in the open courtyard.

Cato looked at him. "Are you now the general of Primigenia, then? I do not recall an application having been made at the Senate house." His voice was light and without threat, but Julius stiffened, knowing he had to watch every word.

"It has yet to be made official, but I speak for them," he replied. Courtesy demanded he offer the senator a seat and refreshment after his journey, but he could not bring himself to utter the fictions of politeness, even knowing Cato would take it as a small triumph.

Renius and Brutus moved to Julius's side and Cato looked from one to the other, seemingly unaffected by the men he faced.

"Very well, Julius. I will speak to you of my son," Cato

said. "I have offered gold for him and had it refused. I have come tonight to ask what you do want for him."

He raised his head and Julius saw his deep-set eyes were bright. He wondered if this man had ordered the killing of Pompey's daughter. Would the risk be lessened from him if he handed Germinius back to his father? Or would it be seen as a weakness that Cato would use to scatter his house in ashes?

"He has taken oath, Senator. There—"

"You are understrength, are you not?" Cato interrupted. "I can have a thousand men here tomorrow morning. Healthy slaves from my own estate to be the backbone of Primigenia."

Renius growled suddenly, "There are no slaves in the legions, Senator. Primigenia are freemen."

Cato waved a hand as if it was of no consequence. "Free them after they have taken your precious oath, then. I have no doubt a man like you will find a way, Renius. You are so . . . resourceful." As he spoke, a fraction of his spite gleamed through and Julius knew to give way to him would be to invite destruction.

"My answer is no, Senator. The oath cannot be bought back."

Cato looked at them without speaking for a moment.

"You leave me no choice then. If my son must serve two years with you, I want him alive at the end of it. I will send the men"—he paused—"*freed* slaves, Renius. I will send them to you to protect my son."

"When you have freed them, they may not do what you want," Renius replied, matching the senator glare for glare.

"They will come," Cato snapped. "Few men are as troublesome to me as you have been."

"They will not be your son's guards if they come to Primigenia," Julius said. "Believe me when I say I will not allow it."

"Will you give me *nothing*?" Cato said, his voice rising in anger. All movement in the courtyard changed as hands began to creep toward swords.

"If the gods allow, I will give you your son two years from now. That is all," Julius replied firmly.

"See that you do, Caesar. If he does not survive..." He spoke through clenched teeth, all pretence at calm gone, "Be *sure* he does."

Turning on his heel, he signaled to his men to open the gate. The soldiers of Primigenia reached it first and Cato climbed into his carriage without a backward glance.

Brutus turned to Julius as the closing gate hid the view of Cato's men.

"What are you *thinking*? How many of his 'freed slaves' will be spies, do you think? How many will be assassins? Have you thought of that? Gods, you have to find a way to stop him."

"Don't you want a thousand more for Primigenia?" Julius said.

"At that cost? No, I think I'd rather give Germinius back to his father, or have taken the gold. If it was a smaller number, we could have them watched, but a thousand! A full half of Primigenia we can't trust. It's insane."

"He's right, you know," Renius added. "A hundred would be more than I'd like to take in, never mind this many."

Julius looked at both of them. They had not been there when he had scoured the coasts for Roman sons, nor when he'd found his veterans in Greece.

"We will make them ours," he said, ignoring his own doubts.

*   *   *

Having slept until the sun rose to its greatest height above the wintry city, Cato suffered with a headache that even hot wine could not shift. It throbbed slightly as he listened to Antonidus, hardly able to bear his posturing.

"Ten thousand sesterces is high, even for a death, Antonidus," he said. He enjoyed watching the prickle of sweat that broke out on the general's brow, knowing as well as the man himself that if the money wasn't paid, a sure death would come from the assassins' spite. Keeping him waiting was a petty response, Cato knew, but still he let the time drag out, tapping his fingers idly on the arm of his couch. Pompey's public enmity was to have been expected, of course, even if the assassin hadn't left a clay token in the little girl's grip, as he had been told to do. Cato could not have guessed the senator would throw away his favors simply to make the point, though he could applaud the subtlety of the move. He had hoped Pompey would act in grief and folly, allowing Cato to have him arrested and removed from the games of power in the Senate. Instead Pompey had shown a restraint that marked him as a more dangerous enemy than he had realized. Cato sighed and scratched the corner of his mouth. If he were judged by his enemies, he was surely a power in Rome.

"I would be tempted to withdraw my support and my funds from your revenge, Antonidus, if it wasn't for the matter of this trial of yours. I have hired Rufius Sulpicius to be your advocate."

"I can argue against Caesar myself, Senator. It is a simple enough case," Antonidus responded in surprise.

"No, I want that young cockerel humiliated. From what I have seen, he is young enough and rash enough to be brought down easily. A public embarrassment in front of the magistrates and the plebeians should remove some of the fresh gloss of his tribune rank. We may even demand his death for the wrongs you have suffered." Cato rubbed his forehead with his eyes closed, his full mouth pursing. "There *is* a price for my son and he must pay it. Use Sulpicius. There are few better minds in Rome than his. He will appoint the jurists for you and find the precedents in custom. I have no doubt that this Caesar will be well prepared. Have you sent the summons?"

"No, I was waiting for a date to be set. I have applied to the praetor, but there has been no reply as yet."

"That, Antonidus, is why you need a man like Sulpicius. Meet with him and let him handle the case. He will secure a date for trial in a month or less. That is his business, you know. Your precious house will be back in your hands, for which I expect you to be suitably grateful and indebted to me."

"I am, Senator. And the money?"

"Yes, yes," Cato said waspishly, "you will have your funds, both for the court and . . . the other matter. Now leave me to my rest. The day has been long and tiring."

Even in the privacy of his own home, he did not speak without care, taking pleasure in the forms of conspiracy that forced him to employ men like Antonidus. He knew that many of the senators saw him as a man only of words, preferring the cut of a reply to their martial posturing. The assassins were a delicious departure from his usual intrigue, and he found the power it gave him quite intoxicating. To be able to point to any man and call down a death on him was a thrill even for a palate as jaded as his own. As the general left, he called for a cool cloth to drape over his face.

CHAPTER 32

The trial began as the sky lightened to the east of Rome, the false dawn that woke the workers and sent the thieves and whores to their own beds. The area in the forum that was set aside for legal proceedings was still torch-lit from the night, and a large crowd had gathered at the boundary, held back only by the solid line of soldiers from the city barracks. Under the direct command of the praetor who would oversee the trial, these were charged with keeping the peace in the event of an unpopular verdict, and the crowd was careful not to come within range of the staffs they carried. Unusually, for a case concerning such an apparently minor matter, the benches on either side of the advocates' square were also full. Many of the people Julius knew from the Senate had come to listen, either at his invitation or the call of Antonidus. His own family had stayed at the estate outside Rome. Cornelia and his daughter had to remain under the protection of Primigenia, and Julius did not want Tubruk anywhere near Antonidus or the senators, for all his assurances that he could not be recognized.

Julius's searching gaze found Brutus in the second row of three, sitting next to a woman who raised her head to look back at him. There was something disturbing in her cool appraisal, and he wondered how she seemed to stand out against the crowd around her, as if she were sitting fractionally closer than anyone else. In a timeless moment, she leaned back slowly, arresting his attention. Her hair was unbound, and before he summoned the will to break the contact, she raised a hand to pull a tendril back from where it had fallen loose over her face.

Forcing himself to relax and concentrate, he breathed in the warm air, going over the points he had prepared with his jurists in the weeks after the formal summons. If the case was judged fairly, he knew they had an excellent chance of winning, but if any of the three magistrates was in the pay of his enemies, the trial could be a mockery, with everything won but the final verdict. His gaze swept over the gathering crowd, all of them oblivious to what was at stake. They had come for the entertainment of oratory, to cheer or curse clever points of debate. Julius hoped too that some had come because of the rumors his jurists had started around the city, that the trial was to be nothing less than a defense of Marius. There did seem to be a lot of the plebeians in attendance, and the sellers of baked fish and steaming bread were doing a fine trade already as the people waited patiently for the magistrates and the praetor to make their entrance.

Julius looked again at the draped shields that Alexandria had completed, and noticed that many of the crowd craned their necks for a glimpse of them as well, pointing and talking amongst themselves. Only Alexandria, Tabbic, and himself knew what was under the thick folds of cloth, and Julius felt a touch of excitement at the response they would get when he unveiled them at last.

Behind him, his three jurists shuffled through their papers and notes one more time, their heads bowed in low mutters. Hiring Quintus Scaevola to help him prepare the case had cost him two talents of gold, but there were few men in Rome with a better command of the twin laws of custom and the Twelve Tables. It had taken such a vast fee just to tempt him out of retirement, but despite his arthritic stiffness, the brain behind the heavy-lidded eyes had turned out to be as sharp as Julius had been told. Julius watched Quintus as he scribbled a footnote to the papers for the trial and caught his eye as he looked upward in thought.

"Nervous?" Quintus asked, waving the sheaf at the court and the shadowed crowds beyond.

"A little," Julius admitted. "There is a great deal at stake."

"Remember the point of value. You always leave that one out."

"I remember, Quintus. We've been over it enough times," Julius replied. He had grown to like the elderly jurist, although the man seemed to live only for the law and cared nothing for the other concerns of the city. As a joke in their first week of preparation, Julius had asked him what he would do if he found one of his sons setting fire to a house in the city. After a great deal of silent thought, Quintus had said that he would not be able to take the case as the law forbade calling himself as a witness.

Quintus pressed the notes into Julius's hands, his expression stern. "Do not be afraid to consult, remember. They will try to make you speak without thought. If you feel the arguments are slipping from you, turn away and I will advise as best I can. Do you remember the passage from the Twelve Tables?"

Julius raised his eyes in exasperation. "The one we all memorized as children? Yes, I know it."

Quintus sniffed at the sarcasm. "Perhaps you should recite it again to be sure," he said, unmoved.

Julius opened his mouth to reply, but a light cheer from the crowd interrupted him.

"It's the magistrates…and the praetor. Only an hour late, Master Scaevola," one of the younger jurists hissed to Quintus. Julius looked to follow their gaze and saw the group come out of the Senate building, where they had been preparing.

The crowd fell silent in anticipation as the group of four men walked slowly with their guards into the court area. Julius scrutinized them carefully. The praetor was unknown to him, a short red-faced man with a bald crown. He walked with his head bowed as if in prayer, taking his seat on the raised platform that had been assembled for the trial. Julius watched as the praetor nodded to the centurion of the guards and signaled for the magistrates to take their seats next to him.

These men were familiar enough and Julius breathed a silent sigh of relief as he saw none of them were faces he recognized from the factions in the Senate. His worst fear was that they would be Cato's creatures, but he brightened as one of them smiled at him. The people's tribune took his place last as the most senior of the magistrates. The crowd let out a ragged cheer for their representative, and the man smiled back at them, raising his hand briefly in acknowledgment. His name was Servius Pella, which was just about all Julius could call to mind about him. His hair was white and cropped close to an angular skull with deep-set eyes that seemed black in the dim light of the torches. Fleetingly, Julius wished he had taken the time to meet the man at one of the Senate meetings, but shoved the thought aside. It was pointless to worry about the magistrates, he knew. If he could deal with the posturing of Antonidus's advocate Rufius, he had a strong enough case. If he was humiliated, he would lose not only the house that had belonged to Marius, but also a great deal of his status in the Senate and the city itself. He could not regret the risks he had taken in forcing the trial. Marius would have expected no less.

Julius glanced over to where Cato sat and found the heavy gaze fastened on him with interest. Bibilus was there at his side, as always, and Catalus. Julius saw that Suetonius was sitting with his father, with the same supercilious smile on each face. Their expressions would have marked them as kin even if he hadn't known it already.

Julius looked away rather than show his anger after the revelations from Cornelia. Cato's supporters would learn to fear in time, as he removed the pillars of their influence, one by one.

Quintus patted Julius's shoulder and sat down with the other jurists. The crowd shuffled and whispered as they sensed the trial was about to start. Julius glanced again at the shields, checking that the drapes hadn't slipped to reveal even a part of them.

The praetor stood slowly, his hands smoothing the folds of his toga. With a motion, he ordered the torches snuffed and everyone present waited as each light was covered, leaving the gray dawn to light the forum.

"This august court is convened on the ninety-fourth day of the consular year. Let the records be marked. I charge all present in the sight of the gods that they shall speak only truth here, under penalty of banishment. If any man declares falsehood in this court, he will be denied fire, salt, and water and sent far from this city, never to return, in accordance with the edicts."

The praetor paused, turning to catch the eye of first Antonidus, then Julius. Both men dipped their heads to show understanding, and he continued, his voice a sharp ring across the silent rows.

"In this case of *rei vindicatio*, who is the plaintiff?"

Antonidus stepped forward onto the floor of the court. "I am, sir. General Antonidus Severus Sertorius. I claim wrongful possession of my property."

"And who will speak on your behalf?"

"Rufius Sulpicius is my advocate," Antonidus replied. His words created a buzz of excitement in the crowd, causing the praetor to look sternly at them.

"Step forward the defendant," he said loudly.

Julius stepped off the platform that held the shields, and faced Antonidus across the floor.

"I am Gaius Julius Caesar, the defendant before this court. I claim possession of the property. I speak for myself."

"Have you brought a part of it for the symbol?"

"I have, your honor," Julius replied. He turned to the row of draped cloths and deftly twitched one away, revealing the first bronze shield to the court. A gasp went up from the crowd and a pleased whispering commenced.

The shield was all Julius had hoped. Alexandria had given everything to its creation, fully aware that in front of the court and Senate, she could make her name in a single day.

The shield was ringed in bronze beading, but all eyes were fixed on the face and shoulders of the main figure of Marius, a life-size relief that glared out at those assembled. The whispering went on and on and then a cheer started in the crowd as they tried to show their approval for the dead general.

Antonidus spoke in fierce conversation with his advocate, and the man cleared his throat for the attention of the magistrates. The noise from the crowd was too much for the praetor, and he sent a flat hand signal to the centurion of the court guards. As one, the soldiers crashed the butts of their staffs into the paving and the crowd settled, wary of attack. Rufius stood forward, a bony vulture of a man dressed in a dark robe. He pointed with a sneer at the shield.

"Honorable Praetor. My client insists that this ... item was not part of the house in dispute. It cannot qualify as the symbol unless it was part of the property."

"I know the law, Rufius. Do not presume to lecture me," the praetor replied stiffly. He turned his head to Julius. "Can you answer?"

"It is true that while Antonidus was in unlawful possession of the house of Marius, no such shield hung on the walls, but it was hanging this morning and will do as well as anything as the symbol of disputed ownership. I can produce witnesses to attest this," Julius said smoothly.

The praetor nodded. "That will not be necessary, Caesar. I accept your point. The shield will be used."

He frowned as a fresh cheer came from the crowd around them, and almost raised his hand for another signal to the guards. At this, the people fell silent, knowing better than to push his patience too far.

"Plaintiff and defendant, approach the symbol and complete the rite of dispute," he said loudly.

Antonidus crossed the court floor, a slender spear held in his hand. Julius stepped up onto the platform with him, keeping his face blank of any triumph that would offend the magistrates. Julius touched his spear to the shield with a tiny ring of metal, then stood back. Antonidus brought his own point down and his mouth tightened as someone in the crowd jeered the act. Then he turned his back on Julius and walked back to his station by Rufius, who stood with his arms folded, relaxed and untroubled by the exchange.

"The property has been marked for dispute. The trial may now begin," the praetor intoned, settling himself in his seat for comfort. His part of the proceedings was now over until the time came to dismiss the court. The three magistrates stood and bowed to him before one of them cleared his throat.

"As plaintiff, your advocate must speak first," the magistrate said to Antonidus. Rufius bowed to him and took three steps out into the floor to better command the space.

"Praetor, Magistrates, Senators," he began. "This is a simple case, though the penalties incurred involve the extremes of our law. Five weeks ago, the defendant brought armed men into the city for the purpose of violence. Such a crime is punishable by death or banishment. In addition, the defendant employed his men in breaking into a private house, that of the plaintiff, General Antonidus. The punishment for that is a mere whipping, but after death that may be seen as unnecessary cruelty." He paused while a titter of laughter ran along the benches of the court. The crowd outside remained silent.

"Rough hands were laid on the servants and guards of the house, and when the owner returned, he was forbidden entry to his own home by the same soldiers.

"He is not a vengeful man, but the crimes against him are many and grave. As his advocate, I call on you to administer the sternest punishment. Death by the sword is the only possible answer to such a flouting of Rome's laws."

A polite clapping came from the men around Cato, and Rufius nodded briefly to them as he resumed his seat, his bright eyes belying the air of relaxation he pretended.

"And now the defendant," the magistrate continued. Nothing in his manner showed whether he had been moved by Rufius's words, but still Julius stepped forward with a hollow feeling in his stomach. He had known they could try for death, but hearing it in court made it a reality that shook his confidence.

"Praetor, Magistrates, Senators, people of Rome," Julius said loudly enough to carry to the crowd. They cheered this, though the praetor frowned at him. Julius ordered his thoughts before continuing. Instinctively, he felt that the defense of Marius would appeal more to the people who had suffered under Sulla than to the silent judges, but playing to them was a dangerous course and could even sway the magistrates against a strong case. He would have to be careful.

"This case has a longer history than five weeks," he began. "It begins on a night three years ago when the city prepared for civil war. Marius was the legally appointed consul of Rome, and his legion had fortified the city against attack—"

"Your honors, I appeal to you to have him cease this rambling discourse," Rufius broke in, standing. "The question is the ownership of a house, not the struggles of history."

The magistrates conferred for a moment, then one stood.

"Do not interrupt, Rufius. The defendant has a right to make his case as he thinks best," he said. Rufius subsided and sat down.

"Thank you, your honor," Julius continued. "That Marius was my uncle is well known. He took the defense of the city on himself when Sulla departed to Greece to defeat Mithridates, a task Sulla left rather incomplete."

The crowd chuckled at this, then fell silent as the praetor swept them with his glare. Julius went on. "Marius was convinced that Sulla would return to the city with the aim of assuming complete power. To avert this, he fortified Rome's walls and prepared his men to defend the people of the city against armed attack. If Sulla had approached the walls without violence, he would have been allowed to resume his consular post and the peace of the city would have remained unbroken. Instead, he had left assassins within the bounds who attacked General Marius in the dark in a cowardly attempt at murder. Sulla's men opened the gates and let their master into the city. I believe it was the first armed attack on her in more than three hundred years."

Julius paused for breath, looking at the magistrates to see how they were reacting to his words. They regarded him impassively, their expressions giving nothing away.

"My uncle was dispatched by a dagger from Sulla's own hand, and though his legion fought valiantly for days, they too fell to the invader."

"This is too much!" Rufius cried, leaping up. "He blackens the name of a beloved leader of Rome under the protection of this trial. I must ask you to condemn him for his foolishness."

The magistrate who had spoken before leaned forward and spoke to Julius. "You are pushing our patience, Caesar. If the case is found against you, be sure we will consider your

disrespect when it comes to the sentence. Do you understand?"

Julius nodded, gulping to clear his suddenly dry throat.
"I do, though the words must be spoken," he said.

The magistrate shrugged. "It's your head," he muttered
as Julius took a calming breath before speaking again.

"Much of the rest you know already. As victor, Sulla
claimed the title of Dictator. I will not speak of that period in
the city history."

The magistrate nodded sharply at this as Julius continued.

"Though he had defended the city under the law, Marius
was declared traitor and his possessions sold off by the state.
His house was auctioned publicly and bought by the plaintiff
of this trial, General Antonidus. His legion was dispersed and
their name struck from the honor rolls in the Senate."

Julius paused and bowed his head as if in shame at the
act. A murmur ran through the senators in attendance as they
whispered questions and comments to each other. Then
Julius raised his head again and his voice rang out over the
judges and the crowd.

"My case stands on three points. The first is that Primigenia
has been restored to the legion rolls without dishonor. If they
have suffered no stain, then how can their general be called traitor? Secondly, if Marius was wrongly punished, then his possessions should have come to his remaining heir, myself. Lastly, my
actions to reclaim my house from the thieves within have been
made knowing the court would pardon them in the light of
Marius's unjust fate. A great wrong has been committed, but it
is *against* me, not by me."

The crowd cheered and the guards once again rapped
their staffs into the ground.

The magistrates put their heads together for a moment,
then one of them motioned to Rufius to speak in reply. He
stood, sighing visibly.

"Caesar's attempts to confuse the issue are admirable for their earnestness, but the law sees all things clearly. I am sure the judges enjoyed the journey into history, as I did, but I suspect they realize that the interpretation is colored by the defendant's personal relationship with the general. As much as I would enjoy arguing the vision he has presented as fact, I am in favor of reducing the case to its fundamentals in law and not wasting the time of those present." He looked at Julius and smiled in a friendly fashion, so that all there could see he forgave the young man for his foolishness.

"In a wholly legal sale, my client bought the house in question at auction as we have been told. His name is on the deed and the bill of sale. To have armed guards steal his property from him is a return to the use of force to settle disputes. I'm sure you all noted the touching of spears to that attractive shield at the start of the trial. I remind you that the symbolic act of struggle is just that. In Rome, we do not draw swords to end arguments without submitting to the law.

"I sympathize with the points young Caesar has raised, but they have no bearing on the case at hand. I'm sure he would want to go back even further and reveal the history of the house right back to its first foundation, but there is no call for such a widening of the issues. I must repeat my call for the sword, though it is with regret that Rome should lose such a passionate young advocate."

His expression showed sadness for the harsh penalties to come as he took his seat and conferred with Antonidus, who watched Julius with slitted eyes.

Julius stood and faced the magistrates once more. "As Rufius has referred to a deed and bill of sale, I feel he should produce them for the court to examine," he said quickly.

The magistrates looked over to Rufius, who grimaced. "If the property was a horse or a slave, your honors, then I could of course produce such items for you. Unfortunately, as a house is in question and one taken by surprise and armed force, the documents were inside it, as Caesar is well aware."

The magistrate who seemed to speak for the others peered at Julius with a frown. "Are these papers in your possession?" he asked.

"I swear that they are not," Julius replied. "There is no sign of them in the house of Marius, on my honor." He sat down again. As he had burned the deed and bill of sale the night before under Quintus's direction, his conscience was clear.

"So no ownership papers can be produced by either party?" the magistrate continued evenly. Julius shook his head and Rufius echoed the movement, his face tightening in irritation. He stood to address the magistrates once again.

"My client suspected that such key documents would 'disappear' before the trial," he said with a barely concealed sneer in Julius's direction. "Instead, we have a witness who was present at the auction and can attest to the legal sale to General Antonidus."

The witness stood forward from his seat by Antonidus. Julius recognized him as one of those who sat near Cato in the Senate house. He was a stooped and fragile-looking man, who constantly pulled a lock of his thinning hair back off his forehead as he spoke.

"I am Publius Tenelia. I can attest to the legal sale."

"May I question this man?" Julius asked, stepping into the floor as he received permission.

"You witnessed the entire auction?" Julius asked him.

"I did. I was there from the start to the finish."

"You saw the bill of sale being signed in the name of Antonidus?"

The man hesitated slightly before replying. "I saw the name," he said. His eyes were nervous and Julius knew he was adding to the truth.

"You glimpsed the document briefly, then?" he pressed.

"No, I saw it clearly," the man replied more confidently.

"What was the amount the general paid?"

Behind the man, Rufius smiled at the ploy. It would not work, as the witness had been thoroughly prepared for such questions.

"It was one thousand sesterces," the man returned triumphantly. His smile dropped at a sudden chorus of jeers from the crowd outside the court. Many heads turned toward the mass of plebeians, and Julius saw with the judges that the streets had filled as the trial went on. Every available space was taken and the forum itself was full of people. The magistrates looked at each other and the praetor firmed his mouth in anxiety. Such a large audience increased the dangers of disturbance, and he considered sending a runner to the barracks for more soldiers to keep the peace.

When the crowd was quiet, Julius spoke again.

"In preparation for this case, your honors, I had the house valued. If it was sold this morning, a buyer would be likely to pay in the region of a million sesterces, not a thousand. There is a passage from the Twelve Tables that has a bearing on the matter."

As he prepared to quote from the ancient script, Rufius raised his eyes in boredom and the witness fidgeted, not yet dismissed.

" 'Property may not pass from vendor to purchaser unless value has been paid,' " Julius said loudly. The crowd cheered the point, with a number of conversations breaking out as it was explained to those around them.

"A thousand sesterces for a property worth a million is not 'value,' your honors. The sale was a farce of favors, a mockery of an auction. With not even a bill of sale to prove it existed, no legal transaction took place."

Slowly, Rufius rose. "Caesar will have us believe that any bargain is in breach of the Tables," he began.

The crowd hooted him and the praetor sent his runner for more soldiers.

"I say again that Caesar attempts to confuse the court with pointless distractions. The witness proves the sale was real. The amount is immaterial. My client is a shrewd bargainer."

He sat down, hiding his annoyance at the point. He could not admit that the auction had been mere show for Sulla to reward his favorites, though Caesar had made that clear to everyone there, if they didn't know it already. Certainly the crowd hadn't known and many angry stares were turned on Antonidus, who visibly shrank in his seat.

"Furthermore," Julius continued as if Rufius had not spoken, "as the matter of the value of the house has been raised by Antonidus's own witness, there is another issue I would like to bring to the attention of the court. If the verdict is with me as rightful heir to the property, I will demand the rent for the two years of occupancy by General Antonidus. A generous estimate of that amount is thirty thousand sesterces, which I add to my claim for the house as money denied my family in his time there."

"What? How dare you ask for that?" Antonidus spluttered in anger, rising from his seat. Rufius pressed him back into it with difficulty, muttering urgently into his ear.

When Antonidus was still, Rufius turned back to the magistrates.

"He adds public scorn to his offenses, your honors, by goading my client. The house was empty when General Antonidus took legal possession after the sale. There is no rent at question here."

"My family chose to keep it empty, as was their right. Still, the money could have been earned for me if not for the tenant you represent," Julius snapped at him.

The magistrate cleared his throat, then bent his head to listen to the other two before speaking. After a conference that stretched on for a minute or more, he spoke again.

"The case is clear enough, it seems. Have either of you anything to add before we deliberate on the verdict?"

Julius racked his brain, but everything he wanted to say had been said. His gaze strayed over to the bronze shields that were still covered, but he resisted the urge to unveil them for the crowd, knowing the judges would see it as a cheap display. He wasn't at all sure which way the verdict would go, and when he turned to look at Quintus, the old man simply shrugged blankly.

"Nothing more, your honors. I rest," Julius said.

The crowd cheered him and called insults to Rufius as he too ended his case. The three magistrates stood and bowed to the praetor before leaving for the Senate building, where they would thrash out their final verdict. The extra soldiers that had come running from the barracks cleared the way for them, armed not with staffs but swords.

When they had left, the praetor stood to address the crowd, pitching his powerful voice to carry over their heads.

"When the judges return, there will be no disturbance, whatever the outcome. Be sure that any hostility will be met with quick and final punishment. You will depart peacefully and any man who does not will suffer my displeasure."

He took his seat again, ignoring the baleful stares that were focused on him from the people of Rome. The silence held for only a few seconds, then a lone voice called "Ma-ri-us!" and was quickly joined by those around him. In a few moments, the whole crowd was stamping and yelling the name, and the assembled members of the Senate looked around them nervously, suddenly aware that only a thin line of soldiers stood between them and the mob.

Moving with stately slowness, Julius decided the moment was right to reveal the rest of Alexandria's work. He caught her eye on the benches as he grasped the rough cloth that covered the first and saw she was grinning with excitement. Then he whipped it away and the crowd cheered raucously. It was the three crossed arrows of Primigenia, Marius's beloved legion. On the benches, Brutus stood on impulse to cheer as wildly as the crowd, and others close by him followed his lead.

The praetor snapped out some order to Julius, but it went unheard over the unruly crowd and Julius moved to the others, pulling away the coverings one by one. With each the crowd grew louder in their roaring as those who could see shouted out descriptions to those behind. Small children were hoisted to their parents' shoulders to see, and fists punched the air in raucous enjoyment. Scenes from Marius's life were shown, his battles in Africa, the Triumph through the streets of the city, his proud stance on the walls as he waited for Sulla.

Julius paused dramatically as he reached the last one, and the crowd quietened as if at an unseen signal. Then he pulled the cloth away to reveal the last shield. It shone in the morning light, completely blank.

Into the silence, Julius spoke. "People of Rome, we cast the last image on this day!" he cried, and they erupted into a bellow of cheering and shouts that had the praetor on his feet, shouting to his guards. The space between the crowd and the court was widened, with the soldiers using their staffs to push the people back. They moved away in confusion, yelling defiance and jeering Antonidus. The name of Marius began again as a chant and it seemed as if all Rome was shouting the name.

*   *   *

Cornelia watched in the gray light as Tubruk leaned toward Clodia and kissed her. He was so gentle, it almost hurt to watch, but she could not look away. She hid from their sight in a dark window, and felt more alone than ever. Clodia would ask for her freedom, she was sure, and then she would have no one.

Cornelia smiled bitterly as she probed the tender places of her memories. It should have been different. Julius seemed so full of life and energy as he took Rome in his hands, but none of it was for her. She remembered the words that used to pour out of him when Marius was still alive. She'd had to put a hand over his mouth to stop her father's servants from hearing as he talked and laughed with her. There had been such joy in him then. Now he was a stranger and though once or twice she had caught him looking at her with the old fire, it had gone as soon as she recognized it. There had been times when she'd gathered courage to demand that he make love to her, just to break the ice that was forming between them. She wanted it, even dreamed of him, but each time the memory of Sulla's rough fingers took her resolution and she slipped alone into her nightmares. Sulla was dead, she told herself, but she could still see his face and sometimes in the wind she thought she could smell his scent. Then terror would curl her into the bedclothes against the world.

Tubruk put his arm around her nurse and Clodia rested her head on his shoulder, whispering to him. Cornelia heard his deep chuckle for a moment and envied them what they had found. It was not in her to refuse if Clodia asked, though the thought of being the forgotten wife while Julius gloried in his city and his legion was unbearable. She had seen them before, those poisonous Roman matrons with nurses for their children and slaves to work in the houses. They spent their days buying rich cloth, or organizing a social circle that Clodia saw as a kind of death. How they would pity her when they clawed out the truth of a loveless marriage.

Cornelia rubbed angrily at her eyes. She was too young to be destroyed by this, she told herself. If it took a year to recover, then she would wait out the healing. Though he had changed in his prison, there was still the young man she'd known in Julius. The one who had risked life and her father's anger to come to her room over the slippery rooftops. If she could only keep that man in mind, she would be able to talk to him again and perhaps he would remember the girl he'd loved. Perhaps the conversation would not become an argument and neither of them would leave the other alone.

A shadow moved in the courtyard and Cornelia raised her head to see. It could have been one of the soldiers on his rounds, she thought, then let out her held breath as the graying night revealed him. Octavian, spying on the lovers. If she called to him, the moment of privacy Clodia and Tubruk had found would be spoiled, and she hoped the boy would have the sense not to get too close.

Julius too had grown up inside the walls and once had been as fascinated by love as Octavian.

She watched in silence as Octavian crouched behind a water trough and peered at Tubruk. The couple kissed again and Tubruk reached down to the ground, his fingers searching as he chuckled again. When he had found what he wanted, Cornelia saw his arm go back and jerk forward, sending a pebble clattering toward where Octavian hid.

"Go back to bed," Tubruk called to the boy. Cornelia smiled, turning away to take the advice herself.

*　　　　　*　　　　　*

"The Senate doors are opening!" Quintus said at Julius's shoulder. Julius turned to see the magistrates returning.

"That was fast," he said nervously to the jurist.

The old man nodded. "Fast is not good in a property case, I think," he muttered ominously.

Julius tensed in sudden fear. Had he done enough? If the decision went against him and the judges accepted the call for a death penalty, he would be dead before the sun set. He could hear their sandals on the forum stones, as if they marked off his last moments. Julius felt sweat trickle down his side under his toga, cold against his skin.

With the rest of the court, he stood to receive the magistrates, bowing as they entered. The soldiers who had accompanied them from the Senate building took up their posts in a second line between the crowd and the court, their hands on their swords. Julius's heart sank. If they were expecting trouble, it could be the magistrates had warned them of the verdict already.

The three judges moved to their seats with slow dignity. Julius tried to catch their eyes as they settled, desperate for some clue of what was to come. They gave nothing away and the crowd became silent as the tension grew, waiting for them.

The magistrate who had spoken throughout the proceedings rose ponderously to his feet, his expression grim.

"Hear our verdict, Rome," he called. "We have searched for truth and speak as law."

Julius held his breath unconsciously and the silence that surrounded them seemed almost painful after the crashing cheers and chants before.

"I find in favor of General Antonidus," the man said, his head and neck stiff. The crowd roared in anger, then a hush fell again as the second judge rose.

"I too find in favor of Antonidus," he said, his gaze swinging over the unruly chaos of the crowd. A fresh bellow of jeers followed his words and Julius felt suddenly dizzy with reaction.

The tribune stood and looked over the crowd and the bronze images of Marius, his gaze at last falling on Julius.

"As tribune, I have the right to veto the judgments of my fellow magistrates. It is not a path I would choose lightly, and I have weighed the arguments with care." He paused for emphasis and every eye was on him.

"I exercise that veto today. The judgment is with Caesar," he said.

The crowd went berserk with joy and the chant of "Ma-ri-us" could be heard again, louder than ever.

Julius collapsed in his chair, wiping sweat from his fore-head.

"Well done, lad." Quintus smiled toothlessly at him. "There's a lot of people who will know your name if you ever stand for higher office. I did enjoy the way you used those shields of yours. Showy, but they like that. Congratulations."

Julius let out a long slow breath, still light-headed from being so close to catastrophe. His legs felt shaky under him as he crossed the floor to where Antonidus sat. Loudly enough for the magistrates to hear him over the crowd, he took the first part of his revenge for Cornelia.

"I lay hands on you for the sum of thirty thousand sester-ces," he said, gripping Antonidus's robe roughly.

The man stiffened in helpless rage, his eyes searching out Cato in the crowd on the benches. Julius too turned, still keeping his grip. He saw Cato meet the general's eyes and then slowly shake his head, his expression one of distaste. Antonidus seemed dazed at the turn in his fortunes.

"I do not have the money," he said.

Rufius interrupted at Julius's side. "It is customary to al-low thirty days to pay such a large debt."

Julius smiled without humor. "No. I will have the money now, or the general will be trussed and sold as a slave in the markets."

Antonidus struggled violently in his grip, unable to break it.

"You can't! Cato! You cannot allow me to be taken!" he shouted as Cato turned his back on him and prepared to leave the court. Pompey was in the crowd, watching the scene with avid interest. The general retained enough sense to stop his mouth from blurting out the secrets of the assassins. Either Pompey or Cato or the assassins themselves would have him tortured and killed at such a revelation.

Brutus stepped from his bench to stand by Julius. He car-ried a rope in his hands.

"Bind him, Brutus, but gently. I want to get as much as I can for him on the slave blocks," Julius said harshly, letting his anger and contempt spill out for a moment.

Brutus completed the task with quick efficiency, finally gagging Antonidus to muffle his roaring. The magistrates looked on without a reaction, knowing the action was within the law, though the pair that had voted against Julius were red with silent anger.

When the job was done, Rufius caught Julius's attention with a hand on his arm.

"You spoke well, Caesar, but Quintus is too old to be a choice of jurist for the future. I hope you will remember my name if you need an advocate yourself?"

Julius stared at him. "I am unlikely to forget you, I think," he said.

With Antonidus bound and claimed for slavery, the praetor dismissed the court and the crowd cheered again. Although Cato had moved first, most of the other senators stepped quickly down from the benches, clearly uncomfortable in the presence of such a large mob of the citizens they represented.

Together, Julius and Brutus dragged the prone general over the floor of the court, depositing him roughly against the platform that held the shields.

Alexandria stepped around the milling senators to reach Julius, her eyes bright with the triumph.

"Well done. I thought they had you there for a moment."

"So did I. I must thank the tribune for what he did. He saved my life."

Brutus snorted. "He's one of the people, remember. They would have torn him apart if he'd judged against you like the others. Gods, look at them!" Brutus waved his arm at the citizens who clustered as close as they could to catch a glimpse of Julius.

"Stand up by the shields and acknowledge them," Alexandria

said, beaming at him. Whatever else happened, she knew her work would be in demand and fetch huge prices from the good and the great of Rome.

Julius stood and the crowd cheered him. A new chant started and a pleased flush started across his cheeks as he heard his own name slowly supplanting that of Marius.

He raised an arm in salute and knew what Quintus had said was right. The name of Caesar would stay in their minds, and who knew where that could take him?

The morning sun had risen to light the forum and gleam off the surfaces of the bronze shields Alexandria had created. They glowed and Julius smiled at the sight of them, hoping Marius could see them, wherever he was.

CHAPTER 33

The first warmth of spring was in the morning air as Julius ran through his beloved woods, feeling his legs stretch away the tensions of the days. With the excitement of the trial behind him, he spent most of his time with Renius and Brutus at the Primigenia barracks, returning home only to sleep. The men he had recruited in Africa and Greece were shaping well, and there was a new excitement amongst the original survivors as they saw Marius's beloved legion alive once more. The men Cato had procured for them were young and unscarred. Julius had been tempted to question them about their pasts, but resisted the impulse. Nothing before their oath mattered, no matter what Cato held over them. They would learn that in time. Renius spent every waking hour with them, using the experienced men to help him drill and train the new ones.

Though they were still at less than half strength, the word had been sent out to other cities and Crassus had promised to pay as many as they could call to the Primigenia standard. The debt to him was at a dizzy level, but Julius had agreed to it. For all the gold from Celsus, it took a fortune to make a legion, and Crassus stood against the Sullans, as he did. The vast sums simmered at the back of Julius's mind, ignored. Every day brought footsore travelers from all over the country, lured by the promises of scouts in distant provinces.

It was an exciting time and as the sun set each evening, Julius left them reluctantly, looking forward only to the coldest of welcomes at his home.

Though they shared a bed, she jumped when he touched her and then she would rage at him until his temper snapped or he left to find a couch in another room. Every night was worse and he went to sleep tormented by longing for her. He missed her old self and sometimes he turned to her to share a thought or a joke only to find her face filled with a bitterness he could not begin to understand. At times, he was tempted to take another room and have a slave girl brought to him just to give him ease. He knew she'd hate him then and he suffered through the long nights until a constant snapping anger colored his waking hours and sleep was the only peace. He dreamed of Alexandria.

Though it shamed him, he had brought Octavian into the city on three occasions just to give him an excuse to stop at Tabbic's shop. On the third occasion, Brutus had been there, and after the three of them had stuttered through a few minutes of embarrassment, Julius had vowed not to go again.

He paused, panting as he crested the hill that overlooked his estate, not far from the new boundary fence hammered in by Suetonius's father. Perhaps it was time to do something about that, at last. With good clean air filling his lungs and a light sweat from the run, he felt a lift in spirits as he surveyed the land that was his. Rome was ready for change. He could feel it even as he felt the subtle shift of seasons that would bring back the heat of summer to the streets and fields.

A thunder of hooves jolted him out of his reverie, and Julius stepped off the path as the noise grew louder. He guessed who it was before he caught sight of the little figure, perched high on the back of the most powerful stallion in the stables. Julius noted the boy's balance and skill even as he forced a frown that brought Octavian to a shuddering stop in the damp leaves of the woods.

The stallion snorted and danced at being held back, tugging at the reins in a clear signal to go on. Octavian slid off his bare back with one hand buried in his mane. Julius said nothing as he approached.

"I'm sorry," Octavian started, flushing with embarrassment. "He needed a run and the stable lads don't like to stretch him. I know I said—"

"Come with me," Julius interrupted.

They walked in silence down the hill, a forlorn Octavian leading the stallion behind Julius. He knew a beating was likely or, worse, he could be sent back to the city and never see a horse again. His eyes filled with tears that he wiped quickly away. Julius would despise him if he saw him weeping like a baby. Octavian resolved to take his punishment without tears, even if it was to be sent away.

Julius called for the gate to be opened and marched Octavian over to the stables. Some of the horses had been sold when Tubruk raised the ransom, but the estate manager had kept the best bloodlines to let them rebuild the stock.

The sun was rising as Julius entered the shadowy stalls, bringing a blessed breath of warmth. Julius hesitated as the horses turned their heads to welcome him, sniffing the air with soft noses. Without a word of explanation, he crossed to a young stallion Tubruk had raised and trained from a foal and ran his hand over the powerful brown shoulder.

As Octavian looked on, Julius buckled the reins and chose a saddle from the rack on the stable wall. In silence, he led the gently snickering horse out into the morning sun.

"Why don't you take your pony out anymore?" he asked.

Octavian stared at him, completely at a loss. "He's too slow," he said, patting his stallion's neck without noticing. The powerful horse towered over him, but stood calmly at the touch, showing nothing of the temper that irked the stable-boys of the estate.

"You know you're kin to me, don't you?" Julius asked.

"My mother told me," the boy replied.

Julius thought for a moment. He suspected his father would have taken a stick to his son if he had risked his best stallion galloping around the woods, but Julius didn't want to spoil the mood of optimism that had come to him. He had promised Alexandria, after all.

"Come on then, cousin. Let's see if you're as good as you think you are."

Octavian's face lit up as Julius led the horses out together and watched as the boy leapt lightly onto his stallion's back. Julius mounted at a more sedate pace, then whooped suddenly and kicked his mount into a gallop up the hill.

Octavian watched him openmouthed for a moment, then a smile stole across his face as he pressed his heels and yelled a response, the wind making his hair fly.

*   *   *

When Julius came back into the house, Cornelia longed to embrace him. Flushed from the ride and with his hair made wild with dust, he looked so young and full of life that it broke her heart. She wanted to see him smile at her and feel the strength of his arms as he gathered her into them, but instead she found herself speaking angrily, the bitterness spilling uncontrollably even as part of her cried for softer words she could not find.

"How much longer do you expect me to live here as a prisoner?" she demanded. "You have your freedom, while I can't eat or walk anywhere without a group of your Primigenia bastards following me!"

"They are there to protect you!" Julius replied, shocked at the depth of her feelings.

Cornelia glared at her husband. "For how long, Julius? You know better than anyone that it could be years before your enemies cease to be a danger. Would you have me confined for the rest of my life? What about your daughter?

When did you hold her last? Do you want her to grow up alone? Those soldiers even searched friends of my father's when they came to visit. They won't be back, you can be sure."

"I have been working, Cornelia, you know that. I'll make time for her, I promise. Perhaps Primigenia has been overcautious," Julius admitted, "but I told them to keep you safe until I have broken the threat of assassins."

Cornelia swore, surprising him.

"All this based on what happened to Pompey's daughter! Has it occurred to you that there might not *be* any danger? For all we truly know, Pompey was attacked for something that had nothing to do with the Senate, yet as a result, I am forbidden even short trips into the city to break the monotony. It is too much, Julius. I cannot *stand* it."

The words would not be held, though she writhed in confusion. This was not how it was meant to be. He must see her love, yet he was pulling away.

Julius looked at her, his expression hardening. "Do you want me to leave my family open to attack? I cannot. No, I *will* not. Already I am moving against my enemies. I broke Antonidus in full view of Cato and his supporters. They will know I am dangerous to them, and that increases the risk to you many times over. Even if their killers strike at me alone, they could stumble into you."

Cornelia took a deep breath to slow her pounding blood. "Is it to save us, then, or to save your pride that we are prisoners in our own home?" She watched as his eyes tightened in anger, and she ached for him.

"What do you want me to say?" he snapped. "Do you want to go back to your father? Then go, but Primigenia will travel with you and make that place a fortress. Until my enemies are dead, you must be safe."

He pressed his hands deeply into his eyes, as if to hold back the frustration that swept over him. He reached out to her and gathered her stiff body into his embrace.

"My pride has nothing to do with it, Cornelia. There is nothing more important in my life than Julia and you. The thought of someone hurting you is ... unbearable. I must know you are safe."

"That's not true, though, is it?" she whispered. "You care more for the city than your own family. You care more for your reputation and the love of the people than for us." Tears came from her and he held her tightly, resting his head on hers. Her words appalled him and he struggled with an inner voice that noted a kernel of truth in them.

"No, wife," he said, forcing a lighter tone. "You are more than all the rest."

She held herself away from him, looking up into his eyes. "Then come away with us, Julius. If that is true, take your gold and your family and leave this ugly dispute behind you. There are other lands to settle in, where Rome is too distant to trouble us and your daughter can grow without fear of knives in the night. She has nightmares even now, Julius. I fear more for what the confinement is doing to her than for myself. If we mean so much to you, then leave Rome."

His eyes closed in grief. "You cannot ... ask me for that," he said, unable to meet her eyes. As he spoke, she broke his grip and stood apart from him and though his arms ached to hold her again, he could not. Her voice was harsh and loud, filling the room.

"Then don't *preach* to me about how much you care for us, Julius. Don't ever say that again. Your precious city keeps us in danger and you wrap yourself in lies of duty and love." Tears of anger spilled from her red eyes once again, and she flung open the door, shoving roughly past the soldiers of Primigenia who kept station on the other side. Their faces were pale at what they had heard, but both men kept their gaze fastened on the floor as they followed Cornelia at a distance, fearful of provoking her any further.

In moments, Julius was left alone in the room and he

sank numbly onto a couch. It was the third time they had argued in the three days since the trial, and the worst. He had come home full of the excitement of his triumph, and as he told her, it had somehow brought her feelings to a head, making her speak with an anger he had never seen before. He hoped Clodia was on hand. Only the old nurse seemed to be able to calm her. Anything he said made it worse.

Glumly, he thought back over the argument. She didn't understand the work he had undertaken in the city, and he clenched his fists in sudden irritation at himself. She was right: he had wealth enough to take them all away. The estate could be sold to his avaricious neighbors, and he could leave the struggles of the Senate and the dominions to others. Tubruk could retire and it would be as if the family of Caesar had never played a part in the greatest city.

A memory flashed into his mind of Tubruk pressing his fingers deep into the black earth of the fields when Julius was a little boy. Julius was of the land and could never leave it, though hurting Cornelia shamed him. She would see, when his enemies were broken, that this was simply a passing grief, and they would be able to watch their daughter grow in peace, in the arms of Rome. If Cornelia could only endure for the present, he would make it up to her in time. At last he shrugged off the dark lethargy that plagued him and stood. It was approaching noon, and with a Senate meeting scheduled for the early evening, he would have to be quick to complete his business with the house of Suetonius before making his way to the city.

Octavian was in the stables helping Tubruk to mount. The stallion Julius had ridden that morning gleamed from the brush. Julius patted the boy on the shoulder in thanks as he threw his leg into the saddle, the memory of the exhilarating ride easing his anger for a moment. Guiltily, he realized he was pleased to get away from the estate, from her.

*   *   *

The lands owned by Suetonius's father were closer to the city than Julius's own, with a great stretch that touched his own borders. Though the senator had no military rank, he employed a number of guards, who challenged the two travelers as soon as they passed the border, then accompanied them to the main buildings with professional caution and speed. Messengers were sent ahead as Julius and Tubruk approached the house entrance, and the two men exchanged glances at the efficiency.

The place where Suetonius had grown up was a sprawling mass of white-walled enclosures, nearly twice the size of the one Julius had inherited. The same stream that fed his own land ran through the Prandus holdings, and the grounds were lush with growth and color. Ancient pines shaded the entrance, and the path up to it was cool from the shadows cast by overhanging branches. Tubruk sniffed in disapproval.

"Impossible to defend, this place," he muttered. "The trees give too much cover and it needs a good outer wall and gate. I could take it with twenty men."

Julius didn't reply, thinking of his own home, with the cleared land all around it. He hadn't realized before what a mark Tubruk's influence had left, especially after the slave riots years before. Suetonius's house was beautiful and made his own seem stark and bare in contrast. Perhaps Cornelia would find time passed more easily if her surroundings were less like a soldiers' barracks.

They dismounted to pass through the entrance, a tiled arch leading into an open garden where they could hear the rush of running water hidden by flowering bushes and plants. Julius removed the heavy packs from the horses and shouldered his, with Tubruk taking the other, passing the reins into the hands of the slaves that came to greet them. They were shown to seats in a cool outer chamber and told to wait.

Julius settled himself comfortably, well aware that the senator could ignore their presence for a good part of the day. Tubruk went to a window to look at blooms that Julius thought might appeal to Cornelia around their own home.

A young male slave entered from the inner house and approached the two men.

"Senator Prandus welcomes you, Tribune. Please follow me."

Tubruk raised his eyebrows in surprise at the speed of the response. Julius shrugged and the two of them followed the slave into a far wing, where the man opened a door for them and bowed as they entered.

Senator Prandus stood with his son in a room that resembled a temple more than a place to live. Rich, swirling marble lined the walls and floor, with the house shrine set into the far wall. The air smelled lightly of a soft and fragrant incense, and Julius breathed it in appreciatively. There was no doubt changes would have to be made at his estate. Every step of his feet brought new and interesting details to the eye, from the bust of an ancestor in the shrine to a collection of Greek and Egyptian relics on a wall that he itched to examine. It was a calculated display of wealth, but Julius took it all in as a guide to the changes he would make and missed the intended effect completely.

"This is unexpected, Caesar," Prandus began.

Julius dragged his attention from his surroundings and smiled openly at the pair watching. "You have a beautiful home, Senator. Especially the gardens."

Prandus blinked in surprise, then frowned as he was forced into courtesy. "Thank you, Tribune. I have worked many years to make it so, but you have not said why you are here."

Julius lifted the pack from his shoulder and dropped it onto the marble floor with an unmistakable chink of coins.

"You know exactly why I am here, Senator. I have come

to buy back the land that was sold to you during my confinement with your son." Julius glanced at Suetonius as he spoke and saw the younger man had his features fixed into an arrogant sneer. Julius did not respond to it, keeping his own face blank. It was the father he would have to deal with.

"I had hoped to build my son a house on that land," the senator began.

Julius interrupted him. "I remember you saying. I have brought the price you were paid and a quarter again to compensate you for the loss. I will not bargain with you for my land. I will not offer again," he said firmly, untying the bag to reveal the gold.

"That is . . . a fair settlement," Prandus said, looking at the bags. "Very well, I will have my slaves remove the boundary."

"What? Father, you can't just . . ." Suetonius began angrily.

The senator turned to his son and gripped his arm tightly. "Be silent!" he snapped.

The younger man shook his head in disbelief as Julius approached to take his father's hand to seal the agreement. Without another word, Julius and Tubruk departed, leaving Suetonius alone with his father.

"Why did you do that?" he asked in furious amazement. His father's mouth twisted to mirror his own sneer.

"You are a fool, my son. I love you, but you're a fool. You were there at the trial with me. That man is not someone you want as an enemy. Is that clear enough for you?"

"But what about the house you were going to build? Gods, I've spent days with the architects already."

Senator Prandus looked at his son, his eyes showing disappointment that hurt the younger man worse than a blow. "Trust me, Suetonius. You would have died in that house so close to his lands. Whether you realize it or not, I have kept you alive. I do not fear him for myself, but you are my eldest son and he is too dangerous for you. He frightens Cato and he should terrify you."

"I'm not scared of Caesar, or his soldiers!" Suetonius shouted.

His father shook his head sadly. "That, my son, is why you are a fool."

*   *   *

As Julius and Tubruk guided their horses through the estate gate, they heard a shout from the main building. Brutus ran out to meet them and their cheerful greetings died on their lips as they saw his expression.

"Thank the gods you've come back," he said. "The Senate is calling everyone in. Primigenia has to be ready to move." As he spoke, a slave brought his own mount out and he swung himself into the saddle.

"What's happening?" Julius snapped as Brutus took up his reins, feeling a surge of excitement.

"A slave rebellion in the north. Thousands of them and hundreds of gladiators who killed their keepers. Mutina has been overrun," Brutus replied, his face pale under the road dust.

"That's not possible! There are two legions there," Tubruk broke in, horrified.

"That was the report. The messengers are out all over, but I thought you'd want the news as fast as I could bring it."

Julius turned his horse's head and gripped the reins tightly. "I can't take away the men guarding my wife, not with the danger of another rebellion spreading here," he said flatly.

Brutus shrugged. "The order was to have every available soldier ready to march north, Julius, but I'll forget those ones," he replied, reaching out to clap his friend's shoulder in support.

Julius gathered in his reins, ready to dig his heels into the horse's flanks. "Make the house secure, Tubruk," he ordered. "If the rebellion spreads, we may come to appreciate the way you have set up the defenses after all. Keep my family safe, as you have done before."

They shared a moment of private understanding as Tubruk looked into Julius's eyes. So Brutus couldn't hear, Julius leaned down over the shoulder of his stallion and whispered into Tubruk's ear.

"I know what I owe you," he said. Sulla's death had saved them all.

"Don't worry. Now go!" Tubruk replied gruffly, slapping Julius's horse on the rump. The two young men bent low over the saddles as they kicked their mounts into a full gallop, raising a mist of dust on the road to Rome.

CHAPTER 34

The Senate building was buzzing with activity as Julius and Brutus approached. They dismounted at the edge of the forum and led their mounts toward the clustered groups of senators who were coming in from all directions, summoned to the emergency meeting from all over the city and beyond.

"How did you get the news so quickly?" Julius asked his friend as they crossed the space. Brutus looked uneasy, then his head came up.

"My mother told me about it. She has a number of... contacts in the Senate. She was probably one of the first to know."

Julius noted a wariness in Brutus's manner and wondered at it. The young man had been pressing for a meeting between Servilia and himself, and Julius sensed how important it was to him.

"I really will have to see this mother of yours," he said lightly.

Brutus flashed him a look, searching for mockery, and then relaxed, satisfied. "She is very interested in meeting you, after that trial. I want you to know her. She is like no one else I've met."

"Perhaps tonight, then, if there's time," Julius replied, hiding his reluctance. Tubruk had already offered a number of opinions on the woman, but he owed it to Brutus, if it was something he wanted.

Brutus took the reins of the two horses in one hand as they reached the bottom of the steps. "Come to the barracks afterward, if you can. I'll have Primigenia ready to march on your orders," he said. His eyes were bright with an excitement that made Julius chuckle.

"As soon as I'm free," he said, walking up the steps and into the gloom beyond.

The Master of Debate and the consul were still on their way, so no official discussion had begun as Julius entered the Senate building. Instead, half the full number of his colleagues were clustered in anxious knots, shouting questions and comments to each other in a clatter of noise that only served to heighten the impression of an emergency. There was no order to it, and Julius took the time to visit those he knew, picking up the details that Brutus had not heard.

Pompey was with Crassus and Cinna, engaged in a heated argument. They acknowledged Julius with a nod as he reached them, then the fast-talking continued.

"Of course you'll have command, my friend. There is no one else of note, and even Cato won't hesitate with only the forces at Ariminum guarding the south," Crassus said to Pompey.

The sun-dark commander shrugged, his face full of bitter knowledge. "He'd do anything to stop me taking military control, you know that. He must not be allowed to put up his own people. Look what happened in Greece! And the pirates that roam at will, attacking our merchants. If these gladiators are the same ones we failed to put down at Vesuvius, then Mutina was lost because of our timid policy since Sulla's death. All because Cato blocks the Senate from sending out a general equal to the task. You think this time will be any different?"

"It may be," Cinna answered him. "Cato has holdings in

the north that must be under threat from the slaves. They could even turn south and attack the city. Cato wouldn't be such an idiot as to ignore a threat to Rome. They must send you out. At least we have the legions back from Greece to join the others."

"There is the consul, coming in. He must use his veto against Cato if the fat fool interferes. This is more than a personal matter between us. The safety of the north is at stake. The safety of Rome herself."

Pompey left them, shoving rudely through the gathering senators to speak to the consul as he entered. Julius watched as he met the man, an elder elected to the position as a compromise between the Senate factions. As Pompey spoke to him, his hands moving with his words, the man looked nervous and intimidated. Julius frowned, tapping his fingers against his stomach in tension as the consul turned his back on the gesturing Pompey to step up to the rostrum.

"Take your seats, Senators," the consul called.

The meeting oath was quickly taken and then the consul cleared his throat to address the tense ranks before him.

"You have been summoned for an emergency meeting to debate a response to the uprising. I have the latest reports with me and they are worrying. It was a revolt of gladiators from a ring school at Capua. At first the local praetor looked as if he could handle it, but he failed to contain the rebellion. It seems they have managed to gather a slave army and flee north. They have plundered a number of towns and estates, killing hundreds and burning anything they could not steal. The legate at Mutina engaged the slaves and the garrison was destroyed with no survivors."

He paused. Those senators who had not heard the news gasped and shouted in outrage, and the consul raised his hands to calm them.

"Senators, this threat cannot be overstated. The legions at Ariminum have been told to secure the city, but with

Mutina gone, the north is completely open. The estimates I have are varied, but they may have as many as thirty thousand slaves under their command, with more coming in as they ravage each town. I can only assume they overwhelmed the Mutina legions with vast numbers. They must be met with the largest force we can muster while still keeping our southern borders secure. I need not tell you that we cannot strip garrisons from Greece without dire risk so soon after their own rebellion.

"At present, they show no sign of turning toward Rome, but if they do so, there are more than eighty thousand slaves who could rally to their cause by the time they reach the south. This is a grave threat and our response must be swift and final."

The consul glanced quickly at Cato, then Pompey.

"I ask at this time that you put aside your grievances for the good of the city and Roman lands. I call on the Master of Debate to hear the responses."

The consul sat down, wiping his brow nervously, obviously relieved to be able to pass the meeting to another. The Master of Debate had held his post for a number of years, his experience giving him a detachment that served to cool the hottest tempers. He waited patiently for quiet before choosing his first speaker.

"Pompey?"

"Thank you. Senators, I ask to be given command of the legions sent against these rebels. My record speaks for me as qualification and I urge you to vote quickly. Every soldier of Rome within a hundred miles has been called back to the city. Within a week, we should have an army of six legions to send against the slaves, joining with the two at Ariminum when we reach it. If we delay, this slave army will grow further until it may be impossible to stop. Remember that they outnumber us, Senators, even in our own homes. Grant me the command and I will destroy them in the name of the Senate."

Pompey sat down to scattered cheers and stamping of feet. He did not respond to the noise, his gaze fixed on the figure of Cato, who had risen slowly, his face flushed.

"Cato to speak," the Master of Debate confirmed.

"Pompey's record is indeed a fine one," Cato began, smiling at the stone-faced senator across the benches. "I agree with him that a force must be assembled and sent to strike quickly before the fire of the rebellion burns the north. However, there are other choices for men to command the force we send, others who bear the rank of general and have experience in fighting for Rome. It strikes me that a man who puts himself forward may not be suitable for such a role. Better we appoint a general who is acceptable to all of us for this difficult task. I confess Pompey's eagerness makes me uneasy given our recent city history, and instead I suggest the command is handed to Lepidus, fresh returned from Greece." He sat down in silence before a babble of angry shouts and conversation broke out, with both factions abusing the other.

"Be silent, gentlemen. You do not serve Rome with your spite," the Master of Debate said across them, bringing a restless stillness back to the benches. He looked around at the seated senators and nodded to Julius, who had risen at the end of Cato's speech.

"I was a witness to the caution of Lepidus against Mithridates. He was late to engage and had barely moved beyond his landing place when I came upon him to hand over the body of the Greek king. I have seen too many such compromises in this Senate. Lepidus is a poor choice, when we need to move quickly and crush the rebellion before it grows out of control. We must put aside our grievances and factions to grant the command to the one who will achieve most and fastest. That is Pompey."

The Master of Debate nodded his agreement, dropping his usually impartial stance, but was then compelled to recognize Cato as the man stood again.

"I am concerned that the threat against us is being used as a blind for ambition, Senators. Lepidus will never endanger us when the battles are over, but Pompey may well have his eyes on a future even as we discuss this choice. My vote will be for Lepidus." The man lowered himself carefully back into his seat, glaring at Julius for a moment.

"Are there any other candidates? If so, let them rise, or we will go directly to a vote." The Master of Debate waited, his gaze sweeping the rows.

Crassus stood stiffly, ignoring the surprise of Cato's supporters. He received the nod to speak and crossed his hands behind his back, like a tutor addressing his wards.

"Senators, I fear that politics will bring us to the wrong choice for the city. I do not know who would win a vote between Pompey and Lepidus as commanders, but if it is Lepidus, that could only lead to disaster. I put myself forward as a third candidate to prevent the waste of lives that would surely result from any command by Lepidus. Though I have devoted myself to business in recent years, I too rest on my previous record with the legions, for your approval."

Once again, the noise of conversation broke out all over the Senate hall as Crassus sat. Pompey was amazed at the revelation from his friend and tried to catch his eye without success as Crassus looked away from him. As the noise died, Pompey stood, his hands tightening into fists unconsciously.

"I withdraw my name from consideration in favor of Crassus," he said bitterly.

"Then we will move to a vote without further delay. Rise for your choice, gentlemen," the Master of Debate replied, as surprised as anyone by the turn of events. He waited a few moments more for the senators to make up their minds, then began to call the names.

"Lepidus!"

Julius craned his neck with everyone else still seated to

judge the numbers, then breathed out in satisfaction. There were not enough to carry the vote.

"Crassus!" the Master of Debate intoned, smiling to himself.

Julius stood with Pompey and the others who had judged the choice correct. The Master of Debate nodded to the consul, who stood and gripped the rostrum before him.

"Crassus is appointed general of the north armies assembling and is ordered to take the field against the rebellion and destroy it utterly," the consul said.

Crassus stood to thank the senators.

"I will do my utmost to preserve our lands and the city, gentlemen. As soon as the legions are brought together in the Campus Martius, I will move against the rebels."

He paused for a moment and smiled slyly.

"I will keep the legates in place under me, but I must have a second-in-command should I fall. I name Gnaeus Pompey as that second."

Curses and cheers broke out all over, with the calls for quiet from the Master of Debate ignored. Julius laughed at the stroke and Crassus inclined his head toward him in acknowledgment, clearly enjoying himself.

"Keep silence!" the Master of Debate bellowed above them, finally losing his temper. The babble subsided under his glare, but slowly.

"We should move on to the details, Senators," the consul said, shuffling through his papers. "Our runners report that the slaves are well armed after Mutina, having outfitted themselves with legionary supplies and armor. One of our people claims to have seen the gladiators training the slaves in sword and spear work, mimicking our formations on the field. After Mutina, they should not be underestimated." The consul licked his fingers nervously as he scanned the sheaf of parchments in front of him.

"Do they have officers?" Pompey called out.

The consul nodded as he read. "It seems they have a structure based on our own legions in every way. I have the original message from the owner of the barracks where the gladiators escaped. It's here, somewhere."

The senators waited patiently as the consul found the paper he was looking for.

"Yes, there were seventy of them and all the guards were killed. The barracks slaves went with them, though whether they were willing or forced, the man does not know. He claims to have barely escaped with his own life. It seems these gladiators form the officer class of the army."

"Who leads this rabble of gladiators?" Pompey demanded, uncaring that his tone went some way to confirm the fiction of Crassus's leadership.

The consul searched through the papers again, and licked his fingers more than once to separate them.

"Yes, I have it. They are led by a gladiator named Spartacus, a Thracian. He began it and the rest followed him. There is nothing more, but I will pass anything further to Crassus as the reports come in."

"With your permission, gentlemen, I would like to leave with my second to prepare for the march ahead of us," Crassus said.

As he turned, he tapped his hand on Julius's shoulder. "I want Primigenia with me when we go, Julius," he said quietly.

"They will be ready," Julius promised.

*　　　　　　*　　　　　　*

Crassus lay back in the warmth of the sunken bath, allowing the difficulties of the day to slide away from him. Darkness had come early outside, but the bathing room was lit with softly flickering lamps and candles, the air thick with steam from the water. He rested his arms along the marble sill, enjoying the coolness against his skin. The water came to his neck, but with the smooth stone seat under the surface, he could relax completely. He exhaled slowly, wondering why the pool in his own estate could never be as comfortable.

Servilia sat naked in the water across from him, only her shoulders above the surface. When she moved, the swelling curves of her breasts eased into view for tantalizing moments before they slid down again, blurred by the sweet oils she'd poured for them both. She'd known it was what he wanted as soon as he came to her from his generals, tired and irritable. That had all gone as her fingers worked away the painful spots from his neck before he stepped into the deep pool, set into the floor of a private part of her home. She could always sense his mood.

She watched as the tension of the day left Crassus, amused by his sighs and groans. She knew what hardly anyone else suspected of the aging senator, that he was a terribly lonely man who had accumulated fortunes and influence without holding on to the friends of his youth. He rarely wanted anything more from her than the chance to talk in privacy, though she knew the sight of her nakedness could still arouse him, if she let it. It was a comfortable relationship, without the sordid worry of payment to spoil the intimacy. He offered her no coin but the conversations, though they were sometimes worth much more than gold.

The oils glittered on the surface of the pool, and she traced patterns in them with a finger, knowing he would be enjoying the sight of her.

"You have brought Primigenia back," she said. "My son is wonderfully proud of the men he's found for the name."

Crassus smiled slowly. "If you'd known Marius, you would understand why it gave me such pleasure to do it."

He chose not to remind her of the part Pompey and Cinna had played, preferring not to hear their names in her house. That was another thing she understood without it having to be said.

Servilia raised herself out of the water, laying her slender arms out to the sides, so that her breasts were fully visible. She was very vain about them and she moved without embarrassment. Crassus smiled appreciatively, completely comfortable with her.

"I was a little surprised to hear he'd given command to Julius," he said.

Servilia shrugged, which fascinated him. "He loves him," she replied. "Rome is lucky to have sons like those two."

"Cato would not agree, my dear. You must be wary of him."

"I know, Crassus. They are both so very young. Too young to see the danger of mounting debts, even."

Crassus sighed. "You came to me for help, remember? I have set no limit on Primigenia's purse. Would you have me cancel the debt? I would be laughed at."

"For raising Marius's legion back from the ashes? Never. You have acted as a statesman, Crassus; they will know that. It was a noble thing to do."

Crassus chuckled, resting his head back on the cool stone and staring up at the ceiling where the steam hung in a cooling mist.

"You are flattering me rather obviously, don't you think? We are not discussing a small sum, for all the pleasure it brought me to see Primigenia back on the rolls."

"Have you thought that Julius may pay the debt? He has the gold for it." As the air cooled on her skin, she shivered slightly and sank back into the water. "So much better for you to make a gift of it, a grand gesture to shame the petty men in the Senate. I know you care nothing for money, Crassus, which is why you have so much. It is the influence it brings that you love. There are other kinds of debts. How many times have I passed on information that you used for profit?"

She shrugged in answer to her own question, making the steaming water ripple away from her. Crassus lifted his head with an effort, letting his gaze play over her. She smiled at him.

"It is a part of my friendship and it has given me pleasure to help you once in a while. My son will always think kindly of you if you gift the money to him. Julius will support you in anything. You could not buy such men with coins, Crassus. They have too much pride, but a forgiven debt? That is a noble act, and you know it as well as I do."

"I will . . . think about it," he said, his eyes closing.

Servilia watched him as he sank into light sleep and the water cooled around her. He would do as she wanted. Her own thoughts drifted back to seeing Julius at the trial. Such a forceful young man. When her son had passed over Primigenia to him, she wondered if they had considered the debt to Crassus. It would not be a burden now. Odd how the thought of her son's gratitude was a minor pleasure compared to Julius knowing she had been a part of the gift.

Idly, she let her hands slide over her stomach as she thought of the young Roman with the strange eyes. He had a force in him that was no more than echoed in the sleeping Crassus, though it was the old man who would take the legions north.

One of her slaves entered the room in silken silence, a beautiful girl Servilia had rescued from a farm in the north.

"Your son is here, madam, with the tribune," the girl whispered.

Servilia glanced at Crassus, then signaled the girl to take her place in the warm water. If he woke, he would not be pleased to find himself alone, and the girl was attractive enough to catch even his interest.

Servilia pulled a robe around her still-wet skin and shivered slightly in anticipation.

She paused for a moment in front of a huge mirror set into the wall and pushed her damp hair back from her forehead. Her stomach felt light with a surprising tension at the thought of meeting Julius at last, and she smiled at herself in amusement.

Brutus sat with Julius in a chamber that had nothing of the artistry she employed for her business rooms. It was simply furnished and the walls were covered in subtly patterned cloth that gave a feeling of warmth. A fire flickered in the grate and the light was golden as both of them rose to greet her.

"It's good to see you at last, Caesar," she said, extending a hand. Her robe clung to her damp skin exactly as she had hoped it would, and his expression gave her pleasure as he struggled not to stare at her.

Julius felt overwhelmed by her. He wondered if Brutus was troubled by the fact that she seemed almost naked, despite the thin cloth that covered her skin. He saw she had been bathing and his pulse thumped at the thought of what might have been going on before his arrival. Not beautiful, he thought, but when she smiled, there was something utterly without pretense in her sensuality. He was dimly aware that he hadn't slept with a woman for so long he had almost forgotten, and even then, he didn't remember Cornelia or Alexandria stirring him as this one did so effortlessly.

He flushed slightly as he took her hand.

"Your son speaks very highly of you. I'm glad we could meet, even for just a moment before I return home. I'm sorry I can't stay longer."

"Primigenia will be mustering to put down the rebellion," she said, nodding. His eyes widened slightly as he took in her words. "I won't keep you and I should return to my bath. Just remember you have a friend if you ever need me."

Julius wondered if there really was a promise in the eyes that looked so warmly back at him. Her voice was low and soft and he could have listened to it for a long time. He shook his head suddenly, as if to break a trance.

"I will remember," he said, tilting his head slightly as he

considered her. As she looked at Brutus, he stole a glance to where the lines of damp cloth curved around her breasts, and flushed again as she caught his glance and smiled with obvious pleasure.

"You must bring him again, Brutus, when you have more time. My son speaks highly of both of us, it seems."

Julius looked at his friend, who was frowning slightly.

"I will," Brutus replied. He led Julius away and left her looking after them. Her fingers brushed lightly over her breasts as she thought of the young Roman, the hard nipples having little to do with the air on her skin.

*   *   *

Brutus found Alexandria's home easily, despite the dark of the streets. In the armor of Primigenia, he was an uninviting target for the raptores who preyed on the weak and the poor. Octavian's mother, Atia, answered the door with a look of fear that vanished as she recognized him. He entered behind her, wondering how many others lived in terror of soldiers coming for them in the night. While the senators surrounded themselves with guards, the people of Rome could afford no protection other than the doors they barred against the rest of the city.

Alexandria was there and Brutus was struck with embarrassment as Octavian's mother prepared their evening meal only feet away.

"Is there somewhere more private for us to talk?" he asked.

Alexandria glanced at the open doorway to her room, and Atia tightened her mouth to a thin line.

"Not in my house," she said, frowning at Brutus. "The two of you aren't married."

Brutus flushed. "I'm leaving tomorrow. I just wanted to..."

"Oh, yes, I understand very well what you wanted, but

it's not happening in my house." Atia went back to cutting vegetables then, leaving Brutus and Alexandria to stifle giggles that would only have confirmed her suspicions.

"Would you come outside with me, Brutus? I'm sure Atia can trust you in the view of the neighbors," Alexandria said. She pulled on her cloak and followed him out into the night as Atia upended her chopping board into the stewpot, unmoved.

Alexandria stepped into his arms and they kissed. Though it was dark, the streets were still crowded. Brutus looked around him in irritation. The little doorway hardly offered shelter from the wind, never mind the kind of privacy he wanted.

"This is ridiculous," he said, and in fact he had been hoping for exactly the kind of meeting Atia had prevented. He was leaving to fight on distant battlefields, and it was almost a tradition to find a welcoming bed for the night before.

Alexandria chuckled, kissing him on the neck, where his armor made his skin cold.

"Pull my cloak around us," she whispered into his ear, quickening his pulse. He arranged the cloth so that it wrapped them both and they were breathing each other's breath.

"I'm going to miss you," he said wistfully, feeling her body press closely against him. He had to grip the cloak with one hand, but the other was free to slide against the warmth of her back and, when his fingers had warmed, under her stola and against her flesh. She gasped slightly.

"I think Atia was right," she whispered, not wanting the woman's sharp ears to hear them. With his broad hand on her hip, she felt as if she were naked with him, and the crowds rushing by in the darkness only added to her excitement. The cloak formed a warm space against the cold and she held him tightly, feeling the hard lines of his armor. He was barelegged, as always, and it was with a shocking sense of daring that she put her hands on his thighs, feeling the smooth strength of them.

"I should call her to protect me from you," she said, moving her hands upward. She found soft cords and loosened them to feel the heat of him against her hand. He groaned softly at the encircling touch, glancing around him to see if anyone had noticed. The crowds were oblivious in the dark and suddenly he didn't care if they could be seen or not.

"I want you to remember me while you are away, young Brutus. I don't want you looking wistfully at those camp whores," she whispered. "We have unfinished business, you and I."

"I wouldn't... oh gods. I've wanted you for such a long time."

Under the cloak, she unbuttoned her stola and eased him into her, her eyes shuddering closed with the movement. He lifted her weight easily and, together, they braced against the doorway, unaware of anything else around them as they moved in silence. The crowd jostled near them, but no one stopped and the night swallowed them.

Alexandria bit her lip in pleasure, gripping the cloak tighter and tighter around them until it almost cut into her throat. His chestplate pressed coldly against her, but she didn't feel the discomfort, just the heat of him inside her. His breath was hot on her lips as she shuddered and felt him begin to tense.

It seemed to last a long time before they became aware again of cramping muscles and the cold. Alexandria moaned softly as he eased out of her. Brutus stayed close in the darkness, stroking the skin he couldn't see in some sort of wonder. Heat swirled into the air, made by them. He looked into her eyes and they gazed back at him. There was a vulnerability there, for all her outward confidence, but it did not matter. He would not hurt her. He struggled to find words to tell her what she meant to him, but she put a hand over his mouth to still the babble.

"Shhh...I know. Just come back to me, my handsome man. Just come back."

She arranged the cloak to cover her disarray beneath it and, after kissing him one last time, opened the door onto light that vanished with her, leaving him alone.

Brutus spent a moment arranging himself to be decent enough to walk the streets. Every nerve tingled with the touch of her and he felt completely alive with the intensity of what had happened. He swaggered a little as he walked back to the barracks, and his step was light.

CHAPTER 35

Gasping slightly in the cold air, Julius turned to look back at the glittering snake that wound down the Via Flaminia below the high pass. The first three days had been hard on him, before the fitness of his time in Greece began to return. Now his legs had hardened into ridges of muscle, and he relished the pleasure that comes from simple exertion with a body that feels inexhaustible. By the end of the tenth day, he was enjoying the march to Ariminum with the legions at his back. In the evenings in camp, he practiced the gladius with the experts Crassus had brought along, and though he knew he would never be a master, his wrists were strengthening day by day and only the sword teachers themselves could break through his guard.

The wind gusted around the marching column and Julius shivered slightly. Although he'd seen many different lands in his time away from Rome, the cold of the Apenninus peaks was new and he bore it with a grim dislike that was mirrored in many of the soldiers around him.

To break the taste of dust in his throat, Julius took a gulp from his waterskin, shifting the heavy weight of his equipment to pull the stoppered mouth toward his lips. The column stopped only twice a day: briefly at noon and then the evening halt, which began with three hours of exhausting work to prepare the camp boundary against ambush or attack. He looked back again at the legion column and marveled at the length of it. From the high pass through the mountains, he could see a huge distance in the clear air, but the invisible rear guard of cavalry was more than thirty miles behind him. As Crassus was pushing a fast pace of twenty-five miles from dawn till dusk, it meant those at the rear were a day behind the front and would only catch up at Ariminum. Each halt had to be relayed along the column by the cornicens, with the blared notes dwindling with distance until they could not be heard.

Ranging up the steep slopes around were the units of *extraordinarii* horsemen, scouting the forward line. Mounted on sturdy breeds and advancing in crisscrossing patterns, they covered three or four times the distance the column marched. It was a standard tactic, Julius knew, though anyone who dared to attack a column of their strength would have to be suicidal.

At the head was the vanguard legion, chosen by lot each day. With Primigenia understrength, they could not take part in the changeovers and were permanently stationed ten miles back, lost to view in the center of the column. Julius wondered how Brutus and Renius were finding the march. Cabera was older than some of the veterans who had fought Mithridates with him. Back in Rome, Julius had thought it would be important to be close to Crassus, but he missed his friends. No matter how he strained his eyes, he couldn't pick out the Primigenia eagle standard from the smudge of banners behind. He watched the legion cavalry ranging up and down the column like the soldier ants he'd seen in Africa, always looking outward for an attack, which they would bear while the fighting lines formed.

Julius marched with the vanguard, within shouting distance of Crassus and Pompey, who rode at walking pace with the men they led. With more than four thousand men ahead of them when the night halt sounded, the generals had arranged it so that the main camp was laid out and the tents erected as they reached it. They were able to begin their discussions and meal while the rest dug the huge earthworks around them, creating a perimeter capable of stopping almost anything.

The three camps were marked out with flags in exactly the same way each evening. By the time the sun finally set behind the mountains, the six legions were enclosed in huge squares complete with main roads: towns sprung from nothing in the wilderness. Julius had been astonished at the organization the older soldiers took for granted. Each night, he hammered in the iron tent pegs with the others at the place marked for them. Then he joined the units digging the trench and staking the top of the earthworks that formed the outer wall of the safe ground, unbroken except for four gates complete with guards and watchwords. Though his tutors had taught him a great deal about the legion routines and tactics, the reality was fascinating to Julius, and from the first, he saw that part of their strength came from mistakes learned in the past. If Mithridates had established a border like the one the legions put down, he knew he could still be in Greece, looking for a way in.

The path for the stones of the Via Flaminia had been cut through a narrow gorge between slopes of loose scree. Though the light was already fading, Julius guessed Crassus would keep the soldiers marching until the van reached clear ground wide enough for the first camp. One of the legions would have to move back onto the plains below for safety, which would leave the pass free except for the guards and extraordinarii who stayed on mounted patrol through darkness. No matter what happened, the legions could not be surprised by any enemy, a precaution they had learned more than a hundred years before, fighting Hannibal on the plains. Julius remembered Marius's admiration for the old enemy. Yet even he had fallen in the end to Rome.

Though the land may once have been savage, now the wide capstones of the Via Flaminia cut through the mountains, with guard posts every twenty miles along its length. Villages had often sprung up around these as people gathered under the Roman shadow. Many found employment in maintaining the road and sometimes Julius saw small groups of laborers, on the grass verge, pleased to be idle for once.

At other times, Julius passed merchants forced off the road, who regarded the soldiers with a combination of anger and awe. They could not move toward Rome while the legions marched, and those that carried spoiling goods watched with dark expressions as they calculated the loss to come. The legionaries ignored them. They had built the trade arteries with their hands and backs and had first call on their use.

Julius wished Tubruk were with him. In his time, he had traveled the same route through the mountains and right across the vast plains in the north where Crassus hoped to engage the slave army. The estate manager would not have wanted another campaign, even if Julius could have spared him from the task of keeping Cornelia safe.

His mouth tightened unconsciously as he thought of the parting. It had been bitter, and though he'd hated having to leave with the anger still fresh between them, he could not delay joining Primigenia in the midst of the great host on the Campus Martius, standing ready to march north.

The memories of the last time he had left the city were still raw in him. Rome had burned on the horizon behind him as Sulla's men hunted down the remnants of Primigenia. Julius grimaced as he marched. The legion lived, while Sulla's poisoned flesh was reduced to ash.

The trial had gone some way to restoring Marius's name in the city, but while Sulla's friends still lived and played their spiteful games in the Senate, Julius knew he could not build the sort of Rome that Marius had wanted. Cato was safe enough while his main opponents were in the field, but when they returned, Julius would join forces with Pompey to break him. The general understood the need as few others could. For a moment, Julius considered the fate of Cato's son. It would be too easy to put him in the first rank of every charge until he was killed, but that was a cowardly sort of victory over Cato. He vowed if Germinius died, it would be as any other soldier, at the whim of fate. Pompey's daughter had been found with Sulla's name on a clay token in her limp hand, but Julius would not stoop to killing innocents, though he hoped Cato would be terrified for his son. Let him lose sleep while they fought for Rome.

Long, bitter months of campaign had to come first. Julius knew he'd be lucky to see the city walls again in less than a year, and much longer if the slaves were as well led as the reports claimed. He could be patient. Only an army could take his estate, and Cornelia's father, Cinna, had remained behind to block Cato in the Senate. They had formed a very private alliance and Julius knew that with the strength of Pompey and the wealth of Crassus, there was little they couldn't achieve.

The cornicens blew the halt sign as Julius marched through the pass into fading sunlight. He could see the Via Flaminia stretching down into a deep valley before working up the heights of a distant black peak that was said to be the last climb before Ariminum. He wished Brutus could be with him to see it, or Cabera, who traveled with the auxiliaries even farther down the column. His tribune rank had allowed him to take station close to the front, but the march in battle order was not a place for friends to idle away the time.

With the sun setting, the first watch took positions, leaving their shields with their units from long tradition. Order was imposed on the broken landscape. Ten thousand soldiers ate quickly and bedded down in the miniature town they had made. Through the night, they were woken in turns to stand their watches, the returning sentries taking the still-warm pallets with relief after the mountain cold.

Julius stood his watch in darkness, looking over the wall of earthworks at the harsh land beyond. He accepted a wooden square from the hands of a centurion and memorized the watchword cut into it. Then he was left alone in the dark, with the camp silent at his back. With a wry smile, he understood why the guards were denied shields: it was too easy to rest your arms on the top rim, then your head on your arms, and doze. He stayed alert and wondered how long it had been since a sentry had been found asleep. The punishment was being beaten to death by your own tentmates, which tended to keep even the weariest soldier from closing his eyes.

The watch was uneventful and Julius exchanged places with another from the tent, willing sleep to come quickly. The problems with Cornelia and Cato seemed distant as he lay with his eyes closed, listening to the snores of the men around him. It was easy to imagine there wasn't a force in the world to trouble the vast array of might that Crassus had marched north from Rome. As he passed into sleep, Julius's last thought was the hope that he and Brutus would have the chance to make a beacon of the name Primigenia in the bloodshed to come.

*   *   *

Octavian yelled a high-pitched cry of challenge to the swarm of adversaries all around him. They hadn't realized that he was a warrior born and every blow he struck left another one dying, calling for their mothers. He lunged to spear the leader, who bore a strong resemblance to the butcher's apprentice in his fevered imagination. The enemy soldier fell with a gurgle and beckoned Octavian close to his bloody mouth to hear his final words.

"I have fought a hundred battles, but never met an opponent so skilled," he whispered with his last breath.

Octavian whooped and ran around the stables, whirling the heavy gladius over his head. Without warning, a powerful hand gripped his wrist from behind and he yelped in surprise.

"What do you think you are doing with my sword?" Tubruk asked, breathing hard through his nose.

Octavian winced in expectation of a blow, then opened his eyes slowly when it didn't come. He saw the old gladiator was still glaring at him, waiting for an answer.

"I'm sorry, Tubruk. I just borrowed it for practice."

Still holding the little boy's wrist too firmly to permit escape, Tubruk reached over and took the sword from unresisting fingers. He brought the blade up and swore in anger as he looked at it, making Octavian jump. The boy's eyes were wide with fear at the expression that crossed Tubruk's face. He had not expected him to return from the fields for another few hours, and by that time the sword would have been back in its place.

"Look at that! Have you any *idea* how long it will take to get an edge back on it? No, of course you haven't. You're just a stupid little fool who thinks he can steal anything he wants."

Octavian's eyes filled with tears. He wanted nothing more in the world than to have the old gladiator approve of him, and the disappointment was worse than pain.

"I'm sorry. I just wanted to borrow it. I'll sharpen it so you can't see the marks!"

Tubruk looked again at the blade. "What did you do, smash it deliberately? That can't be sharpened. It needs to be completely reground, or better still, thrown away for scrap. I've carried that sword through bouts in the gladiator ring and three wars, and all that is undone by one thoughtless hour with a boy who can't keep his hands away from other people's belongings. You've gone too far this time, I swear it."

Too furious to speak further, Tubruk threw the sword onto the ground and let go of the sniveling child, storming out of the stables and leaving him alone with his misery.

Octavian picked up the weapon and ran his thumb over the edge, which had been folded right over in some places. He thought if he could find a good sharpening stone and disappear from the estate for a few hours, by the time he returned Tubruk would have calmed down and he could give him the sword back. A vision of the old gladiator's surprise as Octavian handed him the restored blade came into his mind.

"I thought it couldn't be done!" he imagined Tubruk saying as he examined the new edge. Octavian thought he might not say anything then, but simply assume a humble expression until Tubruk ruffled his hair, the incident forgotten.

The daydream was interrupted by Tubruk's return, and Octavian dropped the sword in fear as he saw the old gladiator had a heavy leather strap in one hand.

"No! I said I was sorry! I'll fix the sword, I promise," Octavian bawled, but Tubruk kept a fierce silence as he dragged him out of the stables into the sunlight. The little boy struggled hopelessly as he was pulled across the courtyard, but the hand that held him was rigid with an adult strength he couldn't break, for all the growing he'd done.

Tubruk heaved open the main gate with the hand that held the strap, grunting with the effort.

"I should have done this a long time ago. There's the road back to the city. I suggest you take it and make sure I don't lay eyes on you again. If you stay here, I am going to beat your backside until you know better. What's the word? Leave or stay?"

"I don't want to go, Tubruk," the boy cried, sobbing in terror and confusion. Tubruk firmed his mouth, deaf to his pleas.

"Right then," he said grimly, and took hold of Octavian by his tunic, bringing the strap down on his bottom with a snap that echoed around the yard. Octavian pulled madly to get away and yelled incoherently in a wail, but Tubruk ignored him, raising the strap again.

"Tubruk! Stop that!" Cornelia said. She had come out into the yard to see the source of so much noise and now faced the pair of them, her eyes blazing. Octavian used the moment to yank his tunic from Tubruk's grasp and ran to her, wrapping his arms around her and hiding his head in her dress.

"What are you doing to the boy, Tubruk?" Cornelia snapped.

The estate manager didn't reply, stepping close to her to grab hold of Octavian once again. Even with his head pressed deep in the cloth of her dress, Octavian sensed him coming and skittered out of the way behind her. Cornelia used her hands to hold Tubruk at bay in a frantic surge of energy that made him take a step back, his chest heaving.

"You will stop this at once. He's terrified, can't you see?" Cornelia demanded.

Tubruk shook his head slowly, his eyes flickering up to hers. "It'll do him no good when he's grown if you let him hide behind you now. I want him to remember this and I want it to come back to him the next time he thinks of stealing something."

Cornelia bent down and took Octavian's hands in hers. "What did you take this time?" she said.

"I only borrowed his sword. I meant to put it back, but it went blunt and before I could sharpen it, Tubruk came back," Octavian wailed wretchedly, watching Tubruk out of the corners of his eyes in case he made another attempt to lay hands on him.

Cornelia shook her head. "You damaged his sword? Oh, Octavian. That's too much. I have to give you back to Tubruk. I'm sorry."

Octavian screamed as she detached his fingers from her dress with firm strength and Tubruk took hold of his tunic again. Cornelia chewed her bottom lip unhappily as Tubruk brought the strap down four more times, then let Octavian run away into the soothing darkness of the stables.

"He's terrified of you," Cornelia said, looking after the boy as he ran.

"Perhaps, but it was called for. I've let him get away with things I never would have stood from Julius or Brutus when they were boys. He spends half his time in a dream world, that one. It won't have done him any harm to have his bottom warmed. Maybe next time he looks to steal, it will slow his hands a little."

"Is the sword ruined?" Cornelia asked, still unsure of herself around this man who had known Julius when he was as young as Octavian.

Tubruk shrugged. "Probably. But the boy won't be, which is more than I could say if he'd gone his happy way in the city for much longer. Leave him in the stables for a while. He'll have a good cry and then come in to eat, as if nothing had happened, if I know him."

Octavian did not turn up for the evening meal and Clodia brought out a bowl of food as darkness fell. She couldn't find him in the stables and a search of the estate brought no sign of the little boy. He and the gladius had gone.

* * *

"You're too ugly to be a good swordsman," Brutus said cheerfully as he moved lightly on the balls of his feet around the angry legionary. As the light faded, the men had gathered in the center of the camp as they had for the previous three nights to watch the bouts Brutus had started.

"You need a certain skill, it's true, but being handsome is also important," Brutus continued, watching the man with a close scrutiny belied by the banter. The legionary turned to face him, gripping his practice sword a little too tightly with tension. Although the wooden weapons were hardly lethal, a solid blow could break a finger or put out an eye. The wood was hollow all along the thick blade and had been filled with lead, making it heavier than a gladius. When the soldiers took up their real swords, they felt almost miraculously light in their hands.

Brutus turned in place to avoid a lunge, letting the blade pass only inches from him. He'd started the bouts at the end of the sixth evening, when he realized he wasn't anywhere near as tired as he'd expected. They had quickly become the main item of entertainment for the bored soldiers, attracted by Brutus's cocky assurance that there wasn't one of them who could beat him. He often fought three or four legionaries in a row, and even the gambling games had ceased in the camp after the second night, with all the money placed in bets on or against Brutus. If he could keep winning, he would end the march with a small fortune.

"People like handsome heroes, you see. You hardly qualify," Brutus announced, turning a sudden attack with a grunt as he finished. "It's not something obvious like a nose or a peculiar mouth. . . ." He launched a spinning combination that was fended off desperately, and Brutus stepped back to let the man recover. The legionary had been just as cocky in the beginning, but now sweat spattered from his hair as he dodged and attacked. Brutus squinted at his face, as if judging his features.

"No, it's accumulated ugliness, as if nothing sits right at all," he said.

The soldier snarled and aimed a blow with enough force to split Brutus's skull if it landed. It sailed past and as the soldier followed it, Brutus tapped his own sword at the base of the man's neck, just enough to force him to overbalance. He went flat and scrambled up with his chest heaving as he spoke.

"Tomorrow? I think I could beat you if I had another chance, ugly or not."

Brutus shrugged and pointed to the line of waiting soldiers. "There's a few ahead of you, but I'll try to have Cabera put you at the front tomorrow evening, if you're willing. You're still holding on too tightly, you know."

The soldier examined his grip and nodded.

"Work on your wrists," Brutus continued seriously. "If you can trust their strength, you'll be able to loosen up a little."

The man retired to the crowd, moving the wooden sword slowly in concentration. Cabera brought up the next, ushering him forward like a favorite child.

"This one says he's good. He was champion of his century a few years back. The quartermaster wants to know if you're going to let the bet ride again. I think you've got him worried." Cabera grinned at Brutus, well pleased that he had eased himself into the Primigenia ranks after the first dull evening near the back.

Brutus looked the latest opponent up and down, noting the powerful shoulders and slim waist. The man ignored the inspection, spending the time stretching his muscles.

"What's your name?" Brutus asked him.

"Domitius. Centurion," the man replied.

There was something about him that caused Brutus to narrow his eyes in suspicion.

"Century champion, were you? How many years ago?"

"Three. Legion champion last year," Domitius replied, carrying on with the exercises without looking at the younger man.

Brutus exchanged a quick glance with Cabera and took in the fact that the crowd around them had grown to the point where everyone except the sentries must have been there. Renius had joined them and Brutus frowned at the sight of him. It was difficult to relax while the man who had taught you was shaking his head in apparent disbelief. He gathered his confidence.

"The thing is, Domitius, I'm sure you are competent

enough, but in every generation, there has to be someone who is better than everyone else. It's a law of nature."

Domitius slowly stretched the muscles of his legs. He appeared to think it over.

"You're probably right," he replied.

"I am right. Someone has to be the best of his generation, and I'm almost embarrassed to say that person is me." Brutus watched Domitius for a reaction.

"Almost embarrassed?" the man murmured as he loosened the muscles in his back.

Brutus felt irritated by the legionary's calm. Something about the almost hypnotic stretching nettled him.

"Right. Cabera? Go to the quartermaster and tell him I'll let the bet ride for one more bout with Domitius here."

"I don't think..." Cabera began, looking doubtfully toward the newcomer. Domitius was almost a head taller than Brutus and moved with control and an ease of balance that was rare.

"Just tell him. One more and I'm coming to collect."

Cabera grimaced and trotted away.

Domitius rose as if he were uncoiling and smiled at Brutus. "That's what I was waiting for," he said. "My friends have lost a lot of money betting against you."

"And that didn't tell you something? Let's get on with it, then," Brutus said curtly.

Domitius sighed. "You short men are always so impatient," he said, shaking his head.

       *   *   *

Octavian wiped his nose along his arm, leaving a silvery trail on the skin. At first the city had seemed a different place. It had been easy enough to slip past the gate guards, using a cart as cover, but once inside, the noise and smells and sheer *hurry* of the crowds were disconcerting. He realized the months on the estate had made him forget the energy of the city, even at night.

He hoped Tubruk was worried about him. In a day or two, Octavian thought, he would be welcomed back with open arms. Especially if he could persuade Tabbic to grind the blade back to a good edge. All he had to do was stay out of trouble until morning, when the little shop opened. The blade was wrapped in a horse cloth and held under his arm. He wouldn't have got far with it otherwise, he was sure. Some public-spirited citizen was sure to stop him, or, worse, a thief could snatch it for the money it would bring at one of the cheaper shops than Tabbic's.

Almost unconsciously, Octavian let his footsteps take him in the direction of his mother's house. If only he could spend the night there, he would see Tabbic and be back in the estate in a day or two with Tubruk pleased with him again. He thought of her likely reaction at seeing him and winced. The sword would be discovered and she would think he had stolen it. For a mother, she was not very trusting, he admitted sadly to himself. She never believed him, even when he was telling the truth, which was always infuriating.

Perhaps he should try to signal Alexandria, get her out to see him without disturbing the rest of the house. She might understand better than his mother what he had to do.

He trotted through the night crowd, dodging around the street sellers and resisting the urge to grab at the hot food that filled the air with tantalizing smells. He was starving, but the empty feeling in his stomach took second place to his need to make things right with Tubruk. Getting himself caught by an angry stall-keeper would spoil things as badly as a conversation with his mother.

"It's the rat!"

The sudden exclamation jarred him from his miserable thoughts. He looked up into the surprised eyes of the butcher's apprentice, and panic flared in him. He jumped down into the street to avoid hands that clutched from behind. They were all there! Desperately, he threw open the blanket roll and got a hand on the hilt of Tubruk's gladius. He brought it up in front of him as the butcher's boy moved in on him, hands clutching in anticipation. A wild swipe nearly touched the outstretched fingers, and the apprentice swore in surprise.

"You're going to die for that, you little Thurin bastard. I've been wondering where you went to. Been stealing swords now, have you?"

As the boy growled at him, Octavian could see the others edging to block his retreat. In a few moments he was surrounded and the bustling crowd moved around them without noticing the scene, or too afraid of violence to interfere.

Octavian held the sword in first position, as Tubruk had taught him. He couldn't run, so he vowed to get a good cut in before they rushed him.

The butcher's boy laughed, closing the space. "Not so cocky now, are you, rat?"

He looked enormous to Octavian and the sword suddenly felt useless in his hands. The butcher's boy approached with his hand held out to knock away any sudden attack, his face lit with feral excitement.

"Give it to me and I'll let you live," he said, grinning.

Octavian gripped the hilt even tighter against this threat, trying to think what Tubruk would do in his position. It came to him as the apprentice stepped inside the range of the wavering sword.

Octavian yelled and attacked, swiping the edge across the outstretched hand. If it had been sharp, the boy could have been crippled. As it was, he yelped and danced backward out of range, swearing and gripping the hurt hand in the other.

"Leave me alone!" Octavian shouted, looking for a gap to run through.

There wasn't one and the butcher's boy inspected his cut

hand before his face twisted evilly. Reaching behind himself, the apprentice took a heavy knife from his belt and showed it to Octavian. It was rusty with the blood of his trade, and Octavian could hardly tear his eyes from it.

"I'm going to cut you, rat. I'm going to put your eyes out and leave you blinded," the older boy snarled at him.

Octavian tried to flee but, instead of holding him, the other apprentices laughed and pushed him back toward the butcher's boy. He raised the sword again and then a shadow loomed over the apprentices and a heavy hand connected solidly with the butcher boy's head, knocking him flat.

Tubruk reached down and picked up the knife from where it had fallen on the stones of the street. The butcher's boy began to rise and Tubruk closed his fist and punched him down into the filth of the street, where he scrabbled, dazed.

"Never thought I'd see the day when I was fighting with children," Tubruk muttered. "Are you all right?" Octavian watched him with openmouthed astonishment. "I've been looking for you for hours."

"I was ... taking the sword to Tabbic. I didn't steal it," Octavian replied, tears threatening again.

"I know, lad. Clodia guessed you were heading that way. Looks like a good thing I came to find you, doesn't it?" The old gladiator glanced at the ring of apprentices who stood nervously around, unsure whether to run or not.

"If I were you, lads, I'd get away before I lose my temper," he said. His expression made the consequences quite clear and they wasted no time disappearing.

"I'll send the sword to Tabbic myself, all right? Now, are you coming back to the estate or not?"

Octavian nodded. Tubruk turned to make his way back through the crowds to the gate. It would be close to dawn before they reached the estate, but he knew he wouldn't have slept with Octavian lost anyway. For all his faults, he liked the boy.

"Wait, Tubruk. Just a moment," Octavian said.

Tubruk turned with a frown. "What is it now?"

Octavian stepped over to the battered apprentice and kicked him as hard as he could in the crotch. Tubruk winced in sympathy.

"Gods, you have a lot to learn. That isn't sporting when a man is down."

"Maybe not, but I owed it to him."

Tubruk blew air out of his cheeks as Octavian fell in with him.

"Maybe you did, lad."

*   *   *

Brutus couldn't believe what was happening to him. The man was inhuman. He had no breath for banter and he'd almost lost the bout in the first few seconds as Domitius had struck with a speed he'd never seen before. His anger had fired his reflexes to match the attack, and the crack of blocked strikes was relentless for longer than he would have believed possible. The man didn't seem to stop for breath. The blows came constantly, from all angles, and twice Brutus had almost lost his sword when he was caught on the arm. With real weapons, that might have been enough to finish it, but in the practice bouts it had to be a clearly fatal blow, especially when there was money riding on the result.

Brutus had regained some ground when he shifted into the fluid style he'd learned from a tribal warrior in Greece. As he'd hoped, the different rhythms had broken Domitius's attack and he caught the man's forearm with a rap that would have taken his hand off at the wrist if there were an edge on the blade.

Domitius had stepped away then, looking surprised, and Brutus had used the moment to force his anger into a calm to match his opponent's. Domitius was hardly breathing heavily and he seemed completely relaxed.

In case it muffled the sound of an enemy attack, the watching soldiers were forbidden to cheer or shout by camp order. Instead, they hissed or gasped as the fight moved around the circle, waving clenched fists and baring their teeth in repressed excitement.

Brutus had a chance to punch as the swords were trapped together, but that too was forbidden, in case the soldiers injured each other too badly to fight or march the following day.

"I . . . could have had you then," he grated.

Domitius nodded. "I had the chance myself earlier. Of course, I have a longer reach than you."

The attack came again and Brutus blocked twice before the third broke through his guard and he looked down at the wooden point pressing painfully into his chest under the ribs.

"A win, I think," Domitius said. "You really are very good. You nearly won with that style you used halfway through. You'll have to show it to me sometime." He saw Brutus's crestfallen expression and chuckled.

"Son, I have been legion champion five times since I was your age. You're still too young to have your full speed, and skill takes even longer. Try me again in a year or two and there might be a different result. You did well enough and I should know."

Domitius walked away into a crowd of soldiers, who clapped him on the back and shoulders in congratulation. Cabera approached Brutus, looking sour.

"He was very good," Brutus muttered. "Better than Renius or anyone."

"Could you beat him if you fought again?"

Brutus thought about it, rubbing his chin and mouth. "Possibly, if I learned from this time."

"Good, because I collected the winnings from the quartermaster before the fight started."

"What? I told you to let it ride!" Brutus said with an amazed grin. "Ha! How much did we make?"

"Twenty aurei, which is the original silver doubled for the seven bouts you won. I had to leave a few on you against Domitius, out of politeness, but the rest is clear."

Brutus laughed out loud, then winced as he began to feel the bruises he'd taken.

"He only challenged me to let his friends win back their money. It looks like I'll get another chance after all."

"I can set it up for tomorrow, if you like. The odds will be wonderful. If you win, there won't be a coin in camp."

"Do it. I'd like another crack at Domitius. You clever old man! How did you know I was going to lose?"

Cabera sighed, leaning close as if to impart a secret. "I knew because you are an idiot. No one beats a legion champion after three other bouts."

Brutus snorted. "Next time, I'll let Renius put the bets on," he retorted.

"In that case, I'll take my share out before you start."

CHAPTER 36

Julius thought he had seen busy ports in Africa and Greece, but Ariminum was the center of the grain trade across the country and the docks were crammed with ships loading and unloading cargoes. There was even a central forum and temples for the soldiers to make their peace and pray for safe delivery in the coming conflict. It was a little Rome, built on the edge of the great Po plain and the gateway to the south. Everything from the north that ended up in Rome passed first through Ariminum.

Crassus and Pompey had commandeered a private home on the edge of the forum, and it was to this that Julius made his way on the second night, having to ask directions more than once. He traveled with ten of the Primigenia soldiers as a precaution in a strange city, but the inhabitants seemed too concerned with trade to have time for plots or politics. Whether the huge force camped in a ring around the city troubled them, he could not tell. The ships and grain caravans went in and out and business continued without interruption, as if the only threat of war was the possibility of raised prices in the markets.

Julius passed easily through the rushing crowds with his men, listening to their chatter as they struck deals while walking, barely noticing the soldiers they stepped around. Perhaps they were right to feel secure, he thought. With the two northern legions they had met at the city, the assembled army approached forty thousand seasoned soldiers. It was difficult to imagine a force that they couldn't handle, for all the shock the Spartacus rebellion had caused after running amok at Mutina.

He found the right place by the sentries that guarded the steps up to the door. Typical of Crassus to find such an opulent house, Julius thought with a smile. For all his personal restraint, he loved to be surrounded by beautiful things. Julius wondered if the true owner would find a couple of empty spaces amongst his treasures when the Romans had left. He remembered Marius saying Crassus could be trusted with anything except art.

Julius was guided in by a soldier and entered a room dominated by a creamy statue of a naked girl. Crassus and Pompey had planted chairs at her feet and more seats in a ring facing them.

Six of the eight legates were already there, and as the last two entered, Julius sat with his hands on his lap and waited. The last to enter was Lepidus, who had accepted the body of Mithridates from him in Greece. It felt like a lifetime ago, but the man still had the same bland, unconcerned expression as he nodded to Julius vaguely and began to clean the nails of one hand with the other.

Pompey leaned forward, the back legs of his chair leaving the floor.

"From this point on, gentlemen, I will expect to see you every night after the sentries are posted. Rather than have a vulnerable line of four camps, I have given orders for only two, with four legions in each. You should be close enough to reach the command position two hours before each midnight."

There was a murmur of interest from the legates as they digested this. Pompey continued over it.

"The latest reports suggest the slave army is heading

north as fast as they can. Crassus and I believe there is a danger they will reach the Alps mountains and Gaul. If we cannot catch them before then, they will disappear. Gaul is vast and we have little influence there. They must not be allowed to win free, or next year will see another rebellion of every slave still on Roman lands. The destruction and loss of life would be huge."

He paused for comment, but the assembled generals were silent, watching him. One or two glanced at Crassus, clearly wondering about the Senate command, but Pompey's companion was sitting relaxed in his chair, nodding as Pompey rattled through the points.

"Your orders are to march west along the plains road until I give the signal to cut north. It's a longer route overall, but we'll make better speed on the road than across country. I want thirty miles a day, then twenty, then another thirty."

"For how long?" Lepidus interrupted.

Pompey froze and let the silence show his irritation.

"Our best estimates are for five hundred miles west and then some distance north that we cannot gauge without knowing the exact whereabouts of the enemy. It depends, of course, on how close to the mountains they get. I expect—"

"It can't be done," Lepidus said flatly.

Pompey paused again, then stood to look down on the general.

"I am telling you what will happen, Lepidus. If your legion cannot match the pace of the others under my command, then I will remove your rank and give it to someone who can make them march."

Lepidus spluttered in indignation. Julius wondered if he had been told how close he had come to outright control of the legions. But for a few votes in the Senate, their positions would have been reversed. Watching Lepidus closely, Julius suspected he knew that very well indeed. No doubt Cato had let the word slip out to him while they gathered in the Campus Martius, in the hopes of fomenting trouble later.

"My men have covered three hundred miles at a hard pace on this trip already, Pompey. They could do it again, but I'll need two weeks to rest them and no more than twenty, twenty-five miles a day afterward. Any more will lose men."

"Then we lose men!" Pompey snapped. "Every day we wait in Ariminum is another that brings this Spartacus closer to the mountains and freedom in Gaul. I am not staying here for a day longer than it takes to load up provisions. If we have a few dozen sprains and limps by the end, it is a price worth paying. Or even a few hundred, if it is the difference between catching them and watching them escape punishment for the Roman blood on their hands. Nine thousand dead at Mutina!" Pompey's voice had risen to a shout and he leaned toward Lepidus, who looked back with an infuriating calm.

"Who *is* in command here?" Lepidus demanded, waving a hand toward Crassus. "I was given to understand that it was Crassus the Senate chose over me. I do not recognize this business of 'second-in-command.' Is it even legal?"

The other legates did not miss the point that Lepidus could have led, any more than Julius did. Like cats, they watched the speakers with claws carefully hidden, waiting for the outcome. Crassus too rose from his seat to stand beside Pompey.

"Pompey speaks with my voice, Lepidus, and that is the voice of the Senate. Whatever you may have heard, you should know better than to question the command."

Pompey's face was tight with anger. "I tell you now, Lepidus. I will have you stripped of rank the first moment you make a mistake. Question an order of mine again and I will have you killed and left on the road. Understood?"

"Completely," Lepidus replied, apparently satisfied.

Julius wondered what he had hoped to gain by the exchange. Did the legate hope to undermine Crassus? Julius knew he could not serve under such a man, no matter how he twisted and turned to gain authority. The threat Pompey had made was a dangerous one. If Lepidus commanded the kind of personal loyalty Julius had seen with Primigenia and Marius, then Pompey had taken a risk. In Pompey's position, Julius thought it would have been better to have Lepidus killed immediately and his legion sent back to Rome in shame. Losing the men was a lighter penalty than marching with ones who might betray them.

"We will march in two days, at dawn," Pompey said. "I have spies out already on the road with orders to meet the main force when we get close. Tactics for the battle will have to wait on better information. You are dismissed. Tribune Caesar, I'd like a word with you, if you could stay."

Lepidus stood with the other legates, beginning a conversation with two of them as they passed out of the room. Before their voices had faded, Julius heard him laugh at some witticism and saw Pompey stiffen in irritation.

"He's the eyes and ears of Cato, that one," Pompey said to Crassus. "You can be sure he's taking little notes of everything we do to report back when we come home."

Crassus shrugged. "Send him back to Rome, then. I'll put my seal on it and we can beat the rebels with seven legions as easily as eight."

Pompey shook his head. "Maybe, but there are other reports I haven't mentioned. Julius, this is to go no further, understand? There's no point having the rumors all over the camp before tomorrow, which is what would happen if I told the others, especially Lepidus. The slave army has grown alarmingly. I'm getting reports of more than fifty thousand. Hundreds of farms and estates have been stripped. There is no way back for them now and that will make for desperate fighting. They know how we punish escaped slaves and the rebellion won't end without a massive show of force. I think we're going to need every legion we have."

Julius whistled softly. "We can't depend on a rout," he said.

Pompey frowned. "It doesn't look like it, no. I'd expect them to fold and run on the first attack except for the fact that they have women and children with them and nowhere to go if they lose. Those gladiators have brought off more than one success already, and they must be more than a rabble." He snorted softly. "If I didn't know better, I'd wonder if Cato was hoping to see us lose, but, no, that's too much even for him. They could still turn south again, and from Ariminum the whole country is open. They have to be crushed and I need good commanders to do it, Julius."

"I have more than two thousand under the Primigenia eagle," Julius replied. He chose not to mention that Cato had supplied half of them to protect his son. Renius had trained them to exhaustion, but they were still of poor quality compared to the established legions. He wondered how many were waiting for the right moment to put a knife in him. Such men at his back didn't inspire confidence, for all his assurances to Renius that they would become Primigenia.

"It's good to see that name in the field again. I can't tell you how much," Pompey replied, losing his grimness for a moment and looking surprisingly boyish as he smiled. Then the mantle of his continual anger settled on him again, as it had ever since his daughter's death. "I want Primigenia to march flank to Lepidus. I don't trust any man who has Cato as his sponsor. When it comes to the fighting, stay close to him. I'll trust you to do whatever has to be done. You'll be my own extraordinarii, I think. You did well in Greece. Do well for me."

"I am at your command," Julius confirmed with a quick bow of his head. He met Crassus's eyes, including him even as he began to plan. Brutus would have to be told.

As he left, with the soldiers of Primigenia falling in around him, Julius felt a touch of excitement and pride. He had not been forgotten and he would make certain Pompey didn't regret the trust.

*　　　　　　*　　　　　　*

The slave sank his hoe into the hard ground, splitting the clods of pale earth with a grunt. Sweat dripped from his face to leave dark marks in the dust, and his shoulders burned with the effort. At first he did not notice the man standing near him, as he was too wrapped up in his own misery. He raised the tool again and caught a flicker of motion out of the corner of his eye. He did not react immediately, his surprise covered in the motions of his work. The blisters on his hands had broken again and he laid down the hoe to tend them, aware of the man, but not yet willing to give his knowledge away. He had learned to guard the slightest advantage from his masters.

"Who are you?" the dark figure asked softly.

The slave turned to him calmly. The man was wrapped in a rough brown robe over a ragged tunic. His face was partially covered, but the eyes were alight with interest and pity.

"I am a slave," he said, narrowing his eyes against the sun. Even in the vine rows, it beat down on his skin, burning and blistering him. His shoulders were mottled with raw redness and loose, flaking skin that itched all the time. He scratched idly at the area while he watched the newcomer. He wondered if the man knew how close the guards were.

"You should not stay here, friend. The owner has guards in the fields. They'll kill you for trespassing if they find you."

The stranger shrugged without shifting his gaze. "The guards are dead."

The slave stopped his scratching and stood erect. His mind felt numb with exhaustion. How could the guards be dead? Was the man insane? What did he want? His clothes were much like the ones he wore himself. The stranger wasn't rich, perhaps a servant of the owner come to test his loyalty. Or just a beggar, even.

"I ... have to get back," he muttered.

"The guards are dead, did you not hear me? You don't have to go anywhere. Who are you?"

"I am a slave," he snapped, unable to keep the bitterness from his voice.

The stranger's eyes creased in such a way that he knew he was smiling under the cloth.

"No, my brother. We have made you a freeman."

"Impossible."

The man laughed out loud at this and pulled the robe away from his mouth, revealing a strong, healthy face. Without warning, he put two fingers into his mouth and whistled softly. The vines rustled and the slave grabbed up his hoe with a rush of fear, his mind filling with images of the assassins from Rome, come to kill him. He could almost taste the sweetness he remembered and his stomach jumped in spasm, though there was nothing to bring up.

Men appeared out of the green shadows, smiling at him. He raised the hoe and held it threateningly.

"Whoever you are, let me go. I won't tell anyone you were here," he hissed, his heart thumping and the lack of food making him light-headed.

The first man laughed. "There is no one to tell, my friend. You are a slave and you have been made free. That is truth. The guards are dead and we are moving on. Will you come with us?"

"What about..." He could not bring himself to say "master" in front of these men. "The owner and his family?"

"They are prisoners in their house. Do you want to see them again?"

The slave looked at the men, taking in their expressions. There was an excitement there he understood and he finally began to believe.

"Yes, I want to see them. I want an hour alone with the daughters and the father."

The man laughed again and it was not a pleasant sound. "Such hatred, yet I understand it. Can you handle a sword? I have one here for you, if you want." He held it out as a test. A slave was forbidden to bear arms. If he took it, he was marked for death with the rest of them.

The slave reached out and gripped the gladius firmly, rejoicing in the weight.

"Now who are you?" the stranger said softly.

"My name is Antonidus. I was once a general of Rome," he said, straightening his back subtly.

The man raised his eyebrows. "Spartacus will want to meet you. He too was an army man before ... all this."

"Will you let me have the family?" Antonidus asked impatiently.

"You will have your hour, but then we must move on. There are more to be freed today and our army needs the grain in the stores here."

Antonidus smiled slowly at the thought of what he would do to the people who had called themselves his masters. He had only seen them at a distance as he worked, but his imagination had provided the sneers and slights he could not see. He ran his thumb across the edge of the blade.

"Take me there first. After I have had my satisfaction, I am yours."

     *   *   *

The warren of filthy streets seemed closed off from the life and light of Rome. The two men Cato had sent trod warily through the refuse and excrement, trying not to react to the scrabbling sounds of rats and larger predators in the dark alleyways. Somewhere a child screamed and then the sound was cut off as if stifled. The two men held their breaths waiting for it to start again, wincing in understanding after the silence went on too long. Life was cheap in that place.

They counted the number of turnings at each stage, occasionally whispering to each other whether a tiny gap between the tenements was part of the count. These were sometimes less than a foot wide and filled with a dark mass they didn't dare to investigate. One of them had a dead dog half sunk in refuse that seemed to lean toward them as they passed, shuddering slightly as the buried part was eaten away by unseen mouths.

The two men were desperately uneasy by the time they reached the crossroads where Cato had told them to wait. It was nearly deserted, with only a few scurrying people moving past them without acknowledgment.

After a time, a shadow detached itself from the darkness under an overhang and moved silently toward them.

"Who do you seek here?" a voice whispered.

Both men swallowed in fear, their eyes straining to make out features in the gloom.

"Look away from me!" the voice snapped.

They turned as if pushed, staring down the rubbish-strewn lane. A sickening smell washed over them as the dark figure stepped close enough to touch.

"Our master told us to mention the name of Antonidus to whoever came," one of them said, breathing through his mouth.

"He has been sold as a slave, far north. Who is your master now?" the voice returned.

One of the men suddenly remembered the smell from when his father had died, and he vomited, bending over and spilling his last meal into the unrecognizable slop that covered the lane. The other spoke haltingly, "No names, we were told. My master wishes to continue the association with you, but there must be no names."

A warm scent of rot sighed over them.

"I could guess it, you fools, but this is a game I know how to play. Very well then, what would your master have of me? Deliver your message while I still have patience for you."

"He . . . our master said you were to forget the one Antonidus asked for, now that the general has been taken for slavery. He will have other names for you and will pay your price. He wants the association to continue."

The figure let out a soft grunt of regret. "Tell him to name them and I will decide. I will not promise service to any man. As for the death bought by Antonidus, it is too late to call back the men I have sent. That one is dead, though she still walks unknowing. Now go back to your master and take your weak-stomached companion with you."

The pressure disappeared and Cato's servant took a deep breath in reaction, preferring the stench of the street to the soft odor that seemed to have sunk into his clothes and skin as they talked. It lingered with the two men as they made their way back to the open streets and a world that laughed and shouted, unaware of the festering alleys so close to them.

CHAPTER 37

A crest of white-topped mountains lined the horizon. Somewhere between the teeth were the three passes they hoped to use to escape the wrath of Rome. The cold peaks brought an ache of homesickness as Spartacus looked up at them. Though he hadn't seen Thrace since his childhood, he remembered scrambling on the lower slopes of the great range there. He had always loved high places where the wind was a constant force against the skin. It made a man feel alive.

"They are so close," he said aloud. "We could cross them in a week or two and never see a Roman uniform again."

"Until they come next year and tear Gaul apart looking for us, if I know them," Crixus said. The man had always been blunt compared to the gladiator he followed. Crixus reveled in the reputation of being a practical man, allowing no dreams or wild schemes to detract from the leaden reality of what they had achieved. He was a short squat figure next to Spartacus, who still retained the litheness that suggested speed even when he was standing still. Crixus had no such grace. Born in a mine, the man was as ugly as he was strong and the only one of the gladiators who could wrestle Spartacus to a draw.

"They couldn't find us, Crix. The Gauls say the land over the mountains is filled with battling tribes. The legions would have to wage war for decades and they haven't the stomach for that. Now Sulla's gone, they haven't a decent leader in the whole pack of them. If we cross the Alps, we'll be free."

"Still the dreamer, Spartacus?" Crixus said, his frustration evident. "What sort of freedom do you see that is such a prize? Freedom to work harder than we ever did as slaves, scratching out a few crops on land threatened by the locals? They won't want us any more than the Romans do, you can be sure of that. It'll be a backbreaker, this freedom of yours, I know it. Get the women and children clear, that's all. Leave a hundred men to take them through the passes and we can finish what we started."

Spartacus looked at his second-in-command. Crixus had a thirst for blood in him that had only been whetted in the triumph at Mutina. After what he had lived through at Roman hands, that was easy enough to understand, but Spartacus knew there was more to it.

"Is it their soft life you want, Crix?" he said.

"And why not?" Crixus demanded. "We have turned over their hive, now the honey should be ours for the taking. You remember the civil war and so do I. Whoever has Rome has their balls. If we could take the city, the rest of them would fall over. Sulla knew that!"

"He was a Roman general, not a slave."

"That doesn't matter! Once you're in, you can change the rules to suit you. There *are* no rules except what you choose when you have the strength. I tell you, if you miss this chance, you will throw away everything we've done. In ten years, the scribes will say the garrison at Mutina were the rebels and *we* were loyal Romans!

"If we take the city, we'll be able to shove their history and their pride down their throats and *make* them accept the new order. Just give the word, Spartacus. I'll see it done."

"And the palaces and great estate houses?" Spartacus probed, his eyes narrowing.

"Ours! Why not? What is there in Gaul but scrubland and villages?"

"You'll need slaves to run them, Crixus, have you thought of that? Who will take in your crops and tend your vines?"

Crixus waved his scarred fist at the man he loved above all others. "I know what you're thinking, but we won't do it like those cursed bastards. It doesn't have to be like that."

Spartacus watched him in silence and he went on angrily. "All right, if you want an answer, then I'll have the Senate work my fields and I'll even pay the bastards a wage."

Spartacus laughed. "Who's dreaming now, Crix? Look, we've come this far. We've reached a place where we can leave all that behind, make a new start to our lives. No, go back to our lives as they should have been. They may come for us in the end, but as I said, Gaul is big enough to hide more than one army. We'll keep going north until we find a place where Rome is just a word, or not even known at all. If we turn south again, even without the women and children, we risk losing everything we've won. And for what? So you can sit in a marble house and spit at old men?"

"You'd let them chase you out of their land?" Crixus asked bitterly.

Spartacus gripped his arm with one of his powerful hands. "You'd wait for them to kill you?" he said gently. The anger went out of Crixus at his words.

"You don't understand, you Thracian whoreson," he said with a tight smile. "This is my land too, now. Here I am your general, the slave hammer who broke a legion on its own ground and two more at Mutina. In Gaul I'm just another tribesman in badly tanned furs. You would be as well. We'd be mad to turn away from all that wealth and power just to spend our remaining years hoping they never find us. Look, we have Antonidus now. He knows where they're weak. If I didn't think we could win, I would turn my arse to them and vanish before I ever saw another legionary, but we *can* win. Antonidus says they're tied up on every one of their borders, in Greece, Africa, everywhere. There aren't enough legions in the country to take us. Gods, the north is open, you've seen that. Antonidus says we can put three men in the field for every legionary. You won't find better odds than that, not in this life. Whatever they have, we can beat, and after them, Rome, the cities, the country, the wealth—it's all ours. Everything."

He put out his hand and whispered the words that had marked each stage of their rebellion, from the first wild days to the dawning belief that they could break the order that had existed for centuries. "All or nothing, Spartacus?" he said.

The gladiator looked at the hand and the bond of sworn friendship it represented. His gaze strayed to the Mutina eagle where it leaned against the wall of his tent. After a moment of silent contemplation, he let out his breath.

"All right, all or nothing. Get the women and children clear away and then I want to see Antonidus before putting it to the men. Do you think they will follow us?"

"No, Spartacus, but they will follow *you* anywhere."

Spartacus nodded. "Then we will turn south and strike at the heart of them."

"And rip the bastard out."

*   *   *

Pompey had ordered Lepidus to the head of the column with his legion, forcing them to set the pace. Behind them, Primigenia marched with Crassus and Pompey at the head. The message was clear and the first hundred miles had been covered at the speed Pompey wanted without losing a man to injury.

The evenings were quieter times in the two great camps than they had been on the Via Flaminia. The pace sapped the energy of the legionaries, and by the time the halt was called, they were ready to eat and sleep and little more. Even Brutus had ceased his sword bouts, claiming a draw with two losses and two wins against Domitius by the end. At intervals, Cabera would bring up the money they had lost with some bitterness.

Riders from the extraordinarii reported back each day, scouting far ahead of the main force. The messages they brought were worryingly brief, with no sign of the slave army within their range. Pompey sent out more and more of the scouts with orders to move north and west to find them. It wasn't said aloud, but the worry was that in such vast country the rebels could slip past them and move against the unprotected south.

Each night, the generals' meeting was fraught with argument and snapping tempers. Rather than take it as proof of Pompey's displeasure with him, Lepidus seemed to delight in leading the column, and Pompey grew less and less willing to hear his complaints. By Lepidus's account, only his authority could force the pace Pompey wanted from the legions, and each night he claimed the final price could be disastrous for them. He was a master at knowing when to stop pushing at Pompey's patience, and the meetings had become almost a battle of wills between the two men, with Crassus powerless to intervene. Julius hoped Lepidus could fight as well as he could argue.

After two weeks on the western road, Lepidus reported triumphantly that men had fallen and been left at the guard posts or in villages with orders to rejoin when they had healed. Every night was an agony of blisters and sprains for hundreds of the legionaries all the way down the column. The legions were approaching exhaustion and the other legates had begun to side with Lepidus in their call to rest the men. Pompey acceded reluctantly rather than see his authority undermined, standing them down for four days. Only the extraordinarii were denied rest as Pompey sent them all out in a last bid to find the slave army.

At last the riders came galloping back into camp with sightings. The rebels were moving south and east back from the mountains to the plains. Pompey gathered his generals that evening to give them the grim news.

"They are striking back toward Rome and the scouts say they have more than eighty thousand men on the march. Every slave in the north has gone over to them."

There was little point in holding back the worrying figures from the generals, with the rebels only a few hundred miles away. Now that the scouts had found them, they would not be allowed to escape. Regardless of numbers, it only remained to choose the best place of attack.

"If they're coming south, we can either march to meet them or wait for them to reach us," Pompey continued. "No matter what happens, they cannot pass or we'll lose Rome. Make no mistake, gentlemen, if they break through our line, Rome will fall and all we love will die, like Carthage before us. We will make a stand here to the last man if need be. Make that clear to your men. There is nowhere to retreat to, no safe haven where we can regroup and strike again. The Republic stands with us alone."

Lepidus looked as shocked as the others. "Eighty thousand! I have as much confidence as anyone in our soldiers, but . . . the legions in Greece and Spain must be recalled. The Senate didn't know the size of the threat when they sent us out."

For once, Pompey bore his outburst without a rebuke. "I have sent messages back to Rome, but we are here now. Even if the borders could be stripped without losing everything we've gained in a hundred years, those legions couldn't reach us in time to make a difference to this battle."

"But we could mount a fighting retreat until support

arrives. Eighty thousand could overwhelm us. We'd be flanked and broken in the first hour of fighting. It's impossible!"

"Speak like that in front of the men and that's exactly what will happen," Pompey barked at the general. "These are not trained soldiers we're facing, Lepidus. They could have escaped across the mountains in all likelihood, but instead they are after riches and plunder, while our men fight for our home city and the lives of everyone in it. They will break for us. We will stand."

"The commander at Mutina probably said the same thing," Lepidus muttered, not quite loudly enough for Pompey to be forced to answer, though he glared at the legate.

"My orders are to engage and destroy, gentlemen. We will do exactly that. If we wait for them, they could go right round us, so we will carry this war to them. Make the men ready to march north. Lepidus, you will take the left flank and keep a wide line to prevent encirclement. They have little in the way of cavalry except a few stolen mounts, so use ours to hold the wings steady. Julius, I want you on the left to support Lepidus if that becomes necessary. Crassus and I will take the right flank as always and I will concentrate the bulk of the cavalry there to prevent them spilling round us and making south and east toward Ariminum. They must not be allowed to reach that city."

One of the two legates from Ariminum cleared his throat.

"I would like to take the right flank with you, sir. Many of my men have families in Ariminum. I do myself. They will fight all the harder knowing what could happen if the right breaks."

Pompey nodded. "All right. The Ariminum legions will be the core of the right flank. The rest of you make the center. I want the *hastati maniples* on the front line instead of the *velites*. We need weight more than speed to break them on the first charge. Bring the *triarii* up quickly if the advance is slowed or turned. I've yet to meet a force that can withstand our veterans."

It was dawn before the meeting ended, and the day was spent breaking the camp ready for the march. Julius stayed with Primigenia, passing on the orders and positions to Brutus and the centurions. By that evening, every man knew the seriousness of the battle to come, and many of the injuries they had taken on the march were forgotten or ignored in the thoughts of the conflict they welcomed. Even with the rumors of huge numbers of the enemy, every soldier was determined they would not leave Rome and their families open to the invader. Better than anyone, they knew that their discipline and skill were unmatched, no matter who came against them, or how many.

*   *   *

The army of Spartacus was sighted at sunset. The order signals went out to create a hostile camp, with the borders twice the normal height and every soldier sleeping on short watches ready to repel a night attack. The soldiers spent the time awake checking their armor and swords, oiling leather and polishing metal. Spears were sharpened or replaced with fresh-cast heads from the smithy. Heavy ballistae and onagers were assembled and stone shot made ready for the dawn, their bulk leaving ruts in the soil. The slave army had nothing like the great war machines, and though they had but one range, the "mule's kick" onager could cut swaths through an enemy charge.

Brutus woke Julius from a light sleep by shaking his shoulder.

"Is it my watch?" Julius said sleepily, sitting up in the dark tent.

"Shhh. Come outside. I want to show you something."

Vaguely irritated, Julius followed Brutus through the camp, stopping twice to give the watchword of the day to alert sentries. Within striking range of the enemy, the camp was far from quiet. Many of the men who couldn't sleep sat outside their tents or around small fires talking quietly. Tension and fear tightened their bladders through the night, and Julius and Brutus saw the urine trench was sodden and stinking already as they passed it.

Julius realized Brutus was making straight for the praetorian gate in the north wall of the camp.

"What are you doing?" he hissed to his friend.

"I need you to get us out of the camp. They'll let a tribune through if you order it." He whispered his idea and Julius squinted at his friend in the darkness, wondering at the wild energy that seemed such a part of him. He considered refusing and going back to his tent, but the night air had cleared his head and he doubted he would be able to sleep again. He didn't feel tired. Instead, his muscles trembled with nervous energy, and waiting idle would be worse than anything.

The gate was guarded by a century of extraordinarii, still dusty from their scouting rides. The commander trotted his horse over to them as they approached.

"Yes?" he said bluntly.

"I want to leave the camp for a couple of hours," Julius replied.

"Orders are no one leaves camp."

"I am the legate of Primigenia, a tribune of Rome, and the nephew of Marius. Let us pass."

The centurion wavered in the face of the order. "I should report it, sir. If you leave, you are disobeying Pompey's direct order."

Julius glanced at Brutus, silently cursing him for putting him into this position.

"I will clear it with the general when I return. Report as you see fit."

"He will want to know what you are doing, sir," the centurion continued, wincing slightly. Julius could admire his loyalty, though he dreaded what Pompey would say if the man carried out his threat to report.

"There is a spike of rock that overlooks the battle-ground," he said quietly. "Brutus believes it would give us a view of the enemy force."

"I know it, sir, but the scouts say it's too steep to be climbed. It's practically sheer," the man replied, rubbing his chin in thought.

"It's worth a try at least," Brutus said quickly.

The centurion looked at him for the first time, his expression brooding. "I can delay reporting it until the watch changes in three hours. If you're not back by then, I'll have to name you as deserters. I'll give that much for a nephew of Marius, but that's it."

"Good man. It won't come to that. What's your name?" Julius asked him.

"Taranus, sir."

Julius patted the horse on his quivering neck.

"Julius Caesar, and this is Marcus Brutus. There are your names. We'll be back before the new watch, Taranus. On my word, we will."

The guards moved aside to let them pass on Taranus's order, and Julius found himself on the rocky plain, with the enemy somewhere ahead of them. When they were out of earshot of the guards, he rounded on Brutus.

"I can't believe I let you persuade me into this. If Pompey hears about it, he'll take the skin of our backs at least."

Brutus shrugged, unconcerned. "He won't if we can climb that rock. His scouts are horsemen, remember. They think anywhere they can't take a horse can't be climbed. I had a look at it before the light faded and the top will give us a good view. There's enough moonlight to see the enemy camp, and that will be useful, no matter what Pompey says about us leaving camp."

"You'd better be right," Julius said grimly. "Come on, three hours isn't long."

The two young men broke into a run toward the black mass they saw silhouetted against the stars. It was a forbidding crag, a tooth in the plain.

*   *   *

"It's bigger close up," Brutus whispered, removing his sandals and sword for the climb. Though it would hurt their feet, the iron-shod sandals would slip and clatter on the stones and could alert the enemy. There was no way of telling how close they were to the patrols, but they had to be near.

Julius glanced at the moon and tried to estimate how long they had before it sank.

Unhappy with the calculation, he removed his sword and sandals and took a deep, slow breath. Without speaking, he reached for the first handhold, jamming his hand into a crack and heaving, his bare feet searching for grip.

Even with the moonlight to help them, it was a difficult and frightening climb. All the way up, Julius was tormented by the possibility that some slave archer would see them and spit them with shafts that would send them down to break on the rocky plain below. The spire of rock seemed to get taller as they climbed, and Julius was sure it was more than a hundred feet high, even two. After a time, his feet became numb blocks, barely able to hold him. His fingers were cramped and painful and he began to worry that they would never make it back to camp before being reported.

By his best guess, it took almost an hour to reach the barren crest of the rock, and for the first few moments, he and Brutus could do nothing more than lie panting, stretched flat as they waited for their tortured muscles to recover.

The top was an uneven space, lit almost white in the moonlight. Julius raised his head and then pulled himself into a sudden crouch, horror flooding through him.

There was someone else there, only feet away from them. Two figures sat watching as Julius's hands scrabbled for where his sword usually hung, almost cursing aloud as he remembered leaving it below.

"Looks like you two had the same idea we had," a deep voice chuckled.

Brutus swore and rose fully, caught in sudden fear as Julius had been. The voice spoke in Latin, but any thoughts that it might have belonged to one of their own were quickly dispelled.

"You won't have managed that climb with swords, lads, but I brought a dagger along and when you're this high and barefoot, it's a good idea to keep peaceful. Move slowly over here and don't make me nervous."

Brutus and Julius looked at each other. There was no way to retreat. The two figures rose and faced them, seeming to fill the tiny space. They too were barefoot and wore only tunics and leggings. One of them waved his dagger at them.

"I guess this makes me king for the night, lads. I see by your clothes that you're Romans. Come to see the view, eh?"

"Let's kill them," his companion said.

Brutus looked him over with a sinking feeling. The man was as powerfully built as a wrestler and the moonlight revealed an expression without mercy. The best he could hope for was to carry the man over the edge with him, which wasn't a thought that gave him any comfort. He edged away from the drop at his back.

The other man placed a hand on his friend's chest, holding him still.

"No need for that, Crix. There'll be time enough at the battle tomorrow. We can all shed each other's blood then, roaring and threatening as the mood takes us."

The wrestler subsided with a grunt and turned his back on the two Romans. He was almost close enough to touch, but something about the man's alert stance warned Brutus he was expecting it. Possibly he was hoping they would try.

"Are you armed?" the first man said pleasantly, gesturing them closer. When they didn't move, he inched closer to Julius with the dagger held ready. Behind him, the shorter man had turned back and was glaring at the young men, daring them to try something.

Julius allowed himself to be patted down and then stood aside as Brutus too was checked for hidden blades. The man was careful and his own shoulders looked powerful enough to give him an edge even without the dagger.

"Good lads," he said when he was sure they were helpless. "It's only because I am a dangerous old sod that I carried one myself. Will you be fighting tomorrow?"

Julius nodded, unable to believe what was happening. His mind raced, but there was nothing to be done. When he realized that, he finally relaxed and laughed, making Brutus jump. The man with the dagger returned it, chuckling softly as he looked at the young Roman.

"You might as well laugh, lad. This is a tight space for a bit of a struggle. Do what you came for; it won't make any difference. There won't be much stopping us tomorrow, no matter what you report back."

Watching the man for sudden movement, Julius sat down, his heart hammering at the thought of one quick push sending him over the edge. The situation was strange to say the least, but the man with the knife seemed to be enjoying it. Whoever he was, he seemed completely relaxed, removed from the struggle they would all face back on the ground.

From the top of the granite spike, the rebel camp seemed incredibly close, almost as if a good leap would have them land in the center of it. Julius looked it over and wondered if they would be allowed to return before the watch centurion reported them missing.

The man with the knife put it away in his tunic and sat

next to Julius, following his gaze. "Biggest army I ever saw," he said cheerfully, motioning toward the rebel camp. "Tomorrow will be hard on you, I should think."

Julius said nothing, unwilling to be drawn. Privately, he had the same impression. The enemy camp was almost too large to take in and looked as if it could swallow the eight legions without trouble.

Brutus and the wrestler had remained standing, keeping a close eye on each other's movements. The man with the knife grinned at the pair of them.

"Sit down, you two," he said, gesturing with a flick of his head. Reluctantly, they edged together and sat close, as tense as wires.

"You must have what, thirty, forty thousand men?" the wrestler asked Brutus.

"Keep guessing," Brutus replied curtly and the man began to rise, held down with the lightest touch from his companion.

"What does it matter now? We'll send the Romans running, no matter how many they have." He grinned at Julius, clearly hoping he would rise to the barb.

Julius ignored him, busy memorizing the few details of the camp he could make out in the dim light. He noted the moon had sunk lower and stood slowly so as not to alarm his strange companions.

"We should be going back now," he said. The tension returned to him then, tightening his sore muscles.

"Yes, I suppose we all should," the man with the knife replied, rising smoothly to his feet. He was easily the tallest of all of them and moved with an efficiency of motion that marked a warrior. Brutus had it and perhaps it was that unconscious recognition that had raised the hackles of the one with a wrestler's build.

"This has been...interesting. I hope you and I don't meet tomorrow," Julius said.

"I hope *we* meet," Brutus added to the wrestler, who snorted in disdain.

The man with the knife stretched his back and winced. Then he clapped Julius on the shoulder and smiled.

"In the hands of the gods, lads. Now, I think my friend and I should climb down first, don't you? I don't really want you thinking better of our little soldier's truce when you have your swords again. Get right over where you climbed up and we'll be away in no time."

The two older men scrambled from sight with casual agility and were gone.

Brutus let out an explosion of breath. "I thought we were dead."

"So did I. Do you think that was Spartacus?"

"Possibly. When I tell the story, it certainly will be." Brutus began to laugh simply to release the awful tension of the meeting.

"We'd better move, or that guard will serve us up to Pompey on a platter," Julius said, ignoring him. They climbed down quickly and bore the scrapes and bruises of the descent without a sound. Their sandals were where they had left them, but the two swords had been taken. Brutus looked for the weapons in the bushes, but came back empty-handed.

"Bastards. There's just no honor anymore."

CHAPTER 38

The legions broke camp and formed the battle line two hours before dawn. As soon as it was light enough to see, the cornicens sounded their wailing notes and the huge squares of legionaries moved forward, shrugging off the stiffness and cramp of the morning as they marched. There was no idle chatter in the ranks with the army of Spartacus filling the plain and seeming to stretch to the horizon. Even the crash of their sandals was muffled in the turf, and each man loosened his shoulders as he came closer and closer to the moment when the silence would rupture into chaos.

All along the legion lines, the heavy onagers and catapults were heaved into position. At colossal range, stones, iron balls, and arrows the weight of three men could be sent smashing into the enemy. The men around them cheered as the heavy horse-hair springs were winched back into firing position.

Julius marched with Brutus and Ciro at his side and Renius one step behind him. Although it would be suicide for any of Cato's recruits to try an attack, the three men around Julius were alert for the possibility. There was no place there for Cabera, who had remained behind in the camp with the rest of the followers, despite his complaints. Julius had been firm with him, but even if the old man had been willing to don armor and carry a gladius, he had never fought in formation before and would disrupt the routine of the Romans around him.

Deep in the eighth rank behind the armored hastati, the four of them were surrounded by the best of the Primigenia, men whom Renius had trained and hardened to be ready for such a day. None of Cato's recruits were in striking range.

Though many ached to charge, they matched the pace of the forward line, teeth bared unconsciously as they left everything of the world behind them. Every violent urge they had to restrain in the cities was welcome in that line, and some of the men choked back laughter as they remembered the strange freedom of it.

The order to halt came and seconds later the air was split with the thunder of the war engines, great arms crashing into their rests as they sent their loads flying. The slaves could not avoid the hail of stone and iron and hundreds were smashed into rags of flesh. Slowly, the arms were winched back again and Pompey waited to give the signal, licking dry lips.

At the third volley, the order came again to advance. One more would be fired over their heads before the lines would join.

As the armies closed, the legionaries shrugged away the smooth skin of civilization, leaving only the discipline of the legion to hold their line against the rising desire to kill. Through the gaps in the ranks, they could catch glimpses of the enemy that waited for them, a dark wall of men who had come to test the strength of the last defenders of Rome. Some carried the gladius, but others wielded axes and scythes, or long swords stolen from the barracks of the legion at Mutina. Bloody smears on the soil marked the wide cuts of the onager stones, but they were quickly swallowed by the men behind them.

Julius found himself panting with excitement and fear, responding to those around him as they became linked and pulses began to pound, filling them with strength and reckless energy. Someone shouted in excitement, close.

"Steady, Primigenia!" Julius bellowed, feeling the urge to run forward himself. He saw Brutus too was filled with the strange joy where every moment before the first jolt of pain was longer than all he had lived before. It was a hundred years to cross the plain, and then sound pierced the calm as the front two ranks heaved their spears into the air with a grunting cough that merged into a roar of defiance. They began to run, even as the spears made the air black and the first of the slaves were cut down by them.

The enemy howled enough to fill the world and raced at the legionaries. The first meeting was a crash that numbed the sounds that came after. The heavy Roman shields were smashed upright into the charging line and the impact punched hundreds of slaves from their feet. Then the swords were plunging into bodies and blood spattered blindingly, until the whole of the first rank were covered in it, their arms and faces wet as the swords cut limbs and life from the men they faced.

With Brutus on Julius's right, Julius could work around his friend's shield, as Ciro stood in the protection of his own. Only the ingrained discipline held the ranks back from the front line, free to watch the carnage only feet from them. Stinging droplets of blood touched them as they saw the hastati storm forward through the slaves. Ciro smashed anything that stood against him with tireless strength. Julius and Brutus moved forward at the pace of the advance, sinking their swords into the bodies as they passed, making certain of the kills. By the time the rear ranks passed over the corpses, they would be little more than white bone and tattered flesh as every soldier blooded his sword on them.

The hastati were the spine of the army, men with ten years of solid experience. There was no fear in them, but after a while, Julius began to feel a slight change in the pace as the advance faltered. Even the hastati tired against such a host, and many in the ranks moved forward to fill gaps, stepping over the writhing bodies of men they knew and counted as friends. Renius walked with them, his shield strapped to his body with heavy buckles. He killed with single strokes, taking blows on the shield to allow him the counterstrike, over and over. It buckled and cracked under the repeated impacts, but held.

The cornicens blew a series of three notes over and over, and all along the vast line there was a shimmering as the maniples of Rome moved with a discipline unmatched in the world. The hastati brought their shields up to protect themselves and moved smoothly back through the ranks as the triarii moved forward. They were panting and tired but still filled with a savage pleasure, and they shouted encouragement to the twenty-year veterans who ran to make the new front line. These were the best in the line, and apart from Renius, Primigenia had only a handful, making up the numbers with Cato's fresh troops. The slaves threw themselves at the legions and Primigenia bore the worst toll of dead, the new recruits dying faster than the experienced men around them. Renius held the Primigenia line steady as they fought to move forward.

The advance surged again through the bodies of the slain. The only way was over the dead as neither side wavered or stepped back from the bloody gash that was the front rank. The triarii were the best of the legionaries, men at their fullest strength. Their family and friends were the legions they served and they were soon splashed as redly as the hastati before them.

Julius stood waiting in the fifth rank, with Primigenia straining to attack. Arms and swords shook in anticipation as they stood close enough to the cutting to have more and more of the blood droplets spatter over them like rain, running down their shining armor.

Some armies broke on the hastati, others when the triarii were brought in to crush the will of the enemy. The bodies they walked over and speared so casually numbered in the hundreds, perhaps thousands along the line, but they had only begun to cut away the outer layers of the army of Spartacus, and soon every man knew they would have to take their place. Once they saw it was inevitable, the nerves settled even in the weakest as they waited to reach the first rank.

"Primigenia—second spears!" Julius ordered, repeating the shout to his left and right. The ranks behind him launched without pause over the heads of their own men and the shafts landed unseen on the mass of the enemy. All along the line the action was repeated, and only distant screams told of the lives the points had taken.

Julius craned onto his toes to see what was happening on the flanks. Against so many, the cavalry had to prevent encirclement. As the line of Spartacus's army bowed before the Romans, a memory flashed into Julius's head of a distant schoolroom and a lesson of Alexander's wars. Huge as it was, the Roman army could be swallowed and destroyed unless the flanks remained strong.

Even as he started to look, he felt the change on his left. He saw the line buckle into Lepidus's legion and the enemy pour into the breach. It was too far away to see detail and as Julius paced forward with Brutus, he lost sight of it and swore.

"Brutus, can you see Lepidus? They're breaking through over there. Can you see if they're holding?"

Brutus stretched up on his toes to see. "The line is broken," he said in horror. "Gods, I think they're turning!"

Julius almost stumbled into the man behind him as his pace shortened. He looked at the line four ranks ahead. The triarii were crushing the slaves there and didn't look like tiring. His thoughts were desperate and fear rushed into him. If he moved Primigenia left to support as he had promised

Pompey, he left the triarii vulnerable. If their line was thinned or cut down, the reinforcements they would expect would be missing and the slaves would have two breaches to pour into, cutting the Roman line into islands of men that would shrink and vanish as they were killed.

As he hesitated, he saw the left flank was compacting as the breach widened and some of Lepidus's men turned away from the enemy, beginning to flee. It would spread like plague as those who ran fouled the ranks behind them and infected them with their cowardice. Julius made his choice.

"Primigenia! Saw left into the flank!" As before, he repeated the order twice and the front ranks heard him though they could not turn. They would know there was no one behind to bolster them and would fight all the harder in the time they were vulnerable.

Primigenia moved fast across the line of advance, a few stumbling into the soldiers who had not heard the order. It was a dangerous maneuver to try in the middle of a battle, but Julius knew he had to use his men to stiffen the legion of Lepidus before the whole left flank crumbled. He raced through the ranks with the others, leaping over corpses and continuing to shout orders to keep them in close and moving. At best he had seconds to prevent the rout.

Brutus arrived first, deliberately knocking a fleeing legionary over with his shield. Julius and Ciro took his sides and together they made the core, with Primigenia forming a wall of grim soldiers around them that the retreating Romans would have to cross to get away. Renius had vanished in the press, separated from them by hundreds of waiting soldiers.

"Level swords!" Julius roared, his face twisted into an animal mask of rage. "No soldier crosses this line alive! Show this Lepidus what we *are*!"

The spread of panicking men skidded to a halt as the ranks of Primigenia ranged before them, blocking the retreat. The light of panic went out of their eyes as they took in the swords held ready to cut them down. There was no question they would be used. The men of Primigenia understood as well as Julius that they would all die if Lepidus's legion ran from the slave flank. They would be overwhelmed.

In moments, something of order had returned to the disorganized rabble Lepidus's men had become. The centurions and optios used the flats of their swords and thick oak staffs to bully the soldiers back into formation. They were barely in time.

The slave army had sensed the weakness and they screamed orders, pushing hundreds into the gap to widen it. Julius was caught between moving forward through the ranks and having Primigenia seal the breach or holding his position in case Lepidus's men broke again. He knew the recovery was still weak, with the terrified soldiers barely controlling the fear of death that had broken them once. It would be easier the second time.

"Julius?" Brutus asked him, waiting for the order.

Julius glanced at his friend and saw his eagerness. There wasn't a choice after all. They had to take the front themselves and just pray Lepidus's men didn't leave them naked behind.

"Primigenia! Forward to the line!" he shouted, and the seven hundred men under his command jogged forward with him, holding their formation perfectly.

The last of Lepidus's men turned to run from the slaves and Primigenia cut them down before they could take the panic back with them. They did it with a vicious efficiency that should have warned the slaves who struggled to seize the advantage they had created.

The shields of Primigenia smashed into the breach and the swords rose and fell as quickly as they could, with every man sacrificing care for speed. They crunched over the wounded, leaving them screaming and often alive, but Primigenia shoved forward at such a pace that they were in danger of leaving the whole front rank behind and being cut off. Renius matched them, bringing the line up with bellowed orders.

Julius fought in a frenzy. His arm ached and one long wound had scored his skin in a red line from wrist almost to shoulder. A blade had skidded off him before he killed the owner. A powerful-looking slave wearing Roman armor leapt at him, but was knocked from his feet as Renius reached the position, stabbing the slave in the side through a gap in the plates.

Julius killed the next man who faced him, but then three more stabbed at him. He was grateful for the thousands of hours of practice that made him move before he had begun to think. He stepped to the side of the outer man and shoved him into the others, giving up the kill for the need to entangle them. The man stumbled into the path of the second and Julius took his throat out from the side, then lunged over his falling body to sink his gladius into the heaving chest of the middle man. It wedged in the ribs and he almost cried out in frustration as his bloody grip slipped completely from the sword as he pulled on it, leaving him unarmed in an instant.

The third man facing him brought a legionary gladius around in a hard, chopping sweep and Julius had to throw himself flat to avoid the blade. He felt panic then as he expected to feel the metal enter him and send his blood mixing with the slippery mess under him. The man died with Ciro's sword in his mouth and Julius scrabbled for his own blade, pulling a body off it and heaving until it came free with a crack of parting bone.

Brutus was a pace ahead and Julius saw him kill two more with a speed and ease Julius had never seen in anyone, never mind the boy he had known all his life. There seemed to be a peaceful space around Brutus and his face was calm, almost serene. Anything alive that came within the range of his sword died in one blow or two, and as if the slaves sensed the boundary, they gave him room and did not press the young soldier as closely as the rest.

"Brutus!" Julius called. "Gladiators in front!"

Racing toward Primigenia were men dressed in gladiator's armor. They wore full helmets that covered their faces, leaving only eyeholes that gave them a look of inhuman ferocity. Their arrival seemed to lift the slaves around them, so that Primigenia staggered to a halt, planting their shields into the soft ground.

Julius wondered if any of them were the men he'd met the night before. It was impossible to be sure in the clash of metal and bodies. They were fast and trained and Julius saw Renius shoulder one down as the ranks closed and another swung at him. Julius brought his shield high with a jerk, feeling twin shocks as his return blow dented armor. His shield entangled the man's sword arm as Julius hammered and hammered at the iron helmet until at last it split and he could move on, panting. His muscles ached and his breath seemed to scorch his throat.

Brutus waited in a pool of stillness that was untouched by the press of bodies all around him. The gladiator he faced feinted once and Brutus read it easily, swaying aside from the real blow. His own sword darted out in response and nicked the man's neck. Blood poured out and, a pace away, Julius heard the soft sound of surprise the gladiator made as he put his hand up to it in astonishment. It was no more than a nick, but a major vein had been severed and his legs collapsed under him. He struggled to rise, panting and groaning like a wounded bullock, then the life went out of him.

Julius hacked his gladius into an exposed neck, and was then knocked over backward as yet another fell against his shield, tearing the straps against his arm. He let it fall and grabbed blindly to hold his attacker long enough with his left hand to sink the gladius into his flesh with the other, though he felt a sting along his back as the man tried to bring a point to bear. He could smell the garlic of the man's last meal as he died.

The men of Primigenia were falling around him and he could see more of the gladiators rushing to take advantage of a breach that still wavered. He glanced behind him and saw with a gasp of relief that Lepidus's legion had re-formed and stood ready to move forward.

"Primigenia! Maniple order. Re-form on the fifth!" he shouted and killed two more raging slaves as they tried to take advantage of the change, charging wildly at the line of Primigenia and dying as quickly. There were so many of them, and without moving fresher men to the front, Primigenia would have been overwhelmed.

Brutus fell back with him and Julius was oddly pleased to see him breathing heavily. For a time, his friend had seemed untouchable by the battle, and it was reassuring to know he could become as tired as the rest of them. Julius watched with approval as Lepidus's men took up the attack and the advance pushed on. It was time to move back to the original position. The left flank was secure.

"Sir?" a voice said at Julius's side. He turned his head sharply in reaction, too tense to see anything except threats. A centurion stood there, without a helmet. A spreading bruise along his cheek and bloody forearms showed he had been in the thick of the battle.

"What is it?" Julius replied.

"General Lepidus is dead, sir. There is no one to command the left."

Julius closed his eyes for a second, willing away the tiredness that had seeped into his aching muscles with every pace away from the fighting. He glanced at Brutus, who smiled.

"Still lucky, Julius," he said with a trace of bitterness.

Julius took his friend's hand in a strong grip, a silent acknowledgment of what he had given up, then he turned to the waiting soldier.

"Very well, Centurion. I will assume command. Get the eagle over to me so the men know where to look for orders. Spread the word that if they break for me, I will crucify every last one of them when this is over."

The centurion blinked as he looked into the young commander's eyes. Then he saluted and ran to fetch the standard-bearer. Four ranks ahead of them, the battle raged on without a pause.

*   *   *

Pompey and Crassus watched the unfolding battle from the high vantage point of their mounts. The sun was rising in the sky and still the hills around swarmed with the slave army. Pompey had ordered the onagers and catapults to keep firing over the front lines until they had exhausted their missiles. They had fallen silent after the first three hours and the battle had only grown in ferocity since then.

The senators could observe in relative safety, more than a hundred feet back from the front ranks of the right flank. A century protected the position, allowing only the extraordinarii messengers through to the two commanders. After so long, the horses arrived at the command point with white sweat and spittle lathering their skin. A rider trotted up to the senators and saluted smartly despite his tiredness.

"The breach is closed, sir. Caesar commands the left. General Lepidus is dead," he said through heavy breaths.

"Good," Pompey replied shortly. "That saves me the task of killing the fool after the battle. Get over to Martius and tell him to bring a thousand to support Caesar there. Leave him in command. I'd say he's earned it."

The horseman saluted and galloped through the guards, his weariness showing in the loose way he sat his mount. Pompey signaled another of the extraordinarii to approach and stand ready for the next order. He scanned the battle, trying to judge the progress.

He knew the Romans should have routed the slaves. Thousands had fallen, but they seemed possessed and the legions were becoming exhausted. No matter how they rotated their front lines with the maniple orders, there was no lack of fresh enemies to sap their strength and will. He had left standing instructions with his archers to send shafts at anyone they could see in gladiatorial armor, but hitting individual targets was almost impossible.

Crassus looked over the right flank, where the cavalry of two legions was struggling to hold the ground they had gained in the first charge. Horses were screaming in pain and already men were spilling around them.

"Pompey, the right!" he snapped at his colleague.

Pompey took in the risk and sent the messenger away to bring in reinforcements. It was dangerous to take too many men from the center. If a breach came there, the army would be cut in half and that would be the finish. Pompey found a sense of desperation growing in him. There was no end to these slaves. For all the Roman skill and discipline, he could not see how to bring them victory. His men killed until they became exhausted and then were cut down in their turn, over and over.

Pompey signaled to the cornicens for another maniple order. He had lost count of the number of times he had sent the call and could imagine what his men were feeling as they were rotated back to the front before they had fully recovered from the last time. He had to keep the intervals short to spare them, but that meant less time to regain their strength.

Pompey and Crassus turned as a warning shout came from the right. The slaves had cut through the last of the cavalry and were surging forward, creating panic in the Roman lines as they threatened to envelop the flank or even hit them from behind. Pompey swore and summoned another rider.

"Right to retreat in battle order. Left to come forward.

We have to turn the whole field before they get round us. The cornicens to sound 'Right Wheel.' Go."

The man galloped away and the two generals abandoned dignity to kneel on their saddles for a better view of the developing action. Pompey's hands were cramped and white on the reins as he knew the whole battle rested on the decision. If the retreat turned into a panic, the slave army would spill around and encircle the Romans. His mouth was dried by the cold air as he breathed in hissing gasps.

The orders took a long time to reach up and down the line. Shouts echoed nearby and the right began to give way in order, shifting the line to a red diagonal across the plain. Pompey clenched his fists as he saw the left push forward to compact the slaves.

The whole battle began to turn and Pompey was frantic with worry. It was the only way to save the overwhelmed right flank, but as the thousands wheeled, the slaves were free to peel off and head for Ariminum if their commanders saw the chance.

*   *   *

Spartacus stood on the saddle of his horse and swore softly as he saw the legions were holding. For a moment, he thought Antonidus was right and the wing would be overwhelmed, but somehow they had swung round, eight legions moving as one, to turn the battle toward the east. He whistled softly in admiration, even as he saw their dreams come to dust on the field. The legions were everything he'd known they could be, and for a moment, he remembered his own days as a soldier with them. It had been a grand brotherhood before it had soured for him. A drunken brawl and an officer dead and nothing had been right since. He'd run because he knew they'd put him up before the man's friends and sentence him to death. There was no justice for a man like him, little more than a child when he'd been recruited in Thrace. Not a true

Roman, to them, and little better than an animal. Those were different and bitter memories: capture and slavery, then the gladiatorial school, where they were treated like violent dogs to be chained and beaten into ferocity.

"*Morituri te salutamus.* We who are about to die salute you," he whispered to himself as he watched his people die. He looked at the sun and saw it had risen past noon, cold and pale on the end of winter. The days had barely begun to lengthen and it would only be a few more hours until dark.

He watched the battle for a long time, hoping to see the legions break, but they stood strong against the multitude and he despaired. Finally, he nodded to himself. When the Romans pulled back to their camps for the night, he would make for Ariminum. His men hadn't eaten in four days and the Roman city was filled with food to make them strong again.

"We're going to have to run, Crix," he murmured.

His friend stood with Antonidus, holding the reins in his hand.

"They could still break before dark," Crixus replied bitterly.

Antonidus growled and spat a wad of phlegm onto the ground in anger. He had promised them a victory and he felt his influence slipping away with the toll of their dead.

Spartacus shook his head. "No. If we haven't beaten them by now, they'll not run from us. They'll move back into those forts of theirs and eat heartily before coming out to finish the work tomorrow. We won't be here when they do."

"*Why* won't they break, though?" Crixus demanded angrily to the air.

"Because if they break, Rome falls to us," Antonidus snapped. "They know the stakes, but we can still win. Pull back the front lines and put in fresh men. Move to surround the left wing. Whether they run or not, we can wear them down to nothing."

Spartacus looked with distaste at the Roman general his men had found. The man had nothing but bile in him and didn't seem to grasp that the lives he urged them to throw away were friends and brothers. The gladiator closed his eyes for a moment. They had all cheered Antonidus when Crixus had first shown him to them, dressed in armor taken from a Roman corpse. He had been paraded like a favorite pet for the men, but his promises had been worthless and his clever tactics nothing more than confusion for slaves who had never held a sword before they took it up in the rebellion.

"Our men are weak with hunger," Spartacus said. "I saw some who were green-mouthed from the boiled grasses they'd eaten. We can't survive another day of fighting after this one."

"We can try for the passes to Gaul," Crixus began.

"How many do you think would reach the high passes alive?" Spartacus demanded. "The legions would hunt us down before we'd left the plains. No, that chance has gone. It has to be Ariminum. We'll take what food we need and build our strength. Somehow, we'll stay ahead of them."

"If we could find ships, they might let us go," Crixus said, looking up at his friend.

"It would take a fleet," Spartacus said, considering. He longed to get away from the power of Rome, bitter with the knowledge that he should have led his men across the mountains. Let them have their little country. He would settle for being free.

Antonidus held his temper with difficulty. They had taken him from slavery to be killed by his own people. Neither man realized that Rome would never forgive a general who let them escape. It would be a shame that would last for centuries and every slave in the country would think of rising against their masters. He listened to their plans with growing anger. The only freedom they would see came from beating the legions on the plain, no matter how many lives it took.

Antonidus made a silent promise to slip away before the

end came. He would not be paraded in Rome as a trophy. He could not bear the thought of a triumphant Cato condemning him with a wave of his fat hands.

*   *   *

"The men are exhausted," Crassus snapped. "You must sound the disengage before they're overwhelmed."

"No. They will hold," Pompey said, squinting against the descending sun. "Send the extraordinarii to ready the camps for the night. We'll pull back when the light goes, but if I order it now, the slaves will think they have broken the only legions between here and Rome. Our men must *hold*."

Crassus twisted his hands together in an agony of indecision. The legions were under his command, and if Pompey waited too long to call them back, it could end everything they had ever worked for. If the legions fell, Rome would follow.

*   *   *

Julius heaved air into leaden lungs as he waited for the horns to sound the next attack. The blood on him had dried long ago and dropped away in dark crusts as he moved. Old blood. He looked wearily at his arms and held one hand up, narrowing his eyes at the shiver of exhaustion he saw there.

Another man panted at his side and Julius glanced at him. He had fought well in the last attack, spending his strength with the confidence of the immortal young. He looked up to see Julius watching him, and a shadow passed over his gray eyes. There were no words to be said. Julius wondered if Cato's son would survive the battle. If he lived, Cato would never understand the changes in him.

Ciro hawked and spat behind him to clear the blood from his throat. His lips were split and swollen and his smile was red when he grinned painfully at his general.

They were all cut and battered. Julius winced with every

movement. Something had torn in his lower back as he'd heaved a dead man off him. It sent sparks of pain up to his shoulders with every movement, and all he wanted to do was sleep. He looked over at Brutus, who'd been knocked unconscious by a berserk slave. Only a swift countercharge had reclaimed the ground and his body. Ciro had dragged him back through the ranks to recover, and as the sky began to darken he'd rejoined them, but he moved more slowly and his skill had almost deserted him. Julius wondered if his skull had been cracked by the blow, but could not send him back to the camps. They needed every man who could still stand.

They were all past exhaustion and pain, entering a sort of numbness that left the mind free to drift. Colors paled and their minds lost awareness of time, seeing it slow down and then rush to frightening speed, over and over.

With a jerk, Julius heard the cry of the cornicen's horn nearest him. He staggered forward for another stint on the front line and shook off Ciro's hand when it touched his arm.

"No more today, General," Ciro said, bracing Julius with an arm to steady him. "The light has gone. That's the call back to camp."

Julius looked blankly at him for a moment, then nodded wearily. "Tell Brutus and Renius to form the lines and retreat in good order. Tell the men to keep an eye out for a sudden charge." His words slurred with tiredness, but he raised his head and smiled at the man he'd found in another continent, another world.

"Better than the farm, Ciro?"

The big man looked around him at the bodies. It had been the hardest day of his life, but he knew the men around him better than he could explain. He had been alone on the farm.

"Yes, sir," he said, and Julius seemed to understand.

CHAPTER 39

Suetonius leaned on the fence in the woods. At the edge of his vision, he saw his father's slaves working unhurriedly to uproot the posts and remove the boundary. In a few hours all signs of it would be gone, and Suetonius frowned as he rested his head on his arms. The house he had planned would have been beautiful, rising above the trees on Caesar's land to look down the hill. He had been going to have a balcony built so that he could sit there on warm evenings with a cool drink. All that had vanished with his father's sudden weakness.

Suetonius picked at a splinter on the post, thinking of the host of petty insults that Julius had forced him to accept when they were prisoners and with the Wolves in Greece. He knew if Julius hadn't been there, the other men would have accepted him more readily, perhaps even agreeing to his command in the end as they had for Julius. He would have handed over the body of Mithridates to the legate Lepidus, sharing a meal with the man rather than rushing off to the port with barely a pause. The Senate would have named *him* tribune and his father would have been proud.

Instead, he had nothing but a ransom that belonged to his father and a few scars to show for everything he had endured. Caesar had taken the Wolves away to the north, flattering and persuading them to follow him, while Suetonius was left behind, without even the small comfort of seeing his own house built.

He tore at the splinter in sudden anger, wincing as part of it scored the skin of his hand. He had applied to go north with the six legions, but none of the legates had accepted him. No doubt who had spread the word there. He knew his father could have called in favors for them to accept his son, but had stopped short of asking. The shame of how he had been treated burned at him in the stillness of the woods.

Another movement caught his eye and he raised his head to see. He almost hoped some of his father's slaves were shirking their work. The flogging he would give them would go some way to break the lethargy he felt. He seemed to feel life more strongly in his veins when the time came to punish the lazy ones. He knew they walked in fear of him, but that was only right.

He took a deep breath to bark an order at them, hoping to see them jump. Then he froze. The men were moving stealthily through the thick undergrowth on the other side of the fence. They were not his slaves. Very slowly, he lowered his head back onto his arms and watched in silence as they passed not far away, oblivious to his presence.

Suetonius felt his heart hammer in sudden fear, and a flush came to his cheeks as he tried to breathe shallowly. They had not seen him yet, but there was something very wrong about the scene. There were three men moving together and a fourth some distance behind. Suetonius had almost stood to peer after the first group, and only some instinct warned him to hold still as they vanished through the trees. Then the fourth had come into sight, moving warily. He was dressed in rough dark clothing like the others and walked lightly over the dead wood and moss, showing a hunter's skill with his silence.

Suetonius saw he too was armed and suddenly he thought the man must see him through the shadows. He wanted to run or to shout for his slaves. Visions of the rebellion in the north came to him, and his mind filled with pictures of their knives in him, vivid and terrifying. He had seen so many die and it was too easy to imagine the men turning on him like animals. His sword was at his side, but he kept his hands still.

He held his breath as the last man passed. The man seemed to sense eyes on him and hesitated, scanning the trees around him. He didn't see Suetonius and after a while he relaxed and moved on, disappearing as completely as his companions before him.

Suetonius breathed out slowly, still not daring to move. They had been heading toward the Caesar estate, and his eyes became cruel as he realized it. Let Caesar have his land, with those men walking on it. He would not give them away. It was in the hands of the gods and out of his.

Feeling as if much of his pain and bitterness had been lifted from him, he stood up and stretched his back. Whoever the hunters were, he wished them luck as he walked over to where the slaves were taking down the fence. He gave orders for them to pack up their tools and return to his father's estate, instinctively wanting to be far away from the woods for the next few days.

The slaves saw his mood had lightened and exchanged glances, wondering what viciousness he'd seen to cheer him as they shouldered their burdens and made their way home.

*　　　　　*　　　　　*

Julius was exhausted, cursing under his breath as he stumbled on a loose stone. He knew that if he fell, there was a chance he wouldn't get up and he'd be left on the road.

They could not stop, with the slave army running before them toward Ariminum. Fleeing the field in the dark had given them half a day's start, and Pompey had sent out the order to run them down. The gap hadn't closed in seven days, as the legions pursued an army far fresher than themselves. Julius knew they could lose many more men, but if the slaves turned south, Rome stood naked for the first time in her history.

He fixed his eyes on the legionary in front of him. He had been staring at that back all day and knew every tiny detail of it, from the patchy gray hair that showed under the helmet to the spatters of blood up the man's ankles where he had stamped for a mile to break his blisters. Someone had urinated up ahead, darkening the dust of the road. Julius trudged through the patch indifferently, wondering when he would next have to do the same himself.

At his side, Brutus cleared his throat and spat. There was nothing of his usual energy showing in him. He was hunched under the weight of his pack, and Julius knew his friend's shoulders were raw. Brutus rubbed cooking fat on them at night and waited stoically for the calluses to form.

They had not spoken since dawn, the battle with endurance and the road going on without a public show. It was the same for most of them. They marched with slack and open mouths, all awareness narrowed to a point just ahead on the road. Often when the horns sounded a halt, men would stumble into those ahead and wake almost from sleep as they were cursed or struck.

Julius and Brutus chewed on stale bread and meat as it was handed out to them without a halt. As they tried to find saliva to swallow, they passed another fallen soldier and wondered if they too would be left on the road.

If Spartacus wanted to exhaust the legions in a chase, he could not have done better, and always there was the knowledge that there would have to be another battle when the slaves and gladiators finally found a place to stand. Only death would stop the legions.

Cabera coughed dust out of his throat and Julius glanced at the old man, marveling again that he had not fallen with the others. The poor rations and the miles had reduced his thin frame further, so that he looked almost skeletal. His cheeks were sunken and dark and the march had stolen away his humor and his talk. Like Brutus and Renius behind him, he had not spoken since the moment they were forced to their feet by weary optios, using their staffs on officers and men alike without interest, their faces as thin and tired as the rest of them.

They were allowed only four hours to sleep in the darkness. Pompey knew they could find Ariminum in flames, but the slaves would barely be able to pause before the legions were on the horizon, forcing them on. They couldn't allow Spartacus to regroup. If necessary, they would chase him into the sea.

Julius held his head high with difficulty, knowing he was seen by Primigenia around him. The legion of Lepidus marched in rank with them, though there was a subtle difference between the groups. Primigenia had not run and every soldier knew that the punishment for that failure still had to be meted out. Fear showed in the eyes of Lepidus's men and sapped at their will as they filled the hours with silent worry. There was nothing Julius and Brutus could do for them. The death of Lepidus went only some way in repairing their moment of panic in the battle.

The cornicens sounded as they reached the site of an old camp. It was two hours early, but Pompey had obviously decided to use the boundary they had erected once before, with only a little work needing to be done to shore up the spilled earth. Once inside, the men fell down where they stood. Some lay on their sides, too tired to remove their packs. Friends untied each other and the dwindling rations were brought out from packs and passed along lines to the cooks, who started fires in the ashes of the old ones. The men wanted to sleep and they had to eat first, so the cornmeal and dried meat was heated through and sent out on iron plates as fast as possible. The legionaries stuffed the food into their mouths without interest, then unrolled the thin trail blankets from their packs and lay down.

Julius had just finished his and was licking his fingers to remove every last crumb of the mush his body needed so desperately when he heard a cornicen blow a warning note nearby. Pompey and Crassus were approaching his position.

He scrambled to his feet and kicked Brutus, who had curled up, already drifting toward sleep. Renius opened an eye at the sound and groaned, heaving himself into a sitting position with his arm.

"Up! Get the men on their feet. Centurions, form Primigenia into squares for inspection. Quickly!"

He hated having to do it as he watched the men drag themselves upright, looking dazed. Some had been asleep and they stood loosely, their arms hanging and only dull awareness in their eyes. The centurions bullied and heaved until some semblance of ranks was produced. There were no groans or complaints; they hadn't the energy or the will to resist anything that was done to them. They stood where they were pushed and waited to be told to sleep once more.

Pompey and Crassus rode through the camp, bringing their horses close to Julius before dismounting. As well they might, both men looked fresher than the legionaries around them, but there was an air of tight-lipped seriousness about the generals that woke some of Lepidus's men to the danger, making them glance nervously at each other. Pompey approached Julius, who saluted.

"Primigenia stands ready, sir," Julius said.

"It is your other command that brings me here, Caesar. Tell Primigenia to rest and have Lepidus's men form ranks in their place."

Julius gave the orders and the three of them waited as the soldiers moved quickly into position. Even after the losses they had suffered in the panic of the battle, there were still more than three thousand survivors. Some were wounded, though the worst of these had already been left on the road, days before. Pompey mounted his horse to address them, but before he began, he leaned down to Julius and spoke quietly.

"Do not interfere, Julius. The decision has been made."

Julius returned the questioning stare impassively, then nodded. Pompey joined Crassus and together they trotted their horses right up to the front rank of the assembled men.

"Centurions stand forward!" Pompey barked out. Then he raised his head to have his voice carry as far as possible. "This legion carries a shame that must be cut out. There can be no excuse for cowardice. Hear now the punishment you will receive.

"Every tenth man in line will be marked by the centurions. He will die at the hands of the others. You will not use blades, but crush and beat them to death with fists and staffs. You will shed your own friends' blood in this way and always remember. A tenth of you will die this day. Centurions, begin the count."

Julius watched in horror as the centurions called off the numbers. As they marched along the ranks, the men around the unlucky one would cringe in fear as the officers came abreast of them, then gasp as the hand fell on a different shoulder. Some cried out, for themselves or for friends, but there was no mercy to be had. Crassus and Pompey watched the whole process with stiff disdain.

It took less than an hour, but by the end, three hundred men stood out from the ranks. Some wept, but others gazed blankly at the ground, unable to understand what was happening to them, why they had been singled out to die.

"Remember this!" Pompey bellowed at the men. "You ran from slaves where no legion has run in generations. Lay your swords down and complete your task."

The lines dissolved as each man standing apart was surrounded by nine of his friends and brothers. Julius heard one of them muttering an apology before he landed the first blow. It was worse than anything Julius had ever seen. Though the optios had staffs, the common soldiers had only their fists to smash the faces and chests of people they had known for years. Some of them sobbed as they struck, their faces twisted like children, but not a single one of them refused.

It took a long time. Some of the battered soldiers died quickly, their throats crushed, but others lingered on and on, shuddering and screaming in a terrible chorus that made Brutus shiver as he watched, transfixed by the knots of bloody-handed men, kicking and punching savagely. Brutus shook his head in disbelief, then looked away, sickened. He saw Renius was standing rigidly, his face pale.

"I never thought I would see this again," Renius muttered to himself. "I thought it had died out long ago."

"It had," Julius replied flatly. "Looks like Pompey's revived it."

Ciro watched in horror, his shoulders sagging. He looked at Julius questioningly, but there were no words for him.

Julius watched as the last blows were struck and the centurions checked each corpse. The men stood back, their energy disappearing as they shambled into ranks. The bodies sprawled before them in circles of bloody grass, and many of the living bore the spatters of the executions, standing with their heads bowed in misery.

"If we were in Rome, I would order you disbanded and forbidden to bear arms," Pompey roared into the silence. "As it is, circumstances may save you yet." He glanced at Crassus and the senator shifted in his saddle. Julius frowned suddenly. For Pompey to give way to Crassus meant that he needed the weight of the Senate authority behind whatever was going to be said. For all their maneuvering, only Crassus had that. The older man cleared his throat to speak.

"It is my order that a new legion be formed, to expunge the stain of Lepidus. You will join with Primigenia and make a new history. Your standards will be changed. You will have a new name, untouched by shame. I appoint Gaius Julius Caesar to command you. I speak with the authority of the Senate."

Crassus wheeled his horse and trotted over to where Julius stood, glaring at him.

"Will they be Primigenia, then?" Julius asked harshly.

Crassus shook his head. "I know what it will do to you, Julius, but this is the better way. If they take arms for you, they will always be apart as they are now. A new name will clear the field for them . . . and for you. Pompey and I have agreed. Obey your orders. Primigenia ends today."

Julius couldn't speak with anger for a moment, and Crassus watched him closely, waiting for a response. The younger man understood what they were trying to do, but still the memory of Marius haunted his thoughts. Understanding this, Crassus leaned down and spoke softly so as not to be overheard.

"Your uncle would understand, Julius. Be sure of that."

Julius clenched his jaw and nodded sharply, unable to trust himself to speak. He owed a great deal to this man. Crassus leaned back, relaxing.

"You will need a new name for them. Pompey thought it should be—"

"No," Julius interrupted. "I have a name for them."

Crassus raised his eyebrows in surprise as Julius walked around his horse and faced the bloody men he was to command. He took a deep breath to send his voice out to as many as could hear him.

"I will take your oaths, if you will give them. I remember that you did not desert the field, but rallied when I asked it of you, even with Lepidus dead." He let his gaze fall to the broken bodies all along the ranks. "The price for the failure has been paid and will never be mentioned again after today. But it must be remembered."

The silence was terrible and the air smelled of blood.

"You are marked with the lives of every tenth man. I name you the Tenth, so you will never forget the payment taken and you will never break."

Out of the corner of his eye, Julius saw Crassus grimace at the name, but he had known from the first moment that it was the right choice. It would hold them through fear and pain when others lost their nerve.

"Primigenia! My last command to you. Form ranks with your brothers. Look at their faces and learn their names. Know this. When men hear the Tenth stand against them, they will be afraid, for they have paid their dues in their own blood."

As the ranks re-formed, Julius walked back to Crassus as Pompey joined the senator. Both generals looked at Julius with guarded interest.

"You speak...well to them, Julius," Pompey said. He shook his head slightly as he watched Primigenia welcomed into the ranks. He had thought Julius would resist the order for the sake of Primigenia's name and had been prepared to force the issue. Watching the ease with which the young commander had assimilated the news and made it work for him was a surprise. For the first time, Pompey had a glimpse of how the young man had been so successful in Greece against Mithridates and the pirates before him. He seemed to know the words to use and that they could bite with greater force than swords.

"I would like to extend the time in camp before we move on, sir. It will give me a chance to speak with the men as well as let them finish their food and get some sleep."

Pompey was tempted to refuse the request. Apart from the driving need to pursue the slaves, his instincts warned him not to make things too easy for the young man who could speak directly to the hearts of the soldiers and lift them from misery in an instant. Then he relented. Caesar would need every advantage if he was to resurrect the dignity of the new legion from the ashes.

"You may tell them I have granted two further hours at your request, Julius. Be ready to march at sunset."

"Thank you, sir. I will arrange for new shields and armor for the men as soon as we are finished with this rebellion."

Pompey nodded absently, signaling to Crassus to ride away to the command position farther up at the head of the column. Julius watched them go, his face unreadable. He turned to Brutus and found Cabera with him, something of the old life and interest in the healer's face. Julius smiled tightly.

"Brutus, stand them down and tell them to finish eating. Then I want to speak to as many as I can before they sleep. Marius would have learned their names. So will I."

"It hurts to see Primigenia lost," Brutus murmured.

Julius shook his head. "They are not lost. The name will remain on the Senate rolls. I will make sure of it. Pompey and Crassus were right to make a new start, though it does hurt. Come on, gentlemen, let us walk amongst the Tenth. It's time to let go of the past."

*   *   *

Ariminum stood under a pall of smoke. The slave army had moved through it like locusts, taking everything that could be eaten and driving sheep and cattle to run before them on the march. While citizens hid behind barricaded doors, Spartacus and his army walked slowly through quiet streets with the sun casting weak shadows behind them. They set fires in the grain stores and abandoned markets, knowing their pursuers might waste time stamping them out before following. With the legion still doggedly on their heels, every hour was crucial.

The guards had run from the city treasury, and Spartacus ordered the gold loaded onto mules for the journey south. It was a fortune from trade, and the dream of a fleet of ships to take them to freedom became reality as soon as the gladiators saw the crates of coins.

The docks were empty of ships, the dark hulks standing clear out to sea where they could watch the horde of slaves looting their city under rising plumes of smoke and ash. The ships were packed with silent people, just watching. Spartacus walked up to the edge of the docks and returned their stares.

"See how many they hold, Crix. We have enough gold to buy every one of us a berth."

"These precious merchants won't stir to save us," Crixus replied. "It has to be the pirates. The gods know, they have enough ships, and spitting in Rome's eye will give them some pleasure, as well."

"But how to get word to them? We must send riders out to each port. There has to be a way to reach them." Spartacus looked over the water at the pale specks of faces clustered in the ships. It was possible, if they could speak to Rome's enemies.

Antonidus walked up to stand at his side, squinting out over the waves with a sneer.

"Brave Roman citizens hiding from us like children," he said.

Spartacus shrugged, tired of his bitterness and spite. "Sixty or seventy ships like those and we can leave Roman lands. A fleet bought with their own gold seems like justice."

Antonidus looked at the two gladiators with more interest. He'd been tempted to slip away at the port, taking off his armor and joining the crowds of people who would surely gather once the slaves were gone. Then he'd seen the gold they'd taken from the treasury. Enough to buy him an estate in Spain or a vast farm in Africa. There were many places for a man to hide that would not shelter an army. He knew if he stayed, their trust in him could give him the chance he needed. Would Pompey forgive him if he brought Spartacus's head? Antonidus frowned. No, he'd faced a Roman court once and that was enough. Better just to run for a place where he could start again.

Spartacus turned, putting the sea at his back. "We will send local men to every port with a few coins to prove their promises. Speak to them, Crixus. Someone must know how to reach the pirates. Let them know the plan. It will raise their spirits on the march south."

"We're heading south toward Rome, then?" Antonidus asked sharply.

A terrible anger creased the features of the gladiator for a moment, and Antonidus stepped back as he answered.

"We should never have turned our backs on the mountains, but now we must keep ahead of them. We'll run those bastards ragged on our trail. Remember, we're the ones who till their fields and work every hour of light for their wealth. It's made us strong. Let's see what sort of state they're in by the time we sight their beloved city."

As he spoke he stared west into the sun, his eyes glinting gold with it as he imagined the legions hunting them. His face was bitter and Antonidus had to look away.

CHAPTER **40**

As the moon rose, Alexandria stood on the walls above the great city of Rome with the rain drumming against the stones. Torches had been lit all round the city, and they spat and crackled, giving only a little light to the defenders. When the warning horns had sounded, they had all come, snatching up tools and knives to hold the wall against the silent mass that tramped past in the darkness, churning the Campus Martius into clotted mud.

Tabbic held his iron hammer in tight hands, his face drawn and pale in the flickering light. There was no give in him, or any of them, Alexandria knew. If the slaves attacked them, they would fight as ferociously as the legions themselves. She looked up and down the line at the faces staring down into the dark and wondered at their calm. Families stood together in silence, even the children awed into stillness by the army passing them by. The moon cast only a little light, but it was enough to show the white faces of the slaves as they looked up at the city that had decreed their death. There seemed no end to them, but the moon reached its zenith and began to fall before the last stragglers disappeared into the night.

The tension eased at last, after hours of painful anticipation. The messengers from the legions had passed the news that they were close behind, and the Senate had ordered the people to the walls until it was safe, setting the example by taking places on the great gatehouses with the swords of their fathers and grandfathers.

Alexandria gulped in the cold air, feeling alive. The rain had begun to lighten and Rome had survived. Sudden smiles and laughter showed her that they all felt it, and for a moment she knew they had shared a bond in the dark that was as strong as any other tie in her life. Yet still she was torn. She had been a slave, as they were slaves, and had dreamed of rising up in a multitude to cast down their owners' precious houses and walls.

"Will they all be killed?" she murmured, almost to herself.

Tabbic turned sharply toward her, his eyes shadowed.

"They will. The Senate has known fear and they won't forgive a single one of them. The legions will make a bloody example of them before it ends."

*   *   *

Pompey allowed the lamps to burn low in his tent as he read the dispatches from Rome, less than thirty miles south of them. Rain drummed against the canvas of the command tent and dripped through in places to make the ground sodden. Food sat on his table untouched as he read and reread each message. Crassus would have to be told.

After a while, he stood to pace and barely noticed as one of the torches guttered and failed. He took another from its stand and held it to illuminate a map that covered the entire wall of the tent. Spots of dark moisture showed on the parchment, and he realized he'd have to take it down if the rain continued. Rome was a tiny circle on the thick skin, and somewhere to the south the slaves were moving ever onward to the sea. He stared at the symbol for the city, knowing he had to make a decision before Crassus arrived.

Around him, only the sentries moved around the silent

camp in damp misery. The Senate had sent supplies out to them as soon as the army of Spartacus had marched south. Pompey could only imagine the fear in the streets as the sea of slaves passed them by, but the gates had been barred against them.

He was proud of his people when he'd heard: the old and the young, women and loyal slaves ready to fight. Even the Senate had armed themselves, as they had centuries before to defend their city with their lives. It gave him hope for them.

A murmur of passwords outside revealed the approach of Crassus, who looked around in surprise at the dark tent as he entered. He wore a heavy leather cloak over his armor and pulled back the hood, scattering droplets.

"Evil night," he muttered. "What news?"

Pompey stopped and turned toward him. "Some of it is . . . awful," he replied, "but it must wait. There are four legions at the coast, just landed from Greece. I'm going to meet them and bring them after us."

Crassus nodded warily. "What else, Pompey? You could send the extraordinarii to them, with our seals on the orders. Why go yourself?"

Pompey grimaced in the shadows. "The man who killed my daughter has been found. The men I left to hunt him are watching him now. I will stop at the city before I meet the legions coming west. You'll have to go on without me until this is done."

Crassus took a taper and oil jug from the table and relit the lamps, his hand shaking slightly as he concentrated. At last, he sat down and met Pompey's eyes.

"If they turn to fight, I will not be able to wait for you," he said.

Pompey shook his head. "Then do not force them to turn. Give them room to run and in a few days, a week, I will be back with fresh men to end this chase at last. Don't risk losing everything, my friend. For all your skill in Senate, you are no general. You know it as well as I do."

Crassus hid his anger. Always they saw him as the merchant, the lender, as if there were some great secret to the legions that only the chosen few could understand. As if there were some shame to his wealth. He could see Pompey was desperate not to lose this victory. How awful it would be if lowly Crassus stole it from under him! Whoever broke the rebellion would be the next consul, he was sure. How could the Senate resist the will of the people after so many months of fear? Not for the first time, Crassus felt regret at his generosity in choosing Pompey in the Senate debate. If he had known then how the campaign would go, he would have risked it alone.

"I will herd them south," he said, and Pompey nodded, satisfied. He lifted another of the dispatches from the table and showed it to Crassus, angling it into the light. As Crassus read, Pompey stood and pointed to the map.

"Those reports of a fleet can only be for the slaves. I'd stay if I wasn't sure they will keep moving, but as long as you don't provoke them, they should head south to meet the ships. I'll call in the galleys against them. There will be no escape by sea, I swear it."

"If that's what they intend," Crassus muttered, still reading.

"They cannot run forever. They must be starving, no matter what they've found to scavenge. Every day weakens them if they're hoping to bring us to another battle. No, they're trying to escape and those reports are the key to it."

"And when they see our galleys gathering to prevent it, you'll ride up with the Greek legions to finish them?" Crassus asked, some of the bile he felt creeping into his tone.

"I will," Pompey replied sharply. "Do not take the threat lightly, Crassus. If we lose now, we lose everything. We need the extra legions I will bring. Do not join in battle until you see my flags. I'd rather see you retreat than be routed before I arrive."

"Very well," Crassus replied, stung by the casual dismissal of his abilities. If Spartacus attacked while Pompey was away, the moment would be his to seize, and the glory with it. "I know you will come as quickly as you can," he said.

Pompey sagged slightly, resting his knuckles on the table. "There is another matter. I'm leaving immediately for the city and I don't know if I should keep it to myself until we're finished here or not."

"Tell me," Crassus said, softly.

      *   *   *

The leather tents were heavy with rain that roared in a broken rhythm as the men slept fitfully. Julius dreamed of the estate. The day had been tiring as the legions forced the pace toward Rome, and when the order had come to set the tents, the legionaries had barely bothered to remove their armor before falling asleep. Those who had lived through the forced marches were harder than they had ever been, tight-skinned over taut muscle. They had seen friends die on the march or just fall off the road, their legs twitching. Some of them had lived to join the end of the column, but many of their wounded had died, losing blood with each step until their ailing hearts finally stopped and they lay where they fell.

Feet that had bled and been caked with a brown rime had become layered in callus, white against their sandals. Torn muscles had healed and the legions became stronger on the march, their heads rising. In the third week, Pompey called for a faster pace on the Via Flaminia and they met it without protest, feeling again the thrill of the chase.

Julius murmured irritably as someone shook his shoulder.

"There's a messenger from Pompey, Julius. Wake up, quickly."

Julius snapped awake, shaking his head to clear it of the dream. He looked out of the tent at the messenger carrying Pompey's bronze seal and dressed quickly, leaving his armor behind. As soon as he stepped out, the rain drenched him to the skin.

*   *   *

The sentry at the command tent stood aside as Julius gave the password of the day. Both Crassus and Pompey were there and he saluted them, instantly wary. There was something strange in their expressions that he had not seen before.

"Sit down, Julius," Crassus said.

The older man did not meet his eyes as he spoke, and Julius frowned slightly as he took a seat on a bench by the table. Julius waited patiently and when the generals did not speak immediately, a spike of worry twisted in his stomach. He wiped water from his face with a nervous scrubbing motion. Pompey poured a cup of wine and pushed it toward the young tribune.

"We...I have bad news, Julius. Messages have come from the city," he began. His expression was uncomfortable as he took a slow breath to continue.

"There has been an attack on your estate. Your wife has been killed. I understand—"

Julius stood up jerkily. "No," he said. "No, that must be wrong."

"I'm sorry, Julius. It happened only days ago. It came with the dispatches," Pompey said. The young man's horror tore at his own memories of finding his daughter in the garden. He handed the parchment to Julius and watched in silence as he read through it, his eyes blurring as he started over and over. Julius's breath shuddered out of him and his hands shook so that he could barely read the words.

"Sweet gods, no," he whispered. "It hardly says anything. What about Tubruk? Octavian? My daughter is not men-

tioned. There's nothing there but a few words. Cornelia..."
He could not finish and his head bowed in mute misery.

"It's a formal dispatch, Julius," Pompey whispered. "It
may be they still live. There will be other letters to follow." He
paused for a moment, coming to a decision. "As close as we
are to the city, I will understand if you take a short leave to see
to your affairs at home."

Julius did not seem to hear him. Crassus crossed to the
young man who had seen so much grief in his life.

"If you want to go back to your estate, I'll sign the orders.
Do you hear?"

Julius raised his head and both men looked away rather
than see his agony.

"I request permission to take the Tenth with me," Julius
said, shaking.

"I cannot allow that, Julius. Even if we could spare them,
I cannot give you a legion to use against your enemies."

"Just a fifty, then. Ten even," Julius said, his voice
breaking.

Pompey shook his head. "I am going back to the city myself, Julius. There will be justice done, I swear it to you, but it
will be under the rule of law, the peace of the city. Everything
Marius worked for. You will come back with me in a few days
to finish the rebellion. That is your duty and mine."

Julius turned as if to leave the tent, holding himself still
with an immense effort of will. Pompey put a hand on his
shoulder.

"The Republic is not to be thrown away when we tire of
the restrictions, Julius. When my daughter died, I made myself wait. Marius himself said the Republic is worth a life, do
you remember that?"

"Not her life," Julius replied. He breathed in sobs that he
tried to talk over even as they wrenched at him. "She wasn't
part of it."

The two generals shared a glance over his head.

"Go home, Julius," Crassus said softly. "There's a horse waiting for you. Brutus will command the Tenth while you are gone."

Julius stood finally, taking deep breaths to find some semblance of control in front of Crassus and Pompey.

"Thank you," he said, attempting a salute. He still clutched the report in his hand, and he noticed it then, placing it on the seat before leaving the tent and taking the reins of the horse that had been brought for him. Some part of him wanted just to dig his heels in and gallop from the camp, but instead he wheeled and rode to where the Tenth lay sleeping in their tents. He pulled back the flap to rouse Brutus, who came out quickly when he saw his expression.

"I'm going back to Rome, Brutus. Cornelia is dead, somehow. I don't...understand."

"Oh, Julius, no," Brutus said. He pulled his friend into an embrace and the contact brought tears from Julius in a rush. For a long time they stood together, locked in grief.

"Do we march?" Brutus whispered.

"Pompey has forbidden it," Julius replied, standing back at last.

"Nevertheless, Julius. Do we march? Give me the word."

Julius closed his eyes for a moment, thinking of what Pompey had said. Could he be any weaker than that man? Cornelia's death had freed him of restraints. There was nothing to stop him throwing an army at Cato and burning him out of the flesh of Rome. Part of him wanted desperately to see flames over the city as they cut out the name and the memory of the Sullans for ever. Catalus, Bibilus, Prandus, Cato himself. All of them had families who could pay in blood for what had been taken from him.

There was still his daughter, Julia. The report had not mentioned her death.

As he thought of her, the bonds of his chosen life returned like a cloak around him, muffling his grief. Brutus was still watching him intently, waiting.

"No, Brutus, not yet. I will wait, but there is a debt in blood that must be paid. Lead the Tenth until I come back."

"You're going alone? Let me come with you," Brutus said, putting a hand to the reins Julius held.

"No, you must take the command. Pompey forbade me to travel with any of the Tenth. Get Cabera out of his tent. I need him."

Brutus ran to where the old healer slept and roused him with a shake. When he understood, the old man moved quickly, though his face was lined with exhaustion as he pulled his robe in tightly against the beating rain.

Cabera held out an arm to mount behind Julius and was pulled up with a heave as Julius wheeled the skittish horse in place. Brutus met Julius's eyes then and took his hand in the legionary grip.

"Pompey never knew about the soldiers we left at the estate, Julius. They will fight for you if you need them."

"If they live," Julius replied.

Overwhelming grief stole his breath then and Julius dug in his heels. Then he was off, crouched low with Cabera behind him, blind with tears in the rain.

CHAPTER 41

Thick clumps of dark cloud obscured the spring sun and the rain fell with no sign of easing as Julius and Cabera rode up to the estate. As he looked at his home Julius felt a deep weariness that had nothing to do with the ride through the night. With the weight of the old man behind him, Julius had slowed his mount to a walking pace through the hours. There was no urgency left in him. He'd wanted the time to stretch endlessly, begrudging every step that brought him closer to this moment. Cabera had been silent on the journey and his old infectious joy had been absent as they arrived back at the place of so many memories. His robe hung wetly on his thin frame, making him shiver.

Julius dismounted by the gate and watched it open for him. Somehow, now that he was there, he didn't want to go in, but he walked the horse into the courtyard feeling numb.

Soldiers from Primigenia took the reins, their faces a reflection of his own agony. He didn't speak to them, but crossed the yard to the main buildings through the swirling mud of puddles from the storm. Cabera watched him go, absently rubbing the soft muzzle of the horse as he held its reins.

Clodia was there, holding a bloody cloth in her hand. She was pale and exhausted looking, with dark pouches under her eyes.

"Where is she?" he asked, and she seemed to crumple in front of him.

"In the triclinium," she said. "Master, I . . ."

Julius walked past her into the room and stopped inside the door. Torches burned at the head of a simple bed, lighting her face with their warmth. Julius crossed to his wife and looked down at her, his hands shaking. She had been washed and dressed in white cloth, her face left unpainted and her hair tied back behind her head.

Julius touched her face and winced at the softness of it.

There was no disguising death. Her eyes had opened a fraction and he could see the whites beneath the lids. With his hand, he tried to close them again, but they eased back open when he took his fingers away.

"I am sorry," he whispered, his voice sounding loud against the fluttering of the torches. He took her hand in his, feeling the stiffness of the fingers as he knelt by her.

"I'm sorry they hurt you so badly. You were never part of it. I'm sorry I didn't take you away. If you can hear me, I do love you, I always did."

He bowed his head as shame shuddered through him. His last words had been angry to this woman he'd sworn to love, and there was no way to call the guilt back. He had been too stupid to help her, somehow sure that she would always be there and that the arguments and the ugly words didn't matter. And now she was gone and he clenched a fist against his head in anger at himself, pressing harder and harder and welcoming the pain it brought. How he'd boasted to her. His enemies would fall and she would be safe.

At last he stood, but could not turn from her.

A voice shattered the quiet.

"No! Don't go in there!"

It was Clodia, calling outside. Julius spun round, his hand going to his sword.

His daughter Julia came running into the silence, halting

as she saw him. Instinctively, he moved to block Cornelia from her sight, stepping toward her and lifting her into his arms in a tight embrace.

"Mummy's gone," she said, and he shook his head, tears spilling out of him.

"No, no, she's still here, and she loves you," he said.

*   *   *

Pompey's men almost gagged at the smell of rot that came from the man they held. The skin they could feel under the cloak seemed to move too easily in their grip, and as they shifted their hands the hooded man gasped in pain, as if something had torn away.

Pompey stood facing them, his eyes bright with malice. At his side were two young girls he had found in the house deep in the warren of alleys between the hills. Their faces were pinched with fear, but there was nowhere for them to run and they stood in terrified silence. The threat was clear. Pompey wiped a line of sweat from his cheek.

"Remove his hood. I want to see the man who killed my daughter," he said.

The two soldiers reached up and pulled back the rough cloth, looking away, nauseated, as they saw what was revealed. The assassin glared at them all, his face a mass of pustules and scabs. There was not an inch of good flesh to be seen, and the scarred and bleeding skin cracked as he spoke to them.

"I am not the man you want," he whispered.

Pompey bared his teeth. "You are one of them. You have a name for me, I know. But your life is mine to take for what you have done."

The man's rheumy eyes flickered to the two girls, creasing in fear. If Pompey hadn't guessed already, he would have known then that they were his daughters. The senator knew that fear very well. The assassin spoke quickly, as if to cover what he had shown them.

"How did you find me?"

Pompey drew a knife from his belt, the blade shining even in the shadowy darkness of the room.

"It took time and gold and the lives of four good men to track you down, but the filth you employ gave you to me in the end. I'm told you're building a beautiful estate in the north, far from this hovel. Built on my blood. Did you think I would forget about my daughter's killer?"

The man coughed, his breath overlaid with the sweet perfume he used to cover the rot.

"It was not my knife that—"

"It was your order. Who gave you the name? Whose gold did you take? I know it anyway, but speak it before witnesses, so that I can have justice."

For a long moment their gazes locked, and then the assassin's eyes dropped to the blade that Pompey held so casually. His daughters looked on, their tears drying. They didn't understand the danger and he could have cried for their innocence as they watched their father so trustingly. They were not appalled by his sores. In fact, without the gentle bathing they administered to their father, he knew he would have taken his own life a long time before. They had none of the disease, their skin perfect under the dirt they used to hide themselves from the predators of the alleys. Who would care for them when he was gone? He knew Pompey well enough to see his own life was finished. He'd had no mercy in him since the death of his daughter, if he ever had.

"Let my daughters go and I will tell you," the assassin wheezed, his eyes pleading.

Pompey grunted softly, then reached out to the youngest one, holding her tightly by the hair. With his other hand, he drew the dagger across her throat and dropped her as she twisted in his grip.

The assassin screamed in unison with his daughter,

straining to break the grip of the men that held him. He began to weep then, sagging in their arms.

"Now you know," Pompey said. He wiped the blade between two of his fingers, the blood falling in heavy soundless drops to the earthern floor. He waited patiently until the assassin had subsided into choking sobs.

"The other one will live, perhaps. Last time of asking. Whose gold did you take?"

"Cato ... it was Cato, through Antonidus. That is all I know, I swear."

Pompey turned to the soldiers around him. "Did you men hear?"

They nodded, grim as their commander. "Then we are finished in this place." He turned to leave, only a slight stain on his hands showing he had ever been there.

"Kill them both, the girl first," he added as he went out into the alleys beyond.

*   *   *

"Is he awake?" Julius asked. The room stank of sickness and Tubruk lay sprawled on a bed that showed rusty stains from his bleeding. Before he entered, Julius had waited out his daughter's tears and gently taken her fingers from around his neck. She had cried again then, but he would not take her into another death room and Clodia had found a young female slave to take care of her. From the way the little girl went into her arms, it was clear the woman had comforted her before over the last, terrible days.

"He may wake if you speak to him, but he hasn't long now," Clodia said, looking into the room. Her face told him more than he wanted to know, and he closed his eyes for a moment before entering.

Tubruk lay awkwardly, fresh stitches showing on his chest and disappearing under the blankets. Though he seemed to sleep, he shivered and Julius tugged the blanket up to cover him. There was a trace of blood around his mouth, fresh and red. Clodia brought a bowl of crimson water from the floor and dabbed at the smear as Julius watched in despair. Too many things had changed for him to take in, and he stood frozen as Clodia cleaned the lips and weeping stitches with tender care.

Tubruk groaned and opened his eyes at her touch. He couldn't seem to focus properly.

"You still here, old woman?" he whispered, a faint smile pulling at his mouth.

"As long as you need me, love," she replied. She glanced up at Julius and back to the man on the bed.

"Julius is here," she said.

Tubruk turned his head. "Come where I can see you," he said.

Clodia stood back and Julius came and looked into his eyes. Tubruk took a deep breath and his whole body shivered again with the release.

"I couldn't stop them, Julius. I tried, but . . . I couldn't reach her."

Julius began to sob softly as he looked down at his old friend.

"It isn't your fault," he whispered.

"I killed them all. I killed him to save her," Tubruk said, his eyes blank. His breathing was ragged and Julius despaired of the gods. They had given too much pain to ones he loved.

"Call Cabera in here. He's a healer," he said to Clodia.

She beckoned him away from the tortured figure on the bed, and he bent his head to hear.

"Don't let him be troubled. There's nothing to do but wait now. There's no blood left in him."

"Fetch Cabera," Julius replied, his eyes fierce. He thought for a moment that she would refuse again, but then she left and he could hear her voice calling out in the courtyard.

"Cabera's here, Tubruk. He'll make you better," Julius said, the soft sobbing starting again in his throat.

Dripping raindrops, the old man entered and crossed quickly to the bed, looking stricken. With deft fingers, he checked the wounds, raising the blanket to see beneath. He looked at Julius's desperate expression and sighed.

"I'll try," he said. He placed his hands on the bruised flesh around the stitches and closed his eyes.

Julius leaned forward, whispering a prayer under his breath. There was nothing to be seen, just the figure of the old healer bent over, his hands still and dark against the pale chest. Tubruk took a long inward breath in sudden spasm, then breathed out slowly. He opened his eyes and looked at Clodia.

"The pain's gone, love," he said. Then the life went out of him and Cabera staggered and fell.

*   *   *

Pompey frowned at the galley captain who stood stiffly before him.

"I don't care what your orders are. These are mine. You will sail south toward Sicilia and hail any other galleys you see on the way down the coast. Every Roman vessel is to guard the south and prevent the slaves escaping. Is that understood, or must I have you arrested and appoint another captain in your place?"

Gaditicus saluted, disliking the arrogant senator with a passion he didn't dare let show. After six months at sea, he had been hoping for some time ashore in the city, but he was being ordered out again without even a chance to clean the ship. Prax would be furious when he heard, he thought.

"I understand, sir. We'll clear the docks on the next tide."

"Be sure you do," Pompey replied, before striding back to his waiting soldiers. Gaditicus watched him go and glanced at the other galleys that had already put out to sea. With them all heading for the strait of Sicilia, Roman ports everywhere would be easy prey. Whatever the Senate was planning, he hoped it was worth the risk.

*　　　　　　*　　　　　　*

As the evening darkened, Clodia came to Julius as he drank himself into a stupor in a dark room. He looked up as she entered, his eyes listless.

"Are you home for good now?" she asked.

He shook his head. "No, I'm going back with Pompey in a few days. I'll see to the funerals for both of them first." His voice was slurred and miserable, but there were no words of comfort she could think to offer. Part of her wanted to make him feel pain for the cruel way he'd treated Cornelia, and it was only with the last of her strength that she didn't speak to hurt him. His face showed he knew well enough.

"Will you stay and look after my mother and daughter?" he said without looking at her.

"I am a slave. I should return to Senator Cinna's house," she replied.

He met her eyes then and waved his hand drunkenly. "I free you, then. I'll buy your paper from her father. I can do that much at least before I go back. Just look after Julia. Is Octavian here?"

"In the stables. I wasn't sure if he should go back to his mother and..."

"Look after him too. He's my blood and I made a promise. I always keep my promises." His face screwed up in anguish. "I want you to stay here and run this house. I don't know when I'll be back, but when I am I want you to talk about her. You knew her before I did and I want to know everything."

He was so young, she thought. Young and foolish and learning that life could be bitterly unfair. How long had she waited for love before finding it with Tubruk? Cornelia would have freed her to marry and he would have asked once he'd gathered his courage. Now there was nothing left for her, and the girl she'd nursed as a baby lay still and quiet in another room. When she had the strength, Clodia knew, she would be the one to wrap Tubruk's battered body and clean his skin for the last time. But not for a while.

"I'll stay," she said, and wondered if he heard her.

CHAPTER 42

Cato stood in the forum under a dark sky, his toga stripped from his shoulders to reveal a mass of white flesh that shone with running beads of water. His back was marked with stripes where the whips had fallen, the pain only an echo of the anger and disgust he felt for the petty men who had brought him down. Not one of them would have disdained to act as he had, if the opportunity had come. Yet they glared and pointed at him as if they were not of his breed at all. He sneered at them, holding his head high even as the executioner came forward, the long sword gleaming in his hands.

Pompey looked on without a show of the pleasure he felt. He had delayed joining Crassus to see this task finished. He would have preferred to see the fat hands nailed to a wooden beam and displayed in the forum for a lingering death. Such an ending would be more fitting for Cato. At least there had been pleasure as Cato's family were sold into slavery despite his cries. The house had been given over to the Senate, and the funds raised by its sale would go some way toward financing the legions Pompey took with him against the slaves.

Julius watched numbly at Pompey's side. The general had ushered him forward in triumph to share in the pleasure of the execution, but he felt nothing. There was no joy in seeing Cato killed. It was no more than ending the life of a dog or crushing a stinging insect. The bloated senator understood nothing of the grief he had caused, and nothing he could suffer would bring Cornelia back. Let this be quick, he whispered to himself as he watched. Let it all end.

Cato spat on the stones of the forum as he looked around at the crowd of senators and citizens that had massed to see the execution. For once, there was no sense of danger from the crowd. He had never been popular with the people of the city—as if anyone could care what they thought or did. He spat again, his mouth curling in anger at the sight of the waiting mob. Animals, all of them, with no understanding of how a great man could bend the law under his hand. Marius had done it; Sulla had. None of them could understand that there was no law but that which could be held.

Footsteps sounded and Cato turned his head to see Pompey striding toward him. He grimaced. The man didn't even have style enough to let him die without a few more jeers and taunts. He was not made for greatness. Sulla would have allowed his enemy the dignity of a private death, no matter what had passed between them. There was a man who understood what power meant.

Pompey moved close enough to speak into Cato's ear.

"Your family will not live long as slaves. I have bought them all myself," the sibilant voice whispered.

Cato looked coldly at him. "Germinius too?" he asked.

"He will not survive the final battle."

Cato smiled at that. He wondered if Pompey would find Julius and Brutus any easier to deal with than he had. He raised his head in defiance. It seemed fitting to have his line end with him. He'd heard of kings in ancient times who had their families thrown alive onto their pyres. Pompey was a fool to try to hurt him.

"You will know a day like this one," he said to Pompey. "You are too small a man to hold this city in your hand for long." He laughed aloud then as Pompey's face contorted with a spasm of anger.

"Take up your sword and finish him," the general snapped at the executioner, who bowed low to the ground in response as Pompey stalked back to the waiting senators. Cato nodded to the man. He felt tired all of a sudden, almost numb.

"Not today, boy. Some things have to be done by a man's own hand," he muttered, removing a heavy bracelet from his wrist. With his thumb, he eased out a razor from the edge of it and turned to face the crowd, sneering at them. With a jerk of his hand, he nicked the side of his throat, cutting the heavy arteries, then stood waiting as blood poured out over his white flesh, drenching him.

The executioner stepped forward nervously, but Cato had strength enough to raise his hand, refusing the blade. The crowd watched with animal fascination as his legs began to shiver and then suddenly he fell to his knees with an audible crack on the stone. Even then, he glared at them all before slumping forward in a heap.

The gathered citizens sighed as the tension of the death was released. Despite the crimes they whispered to each other, the courage of the senator stole the pleasure they had come to find. They began to disperse without a sound, passing the slumped body with bowed heads and more than a few muttered prayers.

Pompey pursed his lips in anger. The joy of vengeance was missing at such an ending, and he felt as if something had been stolen from him. He signaled his guards to remove the body, turning to Julius.

"Now we go south, to finish it," he said.

*　　　　　　*　　　　　　*

The general looked at Crassus in amazement.

"Sir, you're talking about more than twenty miles of

broken land! I urge to you reconsider. We should occupy a central position, ready to stop them breaking through."

Crassus waited until the man had finished, his fingers tapping nervously on his table as he listened. It was the only thing to do, he was certain. The slaves were trapped against the coast, and if Pompey had reached the galleys, there would be no one to take them off. All he had to do was hold them, bottle them up in the spit of land at the base of the country. He glanced at Pompey's map on the wall. It looked such a tiny distance, there.

"My orders to you are clear, General. Fresh legions are coming from the north, with Pompey. We will hold the line until they arrive, and I want a fortification cutting across country. You are wasting my time." His voice held a dangerous edge. Surely the man wouldn't hesitate this way if Pompey were giving the orders. It was insufferable.

"Get out!" he snapped at the man, rising from his chair. When he was alone, he sank back again, rubbing nervously at his forehead as he looked at the map again.

Every noise in the night made him jolt awake, terrified the slaves had broken through to pillage the country. It could not be allowed again. At first he had thought of crushing them against the sea, but what if they fought as they had in the north? With escape barred to them, they would be desperate, and if they overran the Roman lines, Crassus knew he'd be finished, even if he survived the battle. The Senate would call for his execution. He grimaced. How many of them had debts that only his death would erase? He could imagine their pious faces as they discussed his fate in Senate. He understood the pressure a little better since Pompey had left him. There was no one to ask; the decisions were his alone.

He crossed to the map and ran his finger across the narrowest neck of land at the toe of the country.

"We will hold you here until the new legions come," he said, frowning. Twenty miles of banked earth. Such a line had never been built before, and the people of Rome would tell their children about it when it was done. Crassus, who built a wall across a country. He scrubbed his finger across the point again and again until a darker line showed on the skin.

It would hold them unless Pompey had failed to gather enough galleys to stop the slaves escaping. Then he would be the laughingstock of the country, guarding nothing but fields. Shaking his head to clear it, he sat down again to think.

      *   *   *

After the delay for Cato's execution, Pompey pushed the Greek legions south without rest. They were the veterans of the borders of Greece, with huge numbers of hastati and triarii to bolster the younger men. With the Via Appia under their feet, they passed thirty-five-mile markers in the first day. Pompey knew the pace would slow when they were forced to turn off the road, but even if the slaves had run to the farthest tip of the country, he knew he could bring the Greek legions to them in less than two weeks.

Julius rode with Cabera at his side, changing horses as Pompey did, every twelve miles at the way stations. Pompey was puzzled by the young tribune. He had spoken only a few words to him since they stood to watch Cato die in the great forum, but he was like a different person. The inner fire that had unnerved Pompey when Julius had taken control of the new Tenth legion seemed to have been drawn out of him. It was not the same man who now rode without caring, his horse wide-eyed with nerves at the lack of signals from its rider. Pompey watched him carefully as they rode each day. He had known men to break before after a tragedy, and if Julius was no longer fit to command, he would not hesitate to remove him from his post. Marcus Brutus was equal to the task, and in his private thoughts Pompey was able to admit that Brutus could never be a threat to him, as the other could. The way Caesar had taken control of Primigenia and yet kept the friendship of Brutus spoke volumes for his ability. Perhaps it would be better to have him removed before he had fully recovered from the murder of his wife, while he was weak.

Pompey looked ahead along the wide road. Crassus hadn't the nerve to engage the slave army, he'd known it from the moment he'd heard his name chosen in the Senate. The victory would be his alone, and it would take nothing less to unite the factions in the Senate and bring him to power over Rome. Somewhere ahead of him, the fleet of galleys was blocking the sea, and though the slaves could not yet know it, their rebellion was ended.

*   *   *

Spartacus looked out over the cliffs and watched the smoke as another vessel was captured and burned by the galleys. The sea was alive with ships fleeing the Roman fleet, their oars smacking into the choppy sea in desperation as they tried to maneuver round each other without collision. There was no mercy for those who were caught. The navy galleys had suffered too many years of impotent pursuits not to revel in the destruction. Some were boarded, but more were burned as two or three galleys rained fire onto their decks until the pirates died in flames or jumped screaming into the sea. The rest made speed away from the coast, taking the last chance for freedom with them.

The cliffs were lined with his men, just watching as the fresh sea air blew against them. The cliffs were green with spring grasses and a light drizzle of rain darkened their grubby faces unnoticed.

Spartacus looked at them, his ragged army. They were all hungry and tired, heavy with the knowledge that their great run through the country was finally over. Still, he was proud of them all.

Crixus turned to him, his weariness showing. "There's no way out of this, is there?"

"No, I don't think so. Without the ships, we're done," Spartacus replied.

Crixus looked at the men around them, sitting and standing without hope in the thin rain. "I'm sorry. We should have crossed the mountains," he said softly.

Spartacus shrugged, chuckling. "We gave them a run, though," he said. "By all the gods, we scared them."

They were silent again for a long time, and out at sea, the last of the pirate ships were chased or captured, the galleys sweeping back and forth on their long oars. The smoke from burning decks rose against the rain, fierce and hot as vengeance.

"Antonidus has gone," Crixus said suddenly.

"I know. He came last night, wanting some of the gold."

"You gave it to him?" Crixus asked.

Spartacus shrugged. "Why not? If he can get away, good luck to him. There's nothing left for us here. You should go as well. Perhaps a few of us will make it on our own."

"He won't get past the legions. That damned wall they've built cuts us all off."

Spartacus stood. "Then we will break it and scatter. I'll not wait to be slaughtered like lambs, here. Gather the men close, Crix. We'll share the gold out so they all have a piece or two, and then we'll run one more time."

"They'll hunt us down," Crixus said.

"They won't catch us all. The country's too big for that."

Spartacus held out his hand and Crixus took it.

"Until we meet again, Crix."

"Until then."

*   *   *

There was no moon to reveal them to the soldiers on the great scar that stretched from coast to coast. When Spartacus had seen it, he had shaken his head in silent disbelief that a Roman general would attempt such a folly to pen the slaves

against the sea. In a way, it was a mark of respect to his followers that the legions did not dare pursue them, but were content to sit and peer over their trenches in the darkness.

Spartacus lay on his stomach in the scrub grass, his face
blackened with mud. Crixus lay at his side, and behind them
a vast snake of men were hidden, waiting for the shout to attack. There had been no opposition to this last gamble when
he put it to them. They had all seen the ships burn and their
despair had turned into a grim fatalism. The great dream had
ended. They would blow away like seeds on the wind, and the
Romans would never catch the half of them.

"It'll be a thin line guarding a trench that long," Spartacus
had told them as the sun set. "We will be the arrow through
their skin, and before they can gather, most of us will be
through and clear."

There had been no cheering, but they had passed the
word without excitement, sitting back then to sharpen their
blades and wait. When the sun had gone, Spartacus rose and
they came with him, trotting hunched over in the blackness.

The lip of the trench was a dark line against the faint
shine of stars in the clear sky. Crixus looked at it and strained
to make out the features of his friend.

"Ten feet high, at least, and it looks solid." He sensed
rather than saw Spartacus nod and cracked his neck with the
tension. The two men stood slowly and Spartacus gave a low
whistle to summon the group who would be first to the wall.
They gathered around him as shadows, the strongest of them,
armed with heavy hammers and axes.

"Go now. What they have built can be torn down,"
Spartacus whispered, and they set off in a loping run, their
weapons held ready for the first strike. The men behind came
to their feet and ran toward the Roman wall.

CHAPTER 43

Julius muttered his thanks as he was handed a bowl of warm stew. Covering the fields around him for as far as he could see, the soldiers of the Greek legions ate, the thin white snares of their cooking fires looping into the air. The ground was thick with mud and heavy clods stuck to their sandals and slowed them. Those who owned cloaks used them to sit on, turning the inside of the cloth down so the mud wouldn't show when they started again. Many more sat on whatever they could find, flat stones, coarse grass, or even a pile of loose hay that they'd spread around.

It would be a short break, Julius knew. The extraordinarii had come in early that morning from their scouting, and rumors flew around the men, even before the official word had come through the chain of command.

There was nothing good in the reports. Julius had been with Pompey when the general heard the slave army was coming north to meet them and not one of Crassus's eagle standards had been sighted. Pompey had raged at the rider who brought the news, demanding details he could not give. Wherever Crassus was, he had failed to hold the slaves against the sea. Julius wondered if he was still alive, but he could not bring himself to care particularly. He had seen so much of death. One more senator in this disastrous campaign would not make a difference.

Cabera wiped his fingers around his bowl and handed it back to the cook servants as they made their way through the vast encampment. There was never enough to eat, and by the time the bowls were passed out, much of it was as cold as the day. Around them, the men waited in that sleepwalking peace before a battle. None of them had fought the slaves before, but the usual chatter was absent. Somewhere to the south, it was easy to imagine a field like the one where they sat, littered with Roman bodies and crows.

Julius sighed as the rain started again. It would make the ground even softer. It didn't matter. It fitted his mood perfectly, the skies reflecting the depression that had settled on him. The picture of his wife's pale face and the torch-lit bed was as clear as if he were still seeing it in his mind. Tubruk, even Cato. It all seemed so terribly pointless. He'd loved the struggle in the beginning, when Marius was the golden general and they knew they fought for the city and each other, but the lines had blurred along the way and now he was sickened, eaten by guilt.

Julius dipped his fingers into the stew, pushing it into his mouth without tasting it. When Pelitas had died, he had wept, but there were no more tears in him for the others. He had no more lies for them, no more speeches. The grand lie had been that there was anything to fight for at all.

His father had seemed to see something worth saving in the Republic, but there was nothing left of that. There were just small men like Cato and Pompey, who saw no farther than their own glory. Visionless men, caring nothing for the things Tubruk had told him were important. Julius had believed what the great men had taught him, but they had all died for their dreams.

He reached down into the mud between his sprawled feet to trace a line with his finger. None of it was worth the death of one of them. Not Cornelia's, not Tubruk's, not any of the men he had led in Greece. They had followed him and given their lives without complaint. Well, he could do that, at least.

Of all the soldiers, Julius welcomed the battle to come. He would place himself in the front line for one last hour until it all finally stopped. He was tired of the Senate and tired of the path. It made him wince to think back to the day Marius had taken him into the building for the first time. He had been awed then at the heart of power. They had seemed so noble then, before he knew them too well to respect. He pulled his cloak against him as the wind built and heavier rain began to fall, spattering the mud around. Some of the men cursed, but most were quiet, making their peace with the gods before the killing began.

"Julius?" Cabera said, startling him out of his thoughts.

Julius turned to see the old man was holding his hands out toward him. He smiled as he saw what Cabera had made for him. It was a circlet of leaves, gathered from the bushes and wound about with thread from his robe.

"What's that for?" Julius said to him.

Cabera held it out, pressing it into his hands. "Put it on, boy. It's yours."

Julius shook his head. "Not today, Cabera. Not here."

"I made it for you, Julius. Please."

They stood up together and Julius put out a hand to grip the back of the old man's neck.

"All right, old friend," he said, letting out a long breath. He removed his helmet and pressed the ring of wet leaves onto his hair, feeling them prickle against his skin. Some of the men looked at him, but Julius didn't care. Cabera had been there through all of it and he didn't deserve to be waiting to die in a muddy field, far from his own home. Another one who would die at his side.

"I want you to stay away from the front line when they come, Cabera. Live through this one," he said.

"Your path is mine, remember?" the old man said, his

eyes gleaming in the rain. His white hair hung in thin strips over his face, and there was something so bedraggled about him that Julius chuckled.

Around the pair of them, men rose to their feet in silence. Julius raised his head sharply at the movement, thinking it was time to march, but they just stood and looked at him. More and more joined them as the word spread, until every one of them was standing. Plates were put down and cloaks left to grow wet as they faced him and the rain fell.

Wonderingly, Julius reached up to touch the circlet and he felt his heart lift. These were not small men. They gave their lives without caring, trusting their generals not to waste what they offered. They smiled and laughed as he caught their eyes and he felt again the bonds that held them together.

"We are Rome," he whispered, and turned to see thousands standing for him. In that moment, he understood what held Tubruk to loyalty and his father's faith. He would turn his hand to the dream as better men had before him, and honor them with his life.

In the distance, cornicens sounded the long notes to break camp.

*   *   *

"Keep moving, my brothers," Spartacus roared. It was the end, and somehow, there was no fear. His slaves had shown that the legions could be beaten, and he knew there would be a day when the cracks they had made would widen and Rome would fall. The legions behind them glittered in the morning sun, sending up a shout as Pompey's thousands marched down to them, faster and faster like jaws to crush the slaves between them. Spartacus saw his ragged slaves would be engulfed. He drew his sword and pulled his iron helmet over his face.

"My gods, we gave them a run, though," he said to himself as the air darkened with spears.

EPILOGUE

Pompey walked with Crassus between the rows of crosses. With Rome in sight, the line stretched for miles down the Via Appia behind them, six thousand men to serve as a warning and a proof of the victory. Forests had been felled to hold them, and when the legion carpenters ran out of nails, the slaves had simply been tied and speared, or left to die of thirst.

The two generals dismounted to walk the last mile into the city. Crassus would not be shamed, Pompey had promised him. Ending the rebellion erased the disasters that had gone before, and Pompey was willing to let him have his moment of glory. He had nothing to fear from Crassus and there was always his wealth to be considered. He would need wealthy men to finance his time as consul. Perhaps, he thought, it would be fruitful to urge Crassus to take the second consular post when the elections came. They could share the expenses then and Crassus would always be grateful.

In the distance, the generals could hear the tinny sounds of a cheering crowd, catching sight of them on the road. They smiled at each other, enjoying the moment.

"I wonder if we should ask for a Triumph?" Crassus said, breathing quickly at the thought. "There hasn't been one since Marius."

"I remember it," Pompey said, thinking of the young

man who had stood at Marius's shoulder on the ride to the forum.

As if guessing his thoughts, Crassus glanced at him.

"It's a shame Julius isn't here to see this. He fought hard enough for us."

Pompey frowned. He would not admit it to Crassus, but when he'd seen the Greek legions stand for Julius in the mud and rain, it had frightened him. All the great men were dead, but that one stood with the blood of Marius in him, general of the Tenth and with a growing fame that could be deadly if he ever chose to use it. No, he did not want Julius in his city or his precious legion. He'd signed the orders sending them to Spain without a moment's hesitation.

"Spain will temper him, Crassus. I have no doubt."

Crassus looked questioningly at him, but chose not to reply, and Pompey nodded in satisfaction as the roar of the waiting crowd grew. Spain was far enough away for Marius's nephew, and when his five years there were up, the people would have forgotten him.

HISTORICAL NOTE

The fact that, as a young man, Julius Caesar was captured by pirates and held for ransom is a matter of historical record. When they suggested a ransom of twenty talents, he is said to have demanded fifty, as they had no idea whom they had captured. He told the pirates that he would have them crucified, though he would have their officers strangled out of mercy.

When he was released on the north coast of Africa, he set about raising funds and demanding men from villages until he had enough to make a crew and hire ships. It is difficult to imagine the personal charisma that must have been necessary to accomplish this. It should be remembered that he was a young man, with no authority or Senate position.

In the book, I have assumed that he picked up his recruits in Roman settlements, the children of retired soldiers. It is the only way I could explain how he was able to take ship, search the Mediterranean for the pirates, find them, and carry out his grisly promises.

On landing in Greece, he discovered the rebellion raised by Mithridates and gathered an army around him. In fact, the battle he fought to stiffen the resolve of wavering Roman cities was against Mithridates' deputy rather than the king himself. Julius achieved a victory that held the region together in the face of Senate fumbling and indecision. It was Pompey who eventually defeated Mithridates and both men gained in status in Rome. Julius was made a military tribune, with the authority to levy troops, a position he still held when the Spartacus slave rebellion began.

There is no record of Caesar's involvement in the war against Spartacus, though I find it difficult to believe that a tribune with his drive and energy would not have been part of the legions led by Crassus and Pompey.

Though Karl Marx described Spartacus as "the finest fellow that the whole of ancient history has to show," there is little doubt that the Thracian gladiator had the chance to cross the Alps and escape Rome forever. We do not know what prompted him to turn south again, but considering how close he came, perhaps it was a genuine belief that the power of the legions could be broken.

The slave army destroyed and routed a number of the legions sent against them, sending shock waves of fear through the city and Roman lands. Estimates are that Spartacus had upward of seventy thousand slaves with him, roaming Italy north and south for two years in the field.

Crassus built his wall across the toe of Italy, and Spartacus's hope of being taken off by pirates came to nothing. The slaves broke through Crassus's barrier and streamed north once more. It took three armies to stop them in the end, and there is no record of whether Spartacus fell or was crucified with the thousands of others along the Appian Way.

Rome's first Dictator for Life, Cornelius Sulla, managed to retire from office and live comfortably until his death in 78 B.C. He is best remembered for his lists of proscriptions, published each day and naming those who had displeased him or were considered enemies of the Republic at his word. Gangs of raptores would earn a fee by dragging unfortunates out to be executed, and for a while Rome was as close to anarchy and terror as she had ever been. In many ways, Sulla was the architect of the downfall of the Republic, though the cracks would not show for some time.

As with Sulla's manner of death, I have found it necessary

on occasion to make changes to events. Though Caesar fought at Mytilene, earning the oak wreath there for bravery, I have left out his travels to Asia Minor and the cases he prosecuted in Rome during this period.

Octavian was Julius's great-nephew and not a cousin, as I have it. The change in relationship allowed me to avoid including a minor character in the first book. Similarly, for plot purposes, I have included Cato's suicide in *The Death of Kings*, whereas in fact he was Caesar's enemy for years longer.

Julius Caesar accomplished so much that it has always been harder deciding what not to tell than to choose the events that cry out to be dramatized. Sadly, sheer limitations of length prevent me from dealing with every aspect of his achievements. For those who are interested in the details I have been forced to omit, I once again recommend Christian Meier's book *Caesar*.

The minutiae of Roman lives were very much as I have portrayed them, from the birthing chair and jewelry making to the manner and customs of a Roman court, for which I owe a debt to *The Elements of Roman Law* by R. W. Lee.

The events of the books to come will, I hope, be made richer by knowing what has gone before.

C. IGGULDEN

ABOUT THE AUTHOR

Conn Iggulden is the acclaimed author of *Emperor: The Gates of Rome,* the first novel in the Emperor series. He lives with his wife and two children in Hertfordshire, England.

The epic adventure continues with

EMPEROR
THE FIELD OF SWORDS

by

CONN IGGULDEN

Read on for an exciting excerpt from
the next book in the *Emperor* series coming
from Delacorte Press in March 2005.

EMPEROR

A Novel of
JULIUS CAESAR

THE FIELD OF SWORDS

CONN IGGULDEN

EMPEROR
FIELD OF SWORDS

On sale March 2005

Julius stood by the open window, gazing out over Spanish hills. The setting sun splashed gold along a distant crest so that it seemed to hang in the air unsupported, a vein of light in the distance. Behind him, the murmur of conversation rose and fell without interrupting his thoughts. He could smell honeysuckle on the breeze and the touch of it in his nostrils made his own rank sweat even more pungent as the delicate fragrance shifted in the air and was gone.

It had been a long day. When he pressed a hand against his eyes, he could feel a surge of exhaustion rise in him like dark water. The voices in the campaign room mingled with the creak of chairs and the rustle of maps. How many hundreds of evenings had he spent on the upper floor of the fort with those men? The routine had become a comfort for them all at the end of a day, and even when there was nothing to discuss, they still gathered in the campaign rooms to drink and talk. It kept Rome alive in their minds and at times they could almost forget that they had not seen their home for more than four years.

At first, Julius had embraced the problems of the regions and hardly thought of Rome for months at a time. The days had flown as he rose and slept with the sun and the Tenth made towns in the wilderness. On the coast, Valentia had been transformed with lime and wood and paint until it was almost a new city veneered over the old. They had laid roads to chain the land and bridges that opened the wild hills to settlers. Julius had worked with a frenetic, twitching energy in those first years, using exhaustion like a drug to force away his memories. Then he would sleep and Cornelia would come to him. Those were the nights when he would leave his sweat-soaked bed and ride out to the watch posts, appearing out of the darkness unannounced until the Tenth were as nervous and tired as he was himself.

As if to mock his indifference, his engineers had found gold in two new seams, richer than any they had known before. The yellow metal had its own allure, and when Julius had seen the first haul spilled out of a cloth onto his desk, he had looked at it with hatred for what it represented. He had come to Spain with nothing, but the ground gave up its secrets and with the wealth came the tug of the old city and the life he had almost forgotten.

He sighed at the thought. Spain was such a treasure-house it would be difficult to leave her, but part of him knew he could not lose himself there for much longer. Life was too precious to be wasted, and too short.

The room was warm with the press of bodies. The maps of the new mines were stretched out on low tables, held by weights. Julius could hear Renius arguing with Brutus and the low cadence of Domitius chuckling. Only the giant Ciro was silent. Yet even those who spoke were marking time until Julius joined them. They were good men. Each one of them had stood with him against enemies and through grief, and there were times when Julius could imagine how it might have been to cross the world with them. They were men to walk a finer path than to be forgotten in Spain, and Julius could not bear the sympathy he saw in their eyes. He knew he deserved only contempt for having brought them to that place and buried himself in petty work.

If Cornelia had lived, he would have taken her with him to Spain. It would have been a new start, far away from the intrigues of the city. He bowed his head as the evening breeze touched his face. It was an old pain and there were whole days when he did not think of her. Then the guilt would surface and the dreams would be terrible, as if in punishment for the lapse.

"Julius? The guard is at the door for you," Brutus said, touching him on the shoulder. Julius nodded and turned back to the men in the room, his eyes seeking out the stranger amongst them.

The legionary looked nervous as he glanced around at the map-laden tables and the jugs of wine, clearly awed by the people within.

"Well?" Julius said.

The soldier swallowed as he met the dark eyes of his general. There was no kindness in that hard, fleshless face, and the young legionary stammered slightly.

"A young Spanish at the gate, General. He says he's the one we're looking for."

The conversations in the room died away and the guard wished he were anywhere else but under the scrutiny of those men.

"Have you checked him for weapons?" Julius said.

"Yes, sir."

"Then bring him to me. I want to speak to the man who has caused me so much trouble."

Julius stood waiting at the top of the stairs as the Spaniard was brought up. His clothes were too small for his gangling limbs, and the face was caught in the change between man and boy, though there was no softness in the bony jaw. As their eyes met, the Spaniard hesitated, stumbling.

"What's your name, boy?" Julius said as they came level.

"Adàn," the Spaniard forced out.

"*You* killed my officer?" Julius said, with a sneer.

The young man froze, then nodded, his expression wavering between fear and determination. He could see the faces turned toward him in the room, and his courage seemed to desert him then at the thought of stepping into their midst. He might have held back if the guard hadn't shoved him across the threshold.

"Wait below," Julius told the legionary, suddenly irritated.

Adàn refused to bow his head in the face of the hostile glares of the Romans, though he could not remember being more frightened in his life. As Julius closed the door behind him, he started silently, cursing his nervousness. Adàn watched as the general sat down facing him, and a dull terror overwhelmed him. Should he keep his hands by his sides? All of a sudden, they seemed awkward and he considered folding them or clasping his fingers behind his back. The silence was painful as he waited and still they had their eyes on him. Adàn swallowed with difficulty, determined not to show his fear.

"You knew enough to tell me your name. Can you understand me?" Julius asked.

Adàn worked spit into his dry mouth. "I can," he said. At least his voice hadn't quavered like a boy's. He squared his shoulders slightly and glanced at the others, almost re-coiling from the naked animosity from one of them, a bear of a man with one arm who seemed to be practically growling with anger.

"You told the guards you were the one we were look-ing for, the one who killed the soldier," Julius said.

Adàn's gaze snapped back to him. "I did it. I killed him," he replied, the words coming in a rush.

"You tortured him," Julius added.

Adàn swallowed again. He had imagined this scene as he walked over the dark fields to the fort, but he couldn't summon the defiance he had pictured. He felt as if he were confessing to his father, and it was all he could do not to shuffle his feet in shame, despite his intentions.

"He was trying to rape my mother. I took him into the woods. She tried to stop me, but I would not listen to her," Adàn said stiffly, trying to remember the words he had practiced.

Someone in the room muttered an oath, but Adàn could not tear his eyes away from the general. He felt an obscure relief that he had told them. Now they would kill him and his parents would be released.

Thinking of his mother was a mistake. Tears sprang from nowhere to rim his eyes and he blinked them back furiously. She would want him to be strong in front of these men.

Julius watched him. The young Spaniard was visibly trembling, and with reason. He had only to give the order and Adàn would be taken out into the yard and executed in front of the assembled ranks. It would be the end of it, but a memory stayed his hand.

"Why have you given yourself up, Adàn?"

"My family have been taken in for questioning, General. They are innocent. I am the one you want."

"You think your death will save them?"

Adàn hesitated. How could he explain that only that thin hope had made him come?

"They have done nothing wrong."

Julius raised a hand to scratch his eyebrow, then rested his elbow on the arm of the chair as he thought.

"When I was younger than you, Adàn, I stood in front of a Roman named Cornelius Sulla. He had murdered my uncle and broken everything I valued in the world. He told me I would go free if I put aside my wife and shamed her with her father. He *cherished* such little acts of spite."

For a moment, Julius looked into the unimaginable distance of the past, and Adàn felt sweat break out on his forehead. Why was the man talking to him? He had already confessed; there was nothing else. Despite his fear, he felt interest kindle. The Romans seemed to bear only one face in Spain. To hear they had rivalry and enemies within their own ranks was a revelation.

"I hated that man, Adàn," Julius continued. "If I had been given a weapon, I would have used it on him even though it meant my own life. I wonder if you understand that sort of hatred."

"You did not give up your wife?" Adàn asked.

Julius blinked at the sudden question, then smiled bitterly. "No. I refused and he let me live. The floor at his feet was spattered with the blood of people he had killed and tortured, yet he let me live. I have often wondered why."

"He did not think you were a threat," Adàn said, surprised by his own courage to speak so to the general. Julius shook his head in memory.

"I doubt it. I told him I would devote my life to killing him if he set me free." For a moment, he almost said aloud how his friend had poisoned the Dictator, but that part of the story could never be told, not even to the men in that room.

Julius shrugged. "He died by someone else's hand, in the end. It is one of the regrets of my life that I could not do it myself and watch the life fade from his eyes."

Adàn had to look away from the fire he saw in the Roman. He believed him, and the thought of this man ordering his own death with such malice made him shudder.

Julius did not speak again for a long time, and Adàn felt weak with the tension, his head jerking upwards as the general broke the silence at last.

"There are murders in the cells here and in Valentia. One of them will be hanged for your crimes as well as his own. You, I am going to pardon. I will sign my name to it and you will go back to your home with your family and never come to my attention again."

Renius snorted in amazement. "I would like a private word, General," he grated, looking venomously at Adàn. The young Spaniard stood with his mouth open.

"You may not have one, Renius. I have spoken and it will stand," Julius replied without looking at him. He watched the boy for a moment and felt a weight lift off him. He had made the right decision, he was sure. He had seen himself in the Spaniard's eyes and it was like lifting a veil into his memory. How frightening Sulla had seemed then. To Adàn, Julius would have been another of that cruel type, wrapped in metal armor and harder thoughts. How close he had come to sending Adàn to be impaled, or burnt, or nailed to the gates of the fort, as Sulla had with so many of his enemies. It was an irony that Sulla's old whim had saved Adàn, but Julius had caught himself before he gave the order for death and wondered at what he was becoming. He would not be those men he had hated. Age would not force him into their mold, if he had the strength. He rose from his seat and faced Adàn.

"I do not expect you to waste this chance, Adàn. You will not have another from me."

Adàn almost burst into tears, emotions roiling and overwhelming him. He had prepared himself for death, and having it snatched away and freedom promised was too much for him. On an impulse, he took a step forward and went down on one knee before anyone could react.

Julius stood slowly, looking down at the young man before him.

"We are not the enemy, Adàn. Remember that. I will have a scribe prepare the pardon. Wait below for me," he said.

Adàn rose and looked into the Roman's dark eyes for a last moment before leaving the room. As the door closed behind him, he sagged against the wall, wiping sweat from his face. He felt dizzy with relief and every breath he pulled in was clear and cold. He could not understand why he had been spared.

The guard in the room below craned his head to stare up at Adàn's slumped figure in the shadows.

"Shall I heat the knives for you, then?" the Roman sneered up at him.

"Not today," Adàn replied, enjoying the look of confusion that passed over the man's face.

*   *   *

Brutus pressed a cup of wine into Julius's hand, pouring expertly from an amphora.

"Are you going to tell us why you let him go?" he said.

Julius lifted the cup to cut off the flow and drank from it before holding it out again. "Because he was brave," he said.

Renius rubbed the bristles of his chin with his hand. "He will be famous in the towns, you realize. He will be the man who faced us and lived. They'll probably make him mayor when old Del Subió dies. The young ones will flock around him and before you know it—"

"Enough," Julius interrupted, his face flushing from the heady wine. "The sword is not the answer to everything, no matter how you may wish it so. We have to live with them without sending our men out in pairs and watching every alley and track for ambush." His hands cut shapes in the air as he strained to find words for the thought.

"They must be as Roman as we are, willing to die for our causes and against our enemies. Pompey showed the way with the legions he raised here. I spoke the truth when I said we were not the enemy. Can you understand that?"

"I understand," Ciro spoke suddenly, his deep voice rumbling out over Renius's reply.

Julius's face lit with the idea. "There it is. Ciro was not born in Rome, but he came to us freely and is *of* Rome." He struggled for words, his mind running faster than his tongue. "Rome is . . . an idea, more than blood. We must make it so that for Adàn to cast us off would be like tearing his own heart out. Tonight, he will wonder why he wasn't killed. He will know there can be justice, even after the death of a Roman soldier. He will tell the story and those who doubt will pause. That is enough of a reason."

"Unless he killed the man for sport," Renius said, "and he tells his friends we are weak and stupid." He didn't trust himself to speak further, but crossed to Brutus and took the amphora from him, holding it in the crook of his elbow to fill his cup. In his anger, some of it splashed onto the floor.

Julius narrowed his eyes slightly at the old gladiator. He took a slow breath to control the temper that swelled in him.

"I will not be Sulla, or Cato. Do you understand *that* at least, Renius? I will not rule with fear and hatred and taste every meal for poison. Do you understand *that*?" His voice had risen as he spoke, and Renius turned to face him, realizing he had gone too far.

Julius raised a clenched fist, anger radiating off him. "If I say the word, Ciro will cut out your heart for me, Renius. He was born on a coast of a different land, but he is Roman. He is a soldier of the Tenth and he is mine. I do not hold him with fear, but with love. Do you understand *that*?"

Renius froze. "I know that, of course, you—"

Julius interrupted him with a wave of his hand, feeling a headache spike between his eyes. The fear of a fit in front of them made his anger vanish, and he was left feeling empty and tired.

"Leave me, all of you. Fetch Cabera. Forgive my anger, Renius. I need to argue with you just to know my own mind."

Renius nodded, accepting the apology. He went out with the others, leaving Julius alone in the room. The gathering gloom of the evening had turned almost to night, and Julius lit the lamps before standing by the open window, pressing his forehead against the cool stone. The headache throbbed and he groaned softly, rubbing his temples in circular motions as Cabera had taught him.

There was so much work to do and all the time an inner voice whispered at him, mockingly. Was he hiding in these hills? Where once he had dreamed of standing in the Senate house, now he drew back from it. Cornelia was dead, Tubruk with her. His daughter was a stranger, living in a house he had visited for only one night in six years. There had been times when he hungered to match his strength and wit against men like Sulla and Pompey, but now the thought of throwing himself back into games of power made him nauseous with hatred. Better, surely better, to make a home in Spain, to find a woman there and never see his home again.

"I cannot go back," he said aloud, his voice cracking.

*　　　　　*　　　　　*

Renius found Cabera in the stables, lancing a swelling in the soft flesh of a cavalry hoof. The horses always seemed to understand he was trying to help them, and even the most spirited stood still after only a few murmured words and pats.

They were alone and Renius waited until Cabera's needle had released the pus in the hoof, his fingers massaging the soft flesh to help the drain. The horse shuddered as if flies were landing on its skin, but Cabera had never been kicked and the leg was relaxed in his steady hands.

"He wants you," Renius said.

Cabera looked up at his tone. "Hand me that pot, will you?"

Renius passed over the cup of sticky tar that would seal the wound. He watched Cabera work in silence, and when the wound was coated, Cabera turned to him with his usual humor dampened.

"You're worried about Julius," the old healer said.

Renius shrugged. "He's killing himself here. Of course I'm worried. He doesn't sleep, just spends his nights working on his mines and maps. I . . . can't seem to talk to him without it becoming an argument."

Cabera reached out and gripped the iron muscles of Renius's arm. "He knows you're here, if he needs you," he said. "I'll give him a sleeping draft for tonight. Perhaps you should take one as well. You look exhausted."

Renius shook his head. "Just do what you can for him. He deserves better than this."

Cabera watched the one-armed gladiator stride away into the darkness.

"You are a good man, Renius," he said, too quietly to be heard.